# AGENTS
## UNDER
## FIRE

# AGENTS
## UNDER
## FIRE

Second, Expanded Edition

DANA MARTON

ISBN: 1940627176
ISBN: 9781940627175



http://www.danamarton.com/
First edition: June 2011
Second, updated edition: August 2016

# GUARDIAN AGENT

# CHAPTER
# ONE

Dark waters lapped the long-abandoned palace's foundation, eager to claim the forgotten building on one of Venice's rarely used canals. In the distance, tourists still partied on at two o'clock in the February morning, drunk on love, youth, and full-bodied Italian wine.

Over the faint beat of music, Gabe Cannon could hear the eager, predatory water somewhere below him, licking to taste what it wanted to devour. He couldn't hear, however, the nine other men in the forgotten palace with him. His new commando team spread out like ghosts floating through the night.

He cocked his ear as he stood silently on the stairs, but not to listen for his teammates. He hoped to hear their target. He listened for the man they hunted.

*Grab him. Hand him over to the US government. Cash the check.* A straightforward job for Gabe's first op with XO-ST, a private security company, Xtreme Ops Shadow Teams.

"Target on the roof," the team leader's voice whispered through Gabe's earpiece.

Gabe hurried up the crumbling stairs, unburdened by the usual heavy commando equipment. Since tonight he gripped a handgun, a SIG P226, he didn't have to be careful not to bang the stock of his M15 rifle into the peeling frescos behind him.

Centuries ago, the palace had been painted within an inch of its life. The ceiling rivaled the Sistine Chapel. All around on the walls, mythical epic battles raged between good and evil.

That good stood no closer to winning now than when ancient Romans had recorded those myths thousands of years ago would have disheartened another man. Gabe Cannon was still a SEAL, however, even if he'd left the navy—once a SEAL, always a SEAL—and SEALs didn't do *disheartened*.

"East wing cleared." The information came through his earpiece.

He hauled ass toward the warped wooden door at the top of the stairs, ready to capture the rogue SEAL who needed to be brought in before he caused more damage. Jake Tekla had killed two civilians and a naval officer so far, but the list of his casualties was going to end tonight.

Gabe and Tekla hadn't been on the same SEAL Team, had known each other from only a single joint op five years back. Tekla had gone AWOL nine months ago. *What the hell happened to him?*

Gabe passed another fresco of an ancient battlefield massacre, swords dripping with blood. His gaze hesitated on the openmouthed agony of the dying.

*War.*

War had happened to Tekla. War could change a person, could even twist a man's mind. Still, in Gabe's book, nothing excused betraying the US Navy.

"Backstairs cleared," Alvarez, one of his teammates, whispered over the radio.

Gabe reached the top of the stairs and hurried down the hallway, looking for the servants' quarters, the most likely location for the entrance to the attic. Most of the doors stood open, warped by moisture and time. When he spotted one that revealed a narrow set of stairs—no frescos here—he hurried up.

Another door stood at the top of the stairs, this one closed. He twisted the rusty knob, pushed through gun first, and scanned the attic in what little light a few missing roof tiles provided. He had excellent night vision, could see everything but the farthest corners.

No movement.

He stood still, held his breath, and listened. Not the smallest whisper of a sound disturbed the silence. The attic smelled of moldy wood and felt empty. The short hairs at the back of Gabe's neck didn't rise in warning.

He eased his weight onto the floorboards with care as he moved forward. The structural integrity of the building was pretty questionable. The stairs had held up, but that didn't mean he could trust the floor up here.

Static hissed in his earpiece. Then, Brent Foley, the team leader, was saying, "Kill order authorized. Repeat, authorized to shoot on sight."

And for the first time on this op, true unease skittered up Gabe's spine.

They were in Europe—*in freaking Venice, packed with civilians*—not in some Iraqi death trap of a desert. The target wasn't an active shooter—no imminent danger. Jake Tekla was outnumbered ten to one.

The original order had been for capture. Capture made a lot more sense. Gabe's team could gain potentially crucial intel from Tekla during interrogation. Usable intelligence trumped a quick kill, every time.

What if Tekla hadn't worked alone? What if he'd pulled the trigger but someone else had issued the order? He could have killed the two civilians for any reason: self-defense, accident, personal revenge, whatever. But the naval officer he'd shot brought uncomfortable possibilities to the case.

Did the killings have something to do with the navy? Was Tekla a traitor?

Why not apprehend the man and ask at least the most obvious questions?

Although, considering that Tekla was a SEAL, confession was probably a pipe dream. Could be why Brent Foley, the commando team's leader, had changed his mind about the takedown and turned *capture* into *elimination*.

And yet…the target was a US citizen, military—which used to mean something. Capture him, interrogate him—whether he said anything or not—but at least put him in front of a military tribunal.

Sanctioned kills were usually reserved for enemy combatants.

Obviously, the private security industry worked differently than Gabe's previous employer, the US Navy. Paid differently too—as in *way better*, and if Gabe wanted to keep the job, he had to get used to the new MO and roll with it.

*First op. Don't fuck up.*

"I want everyone in position on the roof," the team leader said over the radio.

Gabe headed for the maintenance ladder in the shadows to his left and climbed. He checked the metal trapdoor above his head—the last obstacle in his way.

He focused on the two large hinges that held the door in place. Judging by the condition of the rest of the palace, the hinges were probably rusted from the salty moisture of the sea breezes. When pushed open, they'd creak loudly enough to wake the dead. Or at least loudly enough to alert Tekla that he had company.

Gabe rubbed some greasy camo paint off his face with the tip of his fingers, then reached up to lube the hinges, but his fingers slipped. The hinges were already well-oiled.

His hand paused in the air.

The roof had to be a planned escape route for Tekla. He had taken care of the door.

*What else did he set up?*

The dead last target Gabe ever wanted to go up against was another SEAL. Capture would be damn difficult—maybe the kill order was right. But Gabe didn't like the thought any more now than he had earlier.

He ran a probing finger around the door.

*Rigged or not?*

*No wires*—which didn't necessarily mean anything. A small motion-activated bomb could sit on top of the door, plenty enough to evaporate his head if he carelessly set off the charge.

Sweat beaded on his brows as he gently tapped over the door's entire surface with a single knuckle, moving in regular rows, following an imaginary grid, listening.

The sound never changed; nothing to indicate that a block of C4 was attached to the other side. He pushed the door up with his left hand, kept his gun in his right, and kept his head down as the door silently swung open.

He held his breath as he stuck his head out of the hole. When he wasn't greeted with a flying bullet, he exhaled.

They'd get Tekla tonight. The man was slipping.

*Except…SEALs don't slip.*

*But then why not fully protect the door at his back?* He'd gone rogue. *So why the restraint? Why worry about the body count now?*

Those questions set off a number of alarms in Gabe's mind.

The moon bathed the roof in light. He looked carefully for any movement. Caught none. Nobody in sight.

Plywood patches formed a psychedelic pattern over most of the area around him, an unexpected break. Not having to sneak around on crumbling

Mediterranean roof tiles would make his job much easier. He could move without being heard from a mile away.

He left the safety of the attic and stayed in a crouch as he rushed to the deep shadow of a brick chimney stack, the nearest cover, less than twenty feet away.

No shots rang out.

Maybe Tekla wasn't on the roof after all.

Gabe held still, let one minute tick by, then another, saw no movement, heard no suspicious sounds. He didn't allow himself to relax. He scanned the area again, picking out spots he could use for cover as he moved forward.

His earpiece crackled. "Coming up. Hold your fire."

He caught a silent, nearly invisible shadow at the trapdoor—Troy Hill, another mercenary who'd started out in the SEAL Teams.

Troy was built like a SEAL, and when he left the shadows, he moved like a SEAL, decisively, dominating his environment. He was the best fighter on the team, the one Gabe would prefer at his back should the night turn nasty.

Except, where the hell had Troy been for the past fifteen minutes? Gabe had been last into the building but first on the roof. Where was the rest of the team?

Were they testing Gabe because he was the new guy? *Now???*

*Fine.*

He wasn't afraid of having to earn his stripes. He would just prefer not playing games in the middle of a freaking takedown.

Was the team worried because they were going up against another SEAL? The SEAL brotherhood was definitely a real thing—involving a tremendous amount of loyalty. But if Tekla had gone rogue, Gabe had no problem taking the man out. In this, and everything, country came first.

Troy pulled into cover and folded into a low crouch, the scars on his face hidden under camo paint tonight. He signaled to Gabe, pointing west, and disappeared from sight in three seconds flat, moving with purpose.

He didn't look like he had any trouble with hunting Tekla either. Then again, he hadn't personally known the target. Roughly twenty-five hundred active duty SEALs served at any given time. It wasn't as if they all knew each other and were best buddies.

Gabe looked after Troy, then stole off in the opposite direction.

Dormers, chimneys, and ridges blocked visibility. Clouds began drifting across the moon. None of that bothered him. Compared to some of the ops he'd been on overseas, this was a walk in the park.

*Scan. Move forward. Take cover. Repeat.*

He enjoyed a good night game of hide-and-seek, made more challenging by the fact that the ramshackle roof could open up under his feet any minute. He had to watch where he stepped. Nothing new there. The constant IED threat in Afghanistan and Iraq had taught him how to walk with care.

Then he stole around a dormer and spotted the target at last, so he stopped moving. He barely even drew air.

Jake Tekla blended into the night in black fatigues similar to Gabe's, black ski mask in place. He was much slighter than Gabe remembered. Being on the run had taken its toll on the guy. Had he been sick? Injured?

He wasn't injured now. He crept toward the edge of the roof as smoothly as a cat, his focus on the jump he was considering.

*No visible weapons.*

Yet another thing that didn't add up tonight. Tekla was a seasoned veteran on the run. No way he'd go anywhere unarmed.

Gabe inched closer, watching for a trap. *Come on. Turn.* He needed to make positive ID. He wasn't going to make assumptions, not with a kill order. He moved another step closer, then stopped with his feet apart, SIG raised.

His target sensed him at last and spun around. Froze. And for the first time in his life while on an op, Gabe froze too. Tonight's luck had run out at last.

He'd definitely seen the curve of a...*breast.*

# TWO

*What the hell?* Gabe's finger hesitated on the trigger as he stared at the *woman*.

She had to be Tekla's accomplice or a decoy.

Gabe's brain screamed, *Trap!* at the same time as he registered that he'd moved too far out of cover to dive back.

*Where the hell is Tekla?*

Gabe couldn't afford to look around. He couldn't be a hundred percent sure the woman wasn't armed. Maybe she had one of those bra holsters. He'd turn, and she'd shoot him in the back.

But she wasn't reaching for a weapon. And Tekla, wherever he was, wasn't shooting at Gabe either.

Gabe kept his weapon on the woman, since she was the only visible threat.

He had a kill order.

A lot of men he knew squeezed the trigger each and every time, preferring to err on the safe side. He'd been like that once.

A muscle jumped in his cheek. He gritted his teeth and shoved the North Village incident from his mind, just as the woman startled from her initial frozen reaction and darted to the left, sprinting away.

Or tried. Reaching up with his free hand to turn off his mic, Gabe caught up in three leaps and brought her down hard. He stayed on top of her, using his body weight to keep her down. He had questions, and she was going to give him some answers.

"No!" she gasped, lean yet soft, every inch unmistakably feminine.

But none of that feminine softness showed in her fighting spirit when she shoved against him with all she had, then punched and kicked, and he could almost swear she had extra limbs. *The freaking love child of an octopus and Bruce Lee.*

"Let me go!" she demanded in a low, furious whisper.

Where had Tekla come up with this one? And why wasn't he coming out of cover to help her?

*Because he isn't here.*

The commando team hadn't been chasing Tekla for hours. They'd been chasing his Mata Hari accomplice.

She fought well, but not like a professional, although, whatever training she'd had she used to full effect. Still, she was clearly a civilian. She didn't have the kind of muscle mass that came from boot camp and regular obstacle course runs, regular hand-to-hand combat practice.

"Stop," Gabe hissed into her ear.

She had to know she was conquered, yet she refused to yield, stirring some of Gabe's base instincts as her lithe body pushed against him, full contact, while she struggled.

"Stop." He said the single word into her small ear again as he did his best to hold her down.

Her eyes burned with fury. "You stop."

"I'm not going to hurt you."

At least not until he figured out what was going on. If she was an enemy to his country, he had no trouble taking her down, world-class breasts or no world-class breasts.

Instead of listening to him, she did her best to scratch out his eyes, as silently as possible.

She knew that there were multiple hunters. She'd been playing cat-and-mouse games with them for most of the night. She knew that drawing the other guys' attention wasn't in her best interest.

Did she think she could take Gabe out without the rest of the team being the wiser? She couldn't be that delusional, could she?

Gabe didn't ask. God knew, he'd known his share of delusional women. His share of women, period. Okay, more than his share. But they were usually more cooperative than Mata Hari here.

If he wanted to kill her, he could have snapped her neck three times by now. But subduing her without hurting her was more tricky. And he didn't want to call out to his team, because his instincts, honed in battle, demanded caution. Enough small things about this op had triggered alarms for him to want to see what he had here before he alerted anyone.

"Stay still." He captured her hands and pinned them over her head, pinned her body down with his. He weighed roughly twice as much as she did. She wasn't going to buck him off, although not for lack of trying.

As she struggled under him, he patted her down one-handed, not expecting to find much. If she had a knife or any other weapon, she would have used it on him by now. In seconds, his fingers confirmed what his brain knew already: she was unarmed.

He kept his voice low. "Did Tekla send you?"

She tried to buck him off again, a move that involved slamming her hips up into his, an *interesting* sensation now that they were perfectly aligned.

*Whoa there.*

A visceral response shot through his groin.

*Time to end this game right now.* He reached up and ripped off her black mask.

Wavy dark hair tumbled free, her full lips snarling even as her eyes narrowed with threat. Eyes that reminded Gabe a lot of Tekla's. The nose too, come to think of it.

Even if Gabe hadn't remembered Tekla all that well from their brief acquaintance, he'd spent plenty of time studying the target's photos in the op file.

"Who are you?" But the answer was already forming in his mind.

Tekla had two sisters. Gabe had met both about five years ago at Reagan National Airport when he and Tekla had come back from their joint op, their teams having flown back stateside together.

Gabe vaguely remembered Tekla saying something about raising the girls—that he'd enlisted in the navy so he could support them financially. The younger one would be a teenager by now, and the other probably in college, graduate school even.

The one under Gabe now was all woman. *Definitely not the younger sister.*

And still…Her body was a freaking knockout, but even snarling, in the semidark, her face looked impossibly young, making him think his thirty-year-old ass shouldn't be lying on top of her. He might be a dog, but he wasn't a complete bastard.

His earpiece crackled. "Hold your fire," Alvarez whispered over the radio. "Rest of the team's comin' up." Some more static, then, "Try not to accidentally shoot anyone."

Gabe flipped on his mic, because Alvarez would expect at least a *Roger that.* "Can I shoot you on purpose?"

"You could try, rookie boy."

*Rookie. Right.* So they probably *had* been testing him by letting him reach the roof first. They wanted to see if he could handle a kill order on a fellow SEAL.

They weren't going to like the course of action he'd chosen.

*Shit.*

"Got the east end covered," Gabe said, then flicked off the mic.

Plywood gave an ominous creak on the other side of the roof's main ridge, the remaining eight men from the ten-man team moving into position to inspect all the nooks and crannies.

Gabe kept his attention on the woman under him. What was Jake Tekla's sister doing here in Venice on a rooftop in the middle of the night?

And if she was here, why wasn't that mentioned in the pre-op briefing? Supposedly, the target's sisters were living with some aunt in Kansas. No way could the team's intel fail so badly on an op like this. They weren't fighting in the chaos of some distant battlefield.

Under other circumstances, Gabe would have sworn like the sailor he was, but he found he couldn't say those words in her face.

He wanted to believe that the team leader, Brent Foley, hadn't known that Tekla's sister was on the roof when he'd given the kill order, but being naïve didn't pay in this business.

But if Brent *had* known…

Was he simply making a business decision here?

The team had been hunting Tekla for weeks now. Every day on an op cost a shitload of money. Eliminating one of Tekla's sisters might push Tekla over the edge, bring him out into the open as he came in for revenge.

XO-ST's small army for hire consisted of ex-soldiers, ex-cops, and ex-agents, conducting outsourced ops for the US government and anyone else who met their price. Government contractors wrote the book on how to reach goals by whatever means necessary, with the lowest budget possible. They had to learn how to cut costs if they wanted to stay competitive when bidding for contracts.

Except, Gabe hadn't signed on to kill innocents, no matter how badly he needed his share of the money that this op would bring in.

He motioned to the woman to stay still and stay quiet, then eased his body off her an inch so she could fill her lungs.

"Is your brother here?" he whispered.

She stayed down, breathing hard, despair and anger in her eyes. She shook her head, her wild dark hair sticking out in every direction.

He pushed to his knees and sat back on his heels, straddling her slim thighs, still holding her wrists in his hand. And he had a sudden flashback to the last time they'd met. When he'd kissed her. Totally inappropriately.

Okay, she'd kissed him, but he'd been so startled, he'd kissed her back. He'd been twenty-five, a grown man, and she'd been in high school.

As Gabe had been leaving after grabbing some pizza at the airport together, Tekla had had his back turned to say something to the younger sister, and the older sister—this one—had stepped up to Gabe. He'd thought she wanted a handshake. He was a SEAL; a lot of times, even strangers came up to him and asked to shake his hand.

But the girl hadn't reached for his hand. She'd gone straight for his lips. She'd tasted like strawberry lip gloss.

Gabe bit back a curse. She'd made him feel like a freaking pervert, and he resented that.

His feelings must have showed in his eyes, because her gaze slid to his gun, and she swallowed, her body stiffening. Her eyes widened with fear; her mouth turned down with resignation. She finally accepted that she was beaten. And she expected Gabe to shoot her.

She didn't beg, nor did she offer her brother's life for her own. She simply met Gabe's gaze and lifted her small, feminine chin.

He had a kill order in place, and a team of mercenaries spread out around them. No time to contemplate the situation and draw up a pros-and-cons list. Gabe went with instinct and made a split-second decision.

"Stay here and stay quiet. I'll come back."

He pulled a plastic cuff from his back pocket and, with one smooth move, secured her to the iron scroll that decorated the roof's edge.

He switched on his mouthpiece as he left her, ignoring her silent struggle. "Target escaped the roof. Last seen at north end."

He ran along the edge toward that side where a six-foot gap separated the old palace from the next building.

Dark shapes materialized from the shadows from every direction.

He jumped without giving the steep drop below him any thought. And, as expected, his clear purpose and energy drew the rest of the team behind him.

He dashed forward as if he could see a man's disappearing back somewhere up ahead in the darkness.

Crisp sea air filled his lungs as he ran. He didn't slow until twenty minutes and several rooftops later. Then he braced against the edge of the roof as he stared down onto a dark, abandoned bridge below him. "Lost visual contact."

"Fuck," came through his headset from Brent, followed by, "Did he look hurt?"

"No."

"I could swear I clipped him before we lost him last week." A moment of silence. "Spread out."

As the team scattered, Gabe made his way back to the old palace, trying to think of the woman's name, not expecting much after five years, surprised when the name did pop into his brain: *Jasmine.*

A simple plan formed in his mind as he walked: She was going to take him to Tekla.

Gabe would find the target by himself. He would interrogate the target. Then he would bring the target in. At least Tekla would have a chance for that military tribunal instead of a quick bullet in the back of the head. Gabe figured he owed as much to a fellow SEAL.

He preferred a calm takedown instead of a shootout. And, whatever Tekla had done, his sister didn't deserve to be caught in the crossfire. Things could get out of hand when a cornered person was confronted with an entire commando team.

For all Gabe knew, the younger sister was here too. Was Tekla using his sisters to keep himself safe? If so, then he'd changed fundamentally in the past five years. Gabe had no respect for a man who would use his sisters as a shield.

Moving toward Jasmine's location, Gabe vaulted from roof to roof, watching out for crumbling edges. If he could complete the mission without bloodshed, he wanted to do it. Maybe saving a few lives, after having taken so many, would even the scales a little.

Except he found the palace roof empty.

He stared at the sawed-through plastic cuff next to the sharp, shattered pieces of a roof tile. Anger rolled through him, and he kicked a shard, then swore as it sailed through the air and hit the dark waters below with a barely audible splash.

He kicked off another chunk. That didn't make him feel better either.

How in hell could he lose her this fast?

The answer wasn't flattering. He'd taken one look at Jasmine's large, fear-filled eyes, and like a dumbass, he'd underestimated her.

He moved to peer over the edge of the roof, down at the sidewalk below, not really expecting to see her, and finding exactly what he'd expected.

A few hardy tourists were still awake in the distance, doing the whole "Venice by starlight" thing. Going down among them would be futile. Jasmine Tekla could be anywhere by now.

Gabe looked toward the lit-up city center where he'd go in her place. St. Mark's Square would be busy even at this hour. A lot of visitors had arrived for the Venice Carnival that would start next week. They enjoyed taking their fancy costumes out for a test drive. Jasmine could simply hide under a carnival mask that vendors sold by the hundreds on every corner for a couple of euros. Gabe would never find her tonight.

But he *was* going to find her. And then she would lead him to her brother. Then Gabe would bring Tekla in, and nobody would have to die. And Gabe would still get his check.

He badly needed the money from this op. Lives depended on it.

# CHAPTER
# THREE

Jasmine Tekla hurried along the Grand Canal, dodging a group of die-hard revelers, glancing back over her shoulder for the hundredth time, still shaking inside.

Was Gabe Cannon behind her somewhere, following? No way was she going to let him catch her again.

*Oh, the freaking irony.* She'd spent years in lust with him. She'd *dreamed* of him chasing her. Or doing anything at all with her. Seriously, she would have been ecstatic if he'd noticed she was alive.

And now…Her teenage fantasy man was hunting her brother.

Gabe looked just as amazing as when she'd first met him at that airport five years ago and had fallen instantly in love. It'd been one of those unavoidable pitfalls of life. He'd been more handsome than any of her pop idols, and her teenage emotions had been just begging for a focus.

He'd been a casual acquaintance of her brother's through the SEAL Teams. They hadn't been on the same team, but SEALs were a brotherhood.

In fact, the men considered it extremely bad form for one SEAL to stab another one in the back. So what was Gabe Cannon doing here, trying to catch Jake? Jasmine swallowed back the bitter taste of betrayal that bubbled up her throat.

Gabe was larger and harder than she'd remembered. Then again, he'd never been on top of her before—outside her lurid teenage fantasies. There'd been a time when her number one life goal had been to give Gabe Cannon her virginity.

Tragically for her teenage self, until now, a brief airport encounter had been the first and last time she'd seen him. But she'd fantasized about meeting him again. Embarrassment made her cringe when she thought of all the melodramatic drivel she'd written about him in her high school diary. *Dear God, don't ever let him find out about that.*

Gabe's dark hair was a little longer now and his face had developed harder edges, but the sight of him could still knock the air from her lungs.

*"Is your brother here?"* he'd asked.

He'd recognized her immediately. *How on earth?* Last time he'd seen her, she'd been a gangly high school kid with braces. But he hadn't forgotten her.

Her inner teenager was shaking pom-poms and doing cheers.

Her adult self groaned. She would have much preferred staying unrecognized. Staying anonymous might have given her a slight advantage. And when you had no advantages at all, any small thing might make a difference.

*"Permesso."* She moved around an older woman who took up most of the sidewalk, holding half a dozen poodles on leashes.

Jasmine barely registered the dogs, her mind still back on that rooftop where Gabe Cannon could easily have killed her. She could *not* make another mistake like she'd made tonight.

She rubbed her wrist. God, she hated being tied. *Thank God nothing worse happened.*

That Gabe hadn't handed her over to his team was nothing short of a miracle. He'd cut her some slack. And she'd taken full advantage of it, like her brother had taught her. She'd broken free.

*"You're never unarmed,"* Jake had told her shortly after they'd gone on the run. *"Everything around you can be used either as a tool or a weapon."*

Of course, Gabe might have let her escape. Maybe he thought he could follow her from a distance. *Good luck with that.* She'd become a master of evasion in the past few months. And this past week, since they'd arrived in Venice, she'd learned every island, every canal.

With her twists and turns and doubling back, she was confident that even if Gabe had been behind her at one point, by now she'd shaken him.

The canal to her right glistened darkly in the moonlight, leading to the harbor a few blocks ahead. She'd better avoid all the extra security there. US Senator Richard Wharst's whale of a yacht bobbed in the water, overshadowing the smaller vessels. Because of him, the harbor had an increased police presence around the clock.

Jasmine didn't go that far, just past the hideously expensive gondolas and the only slightly less pricey water taxis to catch a *vaporetto*. The water buses, used by locals, were the least expensive way to get around in Venice. Thankfully, they ran even at night due to all the tourists.

Jasmine bought a ticket from the ticket vending machine, jumped on a vaporetto marked for Soremo, and went to stand in the back. She preferred to be on her feet, ready to leap and run at short notice. Or leap and swim. Hopefully, not tonight. She didn't like the look of the cold, dark water.

She turned from the canal and inspected every person on board. No sign of Gabe or the other muscle heads he ran with.

*Gabe Cannon. Here.* Back on that roof, he'd actually been *on top of her!* For all the wrong reasons, of course.

He was with the enemy.

To push Gabe from her mind, Jasmine let her gaze stray to a young man in his twenties and hesitate over his black silk shirt, red sweater, and designer jeans that he wore with Italian leather loafers.

He immediately sidled up to her with an exaggerated smile and an I-want-to-ravish-you look. "Bella Signora, you're an American, sì?"

His face could have been carved by Michelangelo, he was so perfect. Yet nothing in her body responded to him.

"Antonio show you real good time. I'm very special for ladies. Very confidential. Two hundred American dollars. All night," he added with a salacious smile.

Her body clenched—and not in a good way. A year ago, she would have thought the come-on funny, but since the *incident*…She couldn't stand the thought of a man touching her.

Her tired muscles stiffened. She swallowed past her tightening throat. "No thanks."

"Are you sure?" Her vaporetto Casanova dragged out the last word, making it into two syllables, maybe hoping she just needed encouragement. But when he touched her arm and she flinched, jerking away from him reflexively, he shrugged and moved on to find another potential customer.

Jasmine filled her lungs, shook her head, and shook off the weird vibe. *God, what a night.*

She'd been caught, and then she'd been propositioned. It'd be nice not to have any more excitement at least until morning.

When the vaporetto reached its last stop, she jumped off. *Almost there.* She was aching for rest as she dragged her tired butt down the nearly deserted sidewalk.

Soremo was an out-of-the-way island. In the Middle Ages, it had been famous for its salt warehouses, according to a sign printed in three languages at the vaporetto stop. Jasmine had discovered that in the more recent past, the giant storage rooms had been divided into small flats that now housed teachers, shop assistants, and blue-collar workers. People around here were too busy cranking out a living to pay Jasmine much attention as she came and went, which made the island the ideal hiding spot.

She headed to the dilapidated section and to the broken window of an abandoned building. She looked and listened. Enough moonlight filtered in to give decent visibility.

The large room stood empty. She heard nothing but the water below and rats scurrying in the far corners, so she slipped inside, then hurried to the top floor, careful on the rotting stairs. The salty, humid sea air meant anything ignored quickly deteriorated, and there were buildings in Venice nobody had touched in a hundred years.

She stayed mindful of that as she strode forward.

"It's me," she called out before she opened the door at the end of the hallway.

Her sister, Mandy, lowered the only gun they had left. She was the teenage version of Jasmine, except her hair was shorter, lighter, currently mussed from sleep. Right now she looked exhausted and worried, struggling to hide both behind a smile and failing. "Hey."

Jake lay maybe ten feet behind her. He nodded at Jasmine, relief flooding his face that she was back safely. "Everything okay?"

She faked her best smile. "Am I super spy chick or what?" She struck a pose and put a lethal look into her eyes. "Bond, *Miss* Bond."

Jake flashed his long-suffering older brother expression.

Even injured, even down, he still looked like a warrior. He was taller than both of his sisters, his face wider, his jawline masculine. He had the same dark brown hair as Jasmine, several shades darker than Mandy's. He hadn't been sick long enough to lose substantial muscle mass, but his face had definitely lost color.

Jasmine moved toward them through the cavernous room, thirty feet by thirty feet at least, empty save for their junk and some general rubble left behind by previous squatters.

"Did you bring food?" Mandy checked Jasmine's hands, then caught herself. "I probably shouldn't eat in the middle of the night—might as well glue it to my thighs. It's okay if you didn't find anything. I'm not that hungry."

But her hollow eyes told another story.

Jasmine's heart clenched. Mandy should be able to sleep safely, at home, in her own bed, after a decent meal, and go to school in the morning. She was a junior in high school. She shouldn't be living in a ruin with rats. They couldn't go on like this much longer.

"I do what I promise." Jasmine reached into her shirt and pulled out a panini, then the small bunch of bananas she'd snatched from an all-night snack shop while weaving through the streets on her way back. She gave a third to Mandy before she went to check on her brother.

As she crouched next to Jake, her heart clenched all over again, harder, with true fear. Not even the several days' growth of beard could hide Jake's sunken cheeks. His eyes burned with fever.

"I got antibiotics." She presented the small Ziploc bag that held half a dozen white pills. *God let them work.*

"What did you sell for it?" Jake's voice came out heartbreakingly weak.

"Nothing." She'd stolen the pills earlier in the day, kept them in her boot. She felt a tug of guilt over the theft, and a lot of relief that Gabe Cannon had missed the medicine during his pat-down.

Back when her life had been normal, she used to think the line between right and wrong stood pretty clear, the whole black-and-white thing. Now she lived in gray, slipping toward darker and darker tones every week.

Daily now, she did things she would have thought herself incapable of before. She lied to keep Mandy and Jake hidden. She stole to keep them from starving. If she hadn't sold Jake's backup gun for food weeks ago, she might have shot Gabe on the roof before she recognized him.

She wasn't comfortable with that thought, but she couldn't afford to be caught. Mandy and Jake needed her to handle things until Jake recovered. She could do this for a few more days, keep them all from capture. Then Jake would be better, and he'd figure out how to escape, find a permanent solution. Jasmine had to hang on just until then.

But Jake seemed to have come to a different conclusion while Jasmine had been gone, because he said, "You have to take Mandy and leave." He tossed back a pill and swallowed. "It's not safe for you here."

Jasmine's spine stiffened. "It's not safe for us anywhere."

A moment of desperate silence passed between them, filled with her nightmarish memories.

*Don't think about that.* She threw up walls and doors in her mind in a panicked hurry, locking sounds and smells and images away, locking away the memory of pain. She forced herself to breathe evenly and focus on her brother.

Guilt turned Jake's face even more gaunt. Remorse sat in his eyes, as if deep inside, the truth in her words made him bleed.

"I never meant for you to get hurt." His voice begged for the absolution she'd granted a hundred times but which he couldn't accept.

"Jake—"

He shook his head. "This place is no longer a viable option. I need you to scout out a different location and take yourself and Mandy there. An empty apartment for sale where you can turn on the heat."

"You can't make it down the stairs until your leg heals." Some snap sneaked into her voice. No way was he going to get rid of them.

He'd taken a bullet in his thigh the week before. She'd removed the slug with a pair of knitting needles she'd lifted off an old lady at a café, but infection had set in, immobilizing the whole leg and bringing on fever. That he also had a broken arm from a nasty fall, because he hadn't been able to accept that the leg wouldn't work, didn't help.

"You two go right now," he insisted. "I'll come after you tomorrow. I'll be better by then."

His voice was filled with optimism and encouragement, but Jasmine wasn't fooled. He was thinking about giving himself up, so then she and Mandy would be safe.

*Maybe safe.*

The people who hunted them might still come after them anyway, thinking Jake had told them something. The commando team seemed pretty keen on tying up loose ends.

But even if the plan was foolproof, Jasmine still wouldn't have left her brother. They all lived or they all died. They were family. Nobody was going to be left behind, dammit.

"We're not going anywhere without you." Mandy echoed Jasmine's thoughts around the food in her mouth. Then she coughed.

She'd been coughing last night too.

Jasmine shot her a questioning look.

Mandy shrugged. "I think I'm allergic to mold. Or rat poop."

Jasmine pressed her lips together. That they were living like this now seemed utterly surreal at times. While at other times…their new normal. Their spoiled American life was a dream.

They'd begun this escapade with a grim determination to get their old lives back ASAP. Jasmine was no longer sure if that was possible. Instead of dreaming about going back home, now they were all happy just to survive from one day to the next.

Jake shifted on his folded cardboard box bed, keeping his right arm carefully extended in the makeshift cast they'd made with gypsum she'd stolen from a hotel renovation. "Are the men still in the city?"

Because Jasmine needed a moment to organize her thoughts, she pushed to her feet and went back to Mandy, to the stained, ancient mattress they'd salvaged from a dumpster. She sat next to her sister, pulling the blanket higher around Mandy's shoulders. The temperature in the low fifties wasn't bad for February—the Mediterranean Sea tempered the city's climate—but they were far from comfortable without heat.

Sometimes, on moonless nights when nobody would see the smoke, they burned garbage in a steel barrel that stood next to the last window in the back. But mostly they relied on the sun to warm up their south-facing room during the day, and the thick brick walls to radiate that heat back overnight.

Mandy flashed a sleepy grin, licking crumbs from her lips. "Thanks."

Jasmine tucked in her sister but looked back at her brother, who was still waiting for her answer.

"They were out hunting tonight," she told him. "I tried to fool them into thinking I was you and lead them to the mainland. To the airport in Mestre. I thought I could maybe make them think that you were getting on a plane."

But they'd caught up with her long before that, at the old palace. Jasmine cleared her throat. "Gabe Cannon is with them now. I thought he was your friend. Why is he doing this? I thought he was a good guy."

Jake sat up, struggling. "People change. Don't go anywhere near him. We can't afford to trust anyone. If they caught you—"

Jasmine bit the inside of her cheek. Gabe had caught her already. That the night hadn't turned into tragedy was a miracle. But Jake didn't need to worry about that now, on top of everything else.

Only ten men had been after her tonight, but altogether about twenty mercenaries hunted Jake. Half kept searching the city; the other half secured the railroad bridge and Ponte della Libertà, the five-kilometer long Liberty Bridge that connected Venice to the mainland for car and bus traffic.

Jasmine needed to find a way to outsmart those men, and she needed to find it quickly. She swallowed her share of the food without tasting any of the flavors. Today's plan to lead the hunters to the airport had failed. She would have to come up with something better for tomorrow.

Both Jake and Mandy were in worse shape than they admitted.

She watched her brother. "Can you at least tell me why these men are hunting you? Beyond that it's something that happened overseas? What happened in Lahedeh?"

Other than it was a town in Afghanistan and was the source of her brother's troubles, Jasmine knew little.

Jake's eyes filled with regret all over again. "Everyone who knows is dead. If we get caught, your only chance to survive will be if you know nothing."

Sure. If their pursuers believed her when she claimed ignorance. But she didn't want to waste her brother's energy by arguing with him. Instead, she nodded.

Jake finished his meager ration of food, then struggled to stand and hobbled over to the window just three steps behind him. He looked out into the night, gripping the windowsill with a white-knuckled hand.

Jasmine's throat tightened. "You shouldn't put weight on your leg."

Just standing had to take superhuman effort. He had to be in enough pain to knock out a lesser man.

He stopped her with a wave of his hand. He hated to be this weak, so he pretended to be strong, and they pretended to believe him. Except Jasmine was beginning to suspect that pretense wasn't going to save them. They needed real strength, real help.

"Thanks, Jaz." Mandy finished her food and lay back down onto the mattress—reduced to a fragile, listless heap.

Normally, she had the most energy among the three of them. And the biggest mouth. But not tonight.

Jasmine reached out to feel her little sister's forehead, then squeezed her eyes shut for a second, a sense of hopelessness washing over her. "You have a fever too."

Mandy flashed her best can-do smile, pep squad all the way. "I'll be fine. I'll just sleep a little more."

"It's cold in here."

"The sun will be up soon. That'll help."

Jake turned to them, fighting to keep standing, fighting not to let despair show on his face, winning at the first battle, losing at the second. "Why didn't you say anything?" Enough guilt filled his eyes to drown in. "How bad is the fever?"

Mandy fidgeted with her blanket. When she spoke, her voice came out small and shaky. "Not bad. I won't be any trouble."

The sight of her vivacious, chirpy little sister being beaten down like this just about killed Jasmine.

Her brother looked at her, silently asking for the truth.

"She's burning up," Jasmine told him.

Jake hobbled over to them and sat on the corner of the mattress on Mandy's other side. He would never say it, but his leg couldn't support him longer than a few steps at a time. He pulled the Ziploc bag from his pocket and passed a pill to Mandy, who raised her head and swallowed it obediently.

And they both pretended, for Jasmine's sake, that everything was going to be fine, even if they both needed so much more than antibiotics. They needed real medical care, preferably a hospital, and the sooner, the better.

Jasmine's gut hurt from being scared to death for them.

Jake lay down next to Mandy and gathered her to him, his own teeth chattering. And as Jasmine looked at them, she had to accept at last that her brother wasn't going to get better any day now and take charge again. He was as tough as men came, but not bulletproof, and the infection was overwhelming his body. He wasn't going to lead them out of here to safety.

*She* had to do it.

Cold panic coursed through her veins.

For a moment, she had trouble drawing air into her lungs. Then Gabe Cannon's blue eyes flashed into her mind.

His eyes had always stood out in contrast to his dark lashes and dark hair, a spellbinding combination of coloring. She wasn't going to let him bamboozle her this time.

This time, Jasmine was taking charge of the situation.

She shoved the last of the panini into her mouth as she stood. She looked at Jake and Mandy huddled together, and she steeled her spine. What she was about to do would either save them or bury them.

She had one idea, and she had to try it. Waiting for their fate, giving up without trying, wasn't an option. That wasn't what Jake had taught her.

He opened his eyes and frowned. "You should rest too. Where are you going?"

Better that he didn't know. He might try to stop her.

"You both need something for that fever," she said.

Her brother held her gaze. "Be careful."

"Take the gun," Mandy offered from under the blanket.

"You keep it. If anyone else but me comes through this door, you shoot. Okay?" Jasmine hated putting that kind of burden on her sister, but she could find no other way to make sure they were safe. Jake could barely move his right arm, let alone aim a gun with it.

Jasmine gave them her most confident smile. "I'll be back with something that'll help. I promise."

As she hurried down the crumbling stairs a few seconds later, she hoped fate wouldn't make a liar out of her.

At one point, out of sheer desperation, she'd tracked the commandos back to the *pensione* they rented on the main island. She'd wanted to know what kind of enemy she faced. She'd gotten the answer to that: overwhelming.

Since then, she had stayed away from the place. But now she knew that one of the hunters was Gabe. She hadn't recognized him before. Some of the men she'd seen only from afar. Until tonight, her main goal had been to stay as far from them as possible.

But now she had to accept the stark truth that her brother could no longer protect the family. She had to admit that neither could she. She could keep them hidden and keep stealing food, but Mandy and Jake needed medical attention. Pronto.

The only glimmer of hope Jasmine could see was convincing Gabe Cannon to help them. He was a SEAL. Did that mean as much as she thought it did? Or was she delusional because she'd spent too much time during her teenage years thinking of him as her knight in shining armor?

She wanted to trust him. She was predisposed to trust him. But she was a logical enough person to know that none of that meant she *should* or *could* trust him.

The only indication she had that Gabe might still be a good guy was that he hadn't turned her over to his team on the rooftop. But what if that didn't mean what she thought it meant?

Her feet faltered.

What other choice did she have?

None.

So she kept going, back to the man she'd spent half the night escaping. And as she walked, she planned.

What would Jake do? He would take command and dominate the situation. Jasmine was going to have to do the same.

She *was* going to talk Gabe into helping her. But just in case he'd fully gone over to the dark side, first she was going to find herself a weapon.

# FOUR

"I'm fine. I swear. Just tired. The drug program is starting to work," Gabe's sister, Amy, said over the phone. She was on an experimental drug cocktail regimen for MS, and it looked like the drugs were cutting some of her symptoms in half. "Izzy wants to talk to you."

Gabe had already talked to his other two nieces, Bailey and Elli. Izzy was the four-year-old, the youngest, running circles around everybody already, God help them all.

"Hi, Uncle Gabe!" she squeaked into the phone as soon as she took it over.

"Hey, ya, tootsie."

"Knock, knock," she said immediately. Izzy had a double PhD in knock-knock jokes.

"Who's there?" Gabe humored her.

"Bean."

"Bean who?"

"Bean missing you too much, Uncle Gabe!" Izzy broke out in giggles. "Mom, I remembered!"

Gabe grinned. "I miss you too, tootsie."

"I ate my vegedables," Izzy told him next. "My friend Tori ate her vegedables, and Santa brought her a puppy. Can you tell the Easter Bunny to bring me a puppy?"

"Mmmh." Gabe made noncommittal noises. A puppy was up to Mom. He didn't want to encourage false expectations, then see Izzy disappointed. "You already have a pet."

"But Tootie won't fetch."

She had him there. Tootie was the family cat, named Tootie for…obvious reasons. She farted like a warthog at an all-you-can-eat bean buffet.

While Izzy listed all the good behavior she was going to practice to earn the puppy, Gabe kept his eyes on the TV that ran Italian cartoons on mute. He gave no sign that he'd noticed Jasmine Tekla observing him through his window for the past ten minutes.

Brent should have listened when Gabe had recommended setting up perimeter security. But the team leader was too arrogant to think that someone could turn the tables on him. They'd rented the entire *pensione*—Italy's version of a bed-and-breakfast. Twenty rough and tough commando guys filled the rooms. They were plenty secure, according to Brent.

Tekla was running *from* them, not looking *for* them, so Brent hadn't been worried. Having a standing guard would only draw attention, he'd said. And since he was the boss, Gabe had let it go. He wasn't scared. He could handle what came his way.

Izzy shot off a few more knock-knock jokes, made another passionate plea for her uncle's support in the Great Puppy Project, then handed the phone back to her mom.

"I don't want you to put yourself in danger for us," Amy said, keeping her voice low.

"I'm not in a war zone. I swear. I'm in a safe place, on a routine mission." If the twenty of them couldn't take down Tekla and his sister, they all needed to retire. "How is Seattle?"

"Wet. I miss home. The girls do too."

Gabe believed her. As nice as it was, Seattle was a city, nothing like the small Pennsylvania town nestled between rolling hills where Amy and the kids lived. But the clinical trials for the new MS drug cocktail were run by the University of Washington Medical Center, so Amy needed to be in Seattle. And she needed money, which Gabe was going to earn with XO-ST commando work.

"I'm never going to forget that you're doing this for us." Amy had tears in her voice. "You're the best brother ever."

"Sure, now I am," he teased. "You had a different opinion of me back in the day."

Amy gave a weak laugh. "You intimidated all my boyfriends."

*Not enough.* But he didn't want to bring up Dumbass Dave, who'd abandoned Amy and the kids when she'd gotten sick.

They talked for a few more minutes before ending the call.

Gabe made a show of yawning and stretching. Could he grab the gun hidden in the desk drawer? Probably not a good idea. Jasmine would definitely notice.

He turned the drawer key with a slight motion, then palmed it. At least now he knew she wouldn't be able to commandeer the gun while he left the room to lure her in.

He scratched his chest, unmuted the TV, then stood and headed for the bathroom. *Don't spook her now.* He needed to make her feel as secure as possible.

Maybe Tekla was ready to turn himself in and sent her as a messenger. *Could anything ever be that easy? Not likely.* And yet she was here.

Gabe closed the bathroom door behind him, waited two minutes, then flushed the toilet. If she was smart, she would use the noise to cover any creaking as she pushed the window open. And she was smart. She'd outsmarted him on that roof. Thank God the others didn't know about that, or he'd never live it down.

After a few more seconds, Gabe turned on the tap. She would use the cover of the running water to move into the room, knowing he'd turn the tap off when he was done, and she'd have ample warning before he left the bathroom.

She'd probably have a gun this time. He wasn't overly worried. If she wanted to kill him, she would have shot him through the window. *No,* she was here to talk. She would hold him at gunpoint to make herself feel safe, and tell him what she wanted from him.

And then he would take control of the situation and have her lead him to her brother. Gabe bit back a grin. He'd felt a step behind through this whole op. Time for him to get a step ahead.

He left the water running, put his hand on the doorknob, and listened. Of course, with all the noise the water made, he couldn't hear anything out there, except a squeaky cartoon voice talking rapidly in Italian. If Jasmine hadn't come into the room after all, he was going to feel pretty stupid in about three seconds. *Two. One.*

He slammed the door open and burst forward.

He registered the empty room a blink before she dropped on him from the storage shelf above the bathroom door, nearly knocking him off his feet. She had to know she couldn't take down a SEAL in hand-to-hand combat. Unfortunately, that didn't keep her from trying.

"Hey. Stop that." He tried to twist to get hold of her, but his temple caught her sharp elbow, and he saw stars. "Dammit, Jasmine!"

He staggered toward the bed and flipped her down at last, but she managed to hook her leg behind his neck and fought her way on top somehow. She ended up sitting on his chest. Of course, he wasn't resisting much. She wasn't here to kill him.

She didn't even have a weapon.

"Can I ask you something?" he asked as he put up some token struggle, because if he gave up too quickly, she'd suspect a trap.

"What?" She gasped the word as she fought to keep him down.

"Do you seriously think you're going to take down a Navy SEAL barehanded?"

Maybe she'd hit her head when she'd escaped the roof. Or maybe she was suicidal. She could be a total looney tune for all he knew. A girl could change a lot in five years.

She'd certainly changed plenty on the outside—had definitely grown from a pretty girl into a beautiful woman.

"The bigger they are, the harder they fall," she snapped out in a tone that would have fit an Old West-style gunslinger better than her.

"Did you hear that in a movie?"

Instead of responding, she leaned her full body weight on her hands, her fingers wrapped around his wrists as she held them down to the mattress. He let her. He liked the way her eyes glinted with triumph.

The fight was to establish that she wasn't helpless, that he couldn't do with her as he pleased. She was wrong about that. He could. But for now, he was willing to allow her to keep her illusions. She needed a sense of security. She was scared out of her mind. He understood her need to feel that she had *some* control here.

Her wild dark waves of hair were pulled back into a utilitarian ponytail, her cheeks pink from effort, her chin set with determination. She wore the same black outfit as before, same black combat boots. She looked like a comic book action heroine.

Her eyes were the golden-brown color of the antique Venetian gold that gilded St. Mark's Cathedral. Her chest heaved as she leaned forward to keep his hands pinned next to his head on each side. She ended up with her generous breasts inches from his lips.

He could imagine worse ways to spend the evening.

*Don't think like that.* Last time he'd seen her, she'd been wearing a school uniform, for fuck's sake. He was seven years older than she was, but still too young to turn into an old lecher.

Gabe could have subdued her in two moves, but he left her on top of him. She'd be more likely to answer his questions if she thought she was in control. If their position sent some heat zinging through him, he was prepared to ignore it. No need for her to find out how she affected him.

Of course, if she slid her round ass farther down his body and straddled his groin instead of his chest, she'd find out real fast. *Shit. Okay.* If she started sliding back, he'd free his hands and hold her in place. He wasn't going to let their tussle turn sexual in any way. He hadn't even copped a feel.

"Tell me what you need, sweetheart."

He wished she was older, not related to his mission, and came to him simply to spend the night with him.

*Aaand,* there he went again. *Think about her brother.* Or, really, anything but how much he wished they were naked.

She helped him by pulling a six-inch sharpened length of metal from her boot and holding it to his throat, a chunk of a narrow pipe that she probably had rubbed over rough concrete.

Okay. *That* got his attention.

He went completely still. "Where did you learn to make a shiv?"

"Jake taught me."

*Of course, he did.* Gabe was going to have a talk with the guy soon, about being a positive influence on his sisters, among other topics.

Satisfaction lit up Jasmine's face, her antique-gold eyes, lips, even the tilt of her pert nose fierce. "Don't move."

She thought she'd won—if not the war, then at least the skirmish.

She was so far out of her league, it went way past funny, deep into disconcerting territory. In what universe did she think she was going to sneak into the headquarters of a mercenary commando unit and get what she wanted, unscathed?

But for now Gabe let her keep the shiv, and he kept his voice as nonthreatening as possible. "Anything I can help you with, Jasmine?"

The light of satisfaction on her face turned into a look of anger. "Why are you chasing Jake? You two used to be friends."

"My friends don't turn rogue."

"He was framed." She spoke with conviction, appearing to believe most sincerely what she was saying.

"Your brother killed three men. One of them was a US naval officer."

Her lips narrowed to a thin line. "You don't know the circumstances."

She had gumption, passion, and loyalty in spades. Gabe felt a twinge of respect, and a twinge of something else, but he was going to ignore the latter. He was also going to ignore the way her slim thighs felt around his chest, squeezing to make sure he stayed still. He was *not* going to think about what those thighs would feel like wrapped around his waist, squeezing as he pushed into her.

*Shit.*

"So what changed since we were on the roof?" he asked. "Why run away if you were just going to come back to me?"

"Now I have the upper hand." She allowed a smile that turned her face from beautiful to so striking, his balls tingled.

He had to remind himself that she was in league with his search-and-destroy target. The intimate relationship his body demanded wasn't in their future.

He watched her closely. "You think that since I knew your brother at one point, and because I didn't turn you over to the others on the roof, I'm the weak link on the team."

She stayed silent for several moments, smart enough to know that insulting him wouldn't gain her any favors. But then she said, "You're one of the good guys. You're a SEAL. I think once you know the truth, you'll do the right thing." She paused, her expression turning painfully serious. "I have to trust someone. You seem to be the best candidate."

"Trusting strangers will get you killed."

"Doing nothing will get me killed too."

He couldn't argue with that. His team was too close to Tekla. They'd catch him. And if she got in the crossfire…

Gabe watched the tight set of her shoulders and wished she were a thousand miles from here. "Does your brother always send you to fight his battles?"

What was Tekla thinking to involve her in something as dangerous as this? She might be dressed like a comic book heroine, but her golden eyes were so damned trusting, Gabe couldn't stand it.

She bit her full bottom lip, which caused an answering twitch in his pants. He seriously had to gain control of his response to her.

"Jake doesn't know I'm here." She hesitated for a beat before she went on. "He was set up. He knows something, and people want to kill him for it."

"Let me guess, your brother discovered a vast government conspiracy." Gabe didn't bother to keep the skepticism from his voice. Did Tekla have some kind of severe PTSD? Another reason to bring the man in instead of shooting him on sight.

Jasmine's mouth pressed into an annoyed line before she said, "I don't know what he discovered. All I know is that he discovered it in Afghanistan. Some town called Lahedeh. He won't tell me more. He thinks the less I know, the safer I am."

"Maybe he'd tell me?" Gabe was ready to finish this mission and be back stateside to help his own sister for a while before the team received their next assignment.

They'd been tracking Tekla all over Europe for weeks now. But they should be done soon. The guy couldn't possibly evade them longer than another day or two tops.

Since Gabe wasn't resisting, Jasmine removed the shiv from his throat and held it uncertainly at her side. "He's not anywhere around here."

She was lying through the even white teeth Gabe wanted to run his tongue along. He wanted to do things to her with his tongue that made him contrite with guilt, but at the same time, the images set his body humming.

They were in bed. She was on top of him, her firm ass deliciously straddling his chest. His pants felt tighter by the second. *Not going to happen.* He forced himself to focus on the discussion at hand.

"If he's not here, then why did you do your mama-bird-trying-to-draw-the-snake-from-the-nest imitation and lead us across town tonight?"

Her chin came up. She did have a cute chin. Very kissable—an excellent landing point for a man's lips. He could go up from there to her full, tortured bottom lip, or down, to her graceful neck and beyond to—

He blinked. What the hell was wrong with him?

He forced his gaze up to her golden-brown eyes. "So what is it, exactly, that you want from me, Jasmine?"

If their situation didn't involve multiple murders, he might have given her anything she asked. Not a comfortable thought. He liked women. Liked women a *lot*. Yet he'd never before let one render him stupid. But now he found himself *wanting* to believe Jasmine, *wanting* to help her.

She said, "Distract those thugs you work with so I can get away from Venice and find a safer place."

"You mean you and your brother?"

She held his gaze, trying hard to school her expression. And not succeeding. A career in professional poker was *not* in her future.

God, he hoped she'd have a future. He was starting to like her. What she was doing here…She was admirable.

"Your brother shouldn't have dragged you into his crime spree," he said.

"You don't know what you're talking about."

"I know you're not going anywhere until you tell me where he is."

Once Tekla was in custody, the pressure would be off Jasmine, and she would be safe. Not that she showed any appreciation for Gabe looking out for her.

She shot him a look sharper than her shiv. "How do I know you're not a murderous bastard like the others?"

He said nothing. He would be lying if he said he wasn't.

She interpreted his silence correctly. "Don't you have a conscience?"

"I do."

"Tell me one bad thing you regret doing."

"We're not getting into that right now. We don't have time for this."

"One thing," she demanded.

She tried to look hard and tough, but she felt soft and fragile on top of him. He didn't mind spending time in bed with her, but time was of the essence. He needed her to cooperate.

*Fine. Okay. One* thing.

"You know that first time we met? I really shouldn't have kissed you. I apologize. I was a sailor on shore leave. I had no judgment. I'm sorry."

She stared at him. "You can't apologize for that."

"I just did."

"That was my first kiss."

Okay. His turn to stare. Now he *really* felt like a conscienceless bastard.

"We live in a very small town," she said. "Everyone knows everyone. Everyone knows Jake is a SEAL. Boys in high school are hoping for one thing. They never asked me out, because they said if they messed with me, Jake would break them in half."

Gabe didn't know what to say. He kind of remembered having that conversation with a number of boyfriends Amy had brought home back in the day.

"Tell me something else," she said. "Something really serious that you regret more than anything."

He was so desperate to get her to trust him that he told her something he *never* talked about.

"I once led a team to eradicate a makeshift weapons factory in the Afghan mountains. Small place with an unpronounceable name. We called it North Village. I led the charge. We shot the place to hell. We killed most everyone inside this one industrial-looking building. They were classified as enemy combatants in the attack order."

He drew a slow breath. "They weren't. We had faulty intel. The village was starting some grassroots truck part repair business. Most of the men worked there. Now the village is nothing but orphans and widows."

He looked away from her shocked eyes, then back. "So no, I'm not a good person. But I no longer follow orders blindly either. And no more innocent people are going to get killed on my watch if I can help it."

She drew a breath to say something, but somebody knocked on the door at the same time, and she snapped her mouth shut, her eyes growing wide and panicked.

He flipped her before she knew what was happening, sent the shiv flying across the carpet, and put his hand over her lips to silence her.

And all the trust he'd built until now evaporated just like that.

Her cheeks flushed a deeper red, eyes even wider with alarm, the tip of her tongue darting out in a nervous gesture to moisten her lips, or maybe she was just opening her mouth to bite him. He felt her hot moisture against his palm and bit back a groan.

He yanked his hand back. She was smart enough to know that calling out would not improve her situation. He hoped.

"Brent wants to see everyone in his room," Troy called from the hallway in his distinctively raspy voice.

A string of panicked emotions flickered across Jasmine's face. She clearly knew that Gabe was at the point of decision. He could turn her over to the others, and they could use her as bait to draw Tekla here.

If it weren't for that kill order, Gabe would have. But he hadn't handed her over on the roof, and he wasn't going to do it now.

Brent was pulling out all the stops for this op. Maybe because he was ready to go home, or maybe because he was starting to lose face over Tekla's ability to evade him this long. The team leader seemed ready to end the op by whatever means necessary, a decision that didn't sit well with Gabe. North Village had given him a thing about civilian casualties.

Whatever Jasmine's brother had done, *she* shouldn't have to pay for it.

"On my way," Gabe called back to Troy.

As soon as the man's footsteps faded in the hallway, Jasmine began to struggle. The ninja octopus was back. Gabe had triggered her fight-or-flight response, and she was ready to fight so then she could flee.

"Let me go," she begged in a breathless pant.

"I can't."

She'd come here on her own, but she hadn't been a hundred percent sure that she'd made the right decision. If he set her free, she'd probably leave and not come back. He'd spooked her when he'd rolled her under him. He didn't want to lose her again, not before he could ask more questions. They needed to finish this conversation. He needed her to take him to her brother.

A peaceful handover would ensure that Tekla lived long enough to stand trial for his crimes. Once he was in custody, the pressure would be off his family. And, mission accomplished, Gabe's team could go home to the US and collect their payment. *Everybody wins.*

He could think of only one way to ensure her staying put.

"I'm doing this for your own safety," he said in his best soothing voice.

But as soon as he reached for his belt, she bucked under him. "No! Let me go!"

Her eyes filled with stunned disbelief, then burning hate. She fought him every inch of the way. He could barely get his belt off to tie her right hand to the headboard. Then he grabbed a curtain tie and secured her other hand with that.

"I need to go and see what's going on. I need to make sure you're still here when I come back. Relax. Take a break. Nobody else comes in here. You'll be safe."

She kicked at him, her boot connecting with his solar plexus and knocking the air from his lungs.

He scowled at her. "I wouldn't do that again. Let's do this the easy way."

She kicked lower this time, her foot slamming into his upper thigh, way too close to a place boots had no business being.

"The hard way it is." Two more curtain ties and her feet were tied too, each to a bedpost.

Her fury turned into desperation as she struggled against her restraints more and more violently. "No. Please."

She was scraping her wrists raw, dammit.

He opened his mouth to threaten her, then caught the sheen of tears in her eyes. She hadn't been kicking at him to be mean. She was out of control with fear.

"Listen. Hey." He reached for her shoulders, held her down. "You're hurting yourself. Stop. I'll let you up when I get back. All right?"

But she was suddenly in full panic, and thrashed on the bed, shaking it— an overblown response. He hadn't hurt her. He hadn't threatened to hurt her. He'd told her he wanted to help.

He had a feeling he was missing something here, but he didn't have time to figure out what was making her act this way. Too late to let her go. Now she'd bolt for sure.

She fought so hard, the headboard slammed against the wall.

*Shit.* Somebody was going to hear her from the hallway.

He needed to snap her out of her frenzy. "I'm not going to hurt you, Jasmine."

But she didn't seem able to stop fighting. Panic had pushed her beyond reason.

Maybe she'd calm if he put some distance between them. Gabe stepped back from the bed. "I'm not going to hurt you."

She kept on struggling as if she couldn't hear him.

And yet…Bruised wrists and ankles were survivable damage. All the noise she was making, however…if one of the other guys on the team caught her…They had a kill order for her brother. Brent might decide that extended to whoever aided and abetted.

And the team *would* catch her. Right here, in another minute, if she didn't keep quiet. Gabe couldn't just turn the volume on the TV higher to mask the noise she made. People outside the room would think it was weird. Blaring Italian cartoons made no sense, since they all knew Gabe didn't speak the language. He needed another solution. And he could think of only one thing to calm her, short of letting her go.

He grabbed the duffle bag at the foot of the bed and rummaged through the contents. He didn't want to do what he was about to do, but the alternative was worse.

"This is going to help you settle down." He pulled the syringe of sedative and popped the cap, pushed the drug into her arm in the same motion. He tried to control the dosage. The full vial was calibrated for a large man, someone like Gabe, a fighter who might be twice her weight.

Since the original goal of the op had been apprehension, they had tranqs, in case they cornered Tekla in a high-traffic tourist area and had to get him out of there without drawing attention.

Jasmine arched her body up from the mattress, then crashed down, rattling the bed again.

Gabe held her down. "Stay still."

Past following orders, Jasmine swore at him violently and jerked forward, causing him to push in more of the drug than he'd intended.

*Hell, dammit.*

Boots scuffed outside.

He bent to her ear to whisper, "You'll be safe here. I'll lock you in."

"My brother is going to kill you for this," she slurred, her eyes glazing over.

*Shit.* He'd been hoping to convince her to trust him. He got her to hate him instead. How in hell had the situation gotten out of hand this fast?

As he headed for the door, he didn't have a good feeling about Brent calling this meeting either. What did the team leader want now? He'd already given a kill order, which was pretty damn serious. But every instinct Gabe had said that things were about to take a turn for the worse.

# CHAPTER
# FIVE

Jasmine struggled to breathe. Panic made her heart beat so hard, her chest hurt.

She was tied down.

*It's different this time. It's different.* Gabe had tied her down. And he wasn't going to hurt her. He said he wouldn't.

She tried to hang on to that thought, her mind too fuzzy to think or to plan escape. Her brain kept flashing back to another time. *Ropes on her wrists and ankles. A moldy-smelling basement. A man.*

*Pain.*

Her mouth opened to scream, but for some reason, it was very important that she didn't. She couldn't remember why. She squeezed her lips together anyway.

She listened. Cartoon voices carried on a conversation somewhere nearby. She didn't understand them.

*Did the man leave?*

Her eyelids fluttered closed. She struggled to open them again.

No, the man wasn't here.

Gabe Cannon was. Her heart slowed little by little.

*So strange,* she thought as she dozed. Was she back in high school?

But the images flickering through her mind weren't about high school crushes. As she fell asleep, she dreamt much darker dreams.

***

Brent stuck his head forward, his gaze darting from man to man, like a bull about to attack everything that moved in the arena. He had a fat cigar in hand

and looked like he might crush it before he got it lit. He was full of huff and puff, plenty steamed. "What the fuck happened on the roof today?"

His nose sat at a crooked angle, broken more than once, his right ear notched by a bullet, cold eyes, a stocky body, made of nothing but muscle and grit—an ugly sonofabitch by his own admission. And the only thing he had less of than good looks were scruples.

Ten of the twenty team members had gathered in the team leader's suite, battle-hardened soldiers perching on every available surface. Team A, Gabe's team, the men who'd searched the islands today, were in. Team B was still out, guarding all avenues of exit to the mainland, making sure Tekla didn't slip through the dragnet.

"Maybe he went into the water," Coleman suggested, a forty-something ex-cop, burly guy, fired from the LAPD for using excessive force during a high-profile arrest.

A couple of the other guys nodded at his suggestion.

"Tekla's a SEAL," Troy Hill said. He'd washed off the camo paint like the rest of them, so the scars were visible on his face.

Gabe knew better than to ask about them, even one SEAL to another. You didn't talk about past missions, end of story.

"Venice is the best place for him to be," Troy rasped. The same explosion that had scarred his face had also damaged his vocal cords. "The whole damn city is standing in water. And from here, he can reach the rest of Europe, Africa, or Asia in a matter of hours by ship."

Gabe silently agreed. What he didn't understand was, why hadn't Tekla lit out? No way could anyone corner a SEAL in Venice. With all the canals, the islands, and the entire Mediterranean Sea as his playground, the options for Tekla were unlimited. He had a thousand ways to disappear. Yet he'd stayed in the city for the past week, allowing himself to be hunted, acting as if he *was* cornered.

*Why?*

And why did he have his sister with him?

Gabe glanced toward the door. He needed to get Jasmine away from here.

When he turned back to the boss, he found Brent glaring at him as the man finally lit his cigar with a fancy stainless steel lighter that had a red crest in the middle.

"Next time you see Tekla, you shoot him." Brent's tone made it clear he was issuing a direct order. "Is that understood?"

Gabe understood. He just wasn't going to do it. He wasn't shooting anyone until he figured out what was going on.

He gave a small shrug and let Brent interpret the gesture whatever way he wanted. "I didn't have a good visual. I couldn't make positive ID."

Brent grew quiet, his eyes turning a notch colder. "I gave you a kill order."

Gabe didn't argue. Best to say as little as possible for now.

Brent shot him one last frosty glare, then turned to Harris, the team's tech wiz, and his expression lightened. Before Gabe could begin to wonder why, Brent said, "Harris got us into the traffic cam system. We have one shot of Jake Tekla last week, nothing since. He might be covering his face when he goes out. With the carnival coming, half the tourists wear masks."

Brent opened his laptop and turned the screen toward them. He clicked on a tab on the bottom. But before the computer could navigate to the new screen, Gabe caught the list of a dozen folders, one folder name jumping out at him: Lahedeh.

*"I don't know what Jake discovered. All I know is that he discovered it in Lahedeh,"* Jasmine had said earlier.

A cold feeling spread in Gabe's stomach.

Was there a connection between Brent and Tekla that went beyond this op? What if the Lahedeh folder on Brent's laptop wasn't a coincidence?

Before Gabe could give that more thought, the image of a woman popped up on the laptop's screen. Dressed in black, she stood in line at some food joint, her hand wrist-deep in the purse of a tourist in front of her.

*Jasmine.*

Gabe kept his face carefully expressionless, while Brent said, smug as shit, "Our facial recognition software matched this pic with the photo we have of one of Tekla's two sisters. The older one, Jasmine."

He didn't sound surprised.

So Gabe casually asked, "Did you know she might be here?"

"I had a suspicion. The pre-op research said the sisters live with an aunt in Kansas. I sent some friends to that aunt's house. They found nobody there. Not even the aunt."

*And when was that?* Gabe didn't ask out loud, didn't want to seem suspiciously interested.

Then a disturbing possibility popped into his brain. *What if they're all here?*

*Three women in the middle of a takedown—a surefire recipe for disaster. Oh hell, no. Tekla wouldn't do that, would he?*

On the other hand, if he'd turned traitor…Maybe he'd sold sensitive information to the enemy. Maybe he'd had to kill those three men because they'd caught him. Maybe the Russians—or whoever bought him—were coming to grab Tekla and family and ship him off to the safety of Moscow, and he was just waiting here for that.

Jasmine said her brother was being framed, but family was always the last to accept the truth about things like this. And Tekla might not even have told her what he'd done.

*Shit.*

Brent said, "I think they're on the island of Soremo."

"How do we know that?" Troy asked, not unreasonably. One hundred and seventeen small islands made up the city of Venice—another one of the many reasons that made the place perfect for hiding.

Brent puffed on his cigar. "We have security camera footage of Tekla's sister hopping on the water buses when she's done scavenging on the main island, but no pictures of her getting off anywhere."

"Maybe she swims," Alvarez, a tough-as-nails black man who'd come to the team from Army Special Ops Forces, suggested.

"Not without protective gear," Troy said. "Even the Mediterranean Sea is too damn cold in February. Definitely no swimming without a wetsuit."

No indeed. Maybe Tekla could handle the water as a SEAL without hypothermia, as long as he swam only a short distance. But Jasmine barely had any weight to her, no body fat, nothing to protect her against the cold. Her core temp would drop way too fast in that water.

"She gets off at a station that doesn't have a security camera," Gabe said, because Brent was looking at him again—maybe yet another test for the new guy to prove himself. He had to offer *something.*

Since Gabe needed the job, he didn't tell the team leader where the man could shove his tests.

His response earned him a look of approval from the boss. "Exactly. Away from the tourist center, security cameras are not nearly as common. She's hiding somewhere in a residential district. We find her, we find her brother."

"There are other residential islands besides Soremo," Alvarez put in.

"The water buses she takes when she disappears all have their final stop on Soremo." Brent twisted toward the wall behind him and pointed with his cigar at the tourist map he'd pinned up when they'd arrived in Venice.

Gabe kept a neutral expression. "Are we going back out right now?"

He didn't point out that they'd been hunting Tekla all night and none of them had had any rest, but he let some of his exhaustion show in the slope of his shoulders. He needed time. Jasmine was safe in his room. But if his suspicions were right and Tekla's younger sister and his aunt were with him… They didn't deserve to become casualties.

Brent turned back to his men from the map. "Right now, people are waking up and getting ready for work. I don't want to start a manhunt at rush hour. We'll wait until all the worker bees are at their jobs. The residential district should be half-empty in another hour or two."

He glanced at his watch before he continued. "The B Team will be at the showdown with us. I don't want to leave anything to chance this time. Get some sleep. I want everyone ready to leave at oh nine hundred."

His eyes were on Gabe, but he was talking to the team in general as he said, "Tekla is considered armed and dangerous. You're authorized to use whatever force necessary. The kill order is still in place."

"What about the sister?" Troy asked.

*Thank you, Troy.*

Gabe waited for the answer.

Brent didn't look thankful as he swept his gaze around the room, puffing on his cigar. "She needs to stay out of the way if she knows what's good for her. We're facing a seasoned killer here. If she tries to help the target and gets caught in the crossfire, I doubt we'll catch any flak."

Nobody other than Gabe seemed bothered by that. Maybe Troy. Troy did shoot Gabe a flat look, but then he ended with a microscopic shrug that seemed to say *it ain't the navy, but this is what we signed up for.*

Gabe glanced back at the team leader, who was talking quietly with Harris. Brent's need to catch Tekla seemed over the top. He pulled out too many stops. Almost as if he had a personal agenda.

Gabe stayed put and let the others file out of the room while he tried to figure out how he could convince Tekla that to spare his family from getting hurt, he had to give himself up.

Maybe to NCIS at the US Naval base at Naples. Definitely not to Brent.

"Traffic cams came in pretty handy," Gabe remarked to the team leader, buying time until the others cleared out of the hallway.

He didn't want them to catch a glimpse of Jasmine on his bed when he opened his door. "If we get Tekla this morning, we could be shipping out of here by tonight. Not that being in Venice is a hardship. I was expecting battle-field combat when I signed up."

Brent flashed him a dispassionate look. He picked up his fancy lighter from beside the laptop and ran his thumb over the raised, red enamel crest in the middle. "We've seen plenty of battlefield action, and we'll see more. We take each assignment as they come. I'm sure as hell not itching to go back to the hellhole side of the world."

"I hear you. How much time did you spend in the Middle East?"

Gabe had served ten years in half a dozen countries before he left the navy. When his sister had gotten sick—with three kids under the age of ten and a deadbeat ex—Gabe had returned to the US. Then she'd enrolled into that experimental treatment program for MS that cost an arm and a leg, and she needed money more than she needed her brother's daily presence, so Gabe went mercenary to pay the bills.

Brent knew all that. He'd done a comprehensive background check on Gabe before hiring him. Gabe, on the other hand, had been told very little about the team leader.

"Let's just say I've spent too much time in too many ugly places," Brent said now. "Used to be a combat medic. Switched to private security last year. Pays better."

"And thank God for that." If Gabe was going to get all the money he'd been promised, he could pay for Amy's care and keep supporting the North Village project.

That Brent had been a combat medic was the first thing that impressed Gabe about the man. All navy SEALs received basic trauma training, enough to survive most battlefield injuries until they could get professional help. That professional help came from combat medics, who after finishing SEAL training, went for SOCM—Special Operations Combat Medic—training at Fort Bragg, North Carolina. Each platoon had two combat medics. From what Gabe understood, the training was damn tough. Brent was no dummy.

Gabe moved toward the door, turned back before he stepped out into the hallway. "See you in two hours. I'm gonna catch some sleep."

The team leader was already lost in his laptop. Maybe even in something to do with Lahedeh. Gabe couldn't tell. The guy's shoulders blocked the view of the screen.

Gabe closed the door behind him. Troy Hill was the only one left in the hallway, bent over his door, across the hall from Gabe's, wiggling the key in the lock.

Troy looked up. "Sea air rusts shit like a sonofabitch. Wonder if people here ever heard of WD-40." He bit off a curse, then changed subject to, "Like the work so far?"

"Not a big fan of making war on Americans," Gabe said as he moved forward. "I think Brent should rethink a couple of things."

"Yeah." Troy went back to the lock. "This is the first op I've been on with the team where we have an American target. Given a choice, I'd prefer fighting tangos."

Tango was military speak for terrorist.

Gabe stopped a few feet from him. "You know how in the service you could be begging for a kill order on a group of tangos you've been following for days, knew beyond a shadow of a doubt they were bad guys, but top brass has doubts and they order you to stand down?"

Troy groaned in response. "I hear you, man. I figured private security work without fifty layers of bureaucracy was going to be better. But now with kill orders being tossed around, I'm almost wishing for oversight. Is that fucked up or what?"

Gabe had been thinking the same. He gestured toward the lock. "You need help with that?"

"Almost got it. Have to wiggle the key just right."

Gabe loitered anyway. If he opened his door, Troy would get a full view of Jasmine. *Hurry up, buddy.*

"Maybe we'll get sent to guard a pipeline in some war zone next," he said, so he wouldn't look weird just standing there.

Troy glanced at him. "War zone ops come with premium pay."

"That's what I'm saying."

"You seem eager to go. Nobody waiting for you back home?"

Gabe shook his head, pretty sure Troy meant a girlfriend and not his sister and nieces. He'd never done well with long-term relationships. "How do you expect someone to put up with what we do? Right?"

"Takes a special woman. One in a million." Troy's voice held a darker tone, maybe grief.

Before Gabe could decide whether to ask about it, Troy's key turned at last, and he disappeared into his room with a "See you later."

Gabe unlocked his own door and pushed inside, striding straight to the bed where Jasmine was sleeping like this was the last chance she was ever going to get.

Her dark hair had slipped loose and was spread on his pillow. She had the thickest, longest lashes he'd ever seen, flawless skin, and lips that would probably haunt his dreams.

The determined tilt of her chin softened in sleep. But now was not the time to linger and appreciate her beauty.

He bent low to whisper, "Jasmine. Wake up, sweetheart. We have to go."

Her eyes fluttered but didn't open all the way.

He shook her gently. "Jasmine?" He untied her and pulled her into a sitting position. "You have to take me to your brother. Who else is with him?"

She blinked one eye open. It wasn't a happy eye. In fact, after a moment of confusion, her expression crystallized into a look of pure hate.

Still, she was awake at last. When she opened the second eye, just as unfriendly as the first, he let her go.

She fell back onto the sheets, and her eyes closed again.

He pulled her up. "Brent knows where your brother is."

Her eyes snapped open. This time, she wasted no time on confusion; she went straight to hate. "You drugged me."

She tried to punch him in the face but missed and fell into his arms, struggled. *Not good.* He still hadn't forgotten the way she felt struggling against him on the roof, and again while he'd tied her up earlier. His body had responded then, and it responded now.

He dragged her up and over to the bathroom, leaned her against the sink, and turned on the tap. "Splash some cold water on your face."

When she grabbed on to the sink, he left her and went back to his desk for his SIG. He hid the gun in his waistband under his shirt, pocketed an extra clip, then stepped back to the bathroom door. "Ready?"

Jasmine sat on the closed toilet lid, sleeping, her head resting on the edge of the sink. She looked incredibly young and utterly worn out, but he couldn't give her a break.

He turned off the tap, then pulled her up. "Is your little sister in Venice? Is she with your brother?"

She opened her eyes, swayed a little. "No."

"How about your aunt?"

"I don't know what you're talking about," she slurred.

"This is not a good time to play games. Are your sister and your aunt here?"

She pressed her lips together.

Which probably meant yes. He didn't know much about the aunt, but Tekla's younger sister would be about high school age, a kid. She'd been around twelve when Gabe had met her, so now she'd be around seventeen.

Before he could ask again, Jasmine collapsed softly against him and went back to sleep. He swore and didn't bother to do it under his breath. She couldn't hear him anyway.

He sat on the closed toilet lid with her on his lap, pulled off her boots, scooped her up, and stuck her in the shower. Then he turned on the cold water. Her eyes popped open as she sputtered, fighting to get out while he tried to keep her in. Bathing Tootie, his nieces' cat, would have been easier.

He only released her when she looked like she was fully awake and when he thought he might lose an eye if he didn't step back. She spat water as she turned off the shower, shooting him a glare that qualified as a death threat.

"Jasmine, sweetheart?" He tried to make nice. "Where is your brother hiding?"

The glint in her eyes promised retribution. Okay, so she didn't seem ready to forgive being tied down and drugged. Or the forced shower.

Fine. He could start without her. They were going to Soremo. And between here and there, he *would* get her talking.

But first, she needed dry clothes. He went and grabbed a pair of boxer shorts, T-shirt, sweatpants, and his smallest sweatshirt. He put them on the edge of the sink, then turned his back in the open door.

"Out," she said.

"I want to hear you moving. If I leave you alone, you'll probably curl up in the tub to sleep."

For once, she didn't argue, maybe because she was cold. He could hear her pulling off wet clothes and dropping them on the tile floor. Then she pulled on dry clothes, the cotton whispering as it slid over her skin.

"Everything's too big."

He went to the bed, grabbed the curtain tie he'd used earlier to restrain her, and brought the silk cord over.

She stood in the middle of the bathroom, the bottom of the sweatpants rolled up four times at least. She held the waistband to keep the pants from slipping.

He stepped up to her. "Let me help."

Then he reached around her with the curtain tie and secured the pants in place. He stepped back as soon as he was finished. He didn't dare stay that close to her with her hands free. He had about as many burning scratches on his neck as he'd planned on getting today.

She tugged the sweatshirt down.

*Not bad.* She looked as if she was wearing boyfriend clothes. Not exactly stylish, but people wouldn't be pointing either. The shapeless look was a relief. She'd been way too sexy in her cat burglar outfit.

She grabbed her boots from the floor, pushed by him with a scathing look, and went to the bed to put them on, fell back and asleep halfway through.

He finished tying her bootlaces for her, then measured her up. *Over the shoulder, then out the window. No problem.*

He picked her up. She weighed nothing. Maybe she didn't have enough to eat. He gathered her closer.

Of course, she woke when they were halfway through the window, and—confused again—she kicked and punched the living daylights out of him. He tripped and went down, ended with her on top of him in the laurel bushes.

"Easy," he said, while she snapped, "Don't touch me!"

He let his hands fall away. He'd found her less than three hours ago, and this was at least the third time they'd ended up in a compromising position. He was beginning to think the universe was testing him.

She didn't seem to find the situation as stimulating as he did. She stared down at him with crazy eyes that held the promise of murder.

Thank God, she no longer had the shiv.

Five years ago, she'd looked so sweet and innocent in her schoolgirl uniform. What on earth had happened to her?

# CHAPTER
# SIX

The vaporetto chugged down the busy canal, passing shiny black gondolas and low-in-the-water delivery barges. As prettily as Venice lit up at night, the city looked breathtaking in the light of day, sun glinting off marble statues and all those white bridges. Yet Gabe barely registered the old-world beauty that surrounded the waterways, not with Jasmine curled against him, soft and warm.

She slipped in and out of sleep. Hopefully, she was going to lead him to her brother, and not on a wild-goose chase.

He held the bag of breakfast pastry he'd bought on the street. She'd eaten three in about three seconds. He'd been right. She hadn't had enough food. His chest ached at the thought of her starving, hiding, running like a hunted animal. He was ready to punch Tekla in the face for dragging her into his mess.

"I'm going to fix this," Gabe promised her, even if she couldn't hear him.

She fit perfectly against his side, under his arm. He tried not to like it too much, but he couldn't drag his gaze from her. Her eyes were closed, her dark eyelashes outlined against her pale cheeks. With all her wild hair, she looked like an unruly angel.

As the vaporetto reached Soremo and stopped, he brushed her hair back. "We're here."

She blinked at him with drowsy eyes.

"Come on." He pulled her up, then helped her off the waterbus.

Only two people got off with them, but over a dozen got on, probably heading to work. Gabe supported most of Jasmine's weight as the water bus chugged away. He turned her face toward the cool breeze coming off the water. Maybe that would wake her. "Left or right?"

She looked around slowly, blinked. "Where are we?"

He had only himself to blame, but as contrite as he felt about drugging her, he couldn't turn the clock back.

Not that he didn't appreciate the feel of her in his arms. Under different circumstances…Several instant fantasies flashed into his mind. One was rapidly fulfilled when she began to slide down his body with the kind of delicious friction—

*Dammit*, her knees were folding.

He gritted his teeth as he picked her up in his arms. A middle-aged woman passing by smiled at them. She clearly thought Gabe was being romantic.

"What are you doing?" Jasmine slurred.

"Saving you and your family." He kept a smile on his face for the onlookers.

"Mandy has a fever," she said with a frown.

*Damn Tekla.* So the younger sister too was definitely here.

"We'll take care of her." Gabe remembered the girl from that one time they'd met. She'd tried to hustle him at Uno, won five bucks from him—a pretty spunky kid.

"I want you to help Mandy." A heavy sigh escaped Jasmine as she looked up at him. "But I can't trust you."

"You're just going to have to make up your mind about it, sweetheart. I'm here to help."

"You tied me up and drugged me."

"To keep you safe."

She held his gaze for the longest time, doubts and desperation mixing in her eyes. Then she let her body relax against his, and nodded to the right. "That way."

As he carried her, she fell asleep again, but only for a minute or two before startling awake. He decided to talk to her to keep her that way.

"So what do you do when you're not ducking commando teams?" Her maturity, capability, and ingenuity had more than impressed him. He liked this new, adult Jasmine.

"I dabble in SM stuff," she told him with a yawn.

Like BDSM? Gabe choked on his own saliva. A picture of her in studded leather and thigh-high boots popped into his mind, her slim hand cracking a whip.

Suddenly, he was holding her a lot tighter than necessary.

"Social media consulting," she said in response to what probably was a pretty startled expression on his face. "My old college roommate and I started our own gig."

"Oh." He cleared his throat, his blood pressure slowly returning to normal. "So what happens now that you've been away for so long?"

He needed a moment of small talk while he emptied his brain of images of her in black leather boots with five-inch heels.

A water ambulance zoomed by, spraying him with a mist of cold water. That helped a little.

"Becky keeps things going. We're pretty small right now." Jasmine flashed a self-deprecating smile. Since his body blocked hers, she'd been spared the shower. "I check in whenever I can. I can get on the Internet at the library here."

She owned her own business. *Impressive.*

She squirmed in his arms and abruptly changed the subject with, "Did you leave the navy because of that mission that went wrong?"

"No. My sister got sick."

She tilted her head to look into his face. "I think you're a good man."

"There's a village of orphans and widows in Afghanistan who would beg to differ," he said, more to himself than to her.

"What are you doing to help them?"

"What makes you think I'm doing anything?" God, he didn't want to talk about this. "Don't make me into some kind of saint. You'll be disappointed."

"So you just left North Village, all those widows and orphans, to their fate?"

She'd paid attention. She even remembered the name of the place.

"I'm trying," he said, "to refit the factory with sewing machines for the women. A friend of a friend can get them a Fair Trade contract if the factory is operational by the end of spring."

He'd had combat pay saved up, and he'd given that to the village elders. In their tribal society, paying blood money when you hurt someone was an accepted practice. But then Amy had fallen sick, and Gabe had no money left to give his sister. XO-ST had looked like the right solution. Except, leaving with Jasmine without telling Brent…Gabe was as good as kicked off the team. So there went that.

He was going to need a new job and soon. He'd think about that later.

"We're almost there." Jasmine snuggled her face into the crook of his neck and went back to sleep.

His skin tingled. He was a thirty-year-old hard-ass commando soldier, but somewhere in the middle of his chest, his heart turned over. The unfamiliar feeling left him off-balance. He focused on their surroundings instead.

They reached the poor side of town. The houses he passed were progressively worse: sagging roofs, missing windows, peeling paint.

Gabe nudged Jasmine to make sure she'd be awake to tell him when they reached her hiding place. "How long have you been on the run with your brother?"

She blinked a few times before answering. "Nine months."

"Mandy too?"

She nodded, then gestured toward a ramshackle building that sat a little back from the others. "That one. You can put me down now."

She wiggled out of his arms then headed toward the building, slipped inside through a broken window. He followed her in, the sight of garbage and scurrying rats getting to him for a second. Nobody should have to live in a place like this.

She nodded toward a crumbling staircase. "Up there."

"I'll go. Why don't you stay down here? Rest a little."

She stumbled forward. "I can handle it."

He believed her. She'd managed to escape from the roof. And, despite the inherent dangers, she had managed to get his attention and bring him here to help. Word to the wise: the woman was more dangerous than she looked.

She climbed the staircase without hesitation, and he followed a few steps behind her, far enough so their combined weight wouldn't bring down the structure, but close enough so he could catch her if she fell back.

He hadn't minded carrying her. He liked her in his arms. The closer the better. He wanted to protect her. But walking behind her had advantages too. She looked pretty damn amazing even in his shapeless clothes. The soft cotton managed to cling to the curve of her fine…

Yes, he was ashamed of himself for ogling her at a moment like this. But that didn't stop him from looking.

She stopped when he reached the top.

He listened but couldn't hear anything.

"What is it?" he whispered as he caught up with her.

She turned and brought up a fist, used the momentum to punch him hard in the jaw, a pretty mean uppercut. Since he hadn't expected it, hadn't braced for it, his head snapped back.

*Oow.* He drew away. "What the hell?"

"That's for drugging me." Her eyes managed to look sleepy and unexpectedly scary at the same time.

But then she ruined the effect by cradling her fist in her other hand—probably hurt like a sonofabitch. And then she blinked, uncertainly, as if maybe regretting that she'd let her temper rule her for a second.

She drew a quick breath. "I'm—"

"Don't apologize." He reached for her hand, ran the pad of his thumb over her red knuckles to make sure they weren't busted. "One, you meant that punch. You're only sorry because you think I might turn around and walk away instead of helping."

She pulled her hand back, tucked it under her arm. She didn't deny his assessment. "Two?"

"You had every right to punch me," he told her. "Someone hurts you, you give 'em hell. You hit them so hard, they never think of messing with you again."

The corner of her lips turned up. "That's what Jake says."

"Sounds like your brother and I agree at least on one thing."

"You have to help him."

"I'll do what I can."

She squeezed her eyes shut for a second, as if saying her last prayer, then she turned and stumbled toward the end of the hallway.

She made Gabe's head spin. For a woman who mostly dressed in black, she scattered color and energy into the world. The man who ended up with her wouldn't be bored a day in his life. *Lucky bastard.*

"Don't shoot," she yelled through the last door. "It's me. I'm bringing someone."

Gabe stopped next to her and called out, "It's Gabe Cannon. Remember me?" He wanted to reiterate the *don't shoot* part. "Just want to talk. Don't want anyone to get hurt."

He reached for his weapon, then stopped. The sight of a gun might provoke Tekla. So Gabe left his gun stashed under his shirt, but kept his right hand ready to draw, while with his left hand he swept Jasmine behind him. He handed her the bag of breakfast pastry to hold. No way in hell was he going to let her go first.

He glanced at his watch. They had about an hour and a half before Brent would be here with the rest of the team.

"Okay, we're coming in," Gabe called out a last warning.

But when he pushed the door open, he found the cavernous, ramshackle room empty.

# CHAPTER
# SEVEN

Gabe watched the suspicious lump of blanket on the floor among the stacks of wood, plastic crates, and other rubble. The blanket rose and fell slightly as whoever hid under it breathed.

*To hell with trying to look nonthreatening.* He drew his weapon.

At the same time, Tekla stepped from a column to the side, holding a gun in his left hand, his eyes narrow slits. A homemade cast covered his right arm. He leaned his back against the wall behind him.

With those sunken cheeks, the guy barely resembled the charismatic hotshot he'd once been. Any worse and Gabe might not have recognized the man. Tekla looked twenty years older and twenty pounds lighter than the last time they'd met. And a lot less friendly.

"What's wrong with my sister?" As run-down as he was, he still sounded ready to fight.

"I'm fine." Jasmine stepped forward, still swaying on her feet from the tranq, which pretty much undermined her words.

"Come over here and get behind me." Tekla's cold, hard voice carried homicidal undertones. He kept his gun aimed at Gabe. "What did he do to you? Where are your clothes?"

Her response came after a long, uncomfortable moment of hesitation. "He drugged me a little. It's okay. He's here to help." She rubbed her forehead. "I think."

*Way to go with the endorsement.* Gabe could have pulled her over to use her as a shield, but he'd be damned if he hid behind a woman. Not that he didn't think Tekla was dangerous.

According to the op file, Tekla had killed three innocent men, US citizens. He wouldn't hesitate to shoot now when his family was in danger and he was cornered.

The situation had top potential for going real bad real fast, so Gabe held still. No sense in giving provocation if he could help it.

"The commando guys are coming," Jasmine said with exquisite timing.

Tekla swore, his finger twitching on the trigger as he tried to make a split-second decision. He stood balancing on the knife's edge. And when his expression hardened, Gabe knew the man was about to decide for safety instead of taking a chance.

"I know about Lahedeh," Gabe said in rush.

Tekla froze. "You do?"

"I know Brent was there," Gabe bluffed.

"Brent who?"

*Oh hell.* Tekla had been to Lahedeh. Brent had a file on Lahedeh. That *had* to be the connection between the two, the reason why Brent was so desperate to hunt Tekla down. Something had to have happened in the small Afghan town. Gabe's instincts said the chain of events that brought them here had begun there.

He'd spent the vaporetto ride thinking about all the little things that didn't add up. This op definitely meant something personal to Brent. He wanted Tekla too badly. And he didn't care who died with the target. At that last briefing, he'd sounded as if he *wanted* the whole family to be eliminated.

*Why?*

No way would those kinds of orders come from the US government when the target was a US citizen. And with the family…Civilian casualties were always to be avoided. For one, nobody in politics would want that career-ending nightmare.

Tekla moved his finger back from the trigger by a fraction of an inch, "Was Brent the other medic? Eyes beady as shit, guy as stocky as a freaking butt plug?"

*Here we go.* Brent *had* been a combat medic.

"Yeah." Gabe gambled. "Brent Foley. Ugly sonofabitch, flat nose, broken a couple of times, notch in the right ear where a bullet tasted him."

"Sounds about right." Tekla's gaze hardened with undisguised, cold fury. "Where do you come in? You weren't there. How did you hook up with this asshole?"

"Left the Teams three months ago. I was doing this and that, then Brent recruited me. After he got out last year, he started his own private security firm with some of his old buddies." Gabe paused, then added, "I have nothing to do with what went down at Lahedeh. Just found out about it."

"You have no idea what went down at Lahedeh," Tekla said.

"I might," Gabe bluffed again.

"If you did, you'd be dead already." Exhaustion crept into Tekla's voice, a dead-tired weariness. The kind of tiredness that said if it weren't for his sisters, he might just give up and let Brent catch up with him, maybe go out in a hail of bullets.

As his gaze darted to Jasmine, his fingers tightened on his weapon again. "Everyone else involved in the whole clusterfuck is dead, except me."

"Nobody has to get hurt." Gabe used his calmest tone. "Let me take you in. Forget Brent's mercenaries. You need to go to the US Naval Base at Naples. You surrender to NCIS of your own free will. They'll take that into consideration. The government will give you a fair trial."

Naval Criminal Investigative Service was the best place for Tekla to plead his case. Although, Gabe couldn't see a good outcome even there.

"Listen, I'm not going to lie. You're wanted for desertion. You killed three US citizens. You're probably looking at prison for the rest of your life. But your sisters can get their lives back. They'll be out of danger. How long do you think you can keep them safe on the run?"

He paused for effect. "I have a sister, Amy. She's sick. If I could save her life by going to the brig, however long…" He gave a one-shouldered shrug. "No contest. I'd do it in a blink."

Silence stretched in the room. The cavernous space filled with tension. Both weapons remained aimed.

"Can I come out? I can't breathe in here," a plaintive voice called from under the blanket Gabe had been keeping in his peripheral vision.

"Go into another room with Jasmine," Tekla ordered.

The younger sister peeked from her hiding place, then emerged little by little, hair all mussed and cheeks pink with fever, eyes glassy.

Jasmine went to her immediately. She seemed steadier on her feet. The tranq was wearing off at long last.

She felt her sister's forehead and frowned, worry tightening her voice as she said, "She's in no shape to walk around. Gabe isn't going to hurt us."

He appreciated the vote of confidence.

He scanned the room. "Where is the aunt?"

All he got was funny looks. "The aunt from Kansas," he clarified.

Tekla spoke. "Spending the winter with a friend in Florida."

*Thank God.* The last thing they needed in the middle of this volatile situation was another civilian.

"When is Brent coming with the rest of them?" Tekla asked Jasmine.

She shot a questioning look to Gabe.

Gabe glanced at his watch. "In a little over an hour." He nodded toward the younger sister. "She needs help."

Jasmine rolled her eyes at him. "Why do you think I came to you?"

"Didn't have a chance to ask, what with you trying to cut my throat."

Tekla shot an exasperated look at Jasmine, more resigned than angry. "I told you not to go near him."

"I can't do this alone, okay?" She pulled a bottle of water from the rubble and handed it to her sister before looking back at her brother, her eyes begging. "You need as much help as Mandy does. We can't just hang tough. It's gone beyond that. Neither of us can fix this."

The quiet desperation in her voice stirred up Gabe's protective instincts.

She'd been surviving with no resources, no support, in a foreign country, trying to save her brother and her little sister. And the thing was, she'd done it. She'd taken care of them. She'd evaded an entire commando team, then risked her life again, putting everything on the line when she'd come to Gabe.

"I'll help." Hell, that had been a forgone conclusion probably from the moment he'd caught her on the roof and first faced her spirit and courage, first realized that something was off with the op.

"I'll take you to the naval base," he told Tekla. "Once you're in the system, they can't just lose you. They'll have to give you a fair trial. I'll make sure your sisters get back home safely."

Jasmine shot to her feet. "No. I brought you here to help my brother escape."

*Not going to happen.* "Your brother made some bad choices. He's going to have to face the music for that, but the rest of you don't have to get hurt."

She flashed him a look that said she was about to release the ninja octopus. "You don't understand anything."

"Then tell me what happened." Gabe turned to Tekla. "If there's a rational explanation for what you've done, let's hear it."

"The less you know, the safer you are."

"Like your sisters?" Gabe snapped. "You know it's a damn miracle that they're still alive, right? How long are you prepared to gamble with their lives?"

Instead of acknowledging Gabe's point, Tekla gave a short, sour laugh. "I'll never reach any courtroom. If they were willing to give me a fair trial, NCIS would have come after me, instead of sending some bullshit private army. You know why the government uses bullshit private armies? Plausible deniability. Bullshit private armies can break the law at will, torture, and assassinate. Their contracts indemnify them from liability over collateral damage. The government uses them when it doesn't want to get its hands dirty."

With a disgusted expression and a shake of his head, he added, "This thing goes too high. If I come in, that'll be the end of me."

Gabe considered the possibility and the implications.

From what he understood, Brent Foley was one of four old navy buddies who started XO-ST, the small private security company that specialized in overseas missions. The contract for Tekla had come from the US government. They couldn't send military forces after Tekla into a sovereign country. Maybe they could have justified something like that in the Middle East, but certainly not in Europe.

Standard procedure would be to work with local law enforcement. But the US government didn't want local law enforcement involved, according to Brent. A rogue American sailor, a killer on the loose, wouldn't inspire much confidence in the US.

The Italians were already wary of the foreign military presence in their country, especially since the cable car accident a few years back when a US jet flew too low and cut the cables, sending twenty people plunging to their deaths. Some in the Italian parliament were questioning why they should let the American military have bases in Italy at all.

So sending a private outfit after Tekla and keeping the op under wraps had made sense when Brent first explained it. But, apparently, Brent and Tekla had a shared past in Lahedeh, and it sure looked like Brent had a private agenda where catching Tekla was concerned. What were the chances that his team just *happened* to get the government contract?

Maybe Brent had a contact high up in the government who made sure the contract went Brent's way. *Something about Brent isn't right,* Gabe thought once again.

But Tekla wasn't an innocent party either.

Gabe looked him straight in the eye. He didn't want the man's family to come to harm, but he drew the line at aiding and abetting a murderer. "I need to know about those three men you killed."

# CHAPTER
# EIGHT

Jasmine watched the standoff, panic dancing a jig in her stomach while worry played the music, using her nerves as fiddle strings.

Her brother had his finger on the trigger of his gun. So did Gabe. The two men were one finger twitch away from a shootout.

Fever had weakened Jake. He held his gun with his left, his nondominant hand. His only chance at winning would be a lucky shot. But if the last couple of weeks had taught Jasmine anything, it was that they didn't have that kind of luck.

She and Mandy both stayed motionless, barely daring to breathe.

"How about we step out into the hallway?" Jake suggested.

Jasmine opened her mouth to protest, even as Gabe said, "I think your sisters have a right to hear this. I think they should get a vote in what happens next."

Just for that, she forgave him for tying her up and drugging her. He regarded her and Mandy as equals and gave them a vote. One major point for Gabe.

She also liked the way he sometimes looked at her, a *lot* differently than he'd looked at her five years ago. As if he actually *noticed* her now. Way too late, but definitely flattering.

She'd been crazy about him. Well, that ship had sailed. She wasn't going back to live on Obsession Lane in Gabeville. She'd embarrassed herself over him enough for a lifetime back in the day. Every email she'd sent to Jake had at least one question about whether he'd seen Gabe again, and if so, how he looked, had he mentioned her.

Thank God, this time around she was a lot more mature and a lot smarter. She was *not* going to develop any kind of crush on him again. Even if he looked and acted like a movie hero. Even if he could activate her swoon reflex with a glance. She *was* going to resist.

The two men stared at each other.

Jake wouldn't easily trust someone, not after all they'd been through. And he had a lot of pride. Ever since their parents' car accident, he'd shouldered all the responsibility for the family. He *hated* to ask for help. As far as Jasmine could tell, all SEALs had a superwarrior complex. Well earned, actually. But they had no time right now for Jake and Gabe's duel for dominance.

Maybe Jake got that too, at last, because he said, "All right."

He lowered himself to a sitting position and put his gun down at his feet. The deep etchings of pain on his face eased a little once he took the weight off his injured leg.

Gabe watched him carefully. Jasmine doubted he'd missed a single twitch.

She handed Mandy the bag of food Gabe had bought. Mandy kept her eyes on the guys, but didn't refuse a *cornetto*, the Italian version of the croissant.

"Let's start with what happened in Lahedeh," Gabe said. "What were you and Brent doing there?"

"We were looking for the guy who took lead after Osama."

Mandy swallowed.

Jasmine stared. This was the first they heard about that. They'd known Jake wasn't off touring sites when he was deployed, but this new detail drove home the point how insanely dangerous the missions must have been.

"My team," Jake went on, "Brian O'Neil, Greg Buckner, Eric Rocha, who was the CO, and I, went down into a water cistern system."

*A Fire Team.*

When Jake had become a SEAL, Jasmine had learned as much as she could about them. Naval Special Warfare had eight Navy SEAL Teams. A Navy SEAL Commander led each, composed of an HQs element and eight operational sixteen-man SEAL platoons. Platoon structure was flexible, could be eight-man squads, four-man Fire Teams, or two-man Sniper/Reconnaissance Teams. Adaptability was the name of the game.

"Think underground stone tunnels with reservoirs," Jake said. "Above ground, the water would evaporate, so farmers and goatherds made these water channels hundreds, maybe thousands of years ago. Anyway, we found two locals down there, with half a dozen huge terra-cotta jars, like chest high, big suckers. The locals were damned protective of them too, started shooting the second they saw us."

His voice tightened. "They got Bri before we got them, killed him, and injured Eric. Bucky called in the medics. They showed up pretty fast. I knew one, but not the other, stocky bruiser of a guy, boxer's nose, notched ear."

"Brent Foley," Gabe put in.

Mandy took Jasmine's hand and squeezed.

Jake nodded. "Bucky and Bri were pretty tight, from the same town and all that, enlisted together. So Bucky went nuts over Bri's death. He started pumping more bullets into the dead locals. I told him to knock it off before a ricocheting bullet ended up in his own ass, or in mine. So then he starts kicking over the jars. They were too heavy, but he managed to tip one." Jake shook his head, closing his eyes as he remembered. "Man, I've never seen that much gold."

"What gold?" Jasmine asked the same time as Gabe did.

Jake opened his eyes. "Some warlord's hoard. Old Persian gold coins, worth millions."

Jasmine could have strangled her brother. "Our lives were destroyed because of money? That's the big secret you couldn't give up? I thought it had to do with national security." Steam boiled her brain. "Are you kidding me?"

Jake held up a hand, palm out. "Want to hear the rest or not?"

She kept glaring at him but kept her mouth shut.

"Eric was the team leader," her brother said. "He sealed the jars, told us this was all confidential. Word couldn't get out or we'd have the warlord's army after us, plus all the locals and treasure hunters. He took charge. Later he told us that the treasure was transported to the National Museum in Kabul."

"Let me guess," Gabe said. "The gold disappeared on the way."

Jake rubbed his injured leg with a faraway look in his eyes. "Last day I was in Afghanistan, I had a couple of hours to kill in Kabul and ran into a cute sergeant from the local US Army base. I thought I'd take her to the museum, show her the gold, and tell her the part I played. See how far that got me."

Jasmine rolled her eyes.

"Turns out, the museum never heard of the gold," her brother said. "So when I got back home, I tried to call Bucky. I mean, what the hell, right? So then I find out he'd been killed in action. Friendly fire." Jake's expression hardened. "I called the medic I knew. Friendly fire again. Couldn't track down the other medic, couldn't even get his name. But out of the six of us who went down into that cistern, three were definitely dead. I'm not gonna lie, that made me nervous."

"How does this tie in with you killing that naval officer?" Gabe cut to the chase. "Taking out a naval officer is a BFD. The navy isn't going to overlook *that*, even if the other two kills could be explained and justified somehow."

Jasmine knew BFD. It meant "big fucking deal" in military speak.

"Eric Rocha," Jake said.

Gabe's eyes narrowed. "One of the men you went down into that cistern with?"

"Eric was the CO." Jake wrapped his blanket around his shoulders awkwardly, left-handed, while letting himself shiver instead of suppressing it and acting like a tough guy, like everything was fine. Which meant he truly *had* accepted Gabe's help.

Jasmine relaxed a little.

"Bri was shot in the cistern," her brother said, his voice tight. "Bucky and the one medic were killed by friendly fire. In fact, the whole ambulance was hit. Driver and two medics dead. So I figured there went the two medics."

"Which left only you and Eric alive."

"Right. And I knew I didn't take the gold. I was afraid Eric stole the whole damn hoard and had the others killed. He was newly transferred from another platoon. I didn't know him that well."

"Why not go to NCIS with the information?"

The grim look in Jake's eyes said that maybe he regretted not doing just that. "I had zero proof. I figured Eric never reported us finding that gold in the first place. And you don't go around accusing your commanding officer of grand theft and multiple counts of murder without a slip of evidence. I figured I talk to anybody without proof, and next I know, I'll be in treatment for PTSD and paranoid delusions. *If friendly fire doesn't find me first.*"

"So you killed Eric before he could kill you."

"I had trouble believing things could be as bad as I thought they were." Jake closed his eyes and rubbed his forehead with his fist. "I confronted him. He told me I was half-right, but like me, he was innocent. He'd been investigating. Medic number two was still alive. Somebody else had been in the ambulance with medic number one when that ambulance had been hit."

"And you believed the guy?"

"He was my CO." Disgust crept into Jake's tone. "I wanted to believe him. And he made sense. He said the surviving medic used the ambulance to get the gold out. That solved the logistics that I couldn't figure out before. Eric told me to meet him off base that night. He said he'd identified the mystery medic. We were going to gather evidence against him."

"You went, and Eric turned against you."

Jake hung his head. "Shot at me. I was ready. I had a bulletproof vest on. I wanted to trust him, but at that point, I wasn't about to fully believe anyone, so I was watching for an attack."

"And when you shot back, you didn't miss."

Jake's spine stiffened. "I don't miss." Then his shoulders slumped again. "But I still had no proof. I just killed my CO. If I went to NCIS, they would have tossed me in the brig while they figured things out." He filled his lungs. "I did believe that the second medic was involved. That ambulance had taken the gold out. Made sense. If I found the mystery medic, I could get proof. I had Eric's cell phone. All I had to do was figure out which phone number belonged to the medic, then track down the bastard. I'd be AWOL for a day or two, but I'd come back with solid proof."

Gabe nodded, a thoughtful look in his eyes. "So you ran?"

The muscles in Jake's face tightened. "Talked myself out of it. Nobody knew I was meeting Eric that night. Nobody could connect me to his death. I figured I'd look from the inside first. I went out on my next mission. Someone called in an air strike giving my GPS coordinates instead of the tangos I was following. I survived by sheer dumb luck. I knew I couldn't keep counting on that, so I finally got out of there. I wanted to figure out who the mystery medic was, wanted to stop him before he got another chance to call in an air strike on me."

He took a slow breath and shot an apologetic look to Jasmine, his eyes filling with regret. "That was a mistake."

***

Gabe watched as a hard mask slipped over Jasmine's face. She squared her shoulders as if putting on armor. The way she wouldn't meet anybody's gaze… That guilt-soaked regret in Tekla's voice…Gabe was pretty sure something bad had happened after Tekla had gone AWOL and gone into hiding. And it had happened to Jasmine.

"I don't feel good," Mandy whispered, her face flushed. She drew her blanket tightly around her shivering body, but it didn't seem to help.

They had to take care of her before they could move on from here.

Gabe checked his watch. "Fifty minutes left." He stepped forward. "We have to bring her fever down. Then we need to leave."

Jasmine launched into action. "There's a tub in one of the other rooms. We could bring cold water up from downstairs."

Gabe headed for the doorway. "Do you have any buckets?"

She hurried to the corner and pulled two five-gallon paint buckets she had probably picked up at a construction site.

He took those from her. She grabbed a chipped pot from the windowsill. As he followed her, he kept thinking of Tekla's story. Even if only half was true, they were still ass-deep in trouble.

Jasmine led the way to some kind of utility room in the front corner of the ground floor. The water meter hung to the side, disconnected from the pipes. Looked like the water service to the building had been shut off at one point, but someone—Gabe's money was on Tekla—had rigged it.

Gabe filled the buckets, then waited until Jasmine filled the pot.

"What happened after your brother went AWOL?" he asked on their way up.

She wouldn't look at him.

He should probably let it go. Except he wasn't the let-it-go type. "The more I know, the better I'll be able to help. I need to see the full picture."

They reached the top floor. He followed her into a smaller room, and they dumped the water into the tub in the corner. As she bent to set her empty pot on the floor, her top rode up her hips, revealing a strip of skin. Two half-moon-shaped scars peeked out at Gabe.

"Did you get hurt on the roof?" He hoped he hadn't been too rough on her when he'd knocked her down. Or when he'd restrained her to his bed. He hadn't meant to hurt her.

She yanked down her top to cover the scars. "Old injuries. It's nothing." But the way her voice jumped higher said otherwise.

When she turned to leave, he set down the buckets and reached for her arm, stopped her. "Jasmine?"

She straightened her spine, brought that stubborn chin up. "When the men who were after Jake couldn't find him, they came after us to draw him out."

His free hand fisted. "After you and your sister?"

Jasmine nodded.

Gabe watched her tight expression, cold tension gathering in his stomach. "What happened?"

"Mandy had an emergency prom meeting, so she had to stay after school, thank God. I was home alone."

The urge to kill swept through Gabe. He gathered her into his arms without giving her a chance to resist. "Who were they? How many?"

"I don't know who. Two men." She cleared her throat. "They put a pillowcase over my head and tied me up. They took me someplace in the trunk of a car, and kept me tied up in a basement. They set up a trap for Jake, and I was bait."

Gabe swallowed back a vicious curse. No wonder she'd fought the restraints so violently when he'd tied her to his bed.

He drew a deep breath through his nose, held it for a few seconds before releasing it through his mouth, and kept his arms around her instead of putting his fist through a wall.

He bent to rest his chin on the top of her head. "I'm sorry."

She stood stiffly in his arms at first, but then, little by little, she relaxed against him. A shiver ran through her.

What in hell had they done to her? He wouldn't ask. He wasn't about to make her relive the experience. He would simply give her what she needed: his protection.

The level of protectiveness he felt toward her was what he felt for Amy and his nieces—who were his heart. He would kill for them, die for them, whatever it took to keep them safe. Somehow, Jasmine was suddenly in that circle.

And what protectiveness he felt toward her, Tekla had to feel that and more. Which meant if Gabe messed with the man's sister, Tekla was likely to shoot off his kneecaps, if not his balls. And Gabe would deserve it.

So Gabe was going to give Jasmine his help, and only his help, regardless of all the lust, and need, and want that hit him the second they so much as looked at each other.

"I just squeezed my eyes shut," she said after a moment, "and prayed for Jake and you to come and save me."

She looked up, her lips in a lopsided smile. "That makes me sound like some obsessed whacko, carrying a crush all these years. That's not true. Okay, I had a crush on you in high school. But I've matured since. I swear. I was just thinking of you coming with Jake, because there were two who took me, so I wanted two of the toughest men I knew on my side."

So much information there. But all Gabe could focus on was that she'd been hurt. "I'm sorry I didn't come. I wish I'd known."

"Jake came." She pulled away. "He took care of them on his own." Fierce satisfaction glinted in her eyes. "He got us out of the country."

"I'm glad."

She moved toward the door. "We better get Mandy."

Gabe followed, his mind still on the disturbing information she'd just revealed. Thank God Jake had been able to save her. No wonder Jasmine would do anything for her brother.

That thought led to another. "Wait. Were those assholes the two civilians Jake killed in the US?"

She stopped in the middle of the derelict hallway and turned to him. She didn't confirm. And she wouldn't. She wouldn't incriminate her brother. But the somber look in her eyes was all the answer Gabe needed.

"They were bad men," she said.

The four words meant so much more than just those four words. The haunted look in her eyes twisted Gabe's guts. Murderous rage burned through him, impotent rage since he could do nothing about those men at this stage. He wanted to protect Jasmine from them, but he was too late.

He thought of Brent. *Maybe not entirely too late.*

He wanted to take her into his arms again, but she didn't look like she would welcome anyone's touch right now. And if he held her again, he might not want to let go for a while. So he simply said, "I'm here now. I'm going to do whatever I can to help."

He moved forward. They needed to bring Mandy's fever down.

He went into the other room and scooped up the girl under Tekla's watchful gaze, then he carried Mandy over to the tub. He let Jasmine take it from there.

"Call me when you need me to bring her back," he said before he closed the door behind him.

He strode back to Tekla, stopping just inside the door. "Jasmine told me about the basement."

Tekla's jaw looked so tight, Gabe thought the bone might crack.

"If anybody touched my sister Amy or my nieces," Gabe said. "Shit. Those bastards died too easy."

According to the op file, they'd been shot, an efficient double tap each, chest and head. Suddenly, Gabe admired Tekla's restraint.

"So after you went AWOL, have you been able to gather any proof of all that happened?"

Frustration mixed with guilt on Tekla's face. "I haven't had time to investigate. The day after I went AWOL, Jasmine was kidnapped. I went back to the States as fast as I could to find her. Took me two weeks. Too long. Hell, two hours would have been too long."

Gabe agreed. "I'm glad you got her back."

Tekla nodded. "We've been on the run since."

Gabe understood the guy's dilemma. Tekla couldn't go off investigating without leaving his sisters unprotected. But without proof, he couldn't clear himself. Catch-22. Except, now Gabe was here, a new addition to the equation, and that could change everything.

Brent Foley had betrayed his brothers in arms. For money. Screw Brent and his commandos. They could rot in hell as far as Gabe was concerned.

"We need proof," he said. "Which means we have to find the gold. And then link Brent to the gold. Who were the two men Brent sent to grab Jasmine?"

If they'd been employed by XO-ST, that was a link to Brent right there. Not definitive proof, but more than nothing.

Tekla shivered again. "Hired guns. Disposable muscle. I'm pretty sure Brent was going to take them out once they served their purpose."

"Why not send his private commando team? He's using the team to come after you now."

Tekla shrugged. He was probably too damn sick to think straight.

Gabe racked his brain. "Okay, the best I can figure is, he got out of the service as soon as he could after you all found the gold a year ago. Maybe he faked an injury. He was a medic, knew what to say, how to act. Then maybe he was bored and went into the private army business. Maybe he was on a power trip, wanted to have his own men to order around. Maybe he needed to own a business so he could launder the money from his loot, little by little."

"Tell me more about his commando team," Tekla asked.

"Xtreme Ops Shadow Teams. XO-ST. He started it with a couple of buddies he knew from the service. They go after government contracts. Go in and out of the Middle East. Earn big bucks. I haven't been with them long enough to know more. Most are ex-military, probably half of them with dishonorable discharges."

Tekla bobbed his head. "So he wanted to keep his business in the US clean, hired outside help to grab my sisters." He paused. "But then those asswipes failed. And now I'm a wanted man. Brent somehow finagled a contract to bring me in. I don't think his commando team buddies know about the gold. If they knew, he would have to share."

Gabe agreed. "From the way he's been taking out everyone who knew about the gold in the first place, I'd say it's safe to assume Brent is not into sharing." He thought for a few seconds. "Where do you think the gold is?"

"My best guess? Eric told the truth about Brent using the ambulance to move the hoard to a new location within Afghanistan. Couldn't leave the gold in the cisterns, had to hide it from the warlord it belonged to in the first place."

"But how would he get the loot out of Afghanistan? He couldn't have done it while he was in the service. Not even with a medical evac chopper. Too many people on board. The gold would take up too much space and weight. No way could Brent move it unnoticed while working within the constraints of the military."

Tekla's eyes brightened suddenly, as if he'd stumbled onto something. "So that's another reason for Brent to start a private security company. He could get back into Afghanistan with less oversight and more freedom to come and go as he pleased."

"Right." Gabe perked up too. "As the team leader, Brent could tell his team they were transporting arms seized from the Taliban. One sealed crate looks pretty much like another. A lot of border crossings are controlled by the US Army to prevent insurgents from pouring in. A military contractor would be waved through like it's nothing."

"How does he get the gold through US customs?"

"That's the million-dollar question." Gabe considered all the known parameters. And then he came to a conclusion. "I don't think Brent has his gold back in the US yet. I think if he had the money, he'd give up active work at XO-ST. Why would he be risking his life if he could be sitting on millions back at home? He's got an ego on him. He'd be out on a yacht with hot women and booze and drugs, I bet."

"So he's still working on making his dream come true. He still has to take me out, then smuggle the money back home."

"We need to find that gold."

"I think you're right about him having some kind of a connection high up," Tekla said. "Okay, I went AWOL. But why would they send Brent after me? Why not NCIS? Why not one of the hundreds of other private security companies? Brent is just too much of a coincidence. He knows someone who made sure the contract got thrown to XO-ST. We have to be careful about who we reach out to."

"We could go straight to Admiral Markowsky." No way this mess went *that* high.

But Tekla frowned. "The admiral isn't going to want to hear it. I'm accusing *his* men, *his* navy. And I'm wanted by NCIS for murder and desertion.

He'll use the tools he has at hand. He'll hand me over to NCIS and let them sort me out."

Gabe couldn't disagree. NCIS would have to be involved, no doubt about it. And then Tekla would be locked up, if only until his claims could be confirmed.

The admiral was a good man, but even he had to play by the rules of politics. Which wouldn't let him allow a man accused of murder to go free.

And if Tekla was locked away, even temporarily, his sisters would be vulnerable again. Okay, Gabe could protect the sisters. But Tekla would be vulnerable too. They had no idea what kind of connections Brent had. Pretty good, if he could call in air strikes. What if one of Brent's buddies got to Tekla while Tekla was in custody?

"So we need help from outside the navy." Gabe racked his brain. "How about General Roberts?"

Tekla sat up straight, hope glinting in his eyes for the first time. "You think?"

Gabe glanced at his watch. "We don't have time to come up with a better plan."

# CHAPTER
# NINE

Jasmine helped her sister out of the cold bath, listening for gunshots or sounds of a scuffle from the other room. She wouldn't put it past Jake and Gabe to get into a fistfight or worse. But she heard nothing troubling.

She dressed Mandy in dry clothes, and then she changed too, out of Gabe's sweatpants and sweatshirt and into her own black jeans and black sweater. They each had brought a backpack with them when they'd left the US, and, miracle of miracles, they still had most of their belongings.

At least, with her temperature down, Mandy could stand and walk once again, even if her teeth chattered. Good, but not good enough—Mandy's fever would shoot up again. But maybe the bath bought them enough time to get her to a hospital.

"So that's Gabe Cannon," Mandy said, with a dreamy look on her face that looked a lot less feverish.

Jasmine unplugged the tub. "Mm."

"He doesn't look like I pictured him."

"You didn't remember him from when we met?" How could anyone not remember Gabe Cannon?

Mandy put on her shoes. "We met once. I was like twelve. I kind of forgot about him."

Jasmine began combing her sister's hair. They'd been careful not to get her head wet, knowing they'd have to go outside soon. "When have you been picturing him?"

"What?"

"You said he doesn't look like you pictured him."

Mandy wouldn't look up.

Jasmine stared at her, a horrible suspicion growing in her mind. "You read my diary?"

Mandy glanced at her at last, a defensive expression on her face. "What little sister doesn't read her older sister's diary?"

Jasmine ground her teeth. *Oh God.* Her teenage fantasies had been definitely on the lurid side. And explicit. Very.

*Kill me now.*

"Hey." Mandy tried for her wide-eyed, I'm-too-cute-to-be-yelled-at baby sister look. "I learned everything I know about boys from those pages. I never had a mother to have the talk with me."

Jasmine snatched her hand away. "You're playing the I'm-a-poor-motherless-orphan card right now?"

Mandy squinted hopefully. "Is it working?"

"If I hadn't drained the tub already, I'd drown you."

Mandy grinned. "He's so seriously hot, though, right?"

Jasmine just shook her head, resigned. She remembered what it was like to be seventeen.

"He carried me in his arms." Mandy sighed. "I hope that wasn't just a fever dream." Her face lit up with excitement. "Oh my God, that was like the most romantic thing that ever happened to me."

"Well, he carried me first," Jasmine told her, because a person who would read her own sister's private diary deserved to get her bubble burst.

Mandy finished tying her shoes and straightened, eyes comically wide. "When?"

"All the way here from the vaporetto stop."

"But that's like a mile."

"Then up the stairs."

"He could have put out his back!"

Jasmine swatted at her sister. "No weight jokes. You crossed enough lines today."

Mandy pouted. Then grinned again. "So is he yours, or is he mine?"

Jasmine closed her eyes. Heaven help her. "How about we first survive the day, then we can talk about boys."

Although, Gabe Cannon was wa-a-a-y out of the boy category. And, sadly, way out of both their leagues.

She helped Mandy back into the larger room, where the man in question and Jake were still talking. Without pointing guns at each other. Progress.

Gabe jumped to help as soon as he saw them coming, taking over supporting Mandy's weight. Mandy shot Jasmine a triumphant look and leaned on him more than was necessary.

He helped her back to the mattress. He seemed to truly care. Just being here was help already. Jake could never have carried Mandy over to the tub with his bad arm and leg, and Jasmine couldn't have done it either. Her little sister was taller than she was and weighed almost as much as she did.

But Gabe was here and things were going to turn around. For the first time in a long time, Jasmine saw the light at the end of the tunnel.

Gabe was saying something about a general.

Her brother looked like he was seriously considering it. But then he said, "Or you could take Mandy and Jasmine someplace safe. I'll stay here and deal with Brent."

Jasmine stepped forward. "I'm not going anywhere without you. We've already talked about this."

***

Gabe watched the determination on Jasmine's face. She meant what she said. She wouldn't leave her brother. She had incredible loyalty to her family. And strength. And courage. The woman had character.

She'd also managed to surprise him, more than once: escaping from the roof, tracking him to the pensione, holding him at the point of a shiv. She was good at thinking on her feet.

If she was a man, with fifty pounds of extra muscles, she might have made a good SEAL.

But she wasn't a man, and he was way happier over that fact than he should have been.

*No way.* He could not be looking at her *that* way. And he wasn't. *Definitely not.*

*Shit.* Of course, he was.

She'd changed while she'd bathed Mandy. She was back in black, sleek, ready for anything, guaranteed to raise any man's blood pressure.

*Off limits.*

Gabe turned back to Tekla. "I say we go with General Roberts."

The general was the straightest arrow Gabe knew, and nothing was ever off the table for the man, as long as it got him to the mission goal. People at his level of command were usually wedded to doing things the way they'd always been done. But General Roberts listened to reason and considered possibilities nobody else was willing to consider.

Gabe had met Tekla on one of General Roberts's missions. Army Special Ops Forces had run the mission, and General Roberts called in two SEAL Teams to help. An unheard-of maneuver. The average army general would eat his stars before calling in reinforcements from the navy.

On top of all that, General Roberts personally knew both Gabe and Tekla, because he'd taken the time to talk to the teams before the op, then once again to personally thank them afterward. He was just the kind of man who would remember them.

"Okay," Tekla said. "Let's do it."

So Gabe pulled his phone out and identified himself when the general's aide picked up on the other end. He expected to be called back, but instead, in under two minutes, he was connected to General Roberts.

"Navy still treating you well, son? If they aren't, Army Special Ops Forces could always use a man like you. Anytime you want to come over, just say the word."

"Thank you, General. I'm not with the navy anymore. I work for a private outfit these days. I'm in a situation here, sir."

"Are you in trouble?"

"I'm with people who are in trouble. Jake Tekla and two civilians. His sisters, sir. We're in Venice, Italy."

"I remember Jake Tekla. Used to be a good man. I hear he's wanted by NCIS these days."

Bad news traveled fast.

"Yes, sir. There are…extenuating circumstances."

"Extenuating enough for me to stake my career on it?"

Silence stretched on the line. Then Gabe filled his lungs. "If you can't help us, people will be dead by morning, sir."

"Is this a secure line?"

"No, sir."

"So you can't tell me anything." The man paused. "The US Army Base in Livorno is roughly a three-hour drive from Venice. Hold on."

Gabe did.

"What did he say?" Jasmine asked, her gaze hanging on him.

"Nothing yet. I'm holding."

Tekla said, "He could be calling NCIS."

"He could be," Gabe agreed. "But I don't think so."

Before Tekla could respond, the general came back on the line.

"A convoy of US troops is on its way to the Livorno Army Base from the NATO base in Hungary. They'll be passing through near Venice. I'm sending one of the trucks over to Ponte della Libertà. Can you rendezvous with them at oh nine thirty?"

Gabe glanced at his watch. "Yes, sir. Thank you, sir."

As soon as he hung up, he strode to Mandy. "We need to go. Right now." He caught Jasmine's gaze. "Can you help your brother?"

While Gabe wrapped Mandy in her blanket and picked her up, Tekla pulled a pen drive from under his homemade cast, and he held it out for Jasmine. "If something happens to me, this is all I know, all written down with dates and names."

Gabe's eyes met his. Held.

Jake was handing over the information, because if anything happened, he was most likely to get killed. He was the primary target, and he was in the roughest shape among the three. He couldn't run at all. Jasmine could take care of herself. In an emergency situation, if Gabe had to choose whether to save Tekla or Mandy, he would save Mandy. She was lighter, he could run faster with her, improving the odds for the both of them. And Tekla would want him to save Mandy.

Understanding passed between the two men in that half-second look.

"I'll be back for you," Gabe said. "Then we'll have to book it. We have less than an hour to reach Liberty Bridge."

Jasmine shoved the pen drive into her pocket. Then she took the gun Jake handed her, shoved that into her waistband in the front, and pulled her black sweater down to hide the gun. She hurried after Gabe, followed him down the hallway, then down the stairs.

She stayed with her sister while Gabe went back up for Tekla.

Gabe carried him down the stairs piggyback style. He could afford to have both hands tied up. Jasmine was downstairs with a gun. If anyone was coming, she could signal, Gabe would have time to drop Tekla and rush down with his own weapon in hand.

But no attack came, and Gabe made it down without trouble. Then they were all on the lowest floor, behind the double front door, looking out through the gap. The door was chained on the outside with a rusted iron chain almost as thick as Jasmine's wrist, an old-fashioned padlock in the middle, the size of her fist.

They couldn't get through here, but the door provided great cover for them to observe the outside without being seen.

The sidewalk was about ten feet wide, then the canal. Gabe could see only the single boat he'd seen when they'd arrived earlier. The boat was tied out a few buildings down, probably belonging to another squatter, or maybe a lone security guard working at one of the less derelict buildings used for storage.

The boat was a two-seater. Nothing else in sight. Three passengers might be able to jam in, but not four, especially not since Jake had a cast on his arm and an injured leg he could barely move.

They needed to leave *now*.

Jasmine pulled back to look at Gabe. "I'll take a vaporetto and meet you at the bridge. As long as you can make it to the rendezvous point in time, you can tell them to wait for me."

"I'm not leaving you alone."

She was vibrating with nervous energy. "I have a gun. I know how to use it."

One gun against a commando team meant exactly nothing, but they didn't have time to argue, no time to come up with a better plan. If they didn't show on time, whoever was bringing the truck might think they weren't coming. The rescue team might take off without them.

Gabe held her gaze. "Brent and his men are on their way."

"I'll be off the island before they get here."

She *had* evaded the commandos before, but Gabe still couldn't agree. "You take the boat, I'll take a vaporetto."

She shook her head. "Brent and the others want Jake the most. I want you to be with Jake, in case they somehow find him. Just protect my brother and my sister. Please."

"Who's going to protect you?"

"I will."

She looked ridiculously tough. The quintessential comic book action heroine. Sadly, he was no hero, comic book or otherwise. But for her he wished he could be—

His phone rang. He glanced at the screen. "That's Brent. Probably wondering where I am."

They didn't have time to argue. "Help me get them to the boat."

He carried Mandy to the broken window, while Jasmine supported Tekla's weight, her brother's arm around her shoulders as they hobbled forward. Despite all the impediments, they climbed through the window fairly fast. They were well motivated.

Gabe put Mandy into the boat first, helped Tekla, who half pulled Mandy onto his lap, supporting her with his good hand. Then Gabe hopped in, the boat sloshing in the water.

The key was in the ignition. He appreciated that he didn't have to spend precious time with hotwiring. Now if that luck would only hold a little longer.

"If you run into trouble and you have to leave, just leave," Jasmine said. "I can make my way to Livorno on my own."

"I'm not leaving Venice without you."

A second or two of tense silence stretched between them, then Mandy groaned and Jasmine took off running toward the vaporetto stop a few canals over.

He wanted to call her back. He wanted to kiss her until her lips were swollen and her eyes glazed. The he wanted to toss her on his back and swim to the damn mainland with her if necessary, anything but letting her go right now.

Instead, he turned on the motor and navigated the boat into the middle of the waterway. But the whole time, he couldn't shake the feeling that he shouldn't be leaving Jasmine. He turned, but he could no longer see her. She'd already disappeared around a corner.

*She'll jump on a vaporetto.* She'd catch up to them. She was right, her little sister and big brother needed Gabe's protection more than she did. They looked damn pitiful, huddled under the blanket, one in worse shape than the other. Mandy's cheeks glowed red with fever again.

Gabe reached the main water channel and maneuvered among the water taxis, gondolas, and all the private boats that filled the canals every morning. He watched out for Brent and crew, wishing he'd had the time to put on some kind of disguise. If any of the guys came anywhere near, they'd recognize him from a mile away.

He did his best to slink down in the boat's seat and make himself as small as possible.

He passed Sant'Erasmo first, then the island of Murano, then headed into the last two miles, cutting through the open water, moving away from Venice, towards Mestre, the mainland, the long bridge on his left, stretching across the water like a silver ribbon. When he spotted a green US Army truck idling in the Mestre harbor, near the foot of the bridge, he aimed the boat straight for it.

Tekla gathered his sister closer. "Almost there. I'll have them take us straight to a doctor."

Gabe drove the boat as close as he could, tied it up in the marina, then helped Mandy and Jake out. The bridge waited less than five hundred feet away.

A corporal met them halfway to the truck, a thirty-something black guy, bald head, scarred chin. "Gabe Cannon?"

"Thanks for coming." Gabe didn't introduce the others, wasn't sure how much information the general had passed on. The less everyone knew, the better.

The corporal signaled two soldiers forward who helped Tekla toward the truck, while Gabe picked up Mandy. They all tried to look as inconspicuous as possible under the circumstances.

The corporal shot Gabe a questioning look. "I was told there'd be four people."

"We'll have to wait for my other sister," Tekla said. "She's coming."

As they reached the truck, the back opened, and a soldier reached down to help Mandy up.

Tekla looked toward the water, toward the vaporetto stop that stood a few hundred feet from them on the Mestre side of the bridge.

Gabe too was watching for Jasmine. *Come on, sweetheart. Hurry up.*

The corporal picked up on the strained mood. "I don't have a lot of detail here. Are we to expect trouble?"

"Expect it, prepare for it, pray it doesn't happen." Gabe shared his personal philosophy.

"We're strictly transport." Tension seeped into the corporal's voice. "We are not to engage in any kind of confrontation whatsoever."

Gabe understood. American soldiers could not be involved in a shootout in Venice.

The corporal said, "We can't wait much longer."

Gabe didn't argue. When one country's army crossed the territory of another country, route plans were filed and approved months in advance, strictly negotiated—no side trips, no sightseeing breaks. Any deviation and they could be accused of spying, or the incident could even be considered an act of war.

The last thing Gabe wanted was to cause trouble for General Roberts.

*No.* The last thing he wanted was for Jasmine to come to harm.

*Come on, sweetheart.*

But instead of Jasmine, he spotted Harris, Brent's tech wiz, on the bridge. Then another guy from the team. And another.

*What the hell?*

Gabe's stomach dropped. He hadn't been followed when he'd taken Jasmine back to Soremo, he'd made sure of that. He could think of only one other explanation for the commandos showing up here at the exact wrong moment.

Anger punched through him as he patted down his shirt. *Nothing.* He grabbed his XO-ST cell phone.

They'd all been issued the same gadgets, the same weapons. The same trackers? Gabe tossed the phone on the pavement and ground it under the heel of his combat boot.

*Track that.*

Except…If Brent had been tracking him on his laptop, radioing his movements to the others all this time, then they likely knew where Gabe had spent the last hour and a half. The rest of the team was probably at Tekla's hiding place right now.

"Get out of here!" Gabe shouted to Tekla and the corporal, then ran toward the boat.

"Jasmine—" Tekla was shouting.

"I got her!"

But before he reached halfway, a bullet hit the boat's fuel tank. *Bam!*

The explosion knocked Gabe off his feet.

He could see, as he lay there, dazed, the corporal jumping into the back of the army truck, pulling a protesting Tekla up behind him.

"Go!" Gabe shouted to them, not hearing his own voice, his ears ringing.

But maybe the corporal heard him, because the truck shot forward, and they booked it the hell out of there.

*Good decision.* They needed to take care of Tekla and Mandy, and needed to not get involved in an explosion on Italian soil.

Gabe on the other hand, wasn't officially US military. He didn't have to think about the political ramifications of shit right this second. A good thing, because all he could think about was Jasmine alone against Brent's guys, battle-hardened men with a kill order.

Gabe pushed to his feet and lurched to the water, dove in.

*Mother f*—The sea in February was cold enough to shrink his balls to the size of raisins. He came up, but just for a breath of air, then went under again. He swam as if his life depended on it.

Because Jasmine's did.

He reached the nearest cement pillar of the bridge in record time and pulled himself up, shivering like a sonofabitch, his fingers almost too stiff to climb. He made it to the top anyway. Failure wasn't an option.

The people on the bridge were all watching the burning boat. Since whoever had hit the fuel tank had used a silencer, no shot had been heard. The tourists had no idea what was happening. They probably thought they'd witnessed some kind of an accident.

Traffic came to a halt, but nobody panicked. Here and there, people left their cars to take pictures.

All those unattended cars, and none of them did Gabe any good, since they were stuck in traffic. So he grabbed an abandoned motorbike and flew forward between the lanes of cars before the owner could realize his ride was missing.

Gabe glanced back. None of the commando guys were after him. They might not even have seen him climb the bridge. They were too busy chasing after Tekla, their primary target for the op, which was more than fine with Gabe. The corporal and his men should have no trouble outrunning the bastards.

Gabe pushed the bike to the max, dripping seawater, freezing his ass off. His muscles were stiffening from the cold. He did the breathing exercises he'd learned as a SEAL, and in the back of his mind, ran through an ancient Buddhist meditation that could raise a person's core temperature. The navy had gone to Nepal and studied monks for that one—no kidding. Mind over body. Gabe wasn't going to let hypothermia take him.

He had to reach Jasmine before it was too late.

# CHAPTER
# TEN

Jasmine drew in a slow breath, held it, released. She needed to not be this scared. She had to calm down so the blood would stop rushing in her ears so loudly. She needed to be able to hear.

She'd missed the vaporetto because she'd left her few remaining euros in her soggy jeans on Gabe's bathroom floor at the pensione.

By the time she found someone willing to give her enough money for a ticket—Jasmine had told the nice old man that she'd left her wallet at home in the morning rush—the commando guys were there and she had to make a run for it. She ended up back at the abandoned warehouse, the building she knew best on the island, her best chance to hide and evade.

Except now she was trapped.

"Come on out. We won't hurt you," one of the men called out one level below her.

Okay, she could hear *that,* even through the blood pounding a panicked rhythm in her ears. But she needed to do better, needed to hear if any of them attempted to sneak up on her. She filled her lungs slowly, trying to regulate her breathing. *Don't freak out. Jake wouldn't lose it. Gabe wouldn't either.*

She had to reach the staircase to the roof, but the commando guys had herded her to the east end where the place butted up against another warehouse, solid brick walls—no exit.

She breathed deeply and evenly. At least Gabe had Jake and Mandy. At least they were safe.

God, she wanted to stay alive to see them all again. Jake and Mandy. And Gabe.

She'd been completely obsessed with Gabe five years ago. Then, as she'd matured, she realized he couldn't possibly be as great as she'd imagined. Her idea of him wasn't real. She didn't know him enough. The man she thought of as Gabe Cannon was just a fantasy she'd made up.

But now…Well, he was pretty damn good. He made her heart race faster than ever.

He really was as fantastic as she'd made him out to be in her teenage fantasies. He really was a hero. He charged to the rescue. He put himself in danger to save others.

He was saving Mandy and Jake even now.

And Jasmine was going to stay alive, dammit, so she could thank him. Thank him and see what might happen between them now that they were both adults.

Life was so freaking unfair. Or possibly pretty wonderful. She needed to get out of here to find out which.

"Your brother gave himself up. All we want is to take you in safely," came the next lie from the floor below her.

She kept low and ducked between fallen beams, trying to steal around the men. She had to find a way out. She couldn't engage them and fight them off. There were nine of them. Her gun had only four bullets. She would save those until the very end.

Which seemed to be here suddenly.

She ducked as a man crept into the room on her right. He scanned the rubble without noticing her. She could only see him through a gap in the old wallpaper that hung from the ceiling in the corner where she hid. He turned slowly, gun trained. Then looked right at her.

She shot then ran.

She was looking behind her as much as she looked ahead—a mistake. Steel arms snaked out from behind a column and caught her.

***

Gabe heard the gunshot from outside the crumbling warehouse, and his pulse quickened. The team would use silencers, so it had to be Jasmine shooting. And she wouldn't shoot unless she was in serious trouble.

He vaulted right in through the broken window, ready for battle. Scanned the room. Nobody in there. He ran for the door that led to the rest of the ground floor, but stopped when he reached it.

Impulse pushed him to rush to her, but his training held him back. *Assess. Plan. Execute.* Brent was *not* going to get Jasmine, not if Gabe had to take this whole shithole of a building apart brick by brick with his bare hands. He stole around the doorway with care.

Evans, one of Brent's men, stood at the bottom of the stairs, looking up. He had his back to Gabe.

Gabe sneaked up on him, shoved his knee in the back of the man's to bring him down. A hard tap to the guy's temple with the butt of the SIG, and he was out for the count.

Gabe didn't want to shoot if he didn't have to. He didn't think the men were involved in Brent's private agenda. And a gunshot, even with a silencer, could be heard by other team members who were nearby.

He disarmed the guy, then crept up the stairs. When he saw movement in a doorway, he pulled into the cover of a brick column and waited.

Troy was coming his way. Probably the most decent man on the team, but Gabe had no choice, had no time for explanations. He waited until they were in line with each other, then he went for it. Beyond a small grunt, nothing betrayed him when he brought the man down.

*Shit*, he hated to do that to a fellow SEAL.

"Sorry, man," he said under his breath.

He inched up to the next floor, listening for the slightest noise, the faintest creak. He could hear the soft sounds of movement on the level above him. Then a small, scraping sound came from one of the rooms down the hallway.

He moved forward, reached the door, and looked through the open gap, focusing on the two men in there: Alvarez and Boyle. In about two seconds, Gabe had a plan.

He scuffed his boot on the floor.

Alvarez came to investigate.

Gabe knocked him out from behind, then stepped into the room.

Boyle swung and raised his gun. Gabe shot him in the right shoulder and left thigh. That should keep him down for a while.

He strode over, kicked Boyle's weapon out of reach, and quieted the man's moaning by shoving his hat into his mouth, then secured the guy's hands with a plastic cuff.

"Jasmine?" Gabe whispered to the piles of rubble that littered the cavernous room, in case she was hiding in there somewhere.

No response.

He backed out of the room, cleared the rest of the floor, then retraced his steps to the stairs and stole up to the next level.

A bullet whizzed by his ear at the same time as he heard a small pop. He ducked, rolled, aimed. And didn't miss. Coleman went down, hard—a debilitating hit, but not fatal.

Nobody rushed to investigate.

*The others must be out of hearing distance.*

Gabe sneaked down the hallway, turned a corner, then another. Ahead, Johnson and Martinez were inspecting a giant room, clearing it section by section. Gabe looked at the sagging beam that barely held the ceiling, slammed the door, then shot at the beam until it gave, collapsing the ceiling and sealing the men inside.

Gabe had no time to gloat. He was too busy running, since his impromptu demolition worked only too well. The partial collapse in front of the door created a chain reaction. Bricks were coming down all around him as he ran.

A falling beam caught him in the back and knocked him to the floor, an avalanche of bricks half burying him. He had barely begun to dig himself free when, through the settling dust, he caught sight of Brent.

The team leader had Jasmine by the arm, holding his gun to her head.

*No blood on her. No bruises.*

Gabe wanted to rip Brent Foley's throat out anyway, just for laying hands on her.

"Are you okay?" was the first thing out of Jasmine's mouth.

Brent pressed the gun harder against her temple to quiet her. He sneered at Gabe. "I think your contract is going to end here. Short but productive. Just as I hoped."

Gabe focused on him but kept aware of the whole hallway, the open doors to the storage rooms. Where were the others? Nobody came. Maybe the team leader was the last man standing. Maybe he'd sent most of his men to the bridge.

"I like it when a plan works," Brent spit the words at Gabe with satisfaction.

Gabe never wanted to beat the shit out of someone as much as he wanted to pummel Brent at this moment. *I like it when a plan works.* He knew what that meant. He'd been pegged from the beginning, recruited because of his connection to the target.

"Long shot, wasn't it?" he asked in his best unaffected tone. "Tekla and I were never best friends. Last time we saw each other was five years ago. We had one op together."

Had Brent thought that Tekla would come out of hiding if he figured he could safely give himself up to a friend? It hadn't exactly worked out that way, but Gabe *had* led them to Tekla's hiding place. Brent had Jasmine because of *him.*

Brent said in his usual smug-bastard tone, "I didn't bring you on board because of your friendship with Tekla. You were brought in for your girlfriend here. When the men I hired took her, they searched the house and sent me every scrap of paper. Most of it was crap. But this one little diary…"

He gave a mean laugh. "A teenager's diary from five years ago. Didn't pay much attention to it at first, but after Tekla took out those men, I read the damn thing. I figured I might find a clue to where he was hiding. People go to familiar ground when they run."

He paused. "Nothing about Venice in the diary, I tell you that. But there were pages and pages about you."

Jasmine blushed scarlet and wouldn't meet Gabe's eyes.

He was too angry at Brent, too worried about her being in the middle of all this danger to feel amused. But he promised himself to enjoy the hell out of this little piece of information the second they were safe.

Time for him to start working on that. "Tekla got away. He's talking to the authorities right now. Whoever has been protecting you won't take the fall for this. He'll make you the scapegoat."

Brent flashed a grin of pure conceit, all teeth like an alligator that'd just been challenged by a chicken to a swimming contest. "Not to worry. I have enough on the man to make sure he'll never turn against me."

*Who's he blackmailing and with what?*

Questions for another time. Gabe asked something else.

"What's next?" His gun hand was almost free. He needed to keep the man talking.

Brent looked Jasmine over with slow, creepy care, flashing a leering smile as he turned back to Gabe. "I shoot you now, then wait for the rest of the team to call me with the news that they have Tekla. Once I know I no longer need your girlfriend for anything, I'll have some fun with her before I shoot her."

With the gun at her temple, Jasmine had been pretty still already, but now she froze.

*Fight!* Gabe tried to tell her with his eyes. *Fight now, dammit.*

She'd fought him every step of the way up on the roof when he'd tried to apprehend her, and she'd nearly scratched his eyes out in his room. Where was the ninja octopus now?

Brent rubbed his thumb over her arm. Her eyes glazed, as if she was lost in some nightmarish memory. Of course, Brent had just threatened her. After what she'd already been through…

*Come on, sweetheart. Do something. Anything. All I need is a second of distraction.*

"You know, reading all those teenage fantasies wasn't as bad as it sounds." Brent wouldn't shut up. "Let's see what she does with a real man. Maybe I won't shoot you just yet and let you watch. If you say pretty please."

"Drop dead you sick fuck."

Brent moved his gun from Jasmine's head and aimed it at Gabe's.

Gabe wasn't impressed. "Is that how you get off? Yanking your dick while reading some kid's diary?"

"I'll show you how I get off." Brent moved his hand from Jasmine's arm to the back of her head and grabbed her hair then yanked her to him hard.

As they connected, Jasmine snapped out of her frozen fear, and with an ear-splitting scream, she launched herself at the man who hadn't expected much resistance from her corner. Big mistake. The ninja octopus was back with a vengeance.

She fought well, but Brent had fifty extra pounds of muscle and a hell of a lot more training. He knocked her back.

Gabe yanked his arm free of the debris and took aim. He'd gone out of his way not to kill the others, but he didn't try to go easy on Brent. He drilled a bullet right into the middle of the bastard's forehead.

Another shot rang out at the same time, slamming into the man's chest.

Troy Hill stood in a doorway, grim and determined. His hard eyes said he'd heard Brent's rant.

He lowered his gun. "Let's get the hell out of here."

His scarred face looked even more haunted than usual as he watched Jasmine.

Wasn't there a rumor about the explosion that had messed up his voice and face killing the woman he loved? Gabe vaguely remembered Alvarez saying something to the effect.

For the first time, Gabe had an inkling of what something like that could do to a man. He wasn't sure he'd drawn a breath while Brent had his gun against Jasmine's head.

"Thanks for the help." He crawled from the rubble and pushed to standing, ignoring the pain in his knee and the blood trickling down his calf.

Troy's expression wasn't friendly. He looked as if he was thinking about sending his next bullet into Gabe. "The only reason you got the drop on me is because I knew it was you out there, so I didn't have my gun up to shoot you in the face. I kind of expected you to extend the same professional courtesy."

Gabe winced. "Sorry about that. There wasn't time to talk. I had to get to Jasmine."

Troy stood motionless, watching them, but then he nodded. "Yeah."

When Gabe was sure Troy wasn't going to shoot him, he turned to Jasmine, who was blinking at Brent's spreading blood on the floor.

She tore her gaze away. "It's okay, I'm fine."

Gabe reached for her hand. "You are. But I still wish you weren't involved in any of this."

Troy said, "I'll make sure we have a clear path out of here," and took off.

Gabe pulled Jasmine into his arms. "Just take a second. You're a tough woman. You can handle this."

She buried her face into his neck. "Jake and Mandy?"

"Safely in the care of the US Army."

"You came for me."

"I told you I wasn't going to leave you."

"Thank you." She lifted her gaze. Color was coming back into her face. "I was leading Brent toward a patch of rotten floorboards. I figured either he'd fall through all the way and break something important, or go through halfway and get stuck. I wanted to get his gun away from him."

"I bet you would have." He pressed his lips to her forehead, barely feeling the pain in his knee.

"I'm glad you came." Her gaze softened. She looked at him as if he was some kind of a hero.

"You have to stop looking at me like that, sweetheart," he begged, his voice suddenly low.

"Why?" she whispered, her sweet mouth inches from his.

"Because I'm trying hard not to kiss you."

And then he did, just a slow brush of his lips against hers.

He needed to go easy on her. She'd just been through hell. But then she kissed him back.

He was so damn sunk here.

The kiss was flattering, because she kissed him as if she couldn't quite believe that she was kissing him. She kissed him almost reverently, which was mind-boggling, because he so didn't deserve her.

He kept the kiss civil, when all he wanted was to devour her. Eventually, he was even able to pull back. If he'd ever done anything to deserve a medal, this was it.

He cleared his throat, hoped she wouldn't notice the sudden tenting in his pants. "I don't want to take advantage of you here."

She held his gaze. "Do you think you could take advantage of me somewhere else? Later?"

Her words shorted out his brain. He couldn't come up with an intelligent thought, let alone coherent words.

He was saved from having to answer by Troy shouting up from the floor below, "Could we get going here before anyone else shows up to shoot our asses?"

# CHAPTER
# ELEVEN

Gabe walked into the small reception area outside General Robert's office at Camp Darby in Livorno. One desk, four chairs, nothing else—not even a window.

He'd spent the past three days in a room of similar size, except, instead of table and chairs, that one had a bed. That bedroom seemed more and more like a cage with every passing day.

On the day he'd arrived, they'd allowed him one phone call. He'd checked in on his sister, Amy, and his nieces.

He wanted to track down Tekla and family too, but nobody would tell him anything, except that he was confined to quarters. His body *had* needed a little rest. He'd hurt his knee worse than he'd thought. Today was the first day it wasn't throbbing with pain.

"The general will be with you shortly," the sergeant who'd escorted Gabe said, then left him there.

The clock on the wall showed twenty hundred—eight p.m. Too late for a meeting, wasn't it? But maybe the general had just gotten to Italy. Maybe he'd been in the US or the Middle East when Gabe had called him three days ago. But at least the man was here now, and Gabe would be pretty glad to see him.

He needed to ask some serious questions and demand to be let loose. The US Army had no reason, not to mention right, to hold him a prisoner. As a courtesy to General Roberts, Gabe hadn't attempted to break out on his own. But he could and he would, if he didn't get answers today.

When he heard footsteps outside, he stood. Then the door opened, and Gabe pulled his spine straight and put his heels together out of habit.

But instead of the general, Jasmine walked in, clean scrubbed, hair in a sleek ponytail.

She wore army fatigues—and looked damn fine in uniform.

Lust hit him as always, then another emotion that originated in the middle of his chest, bringing an aching need to hold her. He resisted the urge to reach for her.

She went into his arms on her own, no reservations, no pretense, no games. "Gabe!"

He knew he had to have some foolish, dazed grin on his face, but he couldn't help it. He locked his arms around her slim waist.

Her golden-brown gaze held his, a small, shy smile on her amazing lips. "How's your knee?"

"Fine. Jake and Mandy?"

"In the hospital. Much better after some IV fluids and antibiotics. I think we can go home in a few more days." She moved her hands to his hips and hung on to him loosely. "Thank you for saving my family."

"No thanks necessary." He wanted something else. He wanted her not to walk out of his life.

"Jake has a new cast." Her smile grew a little. "He said the general talked to the admiral. NCIS wants Jake, but they agreed not to lock him up. They just want to debrief him and get all the details. They wanted him down at the naval base in Naples, but the general arranged for them to come up here."

*Probably using Tekla's injuries as an excuse. Smart move.* This way, the general would keep control of the situation. Every time Gabe dealt with the man, he respected him more.

Jasmine snuggled closer and laid her head on his shoulder.

"Is that what you've been doing?" he asked. "Visiting Jake and Mandy?"

"And working. I asked for a laptop, and they gave me one. I'm catching up on my accounts."

He should have thought of that. Maybe they would have given him a laptop too. Mostly, he'd been just asking about her. He desperately wanted to kiss her—a very bad idea, with the general on his way to see them. So Gabe didn't claim her lips, but he couldn't let her go either. He kept her in his arms, pretending he was just providing her with comfort. *Yeah. Right.*

*Say something that's not, "Want to come back to my room later?"*

"Building a social media empire?" He could see her doing it with her courage and determination. He couldn't imagine her trying anything and not succeeding.

She pulled back but stayed in the circle of his arms. "It's just a gig. I don't know what I want to do long-term yet." She paused. "After the last couple of months…"

"You just want to be safely back home."

"No. I want to make a difference. I want to be part of the action like you and Jake."

Over his dead body. And over Jake's too, probably. Between the two of them, they were going to talk her out of any budding action-heroine fantasies. Not that she couldn't handle the job. But Gabe couldn't handle the thought of her in danger.

He tucked her back snugly against him. "So do I get to know what's in that diary of yours?"

She blushed crimson. "That diary got you into this mess. You could have been killed. How can you joke about it?"

"No joke. I'd like every lurid detail. The more lurid the better." He fought a grin. "I'm not scared of explicit."

She groaned. "I was a stupid teenager. I didn't know what love was."

"And now?"

She didn't answer.

A warm, funny feeling filled his chest. He kept holding on to her. "My life is a mess. I don't know if I have anything to offer to a woman like you. I'm pretty sure you'd be a lot better off without me."

She gave a lopsided smile. "Are you asking me out?"

He held her gaze. "I'm asking a lot more than that."

Her smile doubled. God, she was a sight to see.

His heart stumbled. To hell with the general. "I'm going to kiss you, if that's all right."

She lifted her mouth to his without hesitation. That was Jasmine. Never flinching when she could be brave. She was soft yet strong. He wanted to know more of her, all of her. In every sense.

Need surged through him to feel those soft curves of hers, to hear her soft breath hitch in his ear as they tangled in the sheets together. He wanted to be buried as deep inside her as a man could be inside a woman, drink her moans of pleasure—

The door's scraping interrupted his fantasy.

General Roberts strode in—tall and crisp, sharp eyes, authoritative from top to bottom, every inch commanding. He gave them a narrow-eyed look, his gaze settling on Gabe as Gabe hastily pulled away from Jasmine.

"I just had to sit through a very uncomfortable meeting," the man said, his expression as serious as a firing squad, "with the Venetian chief of police and Senator Wharst, who is visiting the troops here ahead of the elections. They're not happy about the shootout on Soremo."

Gabe did his best to surreptitiously adjust his pants. "I apologize, sir."

The general shot him a dark glare, then nodded at Jasmine. "Miss Tekla." He led them into the adjoining room, his office.

The space was nearly as spartan as his reception area—if a little bigger— maybe twenty feet by ten, a single window that looked to an empty obstacle course. The only nod to luxury was a plush leather chair behind the desk, although the desk was nice too, old mahogany, but nothing fancy. Military maps covered the walls.

The general strode behind his desk, then gestured toward the two visitors' chairs. "Do you have proof of any of your fairy tale beyond Tekla's pen drive that's nothing more than hearsay and speculation? *Hard* proof. And by that, I mean, do you know where the gold is?"

Jasmine sat first, then Gabe. "No, sir."

The man watched them. "All right." He didn't sound happy, but he didn't sound as if he was ready to order up the firing squad either. "I've already debriefed Tekla. Now I'd like to hear how you got involved in this."

He shot a meaningful glance at Jasmine, as if he knew *exactly* how Gabe had gotten involved—sucked into trouble by a beautiful woman.

Gabe couldn't really argue with that assumption, so he didn't.

He started at the beginning, XO-ST recruiting him. And he ended with, "So we think Brent Foley got the gold out of Afghanistan, but he hasn't gotten it back to the US yet. He blackmailed someone in power into helping him get the contract to bring Jake Tekla in. I think he planned on blackmailing the same person again to sneak the gold into the US."

"You think it's someone in the navy?" The general's lips flattened. "I'd hate to be the one who has to tell that to the admiral."

Gabe had given this considerable thought over the past three days while he'd sat around with his knee iced and elevated. "Someone who had influence over awarding a government contract, so someone in the government."

The general flashed a narrow-eyed look that did have some firing squad in it. "If there's one thing I hate, it's dirty politicians."

Gabe started to say that it was too bad they didn't have a single lead to go on, when the general pulled a fancy lighter from his back pocket— maybe it'd been uncomfortable to sit on—and began absentmindedly playing with it.

Gabe stared at the red enamel crest. "Sir, may I ask where you got that from?"

The general looked at his hand and blinked, as if he hadn't realized he'd been toying with the thing. "From Senator Wharst. I had lunch on his yacht today. He pulled into harbor this morning."

An aggravated tone crept into his voice as he added, "I'm not a fan of the man. He takes campaign contributions from the defense industry. He'll vote for ordering outdated tanks that'll never enter the battlefield, to make sure the manufacturer will receive a big contract. In the meanwhile, he'll ignore my request for armored Humvees, so I'm sending my boys out there day after day unprotected."

General Roberts tapped the lighter on his desk. "He asked me to lunch to try to persuade me to bring those damned tanks of his back into play. I told him we've moved on to drones. If we want to take out enemy combatants, drones are far superior. And when the fighting is done and we move on to a peacekeeping role in a region, tanks send the wrong message. Their time is over. Not that I could convince the senator."

"Wharst was in Venice for the past two weeks," Gabe said.

"He mentioned that. So?"

"Brent Foley had the same lighter." Gabe remembered the strange red crest clearly. Brent had had the lighter out at the team meeting in his room, used it to light his cigar.

The general's gaze sharpened. "Exactly the same?"

"Yes, sir."

The man held up the lighter so Gabe could see it better, a stainless steel boxy body with a blood-red enamel design in the middle. "That's the Wharst family crest," he said. "The senator gifted it to me with a box of coronas." He dropped the thing on his desk. "I don't even smoke."

Gabe asked the question they were all thinking. "What if he was Brent Foley's connection?"

And Jasmine pushed it a step further. "What if the gold is on the yacht? The senator could definitely get it into the US."

General Roberts looked between them, the expression on his face unhappier by the second. "You better be right about this."

He pushed to his feet, then strode to the door, turning back from the doorway. "Neither of you is to leave the base until I say so. Until we figure out what's going on, we're in damage-control mode. Which means radio silence. Other than each other, you don't talk to anyone."

Before they could say *yes, sir*, the door shut behind him with a firm click, and they were left staring after him. Not for long, just long enough to exchange puzzled glances. Barely two seconds passed before a sergeant stepped in to escort them back to their rooms.

They followed him down the hallway and came to Gabe's room first.

"I'll see you later," he said instead of inviting Jasmine in, recognizing the impulse for a bad idea.

She might be a grown woman now, but she was still Tekla's little sister. She'd been through hell in the past couple of months. She needed rest instead of the things he thought about when he looked at her.

He still didn't fully know what happened to her when she'd been kidnapped. She'd let him kiss her, responded to his kisses, but…

He could absolutely not assume that she wanted to go where he wanted to go.

*"Do you think you could take advantage of me somewhere else? Later?"* she'd said at the warehouse. Jokingly. A lot of people used humor to cover up their scars and fears.

Trouble was, Gabe *did* want more than a few kisses. He wanted everything. And it *would* be taking advantage of her.

She stopped. Smiled at him. But the sergeant kept going. So with a quick, reluctant "See you later," she hurried after the man.

Gabe watched them until they disappeared around the corner.

He could have gone to see where her room was. He didn't, as a safety measure.

He strode into his own room, closed the door behind him, and began pacing, didn't even try to sit on the bed. He needed to work off his pent-up frustrations. He needed the obstacle course.

The general had said Jasmine and he were confined to base, but hadn't mentioned anything about their use of the facilities. Time to test the knee. Gabe opened his door, hoping to catch the sergeant and ask if he could have free rein of the base now.

"Hi." Jasmine stood outside his door, hand up, ready to knock. She looked a little startled by the door's sudden opening, but then she smiled. "Can I come in?"

*No.* He needed to say, *no.*

He stepped back and moved aside. Then, after she walked in, he closed the door behind her. He didn't lock it.

"Jasmine?" Why in hell was his voice so low and raspy now? He almost sounded like Troy. He cleared his throat. "What are you doing here?"

She was staring at the single bed, made with military precision. Swallowed. Then she turned her gaze to him.

He drowned in that gaze, the warm color of antique gold. Her stance held hesitance, but her back was straight with courage. She somehow managed to be strong and vulnerable at the same time. And he was so fricking falling for her.

She was here in his room.

He wanted her here.

Wanted her. Period.

"You probably shouldn't be in my room," he said.

Hurt flashed across her eyes. Then embarrassment. "Oh God, I'm throwing myself at you again, aren't I? I'm sorry." She stepped toward the door. "I thought you felt the same and—"

His mouth went on some disastrous kamikaze autopilot, and he said, "I'd sell my left nut on eBay to be able to have you just one time."

Her eyes widened, then her incredible lips twitched. Mischief put sparkles in her eyes. "Would that be listed under 'cannonballs'?"

He snorted. *Gabe Cannon.* "Very funny."

She burst into peals of laughter.

God, she was beautiful. God, he loved her.

"Wouldn't having me work better with two nuts?" she asked when she caught her breath.

They were talking about him having her. His knees were growing weak. Of course, another part of him was growing strong. And hard. "I meant, I'd do anything to have you."

Explaining it now? Dammit. Way to look stupid.

But she smiled even wider, her eyes dancing. "If it's all the same to you, I'd prefer the nuts, or cannonballs, intact."

He could listen to her talk about his nuts all day. Let her do more than talk. Let her do anything she wanted.

He reached back, locked the door without ever taking his eyes off her, then took a step toward her. She took a step toward him, and they met in the middle.

He reached for her, then she was in his arms, pressed against him. The perfect place for her.

She tilted her head up to look into his eyes, kept smiling.

The need to kiss that smile into a look of passion swept through him. He dipped his head and let his forehead rest against hers. "Do you still feel the same about me as you did when you wrote that diary?"

She shook her head. "Those were some pretty ridiculous teenage fantasies."

He swallowed his disappointment. He wanted her more than his next breath, but he wasn't going to pressure her. He'd let her go, even if letting her go killed him.

But then she slipped her hands under his shirt, her fingertips coming to rest on the naked skin of his back. "This is real. You are better than any fantasy. I want the real Gabe."

Heat shot through him as she caressed his back. They were in his bedroom, and she was going for skin. "Are you sure? I know this is pretty sudden. We just met again."

"Are *you* sure?" she whispered.

He let his hands slide to her firm bottom and brought her closer, let her feel his hard length. He looked into her eyes when he said, "But I'm willing to wait."

Her eyes narrowed dangerously. "Don't you dare. I've already waited five years."

"In all those five years, we didn't spend a lot of time together." See? He could be responsible and the voice of reason. He could give valiant resistance another try. He could become the kind of man who deserved a woman like her. *God*, he hoped.

She arched an eyebrow. "You've never had sex with anyone you didn't know thoroughly?"

And what was he supposed to say to that? Had he taken girls home from bars after a brief conversation and a few drinks, maybe a slow dance? Yeah. He wasn't proud of it, but he had.

"You're different."

"Why?"

"You mean something."

"How do you know? You barely know me."

A sound escaped him, aggrieved and miserable. "That's what I mean. We barely know each other, and I look at you, and I want things I'd never thought I'd want. It's like tasting something for the first time, and knowing it's going to be your favorite food forever. Or hearing a song for the first time, and knowing that's your song, your life."

He was sure he wasn't making any sense, but he was at a loss to explain the vast and disturbing feelings she caused inside his chest. He understood lust, but he'd never believed in true love, the whole one-man-destined-for-one-woman thing.

"If we do something here, I'm never going to want to let you go, and that scares the living daylights out of me, to be honest," he confessed.

She smiled the most brilliant smile that existed in the universe—a smile that could probably achieve world peace and cure cancer, possibly replace fossil fuels. It sure had the power to completely scramble what small part of his brain was still functioning.

And then she was on the tips of her toes, her lips touching his.

Negotiations were over.

He kissed her, with more restraint than he thought he had. Then she made a small, throaty sound of desire, and his restraint disappeared. The time for valiantly resisting was over.

His tongue swept inside her mouth, and he licked his way into her wet heat, exploring her. She tasted incredibly sweet. He slipped his hands lower, under her thighs, and lifted her. She obliged by wrapping her long legs around his hips.

He might have fantasized about this a time or two. Or a thousand.

They were lined up perfectly. If only they didn't have all those clothes between them…But he was a SEAL, and he wasn't held back by problems. He was a man of solutions.

He walked her to the bed and set her down on the edge of the mattress, kneeled between her knees so they wouldn't have to break the kiss. He untucked her shirt and slipped his hands under, onto her smooth, warm skin.

She melted against him. But when he grabbed onto the shirt and tried to pull it up, she froze and squirmed back a couple of inches.

He noted the uncertain look in her eyes. "What's wrong?"

She raked her teeth over her bottom lip. "I have scars."

"I know." He didn't want to think about that now, because every time he did, he felt some serious building-a-time-machine-and-going-back-to-mow-some-asses-down kind of rage.

"I have worse scars than what you've already seen," she whispered.

He let her go, unbuttoned his own shirt, and opened the front. "Worse than these?"

At first, she just stared, then she reached out a tentative hand. When her fingertips touched his chest, a shudder ran through him. He held back, held still, let her look and feel, let her take her time to grow comfortable.

She smoothed her fingers over the worst scars on his chest. "What did this?"

"Shrapnel."

Her fingers moved lower, toward his abdomen. "And this?"

His body responded to her touch. "Bullet."

She flattened her palm against the hole as if wanting to cover it, maybe wanting to heal it. Her gaze lifted to meet his.

He covered her hand with his own. "Let me see you, Jasmine."

She bobbed a slight nod and dropped her hand. And he reached for her shirt again. He pulled the hem up slowly, giving her time to stop if she felt uncomfortable. But she sat still as he inched the shirt up, then over her head.

Her bra was simple black cotton, utilitarian. For a moment, he couldn't look away from her perfect breasts. Then his gaze dropped, and her scars snapped into focus.

His entire body tightened as he looked at the circular white marks. He ran his thumb over one. Looked up into her eyes.

She held his gaze as she said, "One of the men who kidnapped me liked to come down to me in the basement while his buddy was sleeping upstairs at night. He would pull my shirt up or my pants down…" She swallowed. "He liked to bite me."

*Oh man.* The scars were teeth marks.

Gabe's chest tightened. He wanted to take those bastards apart with his bare hands, and hated that he was too late. He moved forward and gathered Jasmine into his arms.

Brent had sent some perverted psycho after Jasmine and Mandy. It'd been only luck that Mandy—a fricking kid—hadn't been taken too. Gabe wanted to kill Brent all over again. Maybe this time a little slower. Somebody needed to invent that freaking time machine.

"He got real excited if he drew blood," Jasmine whispered into his neck. "Sometimes he touched himself."

Gabe didn't want to see the images that popped into his head: the pervert bastard biting her, drawing blood, probably ejaculating on her, while she'd been tied up and terrified.

Her captor was marking her as his. The two men had probably been promised that she'd be given to them once Tekla was captured.

Gabe held Jasmine tightly and thanked God that her brother had saved her.

"We can put your shirt back on if you'd like. I'd be happy just to hold you. We don't have to do anything more."

She pulled back, nothing but courage in her eyes. "I want to feel good things again instead of fear when a man touches me."

He held her gaze.

*No pressure.*

The one place he'd always known what he was doing was in bed, and now he suddenly felt like a virgin. "You say when you want to stop. We'll stop. Immediately."

She raised her hand back to his chest in response, her slim fingers warm against his skin. That brought a little urgency back into the moment.

He shrugged out of his shirt. Then he leaned forward and kissed her. His fingers moved to her torso, caressing her scars. He ran his hands lightly down her back, then up her rib cage, using great control to stop under her breasts.

"I'd like to take off your bra," he said against her lips.

"Yes."

He reached to the back and undid the snap, tugged the straps down her arms, then tossed the bra on the chair. He sat back on his heels so he could fully look at her. "You take my breath away."

A quick smile flashed onto her face.

"You too," she said. "I mean, me too." She laughed. "I mean, I feel the same about you."

He slowly lay her back across the bed, her head almost at the wall, her butt on the edge, her knees bent as he knelt between them, her feet flat on the floor on either side of him.

He moved up and over her, kissed her lips, then her chin, then her graceful neck, nuzzling her warmth and softness, breathing in her light, flowery scent. He kissed his way down her collarbone, then to her breast, covering the perfect mound with kisses in concentric circles until his seeking lips reached her nipple.

He licked the swollen bud, then, as her back arched off the bed, he sucked her nipple into his mouth, and a soft moan escaped her.

He looked up and caught her gaze. "How is it so far?"

A smile of pleasure bloomed on her full lips. "Good enough to record for all prosperity. Maybe I should start a new diary."

He thought about all the things he wanted to do with her. "You'd better get one with a key."

He went back to her nipples and took turns at nibbling them until she moaned and writhed under him. By the time he looked up at her face again, she was glowing with desire. And his entire body throbbed with need.

"I want to strip you naked," he said against her skin.

"Yes, please." Her words were breathless gasps.

He unzipped her pants and tugged them down, his fingertips tingling. Her utilitarian black cotton panties matched her bra.

He sat on his heels, rested his forehead against her belly button and inhaled the sweet scent of her skin. He stayed there for a few seconds, until he gathered some control over himself. And then he removed her panties.

"I want to taste you." His words came out in a rough whisper.

For the first time, she looked uncertain.

He pushed back against the blinding lust that tried to propel him forward like a steam engine. "What is it, sweetheart?"

She chewed the side of her mouth. "It's just…" She looked away, then back. "I'm not very…orgasmic. So if nothing happens, it's not your fault. I don't want you to think…"

He bit back a grin, since she was clearly very serious about this. "I'm in charge of orgasms tonight. How about you let me handle that part?"

She held his gaze as she slowly parted her thighs.

He settled in a little lower and hooked her legs over his shoulders. Then she was open to him, and he couldn't wait any longer. He dipped his tongue between her pink folds. *Sweet. Honey. Heaven.*

The small touch had her back arching off the bed again. Maybe it was stupid, but her instant response to him filled him with some macho, primal pleasure. His blood drummed, *mine, mine, mine,* and he licked her again and again, reveling in every soft moan that escaped her lips.

He let his tongue play with her and lost track of time. They were both breathing hard by the time he lifted a finger to test her opening, found her wet, and went so hard, scientists experimenting with new armor coating for submarines should have studied his dick.

Not groaning out loud took effort. He slipped his finger inside her tight channel inch by slow inch and learned her body, what made her moan, what made her squirm, what made her give that ragged sigh that took his breath away. Only when she was ready and close to begging did he add a second finger. And then he put to good use all the things he'd just learned.

He teased her for a while, settling into a steady rhythm before bending the tips of his fingers forward to massage the inside of her clitoris.

Her hands flailed on the bedcover. Her breath came in ragged gasps.

*There. Right there.*

He bent to her sweet body, closed his mouth over her swollen nub and sucked.

And she shattered in his arms, under his lips, with a surprised cry.

He drank in the sound, the feel of her, the taste of her, rested his chin on her pubic bone and watched her face as she rode the wave, the most beautiful sight he'd ever seen. They should paint frescos of *that* in Venice!

"Oh," she exhaled softly as she gathered herself. Then she flashed him a dazed smile. "Your turn."

But as he shifted her to lie lengthwise on the bed and moved up next to her, as the mattress dipped under his weight, and his hand settled on her hipbone, she couldn't quite disguise a flinch.

And he knew she had memories that still needed to heal, no matter how brave she was, how determined.

He gathered her into his arms. "This *was* my turn. I'm not going to take any more tonight."

Her smile turned to confusion. "Why?"

"I'm going to savor you," he said, and claimed her lips in a kiss.

* * *

Jasmine was still floating, playing footsie with Gabe at the mess hall, when General Roberts's aide found them the next morning as they were having breakfast.

"Let's hope for success." Jasmine took Gabe's hand as the aide escorted them to the general's office.

A heady feeling that, to be able to walk around with him hand in hand. She'd spent the night in his room last night, after he'd *savored* her right into the best orgasm of her life. And she couldn't have put that in her diary even if she still kept one, because words didn't exist to describe the things he'd done to her.

He'd *savored* her again this morning, before breakfast. And the burning look in his eyes at the moment said he wanted to savor her again.

"Navy SEALs are the worst overachievers," she said under her breath.

He struggled with a grin and didn't win. "I'm hoping you can put up with that one small fault."

She tried to look put out. "I could probably learn to live with it."

She liked being *savored*. A lot. She was definitely not as unorgasmic as she'd believed. Instead of the infrequent, small pops of pleasure she'd felt before, with Gabe, fireworks went off inside her. Like, fire at the fireworks warehouse inferno.

But before she could fully relive all that, they reached the general's office and were ushered inside.

"General," she said at the same time as Gabe.

The man pointed them to the two empty chairs, and Jasmine's stomach sank at his somber expression.

Gabe must have read the look the same way, because he said, "There was nothing on the yacht."

But the general responded with a grim "We found the gold."

He sounded about as happy as if he'd found a nest of rattlesnakes in his bed.

"No shit?" The words burst from Gabe before he snapped his mouth shut.

The general's eyes narrowed.

"Sorry, sir. I meant, no shit, sir, General."

The man shook his head. "We confiscated the gold, but now what do we do with it? We can't take it to the US."

"We can't?" Jasmine asked. They had the gold! How was that not good news?

Yet the general clearly wasn't celebrating. "That would be out-and-out theft from the people of Afghanistan. Not to mention, we can't have a US senator implicated in something like this when half the Middle East believes we're only warring over there to steal everything that's theirs."

He seemed to have aged since last night, the furrows on his forehead deeper. "We can't give the gold back to the warlord either, or he'll use it to buy arms against us. And we can't give it to the Afghan government without confessing everything."

He fixed Gabe with a hard look. "You and Tekla stirred up a serious shit storm. Any ideas what I'm supposed to do with twenty million dollars' worth of gold coins?"

Jasmine swallowed hard, suddenly light-headed. "Twenty?"

"Could be more," the man said in a tone of disgust. "We're still counting."

As Jasmine glanced over at Gabe, an idea popped into her mind, and she blurted it out without giving it further thought. "North Village?"

The general flashed them a questioning look.

Gabe explained. "There's this garment factory in Afghanistan. It's a non-profit that gives work to widows and supports orphans."

The general nodded. "I'm going to need more detail, but I'm not ruling it out. We might be able to dribble the money back into the country little by little through charities. That's not a half-bad idea. At least the money would go to the people."

Gabe cast Jasmine a stunned I-can't-believe-this-could-actually-work look.

She grinned at him.

Their happiness was not infectious. The general appeared as sober as ever. "I want to know what Brent Foley used to blackmail the senator. I want to use it to bring down Wharst."

"How can we help?" Jasmine asked.

Gabe shook his head at her and corrected with, "How can I help?"

The general ignored their quibble. "I can't get the army out-and-out involved. We don't have jurisdiction over him."

"If you don't mind my asking, sir," Gabe said, "how did you manage to search the senator's yacht?"

The general allowed an almost smile. "He gave permission. I told him we had credible intelligence that illegal cargo had been stowed on his ship. I told him if the Italian authorities found it, we could not control the media."

"So he agreed to the search if the results were kept confidential?" Jasmine asked.

"Promises were not spelled out, but definitely implied. Then we found the crates. Of course, the senator denied all knowledge of them. He claims they must have been smuggled on board when he wasn't looking."

"And we can't prove otherwise," Gabe said darkly.

"I convinced him that this was too big to sweep under the rug," the general responded. "Somebody had to go down for it. To make a long story short, we went around a couple of rounds. Eventually, I outmaneuvered the senator, and he admitted that the crates were brought on board in response to a blackmailing attempt."

Gabe raised his eyebrows. "Did he tell you the truth about who was blackmailing him? That it was Brent Foley?"

"Yes. But according to the senator, Foley said the crates held high-powered rifles for wealthy US gun enthusiasts. The senator agreed to take them on board because he was backed into a corner, but he meant to turn the crates over to US Customs as soon as he sailed into harbor in DC."

Silence followed the man's words.

Then Jasmine spoke up. "What did he say Foley was blackmailing him with?"

The general's voice was heavily skeptical as he said, "A youthful indiscretion."

"And we can't get the truth out of Foley, because Foley is dead." Gabe said.

A couple of seconds ticked away. The general looked between the two of them. "How familiar are you with the senator?"

Jasmine shook her head. She'd heard his name a few times on TV, but didn't know much beyond that.

Gabe said, "Not very."

The general leaned forward in his chair and folded his hands on the desk. "He's a dangerous man. Back when he was governor, his nickname in political circles was The Thugernor. Rumors were, while big industry handled the contributions to his campaigns, his organized crime connections handled his opponents and anyone who tried to come forward with any dirt on him."

Gabe's expression turned thoughtful. "But Brent Foley's commando soldiers kept Brent safe from the senator."

A frown creased the general's forehead. "Who is going to keep you safe?"

And before Jasmine could ask why they would be in danger, the man leaned back in his chair, reached into his drawer, pulled out a handful of computer printouts, and tossed them on the desk between them.

She gasped at the sight of her brother's picture.

Gabe swore, pulling the papers to him and leafing through. "It's Foley's file on Jake Tekla and his family."

The general was looking at Jasmine. "One of the MPs found it in the senator's cabin and accidentally pocketed it."

*Why would Wharst have those files?* "Do you think the senator was trying to find a way to take out Foley, so he had Foley's laptop hacked?"

The general scooped up the printouts and tossed them back into his drawer. "It's worse than that. I had a long talk with him about Foley and the whole blackmail situation. He seems convinced that Foley had a partner in all his evil doings. He's convinced that partner is your brother."

Her chest tightened. "Which means?"

The man's expression was sober and apologetic. "Whatever secret Wharst has that Foley blackmailed him with, he thinks your brother knows it too. Your family is still not out of danger."

"Why would the senator think that Jake and Foley were partners in crime?" Gabe reached over and took Jasmine's hand, and she let him, grateful for the connection.

"Maybe Foley implied it," the general said. "Foley wanted to be the one to bring in Tekla. He needed the senator to make it happen, make sure XO-ST got the contract. He could have told the senator that Jake used to be his partner, they were in the SEALs together. Foley might have mentioned that Jake knew the senator's secret too, so it was in the senator's best interest to arrange for XO-ST to take Jake out of the equation."

Before Jasmine could say anything, Gabe squeezed her hand. "If the senator sends his thugs after your brother, we're going to stop them."

The general said, "I want that man's rule of corruption to end. The army has no jurisdiction to investigate the senator, but the FBI does. I happen to have a couple of good friends at the Bureau. I talked to one of them this morning. He can authorize a temporary team for a preliminary investigation, two or three men."

He focused on Gabe. "I convinced him to hire you to be part of that team. To be more precise, I convinced him to let you put together that team. You go and turn over some rocks. You'll have the FBI at your back, and my silent support and backing, and any assistance you might need, should you need it."

Gabe had the names immediately. "Jake Tekla and Troy Hill."

"Tekla is out of commission."

"He'll heal. First we'll do computer research, check paper trails, phone records—basically office work."

"What about Hill? Would this be the same man who put the second bullet into Brent Foley?"

As Jasmine nodded, Gabe said, "Yes, sir."

"I'll need to talk to him," the general responded, but he sounded agreeable. Then he pinned his gaze on Jasmine. "And what are your plans for the future, young lady?"

She was sure of only one thing. "I want to help."

"Your brother said you're some kind of a tech whiz."

"I'm pretty good with computers."

"These boys are going to need tech support. Could you provide that from stateside?"

Gabe opened his mouth, no doubt to protest, but before he could say anything, Jasmine snapped out, "Yes, sir."

The man turned back to Gabe. "The pay won't be what private security pays, but it'll be decent. This is a small op, but a very important one. Even without the blackmail issue, the senator's involvement with the gold requires a serious investigation. Stealing from another government is begging to cause big trouble. We need a presence in the region. We're in Afghanistan with the Afghan government's invitation. Should they withdraw that invitation, we'd be an occupying force instead of a peacekeeping force. As far as I'm concerned, the senator is a threat to our national security. I want that cigar-puffing, sanctimonious old bastard."

"Yes, sir," they said in unison.

And that put the first real smile on the general's face that they'd seen.

Smile or no smile, the man still intimidated the hell out of Jasmine. She didn't relax until they left his office.

On the way back to their rooms, Gabe took her hand. He ran the pad of his thumb over the back of her fingers. "I was looking forward to going back to the States with you. After we part ways here, we might not be able to see each other for a couple of months."

Yeah. She hated the living daylights out of that thought.

"I've waited five years already. I can wait another couple of months. I want my family safe," she told him, then cleared her throat. "But maybe we should *savor* each other a little more before we leave here."

His grin started slow, stretched wide, then filled with heat, even as his gaze filled with promise.

"Or go, you know, all the way," she suggested, and hoped she wasn't panting. "I'm not a schoolgirl anymore."

"I noticed." He sounded pained. "But I'm still going to do this the right way. We'll go slow."

"Why?" And what was right? The two of them together were right. Sooo right.

"The truth? You knock me on my ass, Jasmine."

"You knocked me on my ass too. And tied me down," she reminded him.

"I meant metaphorically."

*Oh.* She knocked Gabe Cannon on his ass? She felt a huge smile spread on her face.

"I want us to work for the long term," he told her, his tone and eyes serious.

She lost her breath there a little.

Then she lost it a lot when he picked her up, carried her into his room, and said, "I'm only going to fall in love once, Jasmine. When a SEAL does something, he does it right the first time. No do-overs."

And then she didn't just lose her breath. She lost her heart.

* * *

# AVENGING
## AGENT

# CHAPTER
# ONE

Five minutes into the conversation, Allison Myers already regretted coming to the Afghan police station.

"People think you are an American spy here to steal our water," the police chief said in thickly accented English. Anger creased his bearded face as he dabbed his temple with a rag, then swatted at the flies that buzzed around him.

Allison's stomach clenched. *Fudge buckets.* Bad things happened to people around here who were accused of being Western spies. *God, don't let coming here be a fatal mistake.*

The full heat of summer poured into the small office through the iron bars of the open window. Flies circled around her too, trying to dart in to lick the moisture from her forehead.

The police chief's beady eyes never moved from her for a second, as if he was watching some loathsome snake he would like to cut in half.

At least they had a barrier between them: a gray metal desk that matched the gray metal cabinet in the corner.

On the other hand, a silver ceremonial dagger—an ancient tribal relic—hung on the wall behind him, so the whole cutting-in-half business wasn't entirely out of the question.

The dagger definitely fit him better than the handgun in the tan holster at his side.

"I'm a private citizen," Allison said. "Here on private business. Nothing else."

She stole a glance at the door on her right that stood open to aid air circulation in the cramped space. A swarthy, twenty-something guard stood in the doorway with his back to the room, in a stance the US military called *parade rest*: feet shoulder-width apart, hands together at the small of the back.

Allison was under no illusion that she could leave without the police chief's permission. She needed to get him to believe her. "I'm just looking for my fiancé. I swear."

*Ex-fiancé*, technically. She meant to break the engagement once she found Kenneth, but that was none of the police chief's business. She had learned this past week that without claiming she was family, nobody would give her the time of day.

*Fiancé* was her story, and she was sticking to it. Kenneth was her friend, and she did love him, even if she was no longer *in* love with him. You took care of the people you cared about. If her father had taught her anything, he'd taught her that.

"My fiancé disappeared around here five months ago." She kept her voice deferential, bordering on apologetic, even if being submissive didn't come naturally to her. At work, she was the boss. She negotiated multimillion-dollar real estate deals. She didn't kowtow to anyone.

But here…she'd do what she had to for Kenneth.

"Is your fiancé a spy?" The police chief whacked at the flies again and knocked over his coffee cup, which fell to the tile floor with a clatter.

The cup was richly worked copper, so it didn't break, but the coffee spilled, a dark line of liquid running toward the two-door metal cabinet in the corner that was large enough to hide a camel.

The padlock hung open, the looming cabinet's doors an inch ajar, and for some reason, that inch-wide dark gap kept drawing Allison's eyes. Was there a file in there with Kenneth's name on it? Was the police chief just playing with her? She peered at that slim line of darkness, and for a freaky second, she had a sensation that the darkness was peering back at her.

Despite the heat, a cold shiver ran down her spine. *Get your act together.* She tore her gaze from the cabinet and looked back at the police chief across the cluttered desk.

He glared at her as if the spilled coffee was her fault. He didn't move to touch the mess. Clearly, he was a man of importance; he had people to clean up the messes he made.

He gave a piglike grunt. "I think you've been lying to me."

As a business executive, she'd met people like him before: arrogant, domineering, overly authoritative. They were usually heads of megacorporations, used to an environment where their word was law.

In a business environment, Allison Myers had leverage. She wanted something from her negotiating partners, but they also wanted something from her. Here, at the moment, she was entirely at the police chief's mercy—a perilous position.

She wasn't afraid of the man as much as the power he represented. And beyond the power of the police, he had power over her just because he was a man and she was a woman. She clenched her teeth to keep in the words she really wanted to say to him.

She sat with her shoulders hunched, dropping her gaze to hover around the man's chin. She'd been doing that since she'd been ushered in, except for the brief glances she stole at the man's eyes now and then to gauge his mood. *Do not challenge his authority.*

She was here for Kenneth, not the feminist movement. On the other hand, if there *was* a feminist movement in Afghanistan, she was going to donate some serious money to the cause once she returned home.

The police chief slapped his hand on the table, raising his voice. "Is your fiancé a spy?"

"He's just a businessman. He's here to help this country." She made a supreme effort to sound firm yet deferential, but ended up sounding winded.

She couldn't breathe in the heat. At home, she'd be in a pair of shorts with a tank top in weather like this. Fine, in a business suit at work, but she had an air-conditioned office in DC.

Here, in deference to the local customs, a scarf covered her hair. She wore a long black skirt that nearly brushed the ground when she walked, with a long-sleeved, loose black shirt buttoned to her chin. The longer she sat there, the smaller her collar felt around her neck, like a tightening noose.

She reached for her top button but caught herself in time, dropped her hands, and folded them in her lap, then clasped them together. Better sweat through her clothes than be imprisoned for public indecency. Imprisoned or caned. Or both. She needed to get the information she'd come for, then get out of here.

"Kenneth came on business," she said. "He was only supposed to be in town for a few weeks. He was negotiating with a local company."

"I don't believe you." The police chief's words sounded like a judgment. As if his belief was proof. As if here, whatever he believed replaced both fact and due process.

Allison swallowed past her parched throat. "Kenneth's company designs irrigation systems. He came to research local opportunities. You can call the company vice president and confirm."

She'd already provided the contact information. One of Kenneth's business cards lay on the desk.

The police chief ignored the card. "We don't have any irrigation systems in Lahedeh, just the old underground cisterns and water channels. We don't want foreign companies around here. Your people only come to our country to steal."

The man braced his stubby-fingered hands on the desk and rose to tower over her. "You've been bothering people with your questions. Why do you want to know so much?"

She resisted a groan of frustration. "I just want to find Kenneth."

"Why are you here alone? Where are your brothers? Where is your father?"

"My father is gone. Dead," she clarified, and the old ache stirred in her heart. "I don't have any brothers."

The man bristled as if he blamed her for that, as if she'd somehow purposefully thwarted some natural order of things just to be difficult.

"You understand," he said in a tone thick with judgment, "why I consider a woman traveling without a protector extremely suspicious."

*I understand that you're a misogynistic prick,* she thought. But she kept her mouth shut. She had never been at the mercy of another person like this before. Obviously, she'd underestimated the culture gap.

The police chief leaned even more forward, so far across the desk that when he spoke, some of his spit came close to landing on her face. "Are you spying for an American company that wants to steal our water?"

He kept bringing up water theft. People here seemed paranoid about water, probably because they didn't have enough. They wouldn't be forgiving if they thought anyone was after their water supply.

He dropped his tone. "Are you enticing our god-fearing men with your loose morals to tell you our secrets?"

Allison kept her head down instead of getting right in the idiot's face, threatening him with her lawyers and telling him where he could shove his chauvinistic bigotry. None of that would be in Kenneth's best interest, nor in hers.

"I'm only in Lahedeh to find my fiancé. I'll leave as soon as I find him. I just want to make sure nothing bad happened to him."

A moment of tense silence passed. The police chief sat with a heavy thud, then leaned back in his chair. He folded his hands over his potbelly, linking his fingers together. "All right, Miss Myers. I have come to a decision."

She risked a quick look at his face, and her muscles tensed at his smug expression. Was he about to arrest her? She could end up never seeing the outside of the police compound again. She could simply disappear like Kenneth.

*Is that what happened?* Had Kenneth simply stopped a woman on the street—not thinking anything of it—asked her for directions, and been arrested for harassing her? Lahedeh was definitely another world.

The police chief finally said, "The commissioner will be arriving tomorrow on his annual visit. I think he'll want to talk to you."

He glanced toward the guard.

And Allison's heart lurched. Would they try to lock her up until the commissioner arrived?

She sprang to her feet and looked at her watch. "I'll be happy to come in. Thank you for your time. I'd better return to the hotel. I have some health issues. I should take my medication now."

And then she kept lying. "The consul from the American embassy said he'd call me at the hotel around ten." It was now nine thirty. "I asked for their help with the search. They'll be worried if I'm not there when they ring."

The police chief flashed her a censoring look. He seemed to disapprove of not just the content of her words, but that a woman would talk this much. She held her breath.

He didn't grant her permission to leave, but he didn't order her to stay either.

*Good enough.*

"See you tomorrow, then."

She took advantage of his momentary hesitation and squeezed out past the guard—sideways so they wouldn't touch—then she hurried down a long, dingy hallway, expecting to be called back any second.

Steel doors banged in the distance. Muffled cries sounded from the floor below. The place might be a police station, but it smelled like a prison—sweat and desperation. She walked faster, her shoes slapping on the tile floor.

On the way in, she'd been escorted. Nobody bothered with her now. She took one turn after the other, hoping she got the direction right. She had a feeling that if she took a wrong turn and ended up in the dungeons, they'd be happy to lock the door on her and leave her there to rot.

*Get out. Get out. Get out.*

She perspired through her shirt by the time she reached the outer door that led to the street.

Another guard manned that post. He shot her a hostile glare, but he didn't stop her. Then she was finally outside, her knees suddenly trembling as the door closed behind her.

*Oh, thank God.*

She was out. Free. Her heart stopped racing. She filled her lungs with hot, dusty air. Then she squinted against the sun and looked around for the cab that'd brought her over from the hotel. She'd paid the driver to wait.

Except, the beat-up blue sedan was nowhere to be seen.

*Are you kidding me right now?*

She looked farther up the street. There had to be other cabs.

*Breathe.* At least the police had let her go. And now she knew what she was up against. They weren't going to help her. They were likely to hinder her, in fact. Her best bet was to stay away from them. She'd talk to the commissioner tomorrow but then stay as far from the local police as possible.

The sun beat down on her mercilessly. She pulled the collar of her shirt away from her throat for a few seconds to let some air in, careful not to show skin. The street wasn't completely empty. A handful of people were going about their business around her.

A banged-up delivery van passed her, then a family sedan. No cabs. Not much traffic. The police station was on a side street.

She didn't want to hang around here too long, didn't want to give the police chief a chance to change his mind and call her back. So she gave up on the cab and hurried down the street toward her hotel, a dozen blocks away.

It'd be nice if the US embassy *was* calling. Or would consider helping her a little more enthusiastically than they'd been doing so far. But for some reason, their records were all messed up, showing that Kenneth had entered the country as part of a commando team.

Kenneth William Hatch, old-money millionaire businessman with serious political aspirations. *Ha!* He wore Hugo Boss suits and Armani loafers. She couldn't picture him lacing up combat boots.

Not that Kenneth was pompous or incompetent. But he had been born into privilege. The closest he'd come to the military was investing in the defense industry.

Regardless of her protest that the commando information was clearly in error, the embassy had washed its hands, referring her to the US Army, which brought in the private commando teams on contract. Of course, the army wouldn't give her the time of day—classified information and all that.

The locals, including the police, were even less helpful.

She huffed out a quick burst of air. She was *not* going to quit.

Maybe the police commissioner was worldlier than the police chief and didn't hate women as much. Maybe the commissioner would have some information on Kenneth tomorrow.

Allison kept her head down as she walked, but still caught the angry glares of passersby. Even the old beggar sitting in the dirt frowned at her.

She was covered from head to toe. Nobody could possibly find fault with her attire. Maybe they didn't like that she was a woman out alone. Or that she had light skin and blue eyes, clearly a foreigner.

A group of older men carried on an intense conversation a couple of yards ahead. They wore traditional robes and rolled-up round hats called *pakol*, according to the booklet she had on local customs.

The sidewalk narrowed at the spot where the men stood, barely leaving her room to pass. Hostile disapproval filled their eyes as she approached. She kept her gaze downcast.

"Whore," one called out as she reached them.

She walked faster. But before she could move past the group, a hand reached out and yanked her hair, hard. Pain spread across her scalp.

They were all yelling at her, but she could only understand the one who spoke English. "American whore spy."

She scrambled to pull her scarf tighter around her head, but her fingers touched nothing but hair.

She spun around but couldn't see the black scarf anywhere behind her. *Fudge, fudge, fudge.* The flimsy material must have slipped off as she'd been fleeing the police station, in those winding hallways inside.

The men shouted at her in what she thought was Farsi, the local language. Two shook their fists, their faces distorted with outrage. For about half a second, she pretended she could handle them, that she wasn't intimidated and everything was fine. Then she gave up all pretense and she ran.

Her shoes slapped on the ground. Her heart beat in her throat. Panic squeezed her lungs. She didn't dare glance back until she reached the end of the block.

The old men were now arguing with each other, no longer paying her any attention.

*Thank God.*

She drew a shaky breath and pushed forward. Better put as much distance between those men and herself as possible.

The streets grew narrower and narrower. Houses butted up against each other; tall adobe walls loomed above. Which was disconcerting, actually. She should have reached the main thoroughfare by now.

She slowed, trying to identify a point of reference, but nothing looked familiar. Instead of the colorful shops the cab had passed on its way to the police station, drab houses lined the street.

She had taken a wrong turn and entered a residential area somehow. She was definitely on the wrong side of the tracks and stuck out without other foreigners around. None of the residents appreciated an intruder, which they made clear by shooting her hostile looks. Tension seeped back into her muscles as she kept walking.

The maze seemed endless, following no logic, trapping heat in the narrow passageways. As minute after minute ticked by, she could no longer pretend she wasn't hopelessly lost.

*Turn around?*

She looked back.

Four men followed a hundred feet behind her. Not the same ones who'd taken exception to her uncovered head outside the police station. Her latest pursuers were young thugs, the grins they exchanged predatory and dark. She took the next turn to let them walk by, but they turned after her. Her heart raced as she hurried forward, turned again. They kept coming, watching her.

They advanced on her with menacing speed, their intent clear on their leering faces. Unlike the older men, this bunch meant to do a lot more than just pull her hair.

***

Jake Tekla watched the disturbing procession, half hidden by the branches of a pomegranate tree, crouched low on the top of a mud-brick wall that stood at least eight feet tall and a foot wide.

The woman's long hair, the color of honey, fluttered behind her as she ran. Had no one told her that she must always, *always* cover herself here?

He'd seen her before, checking in at his hotel. She'd stood out even there. Here, on the dusty street, she looked surreal—a princess from a fairy tale who obviously shouldn't have left her palace. A princess from a fairy tale who had taken a wrong turn and was about to end up in a much darker story.

The police chief didn't seem to care for her. They'd come in unexpectedly while Jake had been searching the man's desk for any connection to US Senator Wharst, the man Jake was investigating on behalf of the FBI.

Jake had jumped into the metal rifle cabinet barely in time. Damn good luck that it stood nearly empty, with only two old AK-47s in the back, probably left over from the Soviet occupation. He'd been stuck in that hot cabinet while the local top cop accused the woman, who'd introduced herself as Allison Myers, of being here to steal water.

To be fair, the police chief wasn't just paranoid. International conglomerates *were* buying up water rights around the world.

Maybe she did work for one of them. None of Jake's business. But if she'd been acting earlier, she was the best damned actress he'd ever seen. Better than the ones who needed "wardrobe malfunctions" to stay in the limelight.

Although, Allison Myers *was* having her own wardrobe malfunction, to be fair. Where the hell was her scarf? She'd been wearing it at her interview.

Jake had been in the chief's office twice already this week. He had the bars on the window rigged for easy access. He'd gone through what the man had—nothing useful. So in the interest of a thorough investigation, he was on his way to the police chief's house—just another block from here. If the guy had, say, a suitcase full of US dollars under his bed, that might be a good indicator that he was involved.

Jake needed to get going and see about that. Instead, he watched the chase on the street below. The men were closing in on the woman.

She seemed familiar, but he couldn't place her.

Her long skirt tangled between her legs as she ran, slowing her down. What in hell was she thinking, running around in a backwoods little town like this all alone? Might as well wave a red flag at a bullfight.

The woman ran toward his position, less than a dozen feet away and still without seeing him. Situational awareness was not one of her strengths. She had no sense of direction, no weapons, running blindly without any obvious strategy.

She clearly didn't have any military training. Or much common sense. Because no single woman with a lick of common sense would come here unless she was with the US military.

*Rapunzel, Rapunzel, hide your hair,* he wanted to shout at her, but she needed so much more than his advice.

He shifted his weight to ease the pain that pinged up his thigh from crouching for too long. He absentmindedly rubbed the heel of his hand against the damaged muscle, his focus on the woman.

Her problems weren't any of his business—he had his own agenda here. And yet…he couldn't let her come to harm. He had two sisters. And even if he didn't, he'd been raised to protect those weaker than himself.

He looked ahead to where the street took another sharp turn, then he stole forward without making a sound, keeping low on top of the wall. He waited until she progressed out of sight of the men and was passing right below him.

"Hold your hands up," he called down to her.

She shrieked and scrambled back, as if expecting him to drop on top of her.

The men would be rounding the corner any second.

"Give me your hands," Jake ordered in his best military tone that demanded absolute and instant obedience.

The fact that he spoke English and looked American must have tipped the scale in his favor, because she did raise her hands. He grabbed her and yanked her up, dropping her on the other side of the wall in the same motion. She weighed nothing compared to his SEAL buddies he'd had to drag up and over a million walls on the obstacle course during SEAL training.

He thumped down next to her into the abandoned courtyard, just before the men came around the corner. The damaged muscle in his thigh that'd taken a bullet two months back spasmed from the impact. He'd broken his right arm at around the same time. That didn't hurt anymore, but while he'd been in a cast, his muscles on that side had weakened. He exercised daily to fix that and was certainly in shape for an impromptu rescue op.

Allison Myers stared at him, pink-cheeked and wide-eyed, probably considering whether or not to run. Yet she didn't panic. She was assessing her options, her eyes—the deep, clear blue of the Mediterranean Sea, and eerily familiar—never leaving him.

She smelled like spring rain and daffodils. He had the odd urge to bury his face in her neck, in her hair, and inhale that feminine scent. She made him think about sex. For a second, his brain switched to some primal, evolutionary function that wanted more of what it saw. Wanted her. The connection was instant, but he couldn't tell whether she felt it too. The most prominent emotion on her face was worry.

*Of course, she's worried.* Scared too. He'd been in dangerous situations a thousand times worse than this, but she probably hadn't. He needed to reassure her instead of looking at her as if he wanted to taste her.

Once the young thugs passed outside, Jake extended his hand, "Jake Tekla. We're staying at the same hotel."

Her eyes narrowed, her gaze intense as she tried hard to read him, tried to decide whether or not to trust him. "Allison Myers. I don't remember seeing you."

She wasn't supposed to. He'd been keeping a low profile. "Travel writer." He gave her his cover story. "When I'm not out discovering the sights, I'm in my room on my laptop."

She frowned at him. "Sights?"

"Ancient temple ruins. Whatever's left of them after the Taliban came through and blew them up a couple of years ago." His disgusted tone reflected what he thought of that. "Also, the foothills have some spectacular caves." He flashed a deprecating smile. "All right, it's not exactly a tourist mecca, but people do come here."

Her expression remained doubtful, but at least she held his gaze.

When he looked at local women, their eyes instantly darted away from him. For all he knew, they'd been warned against the foreign devils who invaded their country.

Allison Myers didn't trust him, but she wasn't afraid of him. Being chased had rattled her, but hadn't freaked her out completely. She was functioning, assessing, holding it together instead of crying or screaming.

Jake had a thing for stalwart women. But no matter how stalwart Allison was, she shouldn't be here. She'd arrived at the hotel a week ago. If she made it another week, it'd be a miracle. She stood out too much in Lahedeh.

And that was probably why Jake responded to her. She was the first unveiled woman he'd seen in two weeks. No sense in reading anything into the sudden attraction. His inner horndog needed to seriously back down here.

He had helped her out, and now she needed to help herself. "I don't know what you're doing in Lahedeh," he said, "but you shouldn't stay here. Free advice: go home."

He had to figure out what Senator Richard Wharst had done that was so terrible, he'd let himself be blackmailed over it. The task kept Jake plenty busy, leaving him precious little time to babysit beauties in peril.

But instead of assuring him that she'd be on the first flight out, she lifted her chin, her voice all business as she said, "I'm not finished here yet. Thank you for your help. I'll be returning to the hotel."

She strode resolutely toward the courtyard's door to the street but progressed only a few steps before the door rattled. Somebody was unlocking it from the outside.

Jake grabbed her and dragged her in the opposite direction, toward the house. It either stood empty or not; their chances were fifty-fifty. The chances of getting caught here in the courtyard, however, if they didn't move, were one hundred percent. He kept her behind him as he burst through the wooden door into a kitchen.

*Empty. Thank God.*

He closed the kitchen door to a narrow gap, and mouthed *Quiet* to Allison while he watched as a dozen men filed into the courtyard, all wearing traditional robes. Not the ones who'd been chasing her.

These men carried AK-47s and held the guns as if they knew how to use them. They weren't cops. The local police wore uniforms.

Jake hissed out a single curse.

He pulled back to Allison, his mind running all the options. He wasn't here specifically to look for these men, but he was a SEAL—even if he'd left the navy, once a SEAL, always a SEAL. He could gain useful information here that he might be able to pass up the proper military channels. Except, he couldn't stay and spy on the men. Not with a civilian in tow.

"What is it?" Allison leaned forward to steal a glance. She paled.

He tugged her back. He scanned the kitchen again, then the doorway that led to the rest of the house. "Not our lucky day. Of all the houses in town, looks like we're stuck in one that's some kind of a hideout for insurgents."

# CHAPTER
# TWO

*Insurgents? Here?*

"Are you sure?" Fear kicked Allison in the stomach with steel-toed boots. Her breath caught, so the words came out shaky as she added, "We're in the safe zone, under US military control."

She wouldn't have come if she hadn't been assured that she'd be safe. She *had* done research. "Nobody said anything about insurgents."

What were they doing in the middle of town? The region's last remaining bad guys were supposedly holed up in the mountains.

Her brain screamed a single word: *run!*

But as she moved, Jake Tekla's fingers closed around her wrist in an unbreakable hold. God, the man was big this close. He'd pulled her over that wall as if she weighed nothing, had left her gasping for air, her head spinning. Now he loomed over her, his chocolate-colored eyes darting between her and the crack in the door.

"They might not come in." His whispered voice was a low-timbred rumble. "Maybe they're just dropping off their guns in the shed. They might leave, then we can get out of here. If we go deeper into the house, someone might be in there. Then they scream or shoot, and the bad guys will rush in."

She stared at him. How on earth could he think so analytically right now? He was calm and steady, focused, as if he did this kind of thing every day. What kind of travel guides did he write anyway, *How to Travel Combat Zones for Fun and Pleasure?*

He loosened his hold but didn't let her go. "You okay?"

"A toss-up between passing out or throwing up."

Amusement softened his hard expression. "You keep that sense of humor. That'll help." But in a blink, he turned serious again. "I'm going to give you some advice about situations like this. You don't leave safe cover until it's compromised."

He kept one eye on the courtyard through the crack in the door and added, "Or until you've identified even safer cover."

*Who the hell is this guy?*

A small, still-functioning corner of her mind that wasn't flooded with panic—*Hello! Insurgents!*—said maybe trusting a complete stranger wasn't the smartest course of action, but just now she couldn't think of anything smarter.

And then he turned from the door and tightened his grip on her wrist again. "They're coming in."

Before she could pass out *and* throw up, he dragged her across the kitchen, around the cast-iron cooking stove, and past the crowded shelves. They rushed through the kitchen's back door and ended up in a narrow hallway.

At home, walking down the street, if a stranger grabbed her, pulled her into a yard, and started dragging her deeper into the house, she would have fought with all she had. Here, the fact that he looked and spoke like an American made her trust him. Hey, her other option was men with nasty-looking rifles.

When she tugged her hand again, he let her go, a point in his favor. Of course, she immediately stumbled over a burlap bag of rice, making her look like she couldn't fend for herself. He caught her against his body before she could crash to the floor, then he held still for a moment to make sure she was okay.

She stood pressed against a wide and hard chest, her hands braced on the corded muscles in his arms. He smelled good, the scent of sun-kissed skin, some perspiration that wasn't unpleasant, just male, mixed in with the hint of some kind of masculine shower gel. It made her feel a little too wired, a little too aware of him.

*Behold, the power of pheromones.* Of course, *she* probably smelled like plain old I-just-ran-in-the-hot-sun sweat. She pulled away.

His sharp gaze roved her face, his expression all business. "You have to decide whether you trust me or not. *Now.* If you don't, our paths part right here."

Her heart beat in her ears. She'd known him for all of five minutes. But he *had* already saved her from the men on the street. And the new batch of local guys who'd come into the courtyard *were* armed. She was going to take her chances with Jake Tekla.

*Jake. Tekla. Chocolate-truffle eyes.*

Vague, decade-old memories floated back to her. She squinted at him. "Have you ever worked for Mondini Construction?"

And at the same time, his eyes narrowed too. "Didn't you use to go by Allison Mondini?"

She stared. Nodded. Kept staring. What were the chances of her running into someone she knew, here?

"We need to get going." He was moving forward already, hurrying down the hallway. "We'll talk when we're safe."

"What are we going to do?" She whispered the question as she ran behind him.

"We're going to go back to our hotel without sustaining a single injury. We're going to handle whatever comes our way. You're going to do exactly what I tell you, until I tell you that we're out of danger."

She could hear the insurgents arguing outside and felt the blood draining out of her face. "What if they catch us?"

"Step one: stop operating from a stance of fear. Step two: stay right behind me and stay quiet."

*Okay, then.*

She tried her best to keep up and not trip over her own feet while Mr. Testosterone with a Press Pass moved as quickly and silently as a professional burglar.

*Jake Tekla. Wow.*

He'd gone through an incredible change since he had a summer job on one of her father's construction sites. He'd been in college, if she remembered right. A spindly kid. He'd been there one summer, didn't come back the next. Pretty normal for construction work.

With every move, his muscles bunched and shifted. God, he'd grown. She'd been surrounded by strong men all her life, but she had to wonder how many could have swung her over a wall like that.

They reached a narrow set of adobe stairs and ran up, dashed through two empty rooms, up another set of stairs, then burst out into a rooftop living area. Faded red carpets and cushions covered the floor, a white canvas stretched above for shade. A couple of abandoned copper hookahs—water pipes that the locals used for smoking their flavored tobacco—sat in the middle.

Burqas and other clothes flapped on a clothesline set up at the edge of the roof. Jake grabbed a black scarf and handed it to her. "Cover your head."

She did the best she could, shoving her mass of hair underneath the fabric and not quite succeeding. She tugged the scarf to make sure no blond showed. Her hair would give her away as a foreigner, even from a distance.

"Here." He tucked her escaping tendrils under the soft material. Then he twisted the scarf around so he could tie the corners into a knot that held the bulk of her hair in place at her nape. His knuckles brushed against her cheek.

She felt the slight brush clear to her toes. Probably because she was all raw nerves at the moment.

Before she could start feeling awkward, he was already stepping back and scanning the deserted rooftops around them. Then he was moving again. "This way."

They crossed over to the next roof by vaulting over a waist-high wall that separated the two houses. She'd been climbing scaffolding since she could remember, but now her long skirt kept tripping her. She made sure to keep up regardless.

Since the houses were built into each other, they had a clear path to wherever they wanted to go. On the other hand, they had little cover should the insurgents come up behind them.

They hopped over to the next roof, where two young girls played on a faded carpet in the shade of the wall, gesturing while singing what sounded like a counting song. The girls looked more curious than alarmed, staring with mouths agape at the strangers.

Their mother yelled up from below, probably wanting to know why their song had suddenly stopped.

At the same time, a neighbor popped up to his roof, carrying a prayer carpet rolled up under his arm. He hadn't seen Jake and Allison yet. He kept looking in the opposite direction, toward Mecca.

Prayer time? That'd mean the rest of the roofs would fill with people in a minute.

Allison shot a panicked look at Jake.

They only had one way to go: down.

She glanced over the edge. The fifteen-foot drop to a tiny, dusty courtyard didn't look encouraging. The only thing going for the small space was that at least it didn't hold insurgents.

"I'll go first," Jake whispered. "When I signal, you follow. I'll catch you."

He vaulted without giving her a chance to argue with him, and landed on his feet in a crouch, as perfectly balanced as an acrobat. He stayed low as he scanned the area, his right hand hovering behind his back. He had a lump under his shirt back there. A weapon?

Before she could process that, he stood in a fluid motion and held out his arms.

*Wait*, she mouthed, her heart in her throat. This could be a really bad idea.

But if she got caught on the roof…

They still cut off your hand here if they thought you were a thief. If she was found in someone's rooftop living room, there'd be consequences. And even if she could convince the people that she hadn't been trying to break in… If someone caught her here and turned her in, the police chief might think he'd been right about her being a spy slash thief.

The police tortured suspected spies in this part of the world. She had a feeling the police chief would like nothing more than to make an example out of her. *Fudge it.*

Allison swallowed hard, flexed her knees, then stepped off the ledge. The little girls gave a delighted giggle behind her. Good to know *someone* was having fun here.

*Whoosh.*

She lost her breath.

Then strong arms caught her, held her safe. He didn't as much as wobble. She'd grown up around tough construction guys, but Jake Tekla was a cut or two above. And while she'd seen plenty of muscle in the past, none of that muscle had ever held her like this. The effect sent her heart racing faster than the jump had.

She looked up into dark chocolate-truffle eyes that held approval.

"See? With a little trust, everything gets a lot easier." He set her on her feet but didn't grab her hand this time. Instead, he let her follow on her own as they raced across the courtyard and out to the street.

He took turn after turn and led her to the main thoroughfare. Jake Tekla clearly knew these streets, or had an exceptional sense of direction. The man was like a guided missile.

The street bustled with traffic. While she tried to catch her breath, he flagged down a cab—some old-style Soviet car she couldn't name in a million years.

As they slid into the cab's back seat, Allison was still an inch from hyperventilating, trying to catch her breath.

She was a businesswoman. The only action she was familiar with happened on construction sites and in meeting rooms. Up until now, her worst nightmare had been another real estate bubble. Men with rifles were *waaay* out of her comfort zone and frame of reference.

Jake didn't look rattled by their mad dash. If anything, he looked preoccupied, as if his mind was already on something else, like a phone conference with his editor. While her mind was still on: *Did that just happen?*

The cab had pulled into traffic, the graying driver yelling out the window at people to get out of his way.

Jake turned to Allison. "What are you doing in Lahedeh?"

"My fiancé disappeared here about five months ago." She recounted what little she knew about the irrigation project, her heart rate slowly settling back to normal. "I couldn't get information out of anyone over the phone. I decided to come in person."

Jake watched her without commenting, didn't tell her she was out of her depth, which she appreciated. She *was* out of her depth. Her knowledge of the region came from TV news reports. In hindsight…She hadn't been prepared for reality.

Jake Tekla, on the other hand, had clearly been here for a while, or had spent time in areas similar to this. Nothing seemed to faze him.

"Have you been in town long?" she asked, a wave of hope washing over her. "Maybe you've met Kenneth at the hotel. Kenneth Hatch."

Not many Americans hung out in Lahedeh, and the few who did seemed to be staying at her hotel, the only one in town with full Western amenities, such as ice for the drinks and air-conditioning. She'd been asking around the dining room every evening about Kenneth, without success. Maybe Jake had seen him.

She held her breath. *Please say yes.*

But he said, "Never heard of the guy. Sorry."

Not to be deterred, she produced a photo from the fanny pack she wore for its practicality.

Jake gave the picture a good close look but still shook his head. "Never seen him."

She swallowed her disappointment as she tucked the photo away. Guilt bubbled up inside her. She shouldn't have waited all these months. She should have come right away. But that was something she couldn't take back, something she would have to live with if her search ended badly.

Her stomach dropped. She barely heard when Jake asked, "How is your father?"

She blinked. "He's gone."

"I'm sorry to hear that. He was a good man."

"Thank you."

A moment of silence passed between them as traffic rushed by outside the cab.

Then Jake asked, "So you're running the company now?"

She nodded, liking that he would assume that, wouldn't automatically think that just because she was a woman, she wasn't qualified or couldn't handle the job.

"I almost didn't recognize you," he said.

"You've changed too." A vast understatement. The spindly college boy who had struggled to lift bags of cement had been replaced by a man whose T-shirt stretched over a mesmerizing amount of muscle, a man who could haul her over a wall without breaking a sweat.

How sexy had that been?

She wasn't normally attracted to men like him, not beyond the *oh, nice muscles, lovely to look at* reaction. She was attracted to men in well-cut suits who could walk into a boardroom, dominate the competition, and negotiate a deal like nobody's business. But Jake Tekla could teach those guys a thing or two about dominating their environment. He was the quintessential alpha male who took charge and took care of his woman. Not that she was his woman, but she'd been a woman in need of rescue, and he'd rescued her spectacularly.

He was a man who made her *aware* that she was a woman.

Pretty insane to even think that at a moment like this.

Thank God, the ride to the hotel took all of ten minutes.

He paid for the cab ride. She didn't argue. For one, she didn't want to raise any eyebrows. Women around here didn't argue with men in public. And the cab driver would be more comfortable dealing with a man. She could pay Jake back inside.

While she was edging toward the hotel's front door, still half expecting armed men to jump out at them from nowhere, Jake seemed at ease, in his element. He said something to the driver in the local language. The guy grinned and said something back.

Jake's low rumble of a laugh vibrated its way into Allison's chest.

*A travel writer.*

She could see him as some grand adventurer. He seemed to be made for action and excitement. She was a city girl. She didn't do rugged adventure. She felt out of sorts around Jake Tekla's roguish smile and chocolate eyes, that sharp, probing gaze he'd no doubt developed as a journalist. She was sure he saw more than people realized. Maybe more than she wanted him to see.

She wanted to withdraw to the safety of her room and check her email, catch up on work, but he *had* saved her life, and for that she owed him her gratitude.

"Thank you for the rescue," she said when he left the cabbie and came over. She extended her hand to shake his. Keeping it all business.

His strong fingers enveloped hers. Instant awareness flooded her once again. The pheromones were strong in this one. He was like a testosterone Jedi. He really was quite a man. If he hadn't moved as fast and well as he had…

"I can't believe you just yanked me over that wall." Not that she was stuck on that or anything. "You knew exactly what to do. Were you ever in the military?"

They walked into the hotel together.

"Just sportsy, I guess," he said. "I ran track in college."

She didn't remember that about him. She vaguely recalled that he'd been in some photography club, and the other construction workers ribbed him mercilessly. He'd brought his camera to work a few times.

Now that she thought of it, she remembered him asking her to let him take her picture, and she'd said no. She'd thought it was some kind of a come-on, and she'd been seeing Daniel back then. She'd been with Daniel through most of college.

"I saw you running, and I kind of acted on instinct," Jake said with a self-deprecating smile. "I was up on the wall, looking for an unusual angle for some photos I'm hoping to take tomorrow morning. Rising sun in the background."

Because he was a travel writer, and his books and articles needed photos. Made sense.

"May I invite you for a cup of coffee? Or lunch? I really appreciate that you helped me and brought me back here."

As they stood in the lobby, next to the entrance of the hotel's restaurant, under an exquisite antique tribal rug that hung on the wall, a group of men passed them, heading in to eat. She'd seen two of them before—business-men from Jordan. They'd approached her at dinner the previous day to chat her up.

A woman traveling alone drew all the wrong kind of attention here. She'd shot them down then and stood ready to do it again if they kept bugging her, but today they looked at Jake and gave her a wide berth.

Nothing about his expression or body language was threatening, but he did have a certain hardness in his eyes, a toughness at his core that set him apart from the others, even when doing something as mundane as opening the restaurant door for her to escort her in.

Kenneth was never formidable. He planned on going into politics, and *formidable* came across as *unfriendly* on TV—the wrong vibe altogether. He'd attended master seminars on how to exude all positive vibes and exuber-ance, the kind of attitudes that would draw others to him and smooth his way in business and politics. He'd taken coaching on how to develop charisma.

Kenneth made a point of being steady and predictable. He wanted people to know what they could expect from him. Allison liked that. She understood people like him.

Jake Tekla—travel writer in Afghanistan!—puzzled her.

Not that she had to understand Jake. They were just having a cup of coffee. She was here for Kenneth.

***

"So tell me about your fiancé," Jake asked as they were being seated.

Allison had taken off her scarf. Here in the hotel, nobody was going to harass her. The light from the copper chandeliers glinted off her honey-colored hair.

He wanted to run his fingers through those silky locks. He wanted to kiss her dizzy. The horndog in him kept putting images into his head that came with a soundtrack of heavy breathing.

If she hadn't asked him to coffee, he would have asked her. He couldn't believe he hadn't immediately recognized her. Then again, she *had* changed.

The summer before his senior year in college, he'd picked up some construction work. Allison had been the boss's daughter, working in the admin trailer, doing filing for her father. She had short black hair then, wore glasses. She'd been a cute, skinny kid. A college freshman, although she looked young enough to be in high school.

The other men had warned Jake about her the first day—mess with her and his private parts were going to have an unfortunate accident with the nail gun. Some of the older guys who'd spent years working for her father had been like uncles to her.

She'd had a boyfriend anyway, Daniel something.

Jake had stayed away from her, apart from one failed attempt to get her to let him take her picture for a photography assignment.

Now he had trouble keeping his eyes off her, and he wasn't the only man in the room struggling. Several other guys stole glances at her, some openly watching. And they couldn't even see the curves he'd felt when she'd jumped into his arms. *It'd be nice to see her out of the shapeless tent she's wearing.*

She interested Jake on a number of levels. Kenneth Hatch had disappeared in an area Jake's team was investigating for suspicious activity. Could there be a link? Jake couldn't afford to dismiss the idea out of hand. He needed to find out more about the man, which meant spending more time with Allison Myers.

No hardship there.

She was graceful and feminine even in her shapeless clothes. He remembered her in jeans, work boots, and a hard hat. She could have gone the spoiled heiress route, but she hadn't. His sisters—born tomboys—would like her. His younger sister, Mandy, played baseball. Jasmine, the older sister, was Jane Bond at heart. She was currently providing clandestine IT support for Jake's team from the States. They were both growing into strong women, and Allison was one already.

She hadn't complained once, had rolled with the punches.

She scanned the menu, then scanned it again as if distracted. Then she looked up and finally answered his question. "Kenneth and I got engaged just before he came here six months ago on a business trip. He's in water management. Irrigation systems."

"Why are you here all alone looking for him? Where is his family? Why isn't his company sending people?"

She hesitated for a moment. "He doesn't have much family. He has two second cousins who want nothing more than to have him declared legally dead so they can inherit his share of the business."

*Nice.*

Jake thought of his sisters again. They were a tight-knit team. They would all die for one another. Even their aunt was fully supportive, had raised the girls while Jake had been in the service. His family wasn't large, wasn't rich, but they were a true family. He wouldn't trade that for anything.

"The company *is* looking for him," Allison said, frustration creeping into her tone, "through official channels."

"Which are not working," Jake guessed.

She sighed, a soft and sweet sound. "I just want to find him."

While Jake ordered two spiced coffees, the traditional vehicle of a caffeine fix around here, he glanced at her bare ring finger and wondered why her voice had wavered on the word fiancé. *Trouble in paradise?* That would make tracking the man down, coming halfway around the world to rescue him, even more remarkable.

Still extremely misguided and foolish, but impressive.

She caught his look and rubbed the spot where the ring should have been, a touch of defensiveness seeping into her tone as she said, "I haven't had a chance to go in for a resizing."

*Didn't she now?*

A ring from the man she loved, and in six months she couldn't find time to have it resized. That said something right there. However, other people's castles of denial were none of Jake's business, so he held back a comment. He simply smiled at her with understanding.

After a moment, she smiled back.

*Wowza.*

Okay, so the Kenneth guy was dead. Jake could think of nothing else that would keep a man from coming back to her. She looked stunning enough without the smile, but with the smile…*Lethal.*

Her smile focused the attention on her mouth—full, glistening lips—and brought a certain level of sexiness into play.

He couldn't take his eyes off her.

She rubbed her cheek. "I bet I have dirt on my face. Maybe we should have cleaned up."

He toned down the staring. "You look different. The hair…" He wasn't going to mention the curves.

She tucked a stray lock behind her ear. "I think when we met, I was still in my Goth phase. God, my father hated that." She gave a faint smile. Then she said, "The nose too."

"Your father hated your nose?"

"No, I meant my nose is different now. I used to have a bump in it. I was in a car accident when I was five. I broke some bones. My nose didn't heal right."

There was something in her voice…or rather, wasn't. All the color went out of her tone, out of her. Something about the accident…And then he remembered. He'd heard about that crash from one of the construction crew. The boss's wife hadn't survived it.

"I'm sorry about your mother."

"Thank you." She sipped her coffee. "I don't remember most of that day." Her voice deepened with grief.

Her voice was another thing different about her, another reason why he hadn't recognized her at the police station. Back when he'd first met her, she had a slightly nasal tone, probably because of her badly healed nose. Clearly, she'd had that corrected since.

As if reading his thoughts, she said, "A couple of years ago, some scaffolding collapsed under me. I managed to rebreak my nose, so I decided to have it fixed. That's why I look different and sound a little different."

He'd seen scaffolding collapse before. Construction sites were dangerous places, despite all the million safety regulations. He didn't like the idea of her in harm's way. And right now, here, she was in harm's way again.

While Kenneth's possible demise didn't particularly bother Jake, the thought of Allison Myers in danger did. He had no time to help her, but he could take a few minutes to convince her to go back home.

"So did you hear about the hit on that village yesterday?" He paused while the waiter served them. "All over the news. Not ten miles from here."

She drew her perfectly arched brows together into the most graceful frown he'd ever seen. "I haven't been watching the news." Her eyes turned apologetic. "I don't speak the local language."

"Two years ago, the US Army pushed Khanbaba, the local warlord who ruled this area, up into the hills. But the army presence in the region has been downsized since. Last night, the warlord moved on one of the villages to collect tribute. A dozen people were killed before the village pushed him back."

She turned a shade paler. "That can't happen here, right? Lahedeh isn't a tiny village. It's a town with a police station."

"Depends on whether the police chief sympathizes with the warlord or not. Frankly, I don't think he could be in his post without the warlord's tacit approval. But even if he isn't loyal to the old boss, I doubt someone like him would stick his neck out for a couple of peasants."

Her shoulders tightened as she got his message—the police would care even less about foreigners.

"I'm leaving tomorrow," Jake said, "for a week or so, to see if I can find any seminomadic tribes for a feature article." He wanted her to know that he wouldn't be around on a daily basis to rescue her. "I could probably take you halfway to Kabul."

She did consider the offer. For about two seconds. "Thank you, but I'm not leaving without Kenneth. Anyway, I'm supposed to see the police commissioner tomorrow. The police chief thinks I'm here to steal their water."

She was actually planning on going back to see the commissioner?

She should be packing her suitcase tonight. She didn't seem to realize how much trouble she was in. Jake had seen too many innocent people walk into police stations like the one in Lahedeh and never come back out.

"You should go home. Your fiancé will find you when he's done with whatever he's doing."

She fidgeted with her napkin. Then she looked up and filled her lungs. "The truth is…Ex-fiancé, actually. I'm going to end the engagement when I find him. I didn't mean to lie earlier." Her gaze asked for his understanding. "I just can't tell anyone. I barely get any cooperation from people as it is."

He could see her point. To gain information, she had to claim a close link. And an engagement also kept her somewhat safe. Claiming to be already under the control of a man gave her some protection from others. Her revelation didn't bother Jake, but it did puzzle him. "So you're breaking up with the guy but came to help him anyway?"

"You take care of the people who take care of you," she said simply. "My father lived his whole life by that rule. He took care of his workers, bad times or good, when they got sick, whatever."

Jake remembered that. A lot of the men on the construction site he'd worked had been with Mondini for years and years. He treated them like family, and it made a difference.

Pride crept into Allison's voice as she said, "Our company has a third of the turnover rate of the rest of the industry. And that's because of my father. That's how he grew the business so fast."

Taking care of people was important. Jake took care of his sisters. And others, if needed, over the years. A real man helped those he was in a position to help. And a real woman too, he thought, looking at Allison, who was rapidly earning his admiration.

*Ex-fiancé.* For some reason, that news buoyed his mood immeasurably. It opened up new possibilities that…

He caught that thought and shut it down. He needed to focus on his mission, and she needed to leave.

He considered entertaining her with a few more cautionary tales of the various dangers that surrounded her here, but he happened to glance at the clock on the wall.

He finished his cup. "Thank you for the coffee. Sorry I have to rush. I'm expecting an important call from my editor. I should get back to my room."

He stood, then paused. "What happened to Allison Mondini?"

She'd used Allison Myers at the police station and when she'd introduced herself to him.

"Married Daniel Myers." Shadows crossed her face. "He passed away."

*Myers.* That had been the old boyfriend's name, Jake remembered now. "Of what?"

She looked down at her coffee cup. "Cancer."

He wished he hadn't brought up the subject. He wished he could stay another minute to comfort her, but he had a call coming that he couldn't take in a restaurant.

"I'm really sorry." He wanted to pull her up into his arms and just give her a hug. He couldn't. Not in a public place. And more physical contact between them was probably a bad idea anyway. "Listen, I'm in room 402. If I can help with anything, come and get me, all right? And try to stay safe."

"Thank you. I'm in 207. If you think of anything that might help me find Kenneth."

He nodded and pulled out his wallet to pay.

"No. Please," she said. "My treat."

"Thanks." He left her to her coffee but turned back from the doorway, noting the men who kept watching her.

"I'll see you later," he called to her, flashing her a proprietary look the men couldn't misinterpret.

And he *would* see her again, he decided as the door of the restaurant swung closed behind him. He'd catch her at breakfast and do whatever it took to scare her straight. She was a danger to herself here and a distraction to him. He needed to get her on a plane and out of the country.

As he waited for the elevator, his cell phone rang. He glanced at the display—not the call he'd been expecting, but even better. He picked up. "Hey, Sis."

"T.J. broke up with me," his younger sister, Mandy, sobbed on the other end. "He sent a text message. He said the long-distance thing isn't working for him."

Jake's free hand fisted. Every time one of his sisters hurt, he wanted to punch someone—the big-brother reflex. Right now, he wanted to kick teenage dickhead ass.

T.J. was Mandy's first real boyfriend. They should have gone to the prom together and would have, if Mandy and Jasmine hadn't had to go on the run with Jake a few months back. And even now, his sisters still had to be in hiding at an FBI safe house until Senator Wharst could be taken out of the picture.

"Want me to come back home and beat the crap out of him?"

Mandy sniffed. "Just come back. We miss you."

"I miss you guys too." He was doing the best he could to make everything safe again, so their lives could go back to normal. He felt responsible for messing up his sisters' world. And he wasn't even there with them for support. He was on the other side of the globe.

"I'm sorry T.J. turned out to be a jerk."

Over the years, Jake had learned that the best way to survive was simply not to get attached. But at seventeen, Mandy was too young to adopt a life philosophy as jaded as that, so he kept his thoughts to himself.

His cell phone rang a second time just as he reached his room. He closed the door behind him before picking up. *This* was the call he'd been waiting for. He crossed the room in a few steps—just a bed, a dresser, and a small table with two chairs—and stood at the window, checking the street for suspicious activity, an ingrained habit.

"I'm patching Troy in." Gabe Cannon hooked up the three-man team. "Anything new?"

They were an odd trio. While all three had started out in the Navy SEALs, Jake had barely known Gabe back then. They'd done only a single joint op. He hadn't known Troy Hill at all until they'd both gotten out of the Navy. They'd been brought together by the need to bring down one very corrupt senator. The FBI had hired them on as a temporary special team, just for that purpose.

"I came across an insurgent hideout today." Jake told them about the house and armed men he'd seen. "I'll send that information to General Roberts in a minute."

"Sure. Show off. Find insurgents by freaking accident," Troy grumbled. He didn't like that he'd been left behind in DC. "How about something connected to Senator Wharst?"

"Not a damned thing."

The senator was connected to millions of dollars' worth of ill-gotten gold coins. The man who'd originally stolen the gold and smuggled it out of Afghanistan, Brent Foley, was dead. He'd blackmailed the senator into helping him to smuggle the gold into the US.

But with what?

It had to be big, and it had to be bad. Jake's team had to figure it out before someone else—like the media—stumbled on the senator's secret and made it public. If it had to do with something in Afghanistan…If it was even worse than the theft of twenty million dollars' worth of gold…Something like that coming out would cause an international incident. It could cause the US to lose credibility, which in turn would jeopardize the safety of troops in the region.

Jake was investigating in Lahedeh since Brent Foley had been one of the leaders of a private security firm, XO-ST, a mercenary commando outfit that had their Afghan headquarters here. Gabe snooped around Kabul, where most political and business deals were made in Afghanistan. Troy took on Washington, DC, where the senator worked and lived.

"I have a suspicious disappearance in town," Jake reported to the others. "Kenneth Hatch. Can't see any connection to our business so far, but he's an American who came here about six months ago, then went missing shortly after."

"Might be something." Interest perked up Gabe's tone. "It's more than I have. Nobody I've talked to here in Kabul so far has even heard of Senator Wharst. I can't find any US businesses in the city that I can tie to him. Is he still in Washington?"

Troy took that question, his damaged voice rasping through the line. "I'm keeping an eye on him around the clock. Nothing suspicious so far."

He ran through the details of the senator's breakneck schedule and list of visitors who might or might not be connected to the investigation.

Gabe interrupted with, "Jake, did you say Kenneth Hatch?"

"Yeah. He came here to sell irrigation systems."

"I'm looking at the XO-ST files we have. According to the roster, Hatch was one of their contract soldiers. Signed up, got shipped to Lahedeh immediately, and was killed a month later."

"That doesn't sound right." Jake stared at the elaborate patterns of the carpet without really seeing them. "I got the impression he was more of a trust-fund yuppie. A businessman, according to his ex-fiancée."

He didn't think Allison had lied about that. "Any record of what happened to his body? Why wasn't it shipped back to the States to family?"

"Nothing," Gabe said. "But he's a confirmed kill. Maybe he was buried locally."

"That'd be odd, wouldn't it?" The bodies of soldiers were shipped back home. But maybe private security companies weren't as strict about that as the military. Still…

Jake focused on the possibilities that had opened up suddenly. "I want to check him out anyway."

He'd already decided to ask Allison a few more questions, but now he moved that up on his list of priorities.

"Let's see what we can find out about the man," Gabe put in. "See if we can connect him to the senator. Maybe this is Wharst's dark secret. Maybe he had Hatch killed over there."

They tossed that idea around for a while, then a few others, but stayed mired in pure speculation, without a real breakthrough.

After the call ended, Jake took a shower, using the time to make some plans, then he headed to Allison's room—not without some degree of anticipation.

*Cut it out. No anticipation.* Regardless of Kenneth's death, nothing was going to happen between them. Jake was on an op here. And he didn't mess around on an op—the only rule he'd never broken.

He stopped in front of her door and rapped his knuckles against it. Then, when she opened up, he lost his breath. The sight hit him square in the chest.

An antique ivory clip held up her mass of golden-honey hair, leaving the soft, pale skin of her neck exposed. She'd ditched the shapeless dark clothes she'd had on earlier and wore blue silk pants with a white sleeveless silk blouse, the fine material hugging her figure. *God, those curves.*

A wave of lust washed over him—pure hot need. It drowned out the pangs of guilt he felt over what he was about to do.

*No lust. No guilt. Just the op.*

He pasted on a winning smile and slipped into his travel writer persona. "You know, I was thinking…If it's that important to you to stay in Lahedeh, you could tell the police you hired me as your guide and protector. It'd make the locals more comfortable. I could help you figure out where your fiancé went."

Her eyes managed to look interested and cautious at the same time. His sisters looked at fat-free ice cream like that: *Is this too good to be true or what?* "Do you have time to help me? With your deadlines?"

He let his smile turn rueful. "If I don't help you, I'll be worried about you, and I won't be able to concentrate on my work anyway. This is not the safest part of the world for a woman to be traveling alone."

"I've noticed." Her gaze never wavered, as if she was trying to see inside him. "I could hire you as a guide. If you have a couple of days?"

"I can make time to help out a fellow American and an old friend." The *old friend* part was an exaggeration, but, hey, whatever made her more comfortable around him.

She gave a small, decisive nod. Then she opened the door wider in a silent invitation.

He stepped inside but stopped in the narrow entryway, just inches from her as the door swung shut. Her soft scent reached him. She smelled like cookies. He wanted to taste her. And maybe she could see that in his eyes, because awareness sprang to life between them.

His body tensed. If he dipped his head, his mouth would be on hers in a split second.

*What a stupid thing to think.*

But even as he thought that, he was already going for it.

Her breath caught, but she didn't move away. She didn't close her eyes. Neither did he as he slowly dragged his lips across hers, a tasting, a testing.

A fresh wave of lust shot through him, down to his toes, then back up, stopping at his midsection and settling in, then growing.

He wanted her, all of her, here in the narrow entryway, against the wall, with her legs wrapped around his waist and her round ass filling his palms as he ground himself into her.

The image in his head was so clear, it made his palms sweat. *What the hell?*

He swallowed a curse and pulled back.

"What are you doing?" she asked in a weak whisper.

He gave her the only answer he had. "I don't know." He ran his fingers through his hair. "I'm attracted to you. Clearly." A quick, rueful laugh escaped him. "It took me by surprise just how much."

He reached for her, his hands ending up on her upper arms instead of where he wanted them—all over. "I'm not surprised at the attraction. You're incredibly beautiful. I'm surprised at my lack of control. I don't normally attack women."

He let her go. If he was going to try to convince her that he wasn't going to manhandle her again, it'd probably be best to take his hands off her.

"You didn't attack me," she said. "I know how to say *no*. And I have a knee. Two, actually."

He leaned forward. "I'd like to kiss you again."

"No." She moved away and headed deeper into the room. Only the quickly beating pulse in her neck betrayed that she wasn't as unaffected as she pretended.

She stopped by the window, leaving her back to him. To gather herself? Did he affect her the same way she affected him?

He said, "I can do better."

She turned, a smile playing at the corners of her lips. "I'm sure."

He liked the smile. It meant she wasn't angry, or offended. "You don't believe in second chances?"

"I don't believe in one-night stands."

*Whoa.* He lifted a hand in a gesture of *wait a minute.* "I didn't come here for that. I swear."

Now he felt like a dick. Especially since he had no intention of telling her of Kenneth's death.

He hadn't come with the intention of seducing her, but he *had* come to deceive her, to use her for his own purpose.

He crossed the room and went to sit in the armchair by the window, noticing all the details as he went: the bed—made; the clothes hanging in the closet—expensive; her smartphone on the desk—the latest top model; her laptop open on the desk—ditto. Blueprints covered the screen. She'd been working.

The sight drove home the fact that she was a businesswoman. She shouldn't be here alone.

At least she'd have him for protection for the next few days.

He *would* protect her. But even so, he felt guilt over playing her. He had to let that go. None of this was about her.

He was seasoned spec ops, working for the FBI on this mission as a temporary agent. He'd cheated, lied, and killed in the past. On a mission, he did whatever he had to do to reach the mission objective.

Allison tucked her hair behind her ear as she watched him. The light from the window framed her in an angelic glow. She took his breath away.

He had to forget that. He couldn't look at her as someone he wanted. He had to look at her as an avenue of investigation.

Which would be significantly easier if he hadn't stupidly kissed her. That couldn't happen again.

# CHAPTER
# THREE

Allison sat in the police chief's office at the station, her stomach as heavy as if she'd had construction gravel for breakfast. All right, maybe not *that* heavy. She felt marginally better with Jake Tekla by her side. He certainly didn't seem worried as they waited for the commissioner, the guard keeping an eye on them from the open doorway.

To make sure she wouldn't meet the guard's eyes, which would be viewed as inappropriate behavior, she kept her gaze on Jake. "I really appreciate that you came with me today."

*Don't think about the kiss.* God, that had thrown her for a loop. Completely unlike her. Somehow his body had talked to hers, bypassing her brain. His pheromones hit her, and her common sense evaporated. He'd left her shaken and…wanting more of him, dammit.

It'd been a long time since she'd been kissed. And she wasn't sure she'd ever been kissed quite like that, on a crazy rush of pure passion…

*Don't think about the kiss!*

Jake's presence filled the small office as it had filled the cab the day before, then her hotel room when he'd shown up unexpectedly. Having his guidance and protection made her feel safer and more optimistic about her chances of success. But at the same time, anytime she was near him, she felt wired, all her nerve endings dancing a jig. And there was no way she was ever going to forget the touch of his lips against hers.

She kept having this weird feeling, the same she'd had the first time she'd ridden a roller coaster, a sense that something terrifyingly exciting was about to happen.

The carnival ride had turned out to be mostly terrifying. She was sure there was a lesson in there somewhere.

He leaned back in his chair and flashed her a smile, the picture of relaxed ease. The smile drew her gaze to his mouth. She flushed with heat. Luckily, before she could turn bright red, footsteps sounded in the corridor outside, drawing their attention to the door.

Better be the commissioner. She wanted the interview to be over. She sat up straighter, ready.

A fifty-something man strode in, tall, wiry, his tanned skin stretched tight over his cheekbones, his cold eyes immediately settling on her. The police chief followed him, remaining standing as the commissioner took the chair behind the desk.

Allison reached up to make sure she still had her head covered, then dropped her hand. No nervous gestures. The men might see nerves as a sign of guilt.

The commissioner's gaze dripped with contempt as he looked her over before shifting his attention to Jake. "Who are you?"

"Jake Tekla. Travel writer. I'm hoping to put together a book on the natural beauty of your great country," he said smoothly. "Miss Myers hired me as her guide and guardian for the very brief time she'll be spending here."

The commissioner said something to the police chief in rapid Farsi. The chief responded. Then Jake put in his own two cents.

As soon as he started to speak their language, both the commissioner and the police chief grew several notches friendlier. The conversation went on, switching back and forth between Farsi and English. Allison only understood about half, so she paid close attention to body language.

When the commissioner laughed, Jake laughed with him. Since they didn't look as if they were talking about putting her in jail on charges of spying, she relaxed a little.

The men seemed relieved that they didn't have to deal with her but could talk to Jake instead. The interview ended in twenty minutes, concluding with stern warnings on what she should and shouldn't do while she remained in the country.

They denied any knowledge of Kenneth ever having been in Lahedeh.

Walking down through the grim, gray hallways on the way out wasn't as scary as the day before. And since Jake had given her a ride from the hotel in his rented Land Rover, this time she didn't have to worry about the cab driver leaving either.

"Thank you," she said as they got into the SUV. "That went well. I think. They no longer think I'm here to steal their water, right?"

He turned on the engine, then headed toward the hotel. "I'm not sure if they ever did. They just don't like women like you around here, all confident and asking questions. I think they wanted to intimidate you into leaving." He gave her a playful wink. "I let them know that I'd be keeping you under tight control from here on out."

"I'm glad they didn't decide to keep me."

"I wouldn't have let them." His voice was steady and confident.

"What could you have done? It's not like you could get into a fistfight with the Afghan police."

He held her gaze. "I would have done whatever was necessary."

*Oh.* Her heart thudded loudly in her chest, especially when she licked her dry lips and Jake's gaze dropped to her mouth.

She'd been plenty hot already, but the temperature seemed to jump up another few degrees. She looked away, out the window, at the shops and restaurants they were passing.

She didn't want to like him. Talk about an ill-timed attraction. She was here for Kenneth. She and Jake were going to spend a limited amount of time together here, then never see each other again.

"So what's next?" he asked.

She tugged at her collar. "As soon as I get back to my room, I'm going to change out of this tent I'm wearing. Then I'm going to start working the phone again."

She wanted to be alone. Away from the nearly painful awareness she felt around Jake.

"Who are you calling?"

"First, the US embassy in Kabul. Somebody has to know something. I just haven't reached the right person yet."

"How about we leave the calls for the afternoon?" Jake suggested and turned right at the next light, away from the hotel.

So much for putting some distance between them. "Where are we going?"

"You said the hotel had no record of Kenneth staying with them," he said, watching the traffic.

A guy on a red motorcycle weaved in and out their lane up ahead, a cage tied to the back of the bike holding two little lambs. The man cut off cars and trucks with death-defying speed, doing his best to cause an accident.

"Are you sure Kenneth stayed at our hotel?" Jake hung back so if the guy caused a crash, they wouldn't be involved in the pileup.

"That's what he told me."

Allison watched the kamikaze biker but trusted Jake's reflexes. He was an excellent driver. He'd been pretty good at everything she'd seen him do so far. The interview at the police station had certainly been much easier with him present.

"I didn't get anywhere with the front desk guy," she said, "but you might. Maybe he'd prefer talking to another man."

At her company, she could expect her questions to be answered. Here, she was powerless—a new experience. Even after a week in the country, she still had trouble accepting reality. She had utterly underestimated the difficulty level of the trip.

She loosened her headscarf, but just a little. "I'm sure Kenneth stayed at our hotel. Where else would he go? It's the hotel where all the foreigners stay."

"There *is* one other place." Jake shot her a quick glance. "The locals say there are foreigners at Khanbaba's compound."

"Khanbaba? Is he a local businessman?" Maybe he'd invited Kenneth to stay at his place because they were negotiating some deal. That didn't explain why Kenneth had stopped calling, but still, hope filled her.

Jake crushed that hope the very next second.

"Khanbaba is the local warlord I told you about yesterday."

She gaped at him. "Kenneth wouldn't have anything to do with people like that."

"Khanbaba is no longer at the compound."

Right. She remembered now. "The warlord is up in the hills."

"His compound is utilized by XO-ST these days." Jake slowed the car. "A private security firm here on a contract from the US government."

They had reached the outskirts of Lahedeh, where the town looked a lot more like a village, dirt roads and mud huts and freely roaming animals.

Jake drove around a small herd of goats that blocked the road. "XO-ST is not in town right now. They patrol a pretty large region, so they tend to go out for weeks at a time."

"Then why are we going over to their compound?"

"I want to give their quarters a quick look. If they're not there, I won't have to ask permission."

She couldn't argue with that logic, even if it left her uneasy. Maybe Jake Tekla was more impulsive than she liked but, for Kenneth's sake, she would roll with the punches. She wasn't going to discover anything by sitting around at the hotel.

Then she thought of something. "This could explain why the embassy is confused. They told me Kenneth was here as part of some commando group. They probably think most Americans who come to Lahedeh have something to do with XO-ST."

"The embassy said that?" Jake's gaze sharpened. "Could you run by me again how Kenneth came up with the idea of coming here?"

She'd only told him the basics yesterday. Maybe more detail would help. "A friend of his did some business around here that turned out pretty well. He talked Kenneth into checking out the place. Harvard men stick together. They pass on business opportunities if they can. The whole Harvard Club thing."

"What's the name of the friend?"

"Mitch Wharst. I already talked to him." Many times. "He has no idea what happened to Kenneth. They hadn't talked since Kenneth left the US."

"Any relation to Senator Richard Wharst?" Jake showed genuine interest instead of being bored with all the backstory. He seemed ready, even eager, to help, despite the fact that he wouldn't profit anything by assisting her. He couldn't have been more different from the corporate types she was used to. He was a little rough around the edges with an unhealthy zest for adventure—but he was a good man to have around in a pinch.

"The senator is Mitch's brother," she told him.

Kenneth tended to listen to Mitch, tried to impress him when he could. Kenneth planned on going into politics eventually. He was counting on Mitch's help and connections for that next step.

Allison disliked the idea of a life in politics, but Kenneth needed her full support, so she'd been trying to work up the necessary enthusiasm. And not succeeding. She'd been trying to work on so many things regarding their relationship. And pretty much failed on every front.

Truth was, she felt more alive in Jake Tekla's company than she ever felt with Kenneth.

Jake slowed for more potholes in the road, bigger and deeper out in the countryside. "Was Kenneth friends with the senator too?"

"Just with Mitch."

She scanned the stark landscape that surrounded them—mostly rocks, interrupted by patches of scraggly bushes. The snowcapped mountains looked majestic in the distance.

Jake kept silent, probably thinking about how he could make up for all the time he was spending with her and away from his job.

She turned back to him. "I hope you won't get into trouble with your publisher. You're not on any tight deadlines, are you?"

He hesitated for a second. "I'm all right. Almost have all the material I need. I don't mind putting off the trip to the tribes a day or two. Maybe the heat will break. The trek would be easier in cooler weather."

That made her feel less guilty about taking up his time. She didn't want to inconvenience him more than absolutely necessary.

"I'd be more than happy to pay you for your help," she said again. She'd offered last night when they'd agreed on him helping her, but he'd refused a fee.

She could afford to pay Jake. But she didn't want to push the issue right now, didn't want to offend him.

"I have friends in publishing," she said as she thought of it. "If you ever need help in that area, you have to promise me you'll call me."

He grinned. "I promise you'll be the first to know the next time I have a press release."

The thought of him calling on her after they were both back in the US sent an anticipatory tingle down her spine. His alpha-male aura, the charisma that emanated from him, enveloped her. But a prickle of guilt burst that pleasant bubble.

She needed to focus on Kenneth. He was her friend, and he was missing. She shouldn't be lusting after Jake, getting distracted.

Jake leaned forward and squinted at the dusty road in front of them. She followed his gaze and spotted a sprawling structure in the distance.

He stepped on the gas. "That's it. Khanbaba's compound."

As they drew close, more and more of the structure became visible. The place better resembled a ruin than mercenary headquarters. Part of the front wall had been blown in at one point, maybe in the battle that had chased the warlord away. The compound stood stark and threatening in the barren landscape.

As Jake pulled up in front of the eight-foot-tall mud-brick walls, a sudden, uneasy premonition shivered up Allison's spine. "Do you really think we should go in?"

"Might as well. We're already here." He got out and opened the door for her. Then he headed straight to the hole in the wall.

She followed him. "If XO-ST uses this place, why don't they guard it?"

"A question of manpower." He scanned the courtyard. "They take their equipment when they go out on their long patrols, because they need it. And if they leave nothing behind, they don't need to leave anyone behind to guard anything. They have better use for their men on the front lines."

When Jake moved forward, Allison walked behind him, distracted by his wide shoulders and shifting muscles. "Makes sense."

The courtyard had seen better days, probably back when the warlord and his family had lived here. A lonely tree did its best to shade the well in the middle. In the far corner, a few bare branches stuck out of the dry soil. Once it might have been a rose garden.

The buildings seemed just as deserted close up as they had from afar. When Jake walked through an open door, she stepped into the shade behind him. The inside was several degrees cooler.

"Mud bricks must be a pretty good insulator."

Jake grinned as he scanned the place. "The AC from BC."

She rolled her eyes at the lame joke. Then she took her time to look around inside. Empty rooms opened into each other, holding nothing but broken furniture and garbage. She couldn't imagine Kenneth in this place.

"Amazing that some of the poor don't simply move in here." She'd seen plenty of beggars in town.

"They're probably still afraid of the warlord. To the locals, this will always be his place. And they wouldn't want to run into the XO-ST team either."

They meandered through the ground floor, finding some animal droppings in one of the rooms. Stray dogs or goats must have taken shelter in there at one point. She hurried past, into the next room that was in better condition, then into the next room that stood in ruins.

A fallen beam blocked the door to the next space, a giant kitchen.

Suddenly Jake was behind her, and then she was in his arm as he effortlessly lifted her over the obstacle.

*Oh.*

Her arms went around his neck. For support. *Right.*

He really didn't strain at all. And he didn't put her down either.

She looked up at him. Their eyes met. Awareness tingled across her skin, dancing the dance of a thousand possibilities. The attraction was off the charts, ridiculously so, really, considering how little they knew each other. Yet, because she'd never felt this kind of attraction to anyone before, the draw was irresistible.

His gaze bore into hers and heated. "I'd like to kiss you again."

The words sent a thrill through her. "Why?"

"I can't look at you and not want you."

Her breath caught. She felt the same about him. This was new, the kind of chemistry she'd only read about in books.

She and Daniel had been young. He'd been the perfect gentleman, then he'd gotten very sick, very fast. With Kenneth, the relationship had been half friendship, and only half romance.

She wasn't sure how to handle *this*—pure passion that drilled through her defenses like a jackhammer.

They were both crazy. Maybe there was something in the water.

"Every time I look at you…" His voice deepened, roughened. "I'm picturing you naked. Every time I think about you, my dick is hard. I just want to be inside you."

She had to breathe or she was going to pass out. No man had ever talked to her like that.

Jake held her, his strong arms a protective cocoon around her. "Say yes."

Everywhere they touched, her body was going haywire. Her skin felt hot and cold at the same time, her clothes too tight. She drew a gulp of air at last. "Yes."

The 's' was barely out when his lips descended.

Her head swam. In a split second, she was dizzy with need. He gave a low growl as his tongue swept inside her mouth, and she suddenly felt liquefied.

Nobody had ever wanted her like this. And she'd never felt this kind of instant, primal need. Ever.

Without breaking the connection of their lips, he put her down and backed her against the nearest wall. Thank God, because finally she could take her arms from around his neck, and she could put her hands on him.

And he could put his hands on her.

"This is not normal." She gasped out the words between two kisses, as she kneaded his incredible pecs.

"Fuck normal." He unbuttoned her shirt, drew down the cups of her bra. "God, you're perfect."

And then the next second, his large hands covered her breasts, and her knees nearly folded.

She didn't make a joke of the extra fifteen pounds she'd picked up since she'd taken over the company and the time she spent behind a desk doubled. The way his gaze burned into hers when he pulled back so he could look at her, she did feel perfect. She felt desired.

He dipped his head, and his hot lips closed around her nipple. Her head fell back against the wall. Pleasure shot through her, from the spot he was kissing to the V of her thighs—hot, aching, pulsing pleasure.

He reached for her skirt and pulled up the miles of fabric faster than she would have thought possible, his fingers soon tracing her panties. Then his head moved up, and he kissed her again while he pressed his hard body against hers.

Her mind stopped working, except for the one, very clear thought that this was the single most erotic experience of her life.

He ground against her, and suddenly she was frantic with need, reaching for his belt without thinking about it, needing more, needing *him*.

He put a hand on hers. Looked into her eyes. His tone had a desperate note in it as he asked, "Are you sure?"

She'd never done anything remotely like this. Maybe it was time. "I am."

He kissed her.

*No maybe. Definitely time.*

He helped her with his pants, then he had a condom in hand, and then he was sheathed. Her underwear disappeared a split second before his large hands slipped under her thighs, and then he lifted her effortlessly and spread her, her knees bracketing his hips.

His hardness pressed against her core. And then he pushed in.

Again, she forgot to breathe.

He stretched her, and the pleasure of it stole mewling sounds from her throat. He filled her, and then he tilted her pelvis and filled her deeper.

She drew a great, sobbing gasp of air. A good thing, because his lips were on hers again and he began pumping into her in controlled strokes.

She came on the fourth or fifth pump, her body contracting wildly, bucking against his. He pushed into her hard, one last time, and followed her over.

Then they were still, breathing harshly in the silence.

*No, not silence.* Voices came from the courtyard.

Her body clenched around his, and he groaned, the sound filled with reluctance. She wasn't ready yet for the moment to end, maybe he wasn't either.

But he slipped out of her. "I'll see what it is."

He discarded the condom in the rubble, then pulled up his pants.

She leaned bonelessly against the wall, satisfied, stunned, slightly panicked.

More voices. People were here. She had to come back to earth.

She snapped herself out of her orgasm coma and scrambled for her underwear as Jake buckled his belt.

"Stay inside for now." He moved like a shadow, his boots making no noise on the stone floor as he went to investigate.

On trembling knees, she followed him to the door that led to the courtyard, her steps not nearly as silent as Jake's, but quiet enough so she wouldn't be heard outside. She wanted to be as close to him as possible in case of trouble, but stopped just inside the door while he moved forward, his every step filled with control and self-confidence.

*What had just happened?*

Better yet…*Did that really just happen?*

Her still-tingling body testified that, indeed, she *had* just had fast and furious sex with Jake Tekla. In an Afghan warlord's compound.

*How on earth?* This wasn't her.

But now was not the right time to analyze, so she didn't. She watched their visitors instead.

A couple of older men and a young woman came to a halt in the middle of the courtyard. The men led donkeys laden with wood and food. The woman carried a pottery jar on her shoulder.

"Soldiers they come back?" one of the men asked Jake in broken English.

They had no guns, nothing remotely threatening. They looked like simple farmers.

Jake turned back to Allison and nodded.

She went to stand beside him and felt immediately safer.

"We're just tourists. Looking around," Jake told the visitors. "You know the soldiers who sometimes come here?"

They shrugged, obviously disappointed. They'd probably seen Jake's SUV and thought the mercenaries had come back.

"You stay at hotel?" the taller of the men asked.

Jake nodded.

The man hung his head. People who stayed at the hotel wouldn't need firewood or sacks of figs. He turned around with a dejected set of his shoulders and led his animals back through the hole in the wall. The other man followed him.

The woman, almost a full head shorter than Allison, remained. She'd been standing at a respectful distance behind the men but now set her jar down and approached Allison and Jake, wringing her hands. She wore the local garb of loose, full-length dress and veil, but her coloring was lighter than usual around here.

"You friends of soldiers?" she asked in broken English, with a heavy accent that sounded different from the men's.

"Not really," Jake said.

Allison reached for her fanny pack. If these people came here regularly to trade with the mercenaries, and if Kenneth had been here by some remote chance…She pulled out Kenneth's photo, and showed it to the woman, giving her an encouraging smile. "Have you seen this man?"

The woman's face lit up, tears of joy filling her eyes as she grabbed the picture and held it to her chest. "Yes. He is marry me. He sent you bring me to him?"

Allison's mind stalled. She hadn't fully recovered yet from what had happened with Jake inside. The woman's words pushed things farther into surreal territory.

Thoughts began to form but refused to complete.

Jake put a steadying hand on her shoulder. And while her mind reeled, he asked the woman, "When did you last see him?"

"Five months ago. Me his girlfriend. I'm from Ukraine. Came for job at hospital in Kabul. They no want me, no pay. Friend has parents in Lahedeh. They help. Then Mr. Ken came." She smiled shyly. "He says he take me America. But one day he go away. I ask other soldiers, they chase me. I know Mr. Ken come back someday. He sent you, yes? For me?"

Her dress was soiled and torn, her eyes the eyes of a woman who'd been through things Allison didn't even want to contemplate. An aura of desperation clung to her. She was thin to the point of being malnourished, but her face held so much joy and hope as she hugged that photo, she looked as if she might burst with emotion.

"Sorry," Jake said. "He didn't send us. We're trying to find him too."

The light slid off the woman's face, replaced by dark misery. "He promised take me. He must come back."

Allison felt nothing but compassion for her. She thought of what the woman's life must be, eking out a tenuous living on the charity of strangers here, waiting for a man who'd promised the world to her and who might never return. How long would she last, stuck here alone, in a country that had few opportunities for women?

"I don't think he's coming," Allison told her quietly.

Kenneth had ambitions. He needed a wife who could help him fulfill them. Allison had always known that and never minded that it had been one of the many reasons why he'd chosen her. Relationships were complicated. She believed in him and his causes. She just wasn't in love with him. Had never been in love with him—the truth hit home, suddenly undeniable.

She felt no betrayal. Of course, considering that she'd just had the best sex of her life, she would have been a hypocrite to act betrayed.

The woman wiped her tears with the back of her hand. She was tiny to the point of being waiflike, Allison's opposite in nearly every way. Was this what Kenneth had secretly wanted? He had to be really in love with her if he thought about taking her home with him.

*Dammit, Kenneth. Where the hell are you?*

Allison stared at the weeping woman and didn't have the heart to ask for the photo back. She had others at the hotel. She pulled out her wallet, grabbed a handful of local currency without counting, and held it out. "Please take this and go home to your family."

The woman looked at her with tear-soaked eyes and an expression of profound adoration, then collapsed on the ground and kissed her feet.

"Oh, please, don't do that." Allison dragged her back up. "Just, please go and make sure you're safe, okay?"

# CHAPTER
# FOUR

Jake drove Allison back to the hotel.

She tried to hide it, but talking with the Ukrainian woman had shaken her. Her face turned paler, the set of her shoulders tense.

"Lunch?" he asked as they walked into the building. At half past two in the afternoon, he was starving. The police commissioner had made them wait for hours that morning, and then they'd ended up spending a few more hours wandering through Khanbaba's labyrinth of a compound—among other things.

When Allison nodded, he led her to the restaurant and ordered the couscous lamb platter for them.

She was lost in thought, so Jake let her be. She was probably wrestling with the possibility that Kenneth was dead. Jake decided not to broach that subject.

Or remind her of the sex. He didn't want to hear her say that it'd been a mistake. Because for someone like her, what else could it be?

*Man*, the sex.

First time he could remember that his knees shook. Hell, his hands too. He didn't think she'd noticed, and thank God for that.

He seemed to want her with an unending need. Here and now, again, on the table if it could be arranged. He felt sucker punched, and a little worried, because normally he had more self-control than this.

Their food came. They ate. She still said nothing.

She really was shaken.

When they finished, he walked her up to her room and sat her down. A shot of whiskey might have done her good, but with Islam forbidding alcohol, he couldn't just order up a bottle. The minifridge held an assortment of juices and a single bottle of water. He handed her the latter.

She was sitting in one of the chairs by the small table in the corner. Since he didn't want to leave her, he sat in the other. Clearly, she needed a friend in this situation. So, despite the fact that talking was the last thing he wanted, he said, "Talk to me. It hurts when you're betrayed by someone you love." Which was why he never gave his heart to anyone. "It's okay to be angry and hurt."

But she shook her head. "I feel guilty."

"Why would *you* feel guilty?"

Moisture filled her brilliant blue eyes. "I'm not sure if I was ever in love with him. I thought I was, for a while." She choked out the words.

Jake didn't normally do the emotions-and-feelings talk. He wasn't the "best friend" type of lover. He was more into whirlwind romance: heat, need, passion, then a mutual see-you-later.

What he'd shared with Allison was no different. He just wasn't ready to come to the see-you-later part yet. Maybe by tomorrow morning. *Spend the night with her,* his inner horndog suggested, *then drive her to Kabul tomorrow.*

Leaving was in her best interest.

"Of course you loved him." He took her hand. "You came halfway around the world for him."

She pulled her hand back. "He'd do the same for me."

Jake wasn't so sure.

"Where do you think he is?" she asked.

*Six feet under,* he wanted to tell her, not feeling particularly sorry for the jerk at the moment. But if he told her that Kenneth was dead, she would want to know how Jake knew. And he couldn't blow his cover, even if keeping the truth from her felt more wrong with every passing minute.

"I don't think he's here in Lahedeh. You should go back to the States."

Saying that felt wrong too. He didn't want to let her out of his sight. But if he thought professionally, just for a moment, instead of with his dick, these were the words he needed to say.

He had the information he needed from her. Senator Wharst's little brother, Mitch Wharst, had been here. XO-ST had a base here. This had to be how the senator was tied to XO-ST business. Mitch had done something here that was so bad, Brent Foley used it to blackmail the senator. All Jake needed now were specifics and tangible proof he could take back to the US. Allison Myers couldn't help him with that. He was pretty sure she didn't know any more than what she'd already told him.

She sat with her hands folded on her lap as she considered his advice to leave. And resisted. Because she was possibly the most loyal person he'd ever met.

He wanted to gather her into his arms. He wanted to kiss her, then draw her to the bed, thereby proving his sisters' frequently made point that when it came to women, his stupidity was indeed endless.

"I'll take you to Kabul in the morning." The sooner Allison left, the better for both of them.

For a second, she looked like she might agree, but then she rallied. "I can't leave without finding out what happened to Kenneth. Beyond this other woman…Beyond the engagement…Beyond what happened between us." She drew a shuddery breath. "Kenneth is my friend. He was there for me when Daniel died. He took care of me, and I'm going to take care of him."

Before Jake could figure out how to respond, she went on with, "Daniel and I got married at the hospital." Misery etched new lines around her eyes. "Two days before he died. Kenneth was the best man. He was Daniel's best friend."

She paused as if hesitating over whether to say more, but then she went ahead with, "I lost my mother early. No siblings. All my life, all I ever wanted was a family. Daniel and I planned on having a family as soon as we got married. Kenneth knew that. When he first came to me after Daniel's death and asked me to think of him as more than a friend, he kept talking about the big, happy family we would have. It took me a while to figure out that I'd just been in love with that dream and not really with him. I figured it out too late, after I already said yes to his proposal."

She closed her eyes for a second. "Kenneth isn't perfect, but neither am I. He's missing. If I just leave him to his fate…" Her voice broke on the word. "What kind of a person would that make me?"

*About average*, Jake thought. Except, she was anything but.

He hated the thought of her hurting, hated to see her so crestfallen.

And she didn't even know about Kenneth's death yet. As Jake watched her wrap her arms around herself, guilt sank its sharp talons into his chest. He leaned back in his chair, ignoring the seductive scent of her perfume that tried to pull him closer, and the faint voice of his conscience that recommended telling her the truth.

"Despite the other woman…" She pressed her lips together. "Kenneth is a good man. His parents died when he was very young. He was raised by court-appointed guardians who controlled his trust fund and his entire life. Everything was so difficult for him, but he overcame all that. He made himself a name in business, and he was going into politics. He wanted to accomplish great things for our country. He needed my help."

Her tears spilled over.

Jake clenched his jaw. Kenneth had never deserved her. You just didn't betray a woman like Allison Myers. Or any woman, for that matter.

Enjoying female company was one thing, but Jake drew the line at cheating and had no respect for guys who strayed. He knew firsthand what a brokenhearted woman looked like. He had sisters.

Jasmine, especially, had had a lot of up-and-down relationships in college before she found Gabe a couple of months back. At least now Jake didn't have to worry about her in that regard. Gabe would lay his life down before letting any harm come to her.

Allison bit her bottom lip. "I know you think I'm a good person for having come after Kenneth, but I'm not. You know how I found out that he was missing? I found out when I called the hotel to call off our engagement."

Misery tightened her face. "We got engaged just before he left. And then I had second thoughts. So when he called, I avoided him, or had like two-minute conversations with him, then pretended I had to run off for a meeting."

She pressed her lips together. "Then I worked up the nerve to tell him that we'd made a mistake, and I finally called, but he didn't pick up. I was relieved. It wasn't a conversation I was looking forward to. I thought he'd call me back. I didn't mind when he didn't call for a few days. When he's overseas, especially in third-world countries, they go out surveying away from the cities, and a lot of times, he has no phone reception." She winced. "I waited two weeks before calling him again."

Jake nodded. "Hey, I once jumped off a ship to avoid an uncomfortable conversation with a woman."

Allison's eyes widened. "Really?"

"She was in the coast guard. She was really angry at me. And she was armed." He flashed Allison a rueful grin. "So what happened with Kenneth?"

"I still couldn't reach him. I thought he sensed why I was trying to call him, so he was avoiding me. I let him. Another two weeks passed before I called the hotel to ask when they were expecting him back from the field."

"And they told you they'd never heard of him." Jake could easily imagine how surprised she must have been.

She nodded. "So then I started the embassy odyssey and believed for months that they were looking into it. I believed Kenneth's company was looking into it. But the truth is, other than some phone calls, nobody has put any real effort into finding him."

"You should have hired a professional to come in your place."

"I did hire a PI to come with me. He backed out at the last second."

The guy had probably checked around and found the XO-ST link. Jake didn't blame him for dropping the case. Private commandos had a pretty rough, lawless reputation in the business. A single PI wouldn't stand a chance, and he had to know it. The jerk should have given Allison some warning, though.

"There are companies who specialize in these kinds of things," Jake told her. "Retrieving kidnapped businessmen, negotiating ransom with pirates, whatever."

"I wanted to keep the number of people involved to an absolute minimum. The more people who know, the better chance for a leak. I have no idea what's going on, but Kenneth wants to run for office soon. There can't be any scandals. You can't tell anyone about this. Especially about the girl."

"Why don't you go home, and I promise I'll look for Kenneth."

She tried to smile through her tears, then grabbed a tissue to dry her face. She drew a deep breath, and worked herself back to her composed, ladylike self. "I'm fine. Sorry about losing it. I can handle this. Really."

"Putting yourself in danger here won't solve anything. You don't fit in here. People don't like foreigners asking questions. The police are suspicious of you." And Kenneth was dead. She wasn't going to save him. She had no reason to stay.

Except that Jake *could* use her, even if she had no further information about Mitch Wharst and what the guy might have done in Lahedeh.

Working for her added to Jake's cover. He'd realized that while they'd been at the police station.

He'd had his own run-in with the chief where his reasons for being in town had been questioned. But at that first meeting, Jake had been a pesky foreigner. At this morning's meeting, Jake was suddenly the solution to a problem—someone who would handle the troublesome foreign woman.

In addition to that, she also provided a distraction. While the locals watched her because she looked and acted differently from the women they were used to, Jake could fly under the radar.

She clearly had her uses, and he'd been trained to always use every weapon in his arsenal. He always had before.

"You need to go home," he told her again before he could closely examine why he put her interest before his mission.

"Not until I know what happened to Kenneth." Determination gave her voice strength. She stood from the chair. "I'm going to call the embassy again."

He went to her and drew her into his arms. "Allison…"

She pushed him away and raised a hand to hold him back. "About…what happened."

"When we had the hottest sex ever?"

Color tinged her cheeks. "This is going way too fast for me."

Hell, for him too, but what a ride. He definitely didn't want to get off here. "Then we'll take it slow."

A troubled look came into her eyes. "Will we? You want to continue?"

"Yes. I want to get to know you. But I want you to go someplace safe. I'll find you when I'm done here." He wanted to kiss her, but she'd already said no, and he wasn't going to push her.

He strode to the door, then turned back. "Get some sleep. I'll take you to the airport in Kabul in the morning."

Then he stepped out of her room and closed the door behind him before he could go back and beg her to let him spend the night with her.

Maybe he could have seduced her into it. She was incredibly sensuous, incredibly responsive. But suddenly, he wanted her for more than just tonight. He wanted her for the night after that, and the night after that, and the night after that…

*Stupid much?*

Women were supposed to be entertainment at this stage of his life, not a complication.

He strode down the hallway, walking faster than was strictly necessary.

Allison Myers was too serious by half, definitely not the sun-and-fun type he normally went for. She stuck with things even when they were uncomfortable or downright dangerous. She simply didn't give up. She risked her life for a man because it was the right thing to do, even if she no longer loved him.

How far would she go for a man she loved?

Part of Jake wanted to be the man who would inspire such devotion, even while the rest of him knew it could never happen. With his temporary FBI gig and who knew what after that, Jake wasn't the right guy to give her forever.

The thought bothered him more than it should have as he rode the elevator up to his floor, then strode down the hallway.

As he opened his door, the sound of powerful engines outside reached him through the cracked-open window, drawing his attention from things that could never be. He crossed the small space.

While Allison's room looked to the quiet courtyard of the hotel, Jake's window faced the street. A caravan of Humvees sped down the road, armed men hanging out the windows, people and smaller vehicles scattering out of their way as the Humvees didn't look like they would stop for anything.

XO-ST was back in town.

Jake's muscles tightened. Last time he'd met up with an XO-ST team, in Venice, Italy, they'd tried their best to kill him. And they'd nearly succeeded.

But this time he wasn't injured and half-starved. This time he didn't have his sisters with him to worry about. He checked his gun, pocketed some extra ammo, then headed for the door. Plenty of time to do a little recon while Allison talked with the embassy from the safety of her room.

# FIVE

On his way down to the Land Rover in the parking garage, Jake called Troy and told him about Mitch Wharst, asked him to pass the news on to Gabe. Maybe they finally had something here.

He *was* going to bring Senator Wharst down. And somehow he *was* going to keep Allison from harm in the process.

Jasmine called as he was driving away from the hotel.

"Everything okay at home?"

"Other than the teenage heartbreak drama?" Jasmine sighed. "If we weren't stuck in this FBI safe house, I'd go and sort T.J. out, I swear."

Jake bit back a smile. Jasmine probably would. His sister was no shrinking violet.

"Any idea yet when you'll be coming home?" she asked.

"Maybe soon. Looks like I might finally have a lead here." He bit back another smile. "I'm guessing you're more interested in when Gabe is getting back."

"I don't want to talk to you about Gabe. He keeps thinking of me as your little sister. He wouldn't…" She sighed. "Before he left, and he won't even do it over the phone."

Jake almost drove off the road. Were they having the conversation he thought they were having? About Gabe refusing to have phone sex with Jasmine out of a sense of honor?

"I'm so blaming you for this," Jasmine fumed on the other end.

*No. Just no.* Jake did *not* want to think about his sister's sex life any more than he wanted to think about his aunt's. And—thank you, Jasmine, for bringing up the damn topic—now he'd have to wash his brain with bleach when he got back to the hotel.

"I'm leaving town," he said, smart enough to know when to cut and run. "I'm about to lose reception. Stay safe." And with that, he hung up.

He drove about halfway to the compound, then hid the Land Rover behind a tall stand of bushes. The SUV didn't have camouflage paint, but the tan color was perfect. Nobody would pick it out from a distance.

Jake pulled a few branches strategically in place to make the hiding spot even better, then took off running. An entire armed commando team waited up ahead. He was right in his element. No problem.

* * *

"Could you please tell me where I could get a couple of bottles of water?" Allison asked at the front desk. She'd drank the last bottle she'd had.

The old man behind the counter frowned at her, like he did every time he had to talk to her. He was clearly one of those traditionalists who didn't approve that she was here without her husband.

But he replied in careful English. "In the restaurant, madam."

"Thank you." As she turned, a rumbling sound on the street drew her attention.

She caught sight of a Humvee through the glass entry doors, but only because it had to pause for a cab that pulled over to drop off guests. A ten second pause maybe, but enough for Allison to catch a glimpse of the man in the Humvee's passenger seat, about the same size and coloring as Kenneth, the same jawline, if she saw it correctly under days' worth of bristles.

Her heart thumped hard in her chest. Then the Humvee was gone.

She had her scarf, even if she'd meant to come only as far as the lobby. She'd brought her fanny pack since she'd meant to pay for the water. She had everything she needed.

Or maybe she didn't. Yesterday's little adventure had taught her that she had to be a lot more serious about her safety.

The water forgotten, she ran for the elevator. Jake had told her he was in room 402. She went up, ran down the hall, banged on his door. *Nothing.* He wasn't in.

*Fudge freaking mountain.*

He could be out anywhere. Maybe he wanted to take pictures of the sunset.

She leaned her forehead against his door for a desperate moment and just breathed. Could she wait for him?

But what if XO-ST was just blowing into town for a quick check, then blowing out again? Maybe Kenneth was with them so he could survey the area with armed protection. *Maybe, maybe, maybe.*

She wasn't sure of anything, except that she wasn't going to sit on her hands.

She wrote a note to Jake, slipped it under his door, then hurried back down, sailed through the lobby, and slammed into the back of the cab before the driver could object to a single female passenger.

"I'd like to go to the commando headquarters outside town, please."

The bearded man turned and yelled something at her in the local language, using a lot of hand gestures.

She leaned back in her seat, unperturbed. "Sorry, I speak only English and a little Spanish." Then she added something that sometimes helped. "I'll pay in US dollars."

The driver threw a long-suffering look toward heaven, then turned back to the steering wheel and pulled into traffic.

Allison clasped her hands on her lap. *God, don't let this turn out badly. And please let Kenneth be there.*

*** 

When Jake was close enough to see the compound, he slowed and ran in a crouch. In an hour, it'd be dark, but he didn't want to wait. He crawled the last five hundred feet on his stomach, sticking to indentations in the land, using clumps of dry grass for cover.

Two guys stood guard outside where the wall was busted. At least one other sentry on the roof.

Jake stole around to the back. The bars on the windows were brown with rust. He inched to a spot where he'd be out of sight and had to work only a single bar loose before he could vault in.

He crossed the empty room, exited to the empty hallway, then hurried up an empty staircase. The compound was pretty big, and he was in the wing the commandos weren't using. He found a room upstairs that overlooked the courtyard and settled in for surveillance, staying concealed in the shadows.

A couple of the men were unpacking equipment; others were cleaning their weapons. Two of the guys were shaving, one reading, a couple playing cards. They looked like they were settling in to rest a few days before they'd go out on the next patrol.

In addition to the mercenaries, Jake could see two locals unloading their pack animals, the same guys that'd come earlier. They were back with the food and firewood. The woman Allison had given money to hadn't returned.

Jake counted the men in the courtyard: fewer than a dozen. Which meant they weren't all here yet. The rest might have gone on a supply run to Lahedeh. A full XO-ST unit usually consisted of anywhere from twenty to two dozen mercenaries.

When everyone was here and asleep, Jake would search through their belongings. Until then, he had to content himself with eavesdropping.

They were obviously a team who knew each other well. Unfortunately, they talked only about cars and weapons and, every once in a while, girlfriends. Nobody said anything about Wharst, the name Jake strained to hear.

In fact, they were so boring, they nearly lulled him to sleep. Long minutes passed before Jake realized that two men didn't fit in at all, if you looked beyond the camouflage outfits and the most superficial factors.

They were in their twenties, average looking. They didn't seem to be part of the general camaraderie. They looked half-excited, half-scared. They could have been new team members, except, they didn't look like battle-hardened men, the only kind outfits like this hired. Private commando units didn't recruit through the classified ads. They searched out ex-military, combat experience required.

One of the misfits kept loading his gun over and over, not nearly fast enough, definitely practicing. The other looked like he was giving himself a silent pep talk. They tried to join in the general conversation now and then, and the rest of the team let them but seemed to be only humoring them.

Jake pulled away from the open window and moved to the far corner of the room to call Gabe.

"Can you recheck those XO-ST files we have? How often do they take on new men? I need to know if anything looks funny in their recruiting," he said in a low whisper, then hesitated and added, "Hey, I just wanted to say I'm okay with you and Jasmine. I mean, I'm okay with…you know, whatever."

Stunned silence on the other end.

And because Jake had just given permission for things he didn't even want to think about, he added, "You hurt her, and I'll rip your dick off, tie it around your neck, and strangle you with it. Just to be clear."

A snort came from the other end. "Just to be clear, my dick is certainly bigger than yours, but not as long as a necktie."

Jake hung up and inched back to the window to continue his surveillance of the courtyard.

The locals were leaving. Some of the commando soldiers carried the food supplies inside.

Jake had his eye on their leader and the black laptop the guy had with him. The man stood up, shoved the laptop under his arm, and began to walk toward the building.

He had serious bulk on him—big, flashy muscles. Too big to hide and go undercover, almost too muscle-bound to be really good in a fight. Show muscles. Jake had spent his life around real warriors, he wasn't taken in by the macho display.

Since he wanted to know where that one would be sleeping, he turned to leave the room so he could watch the guy from the top of the stairs. But before he could step away from the window, a shout pulled his attention back to the courtyard.

"Yo, Maddox!"

The team leader stopped.

The sentry who'd called after him lumbered forward, a second figure following behind him, someone too short to see.

"There's a woman here with some questions," the sentry said, an odd undercurrent in his tone.

The men around the fires threw curious glances in his direction, trying to look behind him.

*Probably Kenneth's girlfriend, the local woman. She really should have left.*

But as Maddox gestured to her to step forward, Allison Myers stepped past the sentry.

*What the hell? Why? Dammit!* Jake began to move, then forced himself to stay put, even as fury and worry pumped through him in waves. *If they as much as lay a hand on her...*

She pushed her headscarf back, and her rich honey-colored hair spilled into the fading sunlight. Every eye was definitely on her now.

She pulled a picture from her fanny pack and held it up. "Hi. Allison Myers. I'm looking for Kenneth Hatch, an American businessman who disappeared around here about five months ago. I really hope you can help me. Do you think you could maybe just look at this, please? You might recognize him."

The men around the cooking fire tensed. All conversation ended. Only the two greenhorns went on with their business, yapping as if nothing had happened. And in the sudden silence, Jake could make out the words "combat tourism," or something like that.

Not that the words made any sense.

Maybe they meant they needed to fight tourism, keep tourists away from these areas. Maybe XO-ST wanted to keep the place wild and dangerous so they could keep their fat government contracts.

Maddox sent the two greenhorns a withering look to shut them up, then refocused on Allison and gestured toward the building. "Why don't we go inside?"

His voice stayed neutral, but behind Allison, his men were suddenly on full battle alert.

"Thank you." Allison smiled at Maddox. Oblivious to the change of mood around her, she walked forward—a lamb to the slaughter.

# CHAPTER
# SIX

As Allison walked forward, she stole a last glance over her shoulder at the man she'd thought was Kenneth. He stood by the fire, same height and hair, same body type, but definitely a different face. *Of course, it couldn't be that easy.* Disappointment and the beginnings of anxiety settled into her chest.

The guy leading her into the building towered over her by at least six inches and was incredibly muscular, even more so than Jake Tekla. But while Maddox's physique was seriously scary and his focused attention intimidating, he was nothing but polite, gesturing for her to go first. Yet something she couldn't put her finger on made Allison uncomfortable, made her wish she'd waited for Jake to come with her.

She shook off the thought. She'd spent most of her life proving that she could take care of her own business all by herself, even if she was just a woman.

And the commando soldiers were Americans, most of them ex-US military. She was probably perfectly safe with them.

She'd been smart about the cab, refused to pay until the driver took her back to her hotel, so the man would definitely wait for her. She was learning to navigate her foreign environment.

Since her father's death, she'd had to put up with constant insinuations that she couldn't tie her shoes without his guidance, let alone run the whole company. Real estate development was still a man's world; not many women reached the top. And, of course, she hadn't built the business. Her father had. Nobody ever let her forget that. The papers portrayed her as a trust-fund princess in a photoshopped pink hard hat.

So she made it a point to prove, often even in the smallest things, that she didn't need to have her hand held. She *was* as good as any of the men.

When the PI she'd hired to come with her to Afghanistan quit at the last second, she'd thought about postponing the trip until a new one could be hired. But all those media jabs after her father's death about her being unable to do anything on her own had echoed in her head.

So she'd come alone to prove everyone wrong. She hadn't simply come for Kenneth. She had a deep-seated need to be known as the woman who took care of business.

*Pride goes before a fall.* It might have been nice to remember the old adage a little earlier.

She'd figured that since she was traveling to a country under US military control, she'd be safe enough. But as Maddox showed her into a small upstairs room, empty except for an old brown carpet on the floor and a faded-black, moth-eaten blanket in the corner, she was suddenly assailed by dark premonitions and an urge to flee.

"I'm going to have to ask for your cell phone," he said. "No photos here. For security reasons. Think of this as a military installation."

She handed him her phone from her fanny pack. If she didn't, he could just take it. Right now, they were on polite terms. Instinct told her it was in her best interest not to change that.

Her phone didn't work here anyway. Apparently, she needed a satellite phone like the ones Kenneth used when he worked in remote regions.

Maddox slipped her phone into his shirt pocket, then checked her over, looking like he wanted to pat her down, although he didn't.

She lifted her arms out to the side so he could see that she didn't have any weapons.

"I'd just like some information about my fiancé," she said. "Was Kenneth ever here? I don't understand why he would have been. He works in water management. Irrigation."

Maddox's eyes shifted. "We hired him to do a study on a new irrigation system for the town," he said after a moment. "As long as we're here, we'd like to contribute. We can use all the good PR we can get."

That made *some* sense—the first piece of useful information so far. Allison relaxed a little. Maddox knew Kenneth—a good start. "Could you please tell me where he is now? Is he okay? I haven't been able to reach him."

The man's pale brown eyes shifted again. "He's up north. We'll take you to him in the morning." He tapped his laptop. "I've just been planning the route."

She preferred Jake taking her. "Thank you, but that's okay. I'm sure you have other things to do. I wouldn't want to be any trouble." The way Maddox's smile didn't reach his eyes made her wary. "So where is Kenneth exactly? What town?"

"Up in the mountains. Even satellite phone coverage is spotty up there. And he's been pretty sick." Maddox pulled away from her. "We'll leave at first light."

He sounded as if his mind was made up that she would go with them. Something told her she shouldn't argue with the guy. "I should go back to my hotel until then."

He flashed another one of his cold smiles. "Can't let you back out now that it's getting dark. Not safe. You'll be fine with us."

"I took a cab here."

"I'll send it back. You can't trust the local cab drivers. Half of them are thieves." And with that he left the room, taking her phone with him.

The key turned in the lock from the outside.

Before she could so much as blink, she was a prisoner.

She stared at the door. *Wow. Okay.* She hadn't expected *this.* Although, truth be told, from the moment she'd set foot in Afghanistan, nothing had happened as she'd expected.

She hurried to the door and tried to open it, just in case, but no amount of wiggling made the knob budge.

*Jake will come,* a little voice said in her head. Thank God, she'd let him know where she was going. He would find her note, and if she didn't return, he would come for her.

He was very good at showing up when she needed him. He'd saved her on the street from those thugs and gotten her back to the hotel. He'd gone with her to her meeting with the police commissioner and somehow defused the situation there.

*Oh God.* She froze. Maybe her corporate enemies were right. She *did* seem to need help every other minute. *No way.* Deep breath. *Okay. What would Jake do?*

He wouldn't sit around, waiting to be rescued. He had a certain warrior vibe about him. While she couldn't in a million years picture Kenneth in a camouflage outfit and combat boots, she could definitely picture Jake Tekla in military gear.

He had a way about him as he moved, a certain self-assurance as he talked, as if he knew he could handle whatever came his way. She'd be willing to bet half her company that his self-confidence hadn't come from business training seminars.

He made her feel safe and—out of control, she admitted as she searched the room for something she could possibly pick the lock with. A pang of guilt cut through her that she was thinking about Jake and not Kenneth, who was her friend and sick somewhere up in the mountains.

*Hang on. I'm almost there.*

They would always be friends, but the way she responded to Jake drove the point home that the engagement to Kenneth had been a mistake. With Jake, there was no slow, careful deliberation. He was instant ignition. And it wasn't just the danger, the adrenaline rush as they'd run for their lives yesterday.

She liked that he still remembered her father. That he offered help without hesitation. That he'd immediately respected her decision to slow down.

The attraction she felt wasn't just about the sex. Even if the sex was…

She couldn't believe she was thinking about sex right now. Jake had completely bamboozled her brain. But…

He was the wrong type of guy, at exactly the worst time. And she was too smart to make this many bad decisions in a row.

Mistaking the comfort she'd found in Kenneth's company for love had been understandable. Her mind hadn't been in the right place after Daniel's death. But then she'd let her guilt and pride push her into coming to Lahedeh alone. That had been stupid. She wasn't atoning for anything here. She was putting herself in danger.

Falling for Jake Tekla would be even stupider, no matter how hot and electrifying he was. She needed to stop stumbling from one mistake into the next. She was smarter than this, dammit.

She needed to find Kenneth, then take him home.

And *then* she could think about Jake. And if he really came after her to find her…She'd cross that bridge when she got to it.

But first, she had to get out of here. Which probably wasn't going to happen through the door. The room held nothing she could use to pick the lock, not that she knew how to pick one, but she'd been willing to try.

*Okay, what else?*

She moved closer to the window and silently opened it to investigate the bars outside. The mud brick was as hard as cement, nearly a foot thick, and didn't give when she rattled the iron rods one after the other. She couldn't squeeze through a gap either. The bars were set no more than six inches apart.

Frustration made her want to kick the wall. Instead, she closed the window again. She didn't want to draw the attention of the men in the courtyard.

No matter what Maddox had said, it sure didn't feel like she was being held here for her own safety. The room definitely felt like a prison. Yet Maddox hadn't threatened her. Just the opposite. He'd promised to help. But something was wrong with this situation. Something was wrong with these people. Despite the heat, a chill ran up her spine.

The sound of the doorknob turning made her spin around. Her heart leaped into her throat as she pulled back into the farthest corner. But when instead of one of the soldiers, Jake appeared in the doorway, relief sent her flying across the room and into his arms.

And the next second he was kissing her. Or maybe she'd kissed him first. She didn't care. She was grateful beyond words that he was there. She had her legs wrapped around his waist before she caught herself.

Heat flooded her cheeks as she climbed off him, then moved away from his hard chest and massive biceps, from the reassuring solidity of the man.

He took her by the shoulders so she couldn't go too far. He held her in place, inches from him, concern in his eyes in addition to smoldering heat. "Are you all right?"

"Fine. I'm sorry. I—"

"You shouldn't have come here without me." Anger laced his voice now. "What were you thinking?" He pulled her back against him and held her tightly, as if he'd been worried sick about her.

She had to work to catch her breath. "I left you a note," she mumbled into his neck before looking up into his face.

"I didn't get it. I was here running surveillance. I saw you come in." His gaze captured hers as his jaw worked in silence. A long moment passed before he let her go and stepped back.

"Why did you come here without me?" she asked, now angry too.

"To avoid *this*." His tone filled with exasperation. But then it softened again as he said, "You're okay, and that's the most important thing. We need to get out of here before the rest of the mercenaries arrive. That's only half the team out there."

Before she could say anything, he stepped back out into the hallway, drawing her with him, keeping her in the cover of his wide shoulders.

"Wait." She tried to pull away. As much as she didn't like or trust Maddox, he was her only connection to Kenneth. "Kenneth is alive. Up north, in the mountains. Maddox said he'll take me there in the morning."

A muscle jumped in Jake's cheek. "You're not going anywhere with these men."

She agreed wholeheartedly, so she followed him out into the hallway as he pulled his weapon.

Her gaze hesitated on the gun. "I should have one of those."

"No."

"I need a better plan than just hiding behind you. What if you need backup?" She was familiar with nail guns. How different could a real gun be? "In case we get separated."

"We're not going to get separated."

Then he said something under his breath she didn't catch. Possibly a four-letter word. He bent and pulled a smaller handgun from an ankle holster and handed it to her.

She held the thing with two fingers. It felt alien, scary instead of reassuring. She'd never held a real weapon before. *Why does everything look so easy in the movies?* "Maybe you're right. I don't know if I can actually handle a gun."

"My kid sister can handle a gun," he said with patience as he took it back. But before she could relax, he said, "This is how you take the safety off. Then you point and squeeze the trigger. Even if you don't hit the guy you're aiming at, believe me, he'll still duck. When you just need a second to get behind cover, that'll be enough."

He seemed to have complete faith in her.

So she did what she'd always done at the company: handled whatever came her way, one step at a time. When he handed the weapon back to her, she grabbed it more firmly. "Thanks."

He watched her for a second and must have found whatever he was looking for in her eyes, because he nodded. Then he stole down the hallway.

She followed, but, after just a few steps, pulled up short. Beyond Jake, a man sprawled motionless at the top of the stairs, bloodstains at his temple.

Her heart had been pounding like mad since Jake had come through the door, but now it pounded even harder.

Jake glanced back at her. "He was guarding your room. I had to knock him out."

*Not dead. Thank God.* When Jake moved forward, she went with him, but inside, she was freaking out a little. She'd never been around bloody violence before.

"What else did Maddox tell you?" Jake asked as he reached the guard and bent to the man to check his pulse.

"Nothing." She stopped at a safe distance. "He took my phone."

Jake cast her a sharp glance. "Anything else? Tell me your passport is at the hotel."

"In the room safe." She held the gun awkwardly, making sure she pointed it at the floor. "How are we going to find out where Kenneth is?"

Jake rubbed his hand over his face, and for a second looked worn out— and something else, some emotion she couldn't identify, as if he was on the verge of telling her something. But then he thought better of it and schooled his features. "Maddox has a laptop. I'm going to grab it."

He stashed his gun and picked up the downed mercenary, dragging the man back to the room they'd just left. He didn't even strain.

She followed and closed the door behind them once they were inside, then moved to the window to look out. Half a dozen men sat around the fires still. The others had probably gone to sleep, taking rooms somewhere in the building. Maddox sat apart from the rest, his back resting against the stone circle of the well in the middle, his laptop on his knees.

"How are we going to get the laptop away from him?"

Jake tugged off the unconscious man's boots. "See if you can get his attention. Get him up here."

*How?*

She went with the first thing that popped into her mind.

She cracked the window open. "Excuse me! I have to go to the bathroom. I can't open the door. I think it's stuck. Could you please come up and help?"

Maddox looked at her as if she was a puppy whining at the back door at midnight.

"I'm sorry to be so much trouble." She tried to sound as apologetic as she possibly could.

The man put the laptop down, then stood and lumbered toward the building.

Allison groaned with frustration. "He's not bringing the laptop."

"Don't worry about it." Jake finished with the boots and began working on the man's pants. "Help me with this guy's shirt."

While she worked on that, Jake put the man's pants on over his own. They fit with room to spare.

She undid the shirt buttons as fast as she could. Then she had the shirt at last, and a few seconds later, Jake had on the full commando uniform. He grabbed the unconscious man's hat and shoved it onto his own head as the finishing touch. Now he looked like one of the guys down in the courtyard.

"Stand in the far corner," he said as he dragged the guard to the wall where he'd be hidden behind the door when Maddox pushed it open. "Keep your weapon out of sight."

"What if I need to use it?"

"That'll only happen if I'm dead."

Maddox was calling out somewhere down the hallway. "Bill! Where the hell are you?"

Jake suddenly crowded Allison into the corner, hiding his weapon between them. "Hold still."

Not a problem.

With his lips barely an inch from hers, she was pretty much paralyzed. If she moved, she'd be rubbing up against him. Her mind was clear on the fact that they were in danger, but not all of her body got the memo. That damn awareness tingled through her, like every time they were anywhere near each other.

A second passed, then two, then Maddox was rattling the key in the lock. "Why is this open? I told you to keep your hands off her, dammit. I said I hadn't made a decision yet."

He swore and pushed the door in. His gaze settled on Jake's back, probably taking him for Bill. He strode into the room. "What the hell is going on in here?"

Jake whirled and lunged at him. The two men went down hard.

Allison closed the window with one hand to keep the noise from reaching the courtyard. Her other hand gripped her gun. She couldn't shoot unless she had no other choice, for the same reason Jake hadn't used his weapon. The men outside would hear the shot and rush to investigate.

"Get out of the room." Jake grunted as the two men rolled on the floor.

Instead, she moved closer. Could she knock Maddox out with her weapon? *Stop moving, dammit.* But they didn't.

For a moment, Jake was on the bottom, and Maddox slammed his elbow into his face. Blood spurted from Jake's nose. He didn't even seem to notice. Instead, he used the distraction to push Maddox up and smash his head against the wall.

And while Maddox shook his head, dazed, Jake brought up his gun at last and smashed the butt of his weapon against the man's temple. Maddox went slack, went down, right on top of Jake.

Jake rolled him off. Then he immediately looked at Allison. "You okay?"

The best she could do was give him a wordless nod. The violence…The blood…She was suddenly in a world she'd only seen on TV before.

*Don't fall apart.*

She just concentrated on that while Jake took Maddox's weapon before tying up both Maddox and the guard with their own belts and gagging each with a strip of nasty blanket. The hat he'd taken had been knocked off during the fight. Jake grabbed it now and shoved it back on his head.

He'd beaten the bigger man in the fight. In seconds. Maddox had looked dangerous, but apparently, there were degrees of dangerousness. Jake Tekla stood at the apex of the danger pyramid.

He searched Maddox's pockets. When he came across Allison's phone, she said, "That's mine," and he handed it to her.

"Let's go." He grabbed her by the elbow and pulled her through the door, then locked it on the men. Then he pulled up his shirt and wiped his bloody nose with the inside of his shirttail.

"Is it broken?" Getting her bearings back, she tentatively reached toward his face, but he was already moving on.

"Not this time. We need to get out of here."

He tossed the two guns he'd taken from the men into an empty room, then they hurried down the hallway and down the stairs.

Her heart raced. Her palms sweated. What were the chances of them getting out unnoticed and unchallenged?

Jake looked nothing but calmed and focused. When they reached the downstairs landing, he said, "You stay here."

He wiped his face once again, pulled his borrowed hat lower over his eyes, then stepped out into the courtyard.

By the time she thought of protesting that the laptop wasn't worth getting killed for, he was already striding toward the well where Maddox had been sitting.

A bulletproof vest lay on the ground next to the laptop, and on top of the vest a water bottle. Jake picked up everything as if he'd been ordered to bring Maddox's stuff inside. As he turned to make his way back to Allison, he kept his face hidden.

She couldn't take her eyes off him.

He was incredibly good at this. Of course, as a journalist who traveled to war zones, he had to be. On the one hand, writing travel articles about regions like this seemed insane. On the other hand, as he'd said, ancient temples and monuments were being erased by war. She could understand why he would want to record them. There was something heroic about it, about him.

No wonder her romantic side responded to him. How could she not like a man who kept saving her? The key was not to take the attraction too seriously. Falling for him would be a mistake.

He barely got a few steps from the well when two men stood from the fire and headed for the door. Allison's heart stopped beating. If the men passed close enough to Jake, they'd recognize him as an outsider. But Jake veered toward another entrance as if he'd meant to go that way all along.

She let out a breath of relief before she realized that the men would see her as soon as they came through the door. She darted toward the stairs. *Too far.* No way she'd reach the top in time.

*Handle it.*

She jumped for the shadows, then flattened herself to the wall in the darkest corner, hoping the men would pass by her.

They stopped outside the half-open door.

"Can't wait, man. Wildest damn thing we've done so far, right?" one of them said, slurring his words, sounding more like a drunken frat boy than a commando soldier.

Maybe they'd snuck their booze into the country with their equipment.

The other guy swore suddenly. "I left my gun at the fire. Better get it before Maddox sees me without it and kicks my ass."

"Don't let that jerk intimidate you. We're paying *him*," his buddy said, then stepped through the doorway, less than four feet from Allison.

She pressed herself into the darkness and held still, holding her breath. *Don't look this way. Please, don't look this way.*

She would have been fine if the idiot hadn't stumbled. But he did, swerving precariously to the right. Then he lost his balance altogether, careened forward, and slammed into her. His whiskey breath almost knocked her off her feet.

She tried to push him off.

"Hey there," he mumbled, goofy-happy. Then he groped her, shoving her hard against the wall the next second, one hand painfully squeezing her breast.

He was so wasted, he probably had no idea who she was or what he was doing. He just felt "woman" and went for it. And she couldn't scream for help. She couldn't make any noise at all. She would fare much worse if his buddies came in and discovered what she and Jake had done to their team leader.

Her right hand that held the gun was pinned between them. *What would Jake do? Head-butt?* But what if she knocked herself out instead of knocking out the drunk soldier? *Fudgefudgefudge.* Nothing in her business experience had prepared her for this.

She grabbed his wrist with her free hand, but he roughly yanked up her skirt with his other hand. For the first time, she gave thanks to God that the skirt was ankle length. Gathering all that material took several seconds, especially since she was resisting with all her might.

But too soon, his fingers dug into her thigh. She let go of his wrist that she couldn't hold still anyway, and scratched his face. He didn't even react, clearly anesthetized by alcohol and past feeling pain.

Her heart hammered as she fought against him, trying to get her knee in the right strategic position between his legs.

Then Jake rose out of the darkness, his face a hard mask, his eyes burning with a fierce anger.

She went slack with relief.

The bastard thought she was giving in. He grunted with satisfaction.

"Get your hands off her." Jake kept his voice low, but the menace in it put goose bumps on Allison's arms. *Degrees of dangerousness, indeed.*

The idiot groping her was too far gone to recognize the voice of doom when he heard it. He kept going, refusing to budge when she shoved him with all the strength she had left. But then she had her knee in place at last, and she went for it.

The man bent forward with a harsh, angry grunt.

Jake swung. Instead of pulling back, the man lurched forward. And the next second his head snapped back with a sickening crunch.

He dropped and didn't move again.

Jake wasn't even breathing hard. But he was swearing under his breath.

He stood in front of her like some dark avenging angel. Yet, even though she'd just witnessed the single most violent act in her life, she wasn't afraid of him. Instead, when her knees gave out, she collapsed into his arms.

"Hang on." He handed her Maddox's laptop, then picked her up, tossed her over his left shoulder in a fireman carry, probably to leave his right hand free for his gun. He ran down the hall with her, toward the back of the building.

She couldn't think. Okay, she could, but her thoughts were limited to a single question. *Who on earth is he?*

Because, while she knew little about the XO-ST team or the reasons behind Kenneth's disappearance, she knew this: Jake Tekla was no travel writer.

* * *

"Are you all right?" Jake set Allison down once he reached the back of the building.

He pulled her into his arms and held her tightly for three full seconds, even if they didn't have the time. Then he let her go, unbridled anger pumping through him as he looked her over.

Her face pale, her eyes wide with shock, she cleared her throat. "Thank you. I'm fine."

She sounded…quiet. Her attacker had scared her half to death, and then Jake had lost control and finished the job.

*Dammit.* He had made a point of not killing the man left to guard her, knowing she would see him on their way out. He'd even left the team leader alive. He hadn't wanted to scare her. He wanted her to see him as something other than the stone-cold killer he was.

He could forget about that now. "Hold on for a second."

He squeezed through the window that had let him into the building earlier.

"Okay. Come on." Since the window was low to the ground, he could reach back in to help her through as she scrambled after him.

As soon as her feet were on the ground, he turned to leave, but she grabbed his elbow. "Did you kill that man?"

"Didn't mean to. I thought he knew how to fight. I expected him to evade like a soldier, and I compensated for it. Instead, he moved right into the hit, the idiot." Jake clenched his jaw. "I should have used more restraint. You shouldn't have had to see that." But, hell, when he'd found the guy with his hands on her…"I have two sisters. One of them was abducted last year. Assholes who hurt women push all my buttons."

"Is your sister okay?" Allison let go of his arm.

He took her hand and drew her forward. "She's fine." Fine but still not safe. His sisters would have to remain in hiding until Senator Wharst was brought down and the case was rolled up, until everyone involved sat behind bars.

"I've never seen anyone die before." Allison sounded a little breathless. "I was unconscious when my mom died in the accident. And Daniel died the one night I wasn't at the hospital. God, this was…"

He squeezed her hand. "I need you to be okay with it. At least for now. We need to get out of here as fast as we can."

She sped up. "Given the situation…I'm okay with what you did. Thank you for protecting me."

A shout rose in the building behind them. The danger definitely wasn't over yet. She needed more of his protection.

He held her hand and drew her behind him in the twilight. "Careful where you step."

He kept to the darkest shadows as much as possible, grateful for every bush in the near desertlike landscape. Allison kept up every step of the way without complaint.

After a mile or so, he spotted a dozen peasants herding goats and sheep up ahead, some driving donkey carts, heading into town. He had seen them before in the market square. They'd bed down on the street to be in place for the market at dawn.

He headed straight toward them. "A group of people is probably our best chance to hide."

Allison looked back. "Do you think Maddox's men will catch up to us?"

"Yes."

Sadly, he wasn't wrong.

By the time they reached the small group, the baaing of sheep wasn't the only sound disturbing the night's peace. Car motors roared in the distance.

She moved closer to him. "How long before they reach us?"

"Five minutes, if they head straight this way."

But judging by the zigzagging headlights, they were searching the land in a random pattern, focusing on the stands of scraggly bushes.

"Are you lost, foreigner?" the leader of the shepherds called out to Jake in Farsi.

"We could use your help. With many thanks."

The man watched him, wished him peace. Jake wished it back.

Then the shepherd nodded. "You are welcome to walk with us, you and your woman."

And the rest of his people parted immediately, absorbing the newcomers.

They clearly knew that Allison and Jake were trying to hide. They knew they could get in big trouble for hiding the strangers. But they did it anyway. There was a lot to be said for Afghan hospitality.

Jake thanked them, kept his head down, and kept Allison by his side. With a little luck, from afar, all Maddox's men would see were the locals going to market, something they must have seen dozens of times before. Maybe they wouldn't pay the shepherds much attention.

But in another couple of minutes, Jake could make out the vehicles, definitely on the road now, flying straight at them.

"Keep your head down and stay with these people. Wrap your scarf completely around your face," he told Allison under his breath and gripped his gun, ready to run back down the road and face off with the commandos.

A single man could do a hell of a lot of damage with a single gun if his magazine was full and he was a good shot. He'd hit the gas tank of the first Humvee. That'd block the road. Then he'd take care of the rest of them. If he could find a good hiding spot, a deep enough indentation in the ground he could press himself into, he had a fair chance.

But Allison grabbed his arm and held him back, dragged him toward a donkey cart. "Wait. We can hide."

For a moment he didn't know what she meant, then he recognized the young woman leading the donkey. Kenneth's local girlfriend.

She clearly didn't know what was going on, but maybe she could see in their faces that they were in big trouble, because she gestured at her cart, lifting the edge of the tarp that covered what looked like a dozen goat cheese rounds wrapped in cheesecloth.

The Humvees ate up the distance between them with sickening speed. If bullets started flying, people would get hurt. No time now to come up with another plan. Jake boosted Allison into the cart, then dove after her. The woman blocked the view from behind and, once they were situated, quickly covered them.

Just in time. The ragtag caravan was pulling off the road already to let the vehicles pass, and a minute later, two Humvees slowed as they came in line with them. They rolled forward at the pace kept by the animals.

Jake held his breath, gun ready. The commando guys were probably examining every man and woman.

Allison pressed against him, stiff as the boards of the cart, breathing in quick, scared gulps. He reached out slowly with his left arm and put it around her.

Concealment and evasion had been trained into his blood, but not hers. She was a civilian. If she panicked and bolted, they were finished.

# CHAPTER
# SEVEN

Allison's whole body trembled. She could do nothing to stop the shaking. She was in shock. She recognized the symptoms.

She'd been attacked tonight, then watched a person die in a violent confrontation. She understood that in their given situation, Jake had done what he'd had to do. She was even grateful that he had both the mental and physical strength to do it. But she'd had about what she could take in one night. She wasn't like him. She was rapidly reaching her limit.

*Sweet freaking fudge*, she had to get a grip.

She lay sideways in the narrow donkey cart, wedged against Jake, the laptop behind her, its hard plastic corner digging between her ribs. As the donkey dragged the cart over the rough surface of the dirt road, the whole conveyance shook, causing her to bump against Jake over and over.

Why didn't the shepherds stop? Maybe it wasn't that easy to stop a flock of goats and sheep.

Jake held her steady as best he could, his arm under her head. That helped. She tried to focus on his touch with all her might and shut out everything else, but she couldn't, not when the mercenaries were asking the locals questions.

One of the soldiers spoke some Farsi, apparently. She couldn't understand what he was saying, but she didn't really have to. He'd be asking after two foreigners, a man and a woman. And from his tone, she could tell the questions were peppered with threats.

Other than the Ukrainian girl who'd hid them, nobody had any reason to keep them safe.

Panic pushed Allison to jump up and run. Staying still in the face of imminent danger went against every primal instinct. She gripped Jake's arm, squeezed her eyes shut, her muscles drawn tight as she waited for the bullets she was sure would start flying any second. When the cart hit another rock, she gasped. Louder than she should have.

In the blink of an eye, Jake's warm mouth covered hers.

The sensation short-circuited her fight-or-flight response.

His lips were as firm as the rest of his body, but gentle on hers, the kiss barely a caress, and yet it melted something inside her, relaxing her muscles a little. She found that with his lips on hers, she had trouble focusing on anything else.

She knew he was only trying to distract her—she'd been so panicked, he could probably smell her fear. She went with the kiss anyway, because she desperately needed to be distracted.

She breathed in his masculine scent and tried to get lost in that, tried to block out the arguing voices outside their flimsy shelter.

Then, after an eternity, the Humvees pulled away.

Jake stayed where he was for another second. His thumb stroked her arm once, twice, before he shifted slightly and pushed up the corner of the tarp. He lifted his head to look out, then sat up after a minute while her heart still raced.

He said something to the small group, probably expressing his gratitude.

She sat up too, and simply bowed her head.

More Humvees were coming up the road behind them.

Jake lay back down on his side. He pulled her down next to him and covered them with the tarp again.

God, the place was small. "How long do we have to hide here?"

The Humvees passed by them.

"Just a little longer," Jake said.

They were facing each other but couldn't see each other's faces in the dark. Her head kept banging against the boards of the cart with every bump in the road. Jake reached out and put his arm under her head again. They were like lovers lying in bed. Their position shot her awareness level into the stratosphere.

Every time he was this close to her, her body suddenly remembered that she was still alive. She hadn't died with Daniel. Or Kenneth.

*No.* She stopped that line of thinking immediately. Kenneth was still alive. Maddox had said so. She refused to listen to the small part of her that had been softly suggesting for days now that Kenneth was gone, that if he was still alive, he would have found a way to contact her.

Jake shifted next to her. Her breast pressed against him even tighter. And then she couldn't think of anyone else but Jake. Suddenly she couldn't find enough air in the cart to breathe.

*Wrong place. Wrong man.* She didn't even know who he really was—definitely not a travel writer. But no matter how many times she repeated that in her head, her skin still tingled.

Half an hour passed before he peeled back the tarp to look out again. "We're about there."

She peeked out too. They were in the middle of nowhere.

Jake slipped from the cart, and helped her out. He scribbled something on a crumpled gum wrapper he pulled from his pocket, then handed it to the woman who'd hid them.

"When you get to Kabul, call this man. His name is Gabe Cannon. He's my friend. He's an honest man. He'll help you get out of the country safely."

The woman took the paper with tear-filled eyes, nodded rapidly without quite raising her gaze to Jake.

"You will leave?" Allison asked.

"Tomorrow." A bittersweet smile came onto the woman's face. "If you sure Mr. Ken not come back."

"We're sure," Jake said.

He moved on to the goatherds and thanked them for not saying anything to the commando soldiers, then he led Allison away into the darkness.

The young Ukrainian woman waved shyly after them. Allison waved back.

Jake led her into the fields, setting a fast pace. In just minutes, they were way ahead of the small group. He stayed focused, constantly scanning the darkness. She tried not to jump at every little night noise.

"Thank you for saving me. Again."

"You saved me this time." He glanced back at her. "Your kindness to a woman you owed nothing saved us both. She helped us because of what you did yesterday. She must have told the others. They kept quiet to protect us, because you gained their respect."

His approval tingled inside her chest. She smiled at his back.

"Where are we going?" she asked after a minute.

"I have the Land Rover hidden up ahead."

And sure enough, within a couple of hundred feet, in a clump of thick bushes, his tan SUV waited for them, camouflaged with branches.

He brushed the branches off and unlocked the car. And as soon as they were in, he pulled her to him and wrapped his arms around her.

Her heart thudded against his hard chest.

"Allison, I—"

"Yes."

His lips were on hers the next second.

She melted into him. Maybe it was the adrenaline rush of their escape. Maybe it was the fact that she had no resistance when it came to Jake Tekla. Maybe it was the moon, or Mercury in retrograde or whatever. But everything disappeared except him, his need for her and her need for him.

They both smelled like dust and sweat, and she didn't care.

He kissed her to the stars and back.

They both wanted more, and they knew it, but for once, they were both smart enough to know when to stop. So, after another minute, they pulled apart, breathing hard.

Jake let her go and started up the car.

She slipped back to her seat and put on her seat belt as the SUV rolled forward.

They were heading back to town. Not that their troubles were over. She needed to get her passport, money, and clothes before they went north to find Kenneth. Once she had him, she wanted to get him out of the country and to serious medical help as fast as possible—if he was as sick as Maddox had said.

She didn't plan on coming back to Lahedeh. She would hire Jake to take her and Kenneth straight to Kabul.

But to get her passport, cash, and her luggage, they had to go back to the hotel. The only question was, were the mercenaries waiting for them there?

Okay, that wasn't the only question. She had another one.

She stole a glance at Jake. If he was a travel writer, she was a one-eyed monkey on a tricycle.

So who was he really? She meant to find out before the night was over.

***

They rode in silence, keeping an eye out for Humvees. Jake kept running the tip of his tongue along his teeth, remembering the taste of Allison's lips under his, wanting to kiss her again. No matter how many times he kissed her, he always wanted more. He was beginning to think he might be in trouble here.

"Are you some kind of a spy?" she asked out of the blue.

His gaze snapped to her. "Why would you say that?"

"I understand the need for confidentiality." She remained surprisingly calm. "But I'd appreciate knowing at least the basics. My life is on the line here. Are you with the CIA or the NSA or something? Are you in Afghanistan hunting terrorists?"

He bit back a groan. Had he really thought that she wasn't going to figure it out?

"Not exactly." He lifted his right hand from the steering wheel and tried to reach surreptitiously for the small firearm he'd given her earlier that now lay on her lap.

She deftly moved the gun out of his reach.

He turned down the AC as if that had been his intention all along and put his hand back on the steering wheel.

"Will you have to kill me if you tell me?" She'd begun to smile, but then suddenly turned serious. "I probably shouldn't joke about that."

"I'm not going to hurt you." *How could she even think that?* Because she'd just seen him kill a man. *Ah hell.*

He could probably stonewall her at least a little longer. He didn't want to. A connection had built between them. He wanted that connection. "I'm with the FBI."

Her breath caught. "Does your being here have anything to do with Kenneth?"

Jake didn't like the turn the conversation was taking. He didn't want to involve her any more than she was already involved. But he didn't want to keep lying to her either.

"I never heard of him before I met you, but now I'm starting to think he's somehow connected to the case I'm working."

Long seconds passed before she put forth her next question, a tone of dread in her voice this time. "Is that why you offered to help me find him?"

He wished he had a different answer to give her. He turned to her and held her gaze, unblinking, as he said, "Yes." He wanted to leave it at that but couldn't. "There's something I need to tell you."

They reached the outskirts of Lahedeh. Light traffic. No sign of Humvees. He looked at her again. "Kenneth is dead."

She drew back as if he'd struck her. Blinking rapidly, she turned her head from him, toward the window. Her voice broke on the single word, "When?"

And there he went, rolling down shit mountain in a barrel. His fingers tightened on the steering wheel. *No helping it now.* "He was killed a month after he got here."

She rested her head against the window and closed her eyes, pain etched on her face. The way her chin trembled wrenched his guts. He would much rather have taken a punch in the face than look at her struggling with grief.

A full minute passed before her tears spilled over. "I should have come as soon as he stopped calling."

"This is not your fault."

Strained silence stretched between them, endless seconds ticking by before she said, "I don't know if I would have survived Daniel's battle with cancer and then his death without Kenneth." She covered her face. "And now Kenneth is dead too. I'm like one of those Black Widows."

The need to draw her into his arms was overpowering. Completely illogically, Jake was suddenly jealous of two dead men. "None of this was your fault."

"I should have talked Kenneth out of coming here," she said on a broken whisper, dropping her hands. "We'd just gotten engaged. He wanted to go on an engagement trip. I was too busy at the company. Early spring. Start of construction season. Since I didn't have time, when the opportunity arose to come here, he took it."

"This is *not* your fault," he said again, as emphatically as he could, and reached for her hand, but she wouldn't let him take it.

They rode in silence.

She was in pain, and he could do nothing to help her. He had *added* to her pain by not being honest with her from the beginning. If he wasn't sitting on it, he would have kicked his own ass.

"How long have you known?" she asked.

"Almost from the beginning. His name was on a roster my team looked at."

"You lied to me almost from the moment we met."

"Yes." One word. Acknowledgment. No excuses.

"You should have told me."

He kept his eyes on the road. "You're a civilian. And I'm on a covert FBI mission."

She clenched her jaw.

He looked at her, *really* looked at her, and willed her to see the truth in his eyes. "I'm sorry."

She wrapped her arms around herself. "You used me."

The tone of pain and betrayal in her voice just about killed him. "At first, you were an asset, someone with information I needed. I'm here to complete a mission."

Damn fine time to remember that. He wished he'd found his professionalism earlier. Like when he'd been nailing her against the wall at the compound.

She turned to him, and she must have been thinking along the same lines, because she said. "I wish we hadn't…"

Yeah. He'd really crossed every line there. Hell of a thing was, given the chance, he would do it again.

"What I let happen between us is inexcusable. I know better than that. I'm sorry, Allison." Again, he wanted to take her hand, but now was definitely not the right moment. "I never meant to hurt you. Please believe me."

"I'm not inclined to believe anything that comes out of your mouth. I'm sure you understand." She sounded infinitely tired.

She closed her eyes.

He wished she would rave and rant, or even shoot him in the kneecap, but of course, she wouldn't. Because Allison Myers was a lady to the bitter end.

"After we stop by the hotel, I'm taking you to Kabul. I'm going to get you safely on a plane out of Afghanistan. I swear." The only thing he could do for her now.

She didn't react. They rode in silence for several minutes.

"So what are you after here?" she finally asked, opening her eyes again. "The XO-ST team? I'm guessing that's why you went to the compound tonight?"

Best thing would be to tell her nothing. But keeping her in the dark had only hurt her so far. And the XO-ST team was connected to Senator Wharst via Mitch Wharst, who was connected to Kenneth, who was connected to Allison. Maybe she knew something or had a key piece of the puzzle without realizing she had it.

And beyond that—Jake didn't want to keep lying to her. It shouldn't have mattered. He'd certainly lied before to keep a mission confidential or to make sure people stayed safe. For the most part, people he came across during missions…he'd never seen them again. Chances were, he would never see Allison again either.

Yet part of him thought differently. Part of him planned on finding her when this whole mess was over. Which sounded kind of serious, and he didn't do serious. Damned if he knew what was going on with him. Maybe that infection that had nearly taken him down in Venice had messed up his brain.

He put that disturbing possibility away and made a strategic decision.

"What you want to know is confidential information," he warned. "If I tell you, you'll be in danger simply because you know about it. People tried to kill me because I know about it. My sister was kidnapped and got hurt because I knew about this. In fact, right now, both of my sisters are at an FBI safe house. Do you understand?"

She nodded. "Kenneth is dead. I'm involved already. I need to know." Then she added quietly. "What I don't know can hurt me too."

He couldn't argue with that. She *was* already caught up in all this mess.

He rolled his shoulders. Watched the road. "About a year ago, I was involved in finding Khanbaba's hidden gold in the old cisterns outside of Lahedeh."

"Khanbaba? As in the warlord?"

"Right. The treasure was supposed to be taken off to a museum in Kabul, but instead it was stolen by a guy called Brent Foley. Anyway, one thing led to another, and pretty soon, out of the five people who knew about the gold, Foley and I were the only ones left alive. He wanted to eliminate me." Jake clenched his jaw. "He tried to get to me through my sisters."

"How does Foley link to XO-ST?"

"He quit the military, but he needed a way back into Afghanistan to get the gold out. He started XO-ST with a couple of his ex-military buddies."

"Did he smuggle out the treasure?"

"Yes. Then he tried to get it to the US with Senator Wharst's help."

He paused and made sure he carefully worded what he said next. "Did Kenneth ever tell you anything about the senator?" He glanced at her. "Anything that could be a source of blackmail?"

She paled. "Do you think Mitch had a part in whatever it is?" Then her eyes narrowed as she said defensively, "Do you think Kenneth was involved?"

"I don't think he was." Jake had given this some serious thought already. "I don't think even the senator knew about the gold, let alone his little brother. Foley blackmailed the senator into using his private yacht to sneak some sealed crates into the US. According to the senator, and I believe him, Foley told him the crates contained a few dozen military-grade weapons for wealthy gun enthusiasts."

"What could Foley have possibly been blackmailing the senator with?"

"That's what I'm here to find out. Senator Wharst knows that a few of us know something. His political career would be a lot safer if we disappeared. Which means we won't be safe until we take him down."

"Where's Foley now?"

"Dead."

She gave a slow, stunned blink but didn't ask any details. "Where's the rest of your team?"

He'd told her too much already. "Let's keep that on a need-to-know basis."

She didn't push for more. She simply nodded.

But then she said, "I'm not forgiving you for lying to me and using me. I'm just stifling the overwhelming urge to strangle you, until we're safe."

"Yes, ma'am." He admired her reasonable practicality as much as he admired everything else about her.

He stepped on the brake to stop for a red light. They reached the center of town at last. He didn't want to approach the hotel on the north road, which the XO-ST boys would expect, so he went around when the light turned green.

"It'd help if I knew what Mitch Wharst was doing here. We found nothing so far to connect the senator to Afghanistan other than his brother. Maybe Foley was blackmailing the congressman with something his little brother did in Lahedeh."

She thought for a while, frowning. "As far as I know, Mitch's business interests are in the US. He buys office buildings from the government on the cheap when they do some token downsizing every couple of years to improve their approval rating. He then rents the same buildings back to the next administration that hires new government employees to improve unemployment figures to boost their approval rating. The senator sets Mitch up with connections. It's a lucrative business if you can get it, but to get it, you have to be an insider. Maybe Mitch found a way to do the same thing here."

Jake definitely needed to pass this on to Gabe and Troy. He hated corrupt government shit. "Maybe that's it."

Allison shrugged. "Except there's nothing illegal in what Mitch does. Unethical, yes. It definitely costs the taxpayers a ton of money, but it's not against the law."

*Of course not.*

In general, the SEALs had better equipment than most of the military, but Jake had friends who'd died because they'd driven out on patrols in unreinforced Humvees or gone to battle without a proper bulletproof vest. Because there wasn't enough money in the budget, because politicians like Senator Wharst back in DC were dicking around, rerouting government funds into their friends' and their families' pockets.

"The only strange thing is," Allison said, "I could swear when Kenneth first mentioned Lahedeh, he said Mitch came here on vacation, not on business. Which makes no sense. Mitch is an adrenaline junkie. He's into extreme sports. They don't have much bungee jumping or avalanche snowboarding here. But he must have hooked up with some businessmen, because he brought in Kenneth."

Something pricked Jake's instincts, an idea too vague to take solid shape. "Have you talked to Mitch lately?"

"The last time I phoned him, he swore to me he didn't know what happened to Kenneth. Then he stopped taking my calls. I think he feels guilty because he talked Kenneth into coming here."

They finally reached the hotel. Jake stopped, partially hidden by a delivery truck. A familiar Humvee idled across the road, the two men inside watching the hotel's entrance. A couple of other commandos loitered at key points around the building, men he hadn't seen at the compound.

The rest of the team must have arrived. Just what he didn't need.

He watched them for a few seconds before turning to Allison. "You need to get down."

She released her seat belt and slid off her seat to crouch in the foot well.

Maybe she didn't trust him, but she trusted his skill and judgment when dealing with trouble. For now, Jake would take what he could get.

Since these guys didn't know his SUV and had never seen his face, he pulled out from behind the truck, drove up to the hotel, then into the attached, multilevel parking garage, all the way to the top floor, to the very back. He stashed Maddox's laptop under the seat.

Those XO-ST boys had no way to connect Jake's SUV to Allison, so the laptop should be safe there. "Tell me the combination to the room safe. I'll go up and grab your stuff. You need to stay out of sight."

She hugged her knees. "And if they search the parking garage?"

She didn't say that she was scared, but Jake could see it in her eyes, in spite of the especially determined and brave expression she was doing her best to fake.

*Would the men search car to car?*

Truth was, he didn't want to leave her. He would never forget what had happened to Jasmine when he hadn't been there. He would never forgive himself.

"On second thought, let's go together." He handed Allison the keys to the SUV. "Anything goes wrong in there, you get back to this car and get out of here. Understood?"

She couldn't get out of the car fast enough.

The lingering smell of exhaust and leaked motor oil filled the closed space. He led her to the back of the garage. "We can't go through the lobby. They'll be watching the elevators."

He helped her scale the metal service ladder to the roof. She didn't need much help. Despite the long skirt she wore, she moved nearly as fast as he did.

They stole across the parking garage roof to the open window of the third-floor utility room of the hotel.

When he pushed in the window, she asked, "How did you know we can get in this way?"

The words "lucky guess" were on his lips, but he caught himself. No more lying to her, not unless he absolutely had to keep some vital information confidential. "I make sure every day that the window is open, in case I need a quick way in or out in an emergency."

He went through first.

The smell of cleaning supplies hung in the air. Boxes and boxes of the stuff lined the walls, stacked on metal shelves, all the print on the boxes in Chinese. Welcome to the global economy.

He crossed the small, narrow room in half a dozen steps and looked out into the hallway. All clear. Of course, he could only see to the turn in the hallway in each direction, less than ten feet. Someone could be standing just around the corner, and Jake wouldn't know it. If Maddox had a man out there, Jake would just have to deal with him.

He stepped back to help Allison, but she'd already climbed in.

"Do you have your weapon ready?"

She nodded, but her forehead wrinkled with self-doubt. She had no experience with guns. He hated to put her to the test if he didn't have to.

"Your room is only one floor down. You could stay here and hide," he offered.

But the door opened before she could answer.

Greenhorn Number Two from the commando team exploded in, all wild-eyed and jumpy with surprise to discover people in the tiny room. He looked disappointed, almost as if he'd been hoping to hide in there, breathing hard, as if he'd been running.

As he looked at Allison, his eyes flared with recognition. He immediately raised his weapon.

# CHAPTER
# EIGHT

Jake attacked the man, bringing him down and yanking his gun away from him in the same movement. He rolled them and used the guy's body to shove the door shut, then he pressed his elbow into the man's neck. The sucker was done.

Way too fast.

Jake was good, but taking down a US soldier shouldn't have been *this* easy. No way.

Where the hell did Maddox find his new recruits? Sure as fuck not in the military. No way this guy had been through battle. He looked like he was shitting his pants: panting, eyes darting with panic, limbs frozen in defeat. If Jake had to guess, he'd guess that the man hadn't even seen basic training.

"Who are you and what are you doing with XO-ST?" Jake kept his voice down so anyone who might be outside in the hallway wouldn't hear, but he made sure the tone was sharp enough that Wimp Boy here would know a response was expected.

"I'm sorry." The idiot sucked in air in ragged gasps. "The targets aren't supposed to be American." His voice broke. "Oh God. Alex is dead. Oh God. Don't kill me. Please. I didn't sign up for this. It's not my fault. I swear."

Who the hell was Alex? Greenhorn Number One? Jake didn't really care. His mind grabbed on to *I didn't sign up for this.*

"What did you sign up for?"

Tears sprang into the guy's eyes, which made him look ten years younger— a freaking kid. "I can't say." He gasped. "Maddox will kill me if I tell anyone." More gasps. "I signed a confidentiality agreement."

Jake growled into the idiot's face and pushed harder into his neck.

"One month." Greenhorn croaked out the words. "Training. Real-life combat action. One kill." He struggled for air pretty seriously now. "I'm sorry."

*Combat tourism.* The expression Jake had overheard in the courtyard now hit him like a torpedo in the face. As the puzzle pieces came together at last, disbelief was quickly followed by anger that gained heat as it filled him.

*Combat tourism?*

He seriously wanted to hurt whoever had come up with the idea.

But right now, his top priority was getting Allison out of here safely. He would have to sort out the combat tourism goatfuck later.

He made sure the man was completely disarmed, then got off him, yanked him up and shoved him toward the window. "Get the hell out of here. Catch a cab. Go straight to the airport. Don't come back." He made sure his face reflected that he was as serious as a fire on a submarine. "I see you again, you're dead."

The idiot scrambled through the window as if his life depended on it, which it did.

*Of all the stupid, unconscionable, unforgivable things to do—*

"Do you think Kenneth…" Allison started, then stopped. She was still wedged in the corner, her face pale, her eyes round with shock.

Before Jake could say anything, the door burst open and Maddox charged in.

*Should have snapped the bastard's neck earlier.*

If Jake had known what *combat tourism* meant back when they'd fought at the compound, he might have. Once again, he lunged for the man instead of going for his weapon. He didn't want any stray bullets with Allison in the small room.

Of course, as soon as he tackled Maddox to the ground, two other assholes rushed in—one bald, one bearded—filling the small room to capacity. Their guns aimed, they shouted at Jake to stop. He rolled around enough so they couldn't fire without hitting their team leader.

They were three against one. And unlike Greenhorn, these were seasoned commando soldiers who weren't afraid to fight dirty. Jake wasn't going to last long, but he wanted to last long enough to give Allison a chance to escape.

Baldie tried to grab him from behind. Jake smashed his elbow into his face, kicked him into his buddy. Then he struggled to his feet while beating off

Maddox, but the bastard was back on him the next second. Still, Jake managed to keep himself between Allison and the men, giving her time to jump out the window.

She had the car keys. What the hell was she waiting for? He'd told her to run at the first sign of trouble, dammit.

He got in a good punch, then ducked before Maddox could reciprocate. He grabbed the man, went for a chokehold, plowed their combined weight into the other two, and yelled at Allison. "Go!"

But instead of darting for the window, she stepped forward, raising her gun. "Stop!"

Of course, she couldn't shoot, for the same reason Maddox's boys couldn't. No telling who'd get shot in this situation.

The bearded guy tried to put a wrestling hold on Jake. Jake head-butted him backward and put him down. The other one—the bald piece of shit built like a freaking navy destroyer—shoved by the whirling mess of elbows and fists and went for Allison.

Jake struggled to block his way, but Maddox used the momentary distraction and clocked him full force. His head snapped back.

His face hurt like a sonofabitch, as if this time Maddox had driven his nose into his brain. Jake shook off the pain, turned his head in time to see Allison focus on the man coming for her.

"Go!" Jake shouted.

She still could have run. She didn't.

Jake clocked Maddox, fighting off the other guy with a kick, trying to keep an eye on Allison.

"I'm sorry." Allison locked her elbows and shot Baldie in the chest.

The bullet brought the guy to his knees. He swayed for one second, then head-planted into the floor. No second shot necessary.

*Did she just apologize for plugging the guy?* Jake grinned at her from under his two attackers, his ears ringing. *Once a lady, always a lady.*

He could so fall in love with her.

The thought, and Maddox's mad boxing skills, distracted him for a split second—long enough for a respectable left hook to catch him in the chin from Beard Boy.

Maddox pinned Jake down while Beard Boy lunged toward Allison next.

*Oh hell, no.*

Jake knocked back Maddox, then caught the other guy's foot and yanked him down, put him in a headlock, and rolled over him. Maddox drew away, but only to throw himself onto the pile. With his added weight on top of Jake, the other guy's neck broke with a snap.

Maddox didn't even slow down. He was like a freaking machine.

But Jake had better training. In a few more seconds, he was on Maddox, holding him down—elbow to the throat, knee to the chest—blinking blood out of his eyes as he asked, "What happened to Kenneth Hatch?"

He was pretty sure he knew. But he hoped to hell he was wrong about what he thought adrenaline-junkie Mitch Wharst had been doing here, what Mitch had gotten Kenneth into. If Jake was right, it had nothing to do with a business opportunity in irrigation.

"I want the truth." And he was ready to break ribs to get it. He pressed his knee into Maddox's sternum.

With a grunt, Maddox went for the knife tucked into his combat boot.

"Jake!" Allison shouted a warning from behind them.

But Jake had already grabbed the knife and pressed it against Maddox's neck. "Combat tourism. Is that what happened?"

Anger boiled in his blood. Freaking fireworks were going off in his head. "Do you have any idea how much effort the US military puts into getting the locals to trust us, trying to convince them that we're not the bad guys?"

It made a big difference when people cooperated instead of looking for every opportunity to shoot you in the back.

He could barely breathe from the fury that coursed through him. "Then idiots like you come along…"

"You gonna kill me over this?" Maddox goaded him. "One of your own, over a couple of dead camel jockeys? Come on, man."

"You're not one of my own. You're nothing like me. You're one of the bastards who gives my country a bad name. A country I happen to love and believe in." Jake said each word with emphasis.

Maddox still didn't grasp that this was his come-to-Jesus moment. He still didn't look scared. He was looking at Jake as if he couldn't believe Jake didn't get it. "You think it's fun babysitting those greenhorns? You think I'd do it if it weren't for the money? Our government contracts are getting smaller and smaller. The local authorities are riding my ass every waking minute with complaints. You know how much I have to pay out in local bribes? The media is portraying us as—"

"What happened to Kenneth Hatch?" Jake sure as hell didn't need excuses or some twisted explanation. He just wanted Allison to have her answer.

Maddox grunted. "That idiot didn't follow orders and got himself killed in his first exchange of fire."

Allison gasped behind them. Jake wished he could see her face, wished he could go to her to comfort her, but not yet. He had to see this through to the end.

"Was Mitch Wharst one of your *tourists?*"

At the mention of the Wharst name, Maddox clamped his mouth shut, his eyes blazing with defiance.

Jake pressed the blade harder against his neck and waited.

"What do you think?" Maddox said at last, going slack, as if giving up, but then he bucked up suddenly the next second, taking a nick that drew blood, swiping Jake aside as he dove for Allison, and Jake knew exactly what the bastard planned, but didn't have time to stop him.

Maddox grabbed Allison, twisted the weapon from her hand, and pushed the barrel against her temple.

"Drop your weapon and kick it over to me." He barked the words at Jake, a look of superiority on his face. He thought he had them.

So Jake let him think he'd won. He kicked his gun away. "Let's talk about this. Think about what you're doing."

"We're leaving." Maddox dragged Allison toward the window. "But don't think this is over. You messed with the wrong people."

He half turned to the window to shove Allison out in front of him. But Jake still had the knife and threw it with all his strength, hard enough to embed it in the man's neck.

Maddox went down with a thud, his inert weight dragging Allison to the floor with him.

She didn't scream or panic. She smacked him in the head with her elbow. And judging by the way his face squirted blood, she'd broken his nose.

She didn't apologize this time.

She was losing a little bit of her polish. For some weird reason, the thought made Jake laugh, which earned him a questioning look.

"I'm a bad influence on you," he said as he picked up his gun.

"Are you okay?" he asked Allison, instead of dragging her into his arms and kissing her, inhaling her, as he wanted. He couldn't stand seeing her in danger.

Her eyes were wide with shock. "Are we just going to leave him here?"

"Can't save him without a med kit."

Maddox was unconscious already. He was losing blood too fast. The knife had sheared his main artery in half.

Allison carefully stayed away from the spreading pool of crimson and kept her gaze on Jake, making a concentrated effort not to look at the dead and the dying.

"Kenneth would…" Tears filled her eyes. "I can't believe Kenneth would do something like this. If he did, he only did it to impress Mitch."

A police siren sounded outside before Jake could respond. Hotel staff, or maybe one of the other guests, had reported the gunshot.

"We need to get going."

He looked out into the hallway. All clear.

"Let's finish this." He stepped out. "Our safest bet is the fire stairs. We could be cornered in the elevator."

They stole down to the floor below without being seen, but one of the XO-ST mercenaries stood guard at the door to Allison's room. Trying to control the body count was a lost cause at this point, but Jake held back, anyway. He shot the guy in the right shoulder, disabling his gun arm, but not killing him.

The man went down, screaming threats and obscenities. Jake rushed up to him and kicked his gun far down the hallway, then he pushed into the room with Allison.

The place had been tossed, but at least the safe was intact, although it looked like it'd taken a couple of good whacks. Allison grabbed her laptop, passport, and money while Jake threw what clothes he could grab into her suitcase, then they were out of there, running back down the hallway while the shot man cursed after them.

"What about your stuff?" Allison asked, breathless as they ducked into the staircase.

Jake thought of the extra guns and ammo in his room. He was supposed to return those to US Air Force Forward Operating Base Oqab, a small compound tucked in a corner of Kabul International Airport.

Except, he wasn't going to risk Allison's life for a bagful of guns. The Air Force had lots of others. He had his passport on him. "I'm good."

He checked the hallway before they exited the stairs. All clear. They ran back to the supply room and stepped over the bodies on their way to the window. No way to avoid the blood now.

Maddox had bled out, the neck wound no longer pulsing.

Allison wouldn't look at any of the men. She carefully kept her gaze straight ahead. She looked shaken but held herself together as she climbed out. She followed right behind Jake as they ran across the roof to the emergency ladder.

Jake went first, gun still in hand. "Almost there."

"I'm fine." She held the smaller gun as she scanned their surroundings, alert, ready for anything.

She looked nothing like the woman who'd run blindly from the street thugs when he'd first seen her. That woman he'd been attracted to, drawn to her sheer beauty. This one…looked like a woman he could fall in love with.

He didn't have time to ponder all that under the circumstances. He needed his full focus to make sure they weren't seen and captured.

The Land Rover waited where they'd left it. Still no sign of XO-ST in this corner of the garage. As soon as Allison got in, she ducked down without having to be told.

Jake jumped behind the wheel and got going, not too fast, not too slow. He grabbed a map, laid it over the steering wheel like a tourist trying to figure out where he was going. He passed right by the police cars at the entrance.

No Humvees in sight. Maddox's men had probably taken off when the cops got here.

Jake kept an eye out for them as he drove the main road out of town, toward Kabul, kept checking the rearview mirror, scanning not just the road but the sidewalks and the rooftops too. He didn't want any nasty surprises.

He was *not* going to let Allison get hurt.

***

When Jake said, "It should be safe now," Allison moved up into the passenger seat and stretched her cramped legs.

They were on the outskirts of town, riding into an empty landscape.

She put on her seat belt, but she was still seeing Maddox in that pool of blood. And the other two. *God.* Her hands trembled. *Fudgefudgefudgefudgefudge.*

Jake reached over and took her hand. "Breathe slowly and evenly. You'll be fine. You had a pretty tough couple of days. This is normal after major shock. It'll get better."

"I shot that guy."

"It was either you or him. I'm glad it was him."

"Me too," she said. She wanted to live. She felt terrible over squeezing the trigger, but she hadn't gone after them. They'd come after her. And she'd fought. And she'd fight again.

She drew a deep breath, filled her lungs. Her hands stopped trembling.

Jake let her go to hold on to the steering wheel. Outside of town, the road was in rough shape, the SUV bouncing around as he drove around potholes big enough to swallow a wheel.

She missed his touch immediately. She probably shouldn't. She was supposed to be mad at him for lying to her. But somehow all that seemed pretty distant and insignificant after the bloody battle they'd just fought together.

At this very second, all she could think of was that he was the man she'd want by her side if she was in trouble. And maybe even when she wasn't. A heavy feeling settled into her chest at the thought that in a couple of hours, he would drop her off at the airport and she might never see him again.

"So what's next for you?" she asked, not sure if he would be at liberty to tell her. She hoped he wouldn't head straight back to danger.

"I'm going back to the US with you. I got the information I was looking for here."

Some of the tightness in her chest relaxed. She did care about him. She didn't want him hurt. She wished…

*No.* She couldn't wish *that.*

So she wished she hadn't gotten tangled in his secret op. She wished Kenneth hadn't been involved with XO-ST. She wished she could rewind and restart.

"If I'd been a better friend to Kenneth," she said on a sigh, "maybe he would have confided in me that he was so desperate for Mitch's approval. If I'd known, I might have been able to talk him out of this whole trip."

"He made his own choices," Jake said quietly.

Tears choked her. "I don't understand how. Not something as abhorrent and wrong as this. You didn't know him, but this was not Kenneth."

"People do stupid shit under peer pressure."

She shook her head. There had to be limits. But she knew how desperately Kenneth had wanted Mitch's approval, wanted to be best buddies, wanted that link to Mitch's brother, Senator Wharst.

Her grief for a friend mixed with the bitterness of disappointment.

She was mad at Kenneth for the whole combat tourism insanity. And she was so freaking mad at herself for not figuring it all out sooner.

She tried to make sense of what she'd learned, and still couldn't. She hated knowing what she knew. But she would have hated not having any answers even more.

And she owed the answers to Jake.

"I'm just going to forgive you for lying to me. Because I think you had the right reasons at heart. And because I can't be mad at everyone all at once."

"Thank you." His eyes held relief and something more. Concern. For her.

She had something else she needed to say. "Thank you for seeing this through with me."

He *had* kept her safe. And he was still doing it, driving her to Kabul.

She had to let go of some of the anger and disappointment that swirled inside her, so she let go of the part that related to Jake.

"Your sisters will be glad that you're going home," she said. "Jasmine and…"

"Mandy."

"They'll be safe now?"

"Soon." His features were etched with determination.

He clearly felt protective of his sisters, making no secret of the fact that he cared a great deal about Mandy and Jasmine. Allison liked that about him.

"I always wanted a brother. Especially when I was younger. It would have been nice to have someone to play with."

"Were you a lonely child?"

"A little. But it was a lot better than it could have been. After my mother died, my father left his office job and started up his own construction business so he wouldn't have to shove me into day care and never see me. He took me to the work sites." She smiled. "I don't even want to think about how many safety regulations we broke."

Jake grinned at her. "I can see you with pigtails and in a hard hat."

"No joke. I wore hard hats like other girls wear princess tiaras. I had my own overalls and work boots. Still, if a safety inspector caught us, that would have been that."

"You loved it."

Her smile grew. "I was with Dad. Of course, I loved it."

"You miss him."

She lost the smile.

"When did he die?" Jake asked.

"Two years ago. Almost at the same time as Daniel." Her father and her fiancé had died three weeks apart. A heart attack stole her father; cancer had stolen Daniel.

"That had to be tough." Jake glanced at her. "And through all that loss, Kenneth was there for you."

She gave a tight nod. "I'm so incredibly grateful to him still, and I'm so mad at him, I can barely see straight." She sighed. "Not about the other woman." She clenched her jaw, then had to work on relaxing it. "But that he would get involved with the combat tourism insanity."

She just couldn't comprehend it. She couldn't comprehend anyone coming up with the idea, let alone participating, least of all Kenneth.

They rode in silence for a while. Then Jake asked, "Would it help if I found his body for you?"

Her head snapped to him, the air caught in her chest. "Do you know where he's buried?"

"No. But I could try finding out."

He could stay. He could investigate. He would be in danger.

"No," she said after a long moment. "If he's resting on some hillside here, let him rest. Digging his body up and dragging him halfway around the world is not going to change anything at this stage. I'll let his cousins and the company know, in case they don't agree with me."

They passed another mile in silence. Then another.

Too many thoughts crowded in her head. Daniel, Kenneth, Jake…She'd made so many mistakes. She didn't want to make another.

But what would be the bigger mistake, letting Jake go, or holding on to him?

# CHAPTER
# NINE

As they approached Kabul, Jake did his best to avoid as many potholes as possible while Allison slept next to him.

Exhaustion had knocked her out, and she slept through most of the four-hour drive to the capital city. He couldn't blame her. The only surprise was that she hadn't crashed sooner. Neither of them had slept since the night before, and she'd had one shock after the other. She needed the rest.

He was glad that she slept.

Too many crazy thoughts circled around in his head. Like he didn't want to let her go when they got back to the US. Like he was falling in love with her.

To reroute his attention, he called Gabe and Troy. His proximity to Kabul and its towers meant he had cell phone reception. He got through on the first try and gave a quick update.

"Let me get this straight." Gabe's tone dripped with anger. "XO-ST brings civilians onto the team for a month, gives them some half-assed training, and if they're willing to pay for the privilege, then takes them on patrol and lets them take shots at *suspected* insurgents?"

"Combat tourism." Jake's blood boiled all over again just from saying the phrase.

"Sounds like the ultimate adrenaline shot," Troy rasped. "For jerkoffs who liked to play those shoot-'em-up video games when they were kids but didn't have the actual balls to join the military when they grew up."

Troy's vocal cords had been damaged in the same explosion that had scarred his face and killed the woman he loved. Troy never talked about the incident. Gabe had told Jake this much only as a warning so he wouldn't ask questions.

Jake glanced over at Allison, grateful to have her safe and right next to him.

"Mitch Wharst is not in the XO-ST roster." Gabe was clicking away on his keyboard on the other end. "I bet he came in with fake papers."

Right. Because nothing was ever easy. Luckily, difficulty was their specialty.

"Wait," Troy rasped. "So now we know that Brent Foley blackmailed Senator Wharst with his little brother's participation in this lovely little piece of goatfuckery. But we still have no hard proof that Wharst knew about combat tourism."

"At least we have enough information to close down XO-ST." Jake was damned happy about that. "Those idiots need to be done and gone."

Gabe had rosters of the teams that showed civilian names mixed in with the professionals. They had Kenneth Hatch's death. And Mitch Wharst sounded like a weak-ass yuppie. Lean on him hard enough, he'd squeak.

"We'll bring Senator Wharst down too," Gabe said, "now that we know what we're looking for. We just need one piece of physical evidence."

A moment of frustrated tension filled the line. They all wanted the senator. The man was more slippery than a swarm of eels in a barrel of oil on ice.

"How did Foley blackmail him?" Jake asked the question he'd been chewing on. "Phone? Email? There has to be a record."

They would bring Wharst down because they had no other choice. They had to get him before he came after them.

And even if Wharst wasn't a personal threat, Jake could never let him go now. He'd known about combat tourism. A high-level politician sworn to uphold American values, he'd known about these hideous and outrageous acts and had done nothing to end them.

"I'll see if I can find how Foley initially contacted Wharst," Troy said from DC. "There has to be some kind of a trail. We'll find it."

They talked a few more minutes about how they were going to do that.

After the call ended, Jake dialed the airport and booked tickets on the next flight out. Since the plane wouldn't leave until two p.m., he reserved a hotel room as well. Both he and Allison could use a chance to clean up before the long flight to the US.

He drove in silence the rest of the way, thinking about the XO-ST teams, Senator Wharst, Kenneth Hatch, but mostly about Allison Myers.

She looked like Sleeping Beauty, her long lashes fanning her pale cheeks. Even disheveled as she was, she was still a princess, her honey-colored hair spread over her shoulders. She was so far out of his league, out of his world. And he wanted her anyway.

Worse. Way worse. He felt that he *needed* her.

He'd never needed a woman before. Physical need, sure, but not needing someone's company, not feeling bereft at the thought that they wouldn't be together a couple of days from now, a couple of weeks from now, a couple of years from now.

He'd never wanted that with a woman before. Never wanted to want it.

Thank God, she stayed asleep so he couldn't do something completely moronic like tell her.

She didn't wake until he stopped the car at their hotel.

A wave of tenderness rose inside him as he took in her rumpled appearance.

He wanted to pull her into his lap. He wanted her to finish waking up with her legs wrapped around him. His fingers flexed on the steering wheel.

He cleared his throat. "We have some time before we have to leave for the airport. I got us a room so we can clean up and rest."

Her eyes closed, then opened in a sleepy blink. "Thank you. I'll pay you back."

"We'll worry about that when we're back in the US."

She ran her fingers through her hair and twisted it into a knot at her nape. With her arms lifted, her breasts lifted too. His gaze hesitated on her torso. His hands itched to touch her.

She glanced at him and caught him looking. In a split second, thick tension filled the cab.

"Once we're back in the US, I'll have to report to Quantico for debriefing," he told her, holding her gaze. "But then I'm coming to find you."

She dropped her hands to her lap and twisted her fingers together. "I'm bad news for men."

Which wasn't the same as saying that she had no interest in him. He grinned, relieved. "I'm willing to take that chance."

He leaned forward and kissed her. She gave a soft puff of a sigh against his lips, and melted against him.

Heat and need flooded him. He *was* falling in love with her—a stun grenade of a thought. The feelings that spread through him knocked him on his ass, metaphorically speaking.

He didn't kiss her gently. He kissed her with full-on lust and desperation. Cards on the table.

And she responded, and left his head spinning.

He would have kept on kissing her if they weren't in a parking lot in a country where displays of public affection were forbidden.

He pulled away from her with reluctance. Cleared his throat. "Better check in."

Cheeks flushed, she stared at him for a second, then scrambled out of the car.

He went and grabbed her suitcase. His luggage was back at the hotel in Lahedeh. He didn't care. His mind was elsewhere.

"Do you believe in love at kind of first sight?" he asked by way of a reality check as they headed inside.

An uncertain expression crossed her face. But she answered him. "With Daniel and Kenneth…we were friends a long time before we decided…"

"Not that I know anything about the subject, but I don't think love is the type of thing that gets decided." He stopped at the hotel's entrance. "We have something here, right?"

The pink in her cheeks deepened. "Lust?"

A pure shot of happiness filled his chest. So she lusted after him. Definitely a good start. He wanted her so much, he could barely see straight. Any corresponding lust on her part was more than reassuring.

But he wanted more. He wanted her courageous heart, her loyalty—he wanted the entire Allison Myers package.

They went inside, checked in without trouble. The lobby was mostly empty, chrome and mirrors, antique carpets on the walls like at their Lahedeh hotel. They weren't alone in the elevator, so they didn't talk on the trip to the third floor. They simply moved along until he stopped in front of the right door.

His hand hesitated with the card key halfway to the reader. "I got only one room, if that's all right. Two beds."

He opened the door and stepped back. "I don't expect you to jump into bed with me. I just don't want to let you out of my sight until we're safely back home."

She walked forward. "It's fine."

He followed her in, letting the door swing closed behind them.

The two beds pretty much took up the space. He kept his gaze on her and tried to block out the dozen X-rated thoughts that assailed him. *Take it slow. Nothing has to happen here. You have a lifetime.*

His brain said that. His body said, *Bed! Naked! Now!*

But there was one thing he wanted even more than sex with Allison. He wanted her safe. So he focused on that.

"You shouldn't go home right away." And before she could protest, he added, "I'm sure your business needs you, but XO-ST has your name. We have to assume they already have your hotel records from Lahedeh. XO-ST's main office is in the US. They probably have your home address by now. There are some seriously rough guys involved here. My team and I are going to go after them. When we strike, they'll strike back. You know too much. You wouldn't be safe."

She held his gaze. "Okay."

"Just like that?"

"I trust your judgment."

Those words filled his chest with warmth. "Thank you. I'll arrange for a safe house. I'm sure your crew bosses can handle everything for another week or two at work."

"Will you be able to visit me?"

He took her hands. When she didn't protest, he drew her into his arms. "Probably not until this op is over."

She rested her head on his shoulder. He pressed a kiss on the top of her head, on her silky hair. And then she raised her head, and he pressed the next kiss on her lips.

He kissed her, his blood heating, need rising and sweeping through every cell, an overpowering tide. She tasted sweet and…his. He needed every ounce of self-discipline he'd learned during his military career to keep from tumbling her onto the closest bed.

*Easy now. No rush.* Because he was going to find a way to make this last forever.

When she said, "I need a shower," and pulled away from him, he didn't think he could move an inch, his body was so hard.

But he let her go. And ached, unable not to picture her under the spray of water naked. In his imagination, fat drops ran down her bare skin, exploring all the curves his fingers craved.

Was the bathroom door locked? And if it wasn't, if he opened that door, would she invite him in?

*Don't push.*

To distract himself, he ordered room service, then when the tray came, he set everything out for her, grabbing a few bites to sate his own hunger. The hunger that could be satisfied with food.

As soon as she came out of the bathroom, tightly wrapped in a white terry robe, he went in with, "I ordered lunch. Help yourself."

He didn't even bother to turn on the hot water, just went with straight cold. He needed to calm his body down. He wanted her, but he wanted to give her time. He didn't just want a blind rush to release, a repeat of what they'd had at the warlord's compound. He wanted deliberate choice, Allison choosing to be with him.

When he left the bathroom—in a robe that matched hers, with nothing but his boxers underneath—she was sitting on the edge of one of the beds. He went to the other and lay on top of the covers, reached over to his cell phone on the nightstand, and set the alarm.

He tried to pretend he wasn't acutely aware of every breath she drew, every move she made. In. Bed. "We can sleep until noon, but then we better head over to the airport."

"Three hours."

"Not a lot, but we can sleep more on the plane."

She didn't say anything for a long moment, then, "Thank you for lunch."

He heard rustling. When he looked, he found her hidden under the covers. "You're welcome."

"Thank you for everything."

She was literally within arm's reach. The knowledge that she was probably naked under her robe didn't help his lust attack. "Sleep."

She obediently closed her eyes.

Jake closed his. In the navy, he'd learned how to sleep on command. Sometimes all they got were quick combat naps in the twenty- or thirty-minute chopper flight on their way to a fight. The ability to be able to turn off his brain was a valuable skill. He used that skill now and slept.

He woke at eleven to a door slamming out in the hallway, then the creaking of a cleaning cart. Someone turned on a vacuum cleaner that was louder than some tanks he'd been in.

Allison gave a soft, protesting groan in the next bed before her eyes fluttered open and her gaze met his, slowly focusing on him. "Is it time?"

"Not yet. Go back to sleep."

She closed her eyes. Opened them again after a few seconds. The vacuum cleaner growled and whined on in the next room.

Jake got out of bed, grabbed his wallet, and walked out, gave a twenty to the cleaning guy to go start on the other end of the hallway. When he came back in, his legs slowed by Allison's bed on their own.

She lay on her back under the covers, only the collar of her bathrobe showing, her hair spread out on the pillow around her.

"You look like a fairy-tale princess," he said. "Sleeping Beauty."

She rolled her eyes. Sat up. "You should see me in steel-toe boots and a hard hat."

*And nothing else*, his brain added, and he grinned. "I'd like that."

She reached up to braid her hair. "I don't think I can go back to sleep. I napped in the car too."

He sat down next to her. "Should I order more food?"

"I'm good. Thanks."

Every cell of his body protested at the idea of moving away from her. His brain scrambled for an excuse to stay. "Turn."

She did, flashing him a questioning look over her shoulder.

He scooted closer and took over the braiding.

"Two sisters," she said with a grin.

"I want you to meet them." Which would make her the first woman he'd introduced to his family.

"Will they stay at the FBI safe house for a while longer?"

Allison always paid attention. He liked that about her. Among a great many other things. "Yes."

"And I'll be sent to an FBI safe house?"

"Yes. What we uncovered is too big, and it goes too high. People kill to keep these kinds of secrets."

"Maybe we could be at the same safe house," she said.

"I think that could be arranged." A great idea, actually.

"Your face lights up every time you talk about your sisters. You love them very much."

"More than life itself."

"They're lucky girls."

With her half turned, he could see she was smiling, but he could also see that her eyes held worry and uncertainty.

She'd had a rough week here. And she was still in danger, heading to a safe house instead of home.

"They do have an amazing big brother. I can even do nail polish," he bragged, just to make Allison smile. "Mandy is six years younger than Jasmine. When Jasmine got into makeup in her teen years, there was no holding Mandy back from copying her big sister. Except, Jasmine was usually out with friends, having no time for the baby of the family. So if I didn't want nail polish all over the furniture, I had to learn how to give a princess manicure. With sparkles. And, by the way, all of that *is* top secret."

"My lips are sealed." She laughed at last, a free, joyous sound that went straight to his heart.

"Not yet," he murmured, then finished her hair and turned her to face him. He left his hands on her shoulders.

As he held her gaze, the mirth in her eyes slowly turned into something else, awareness first, then desire.

His body filled with heat and need. "Let's take it slow." He shook his head. "I think that's the first time in my life I've ever said that."

Allison laughed.

***

Jake wasn't kidding about going slow, apparently, because he just sat there and let Allison close the distance between them. And then they were kissing. In bed. Not a blind rush like on previous occasions, but a slow seduction that felt a lot like it was going someplace serious.

Despite what he said, she still expected him to take charge in a moment, because he was a take-charge type, pedal-to-the-metal kind of guy, but he kept the kiss so gentle, it completely melted her heart. His lips were featherlight on hers, coaxing instead of demanding. Even when he swept inside her mouth, his tongue caressed, it didn't conquer.

He pulled her onto his lap and cradled her body against his in a protective cocoon. His strong arms surrounded her; his masculine scent enveloped her. He kissed her almost reverently.

Emotions built first, inside her chest, then hot and heavy heat built next, slowly, and spread through her body. Tingly sensations filled her. She felt like her body was a great city, the lights blinking on one by one in the evening, until the whole city was ablaze.

She shifted restlessly against Jake.

He immediately understood what she wanted and laid her on the bed without breaking the connection. Their legs tangled together on top of the covers.

He was half on top of her but kept his weight off her, supporting himself on his elbows as he thoroughly explored her mouth, then nibbled down her neck, then parted the robe and trailed kisses toward her breasts.

"I don't think I've gone a full minute without thinking about this from the moment I first saw you on the street," he said in a hot whisper against her skin.

She could only moan in response. Her fingers tunneled into his thick hair. The feel of his lips, brushing, nibbling, teasing was a revelation.

She'd thought she wanted someone with whom she could trade the *Wall Street Journal* and the *Financial Times* back and forth over breakfast.

She'd been wrong.

*This* was what she wanted, this great slow river of blinding heat, something that until now she hadn't even known existed. She wanted Jake's warrior spirit, the calluses on his hands, and his straight-talking ways. She wanted the way he looked at her like she was someone out of a fairy tale. Then his eyes would change and suddenly fill with breathtaking hunger as if he wanted to devour her, as if he simply couldn't help it.

She felt alive every second she spent with him.

When he sucked her right nipple into his mouth, her breath caught. Desire flooded through her. Need pulsed between her legs.

When he growled, "I want to make love to you, Allison," as he captured her other nipple, she was already nearing orgasm.

And way past speech. So she stayed silent—discounting helpless moans—and showed her agreement by slipping out of her robe.

He went with the program and discarded his, while he somehow managed to never stop touching her.

They were down to underwear. God, he was magnificent.

He hooked his fingers under the band of her panties and tugged them off her slowly, bending his head to trail kisses behind the silk. She couldn't think. All the blood rushed out of her brain to hurry to the places he was kissing.

He dropped her panties to the floor, then, holding her gaze, he stood up and pushed down his boxers, then stepped out of them.

*Oh. Okay.* The air in the room was suddenly too thick to breathe.

At the compound, in the dim room, in their frenetic coupling, she hadn't fully seen him. She saw him now.

He moved to get on the bed, but then caught the look in her eyes and stilled. "What is it?"

"You're a little intimidating naked." Then, because using the words *little* and *naked* together in relation to him seemed nuts, she corrected. "You're enormously intimidating."

He grinned. "My macho ego would like to think there's a compliment in that, but I can't tell because my mind has melted. You're mind-meltingly beautiful."

He joined her on the bed and kissed his way down her stomach, over one hip, down one inner thigh, up the other. The feel of his hot mouth on her sensitive skin drove her wild. When his lips settled against her seam, her trembling fingers found their way back into his hair.

His hot tongue parted her, and she about came off the bed.

And then he licked her, and she lost it, tumbled over the edge in a slow, mind-bending roll of pleasure that went on and on without end.

She was only vaguely aware of him reaching for his wallet. But then he was sheathed and pressed against her opening, and she was more than aware of *that*.

Everything inside her was still quivering, her brain still in a pleasure fog, her heart madly beating. But as he pushed inside, one deliberate, hard inch at a time, the buildup started all over again, even if she thought she couldn't possibly be ready.

"Look at me, Allison." He said the words in a raw whisper.

She opened her eyes.

The intensity of his gaze captured her. His wide shoulders rose above her, muscles bunching, a fierce concentration on his face as he filled her fully, stretching her in the most amazing way, and made her his.

"This is not the end," he promised. "I want to figure out how we can have a relationship. We *will* give this a chance."

She was on the edge of the next orgasm. She couldn't speak.

"This is something." He drew back at an antagonizing pace, and once again, she felt every inch of him. "What we have. This is real. Tell me that you feel it too."

"I feel it." She breathed the words, her heart full.

He made love to her in a way that reminded her of poetry, the kind of poetry they made into long, sweet ballads of love. He was true to his word. He took it slow. And tender, and heart melting, and erotic beyond anything she thought was possible.

She called out his name as her body pulsed and she flew.

He kissed her one more time and flew with her.

***

They were at the airport, waiting for their connecting flight, when Jake's cell phone rang.

He was standing by the floor-to-ceiling window of the terminal with Allison, watching planes land and take off, wishing they were somewhere private so he could make love to her again.

He couldn't wait to introduce her to his family. He couldn't wait for this case to be over, so they could start spending serious time together. She was it for him. He knew when he was sunk. He wanted to drown in her and never come up for air.

He smiled at her before he stepped back to answer the phone.

"Something went wrong in DC," Gabe said on the other end, tension vibrating through the line. "I can't reach Troy. He's missing."

"What do you mean—"

"Hang on. Shit. What the hell—" Gabe grunted.

The next thing Jake heard was the distinctive clap of a gunshot. *Bang!*

Then the line went dead.

# WARRIOR
## AGENT

# CHAPTER
# ONE

Former Navy SEAL Troy Hill hadn't begun his day with giddy-eyed optimism, but neither had he expected to end it in a dog cage.

Getting caught sucked. The security goons trapped him in the basement, in a steel cage enclosure that normally housed the Rottweilers that guarded Senator Wharst's DC mansion.

Troy shifted on the cold cement floor, carefully working the plastic cuff that trapped his hands behind him.

The burly guard left behind to watch Troy perched on an undersized barstool near the stairs—a circus bear doing a balancing act—playing some kind of game on his phone. He rarely looked up. The only time he spoke was when his bear-paw-sized thumbs missed and he cursed.

Troy painted a bored expression on his face while behind his back, he pulled the plastic with all his strength.

Step One: Get hands free.

Step Two: Deal with the two-inch-wide metal chain and the padlock that kept the door secured.

He had to get out fast or he wasn't going to live to see the morning.

If the senator's security goons were going to turn Troy over to the authorities, they would have done so the moment they'd caught him. But they were holding him, which meant they were going to turn him over to someone else.

Back when the senator had been a governor, his insider nickname was the Thugernor—in reference to his connections to organized crime. The man had the kind of friends who could make a problem like Troy permanently disappear.

Troy had been caught shortly after eight p.m. It had to be around midnight now—hard to tell in the basement that had no windows. The *cleanup crew* would have been notified already. They were on their way.

He tugged hard on the plastic cuff, and with the resulting pain, he also felt wetness on his wrists as he broke the skin. He kept on tugging anyway. But as minutes ticked by, the plastic didn't give.

*Try something else.*

He pushed to standing and cleared his throat. "I have to go to the bathroom."

Maybe on the way to the bathroom, he could grab something to use to cut the plastic ties. He scanned the cardboard boxes against the walls that probably held election flyers. A pile of election lawn signs filled one corner, posters another. Not very promising. But maybe the bathroom would yield something usable.

"Hey. I need to take a leak."

The guard just adjusted his bulky frame on the barstool, engrossed in hitting the right buttons.

He was a fricking meat mountain. Troy wasn't crazy about going up against him—not with at least one cracked rib, the busted knuckles on his right hand, and a swollen kneecap that had met with a baseball bat when they'd questioned him earlier. But he'd do what he had to, even if it meant further injury.

"Five minutes, all right?" he said. "Then I'll leave you in peace. I swear. You won't hear another peep out of me."

*Just open the damned cage.*

But the guard didn't even look up from his phone screen.

So Troy slammed his shoulder into the bars.

The goon got up at last and strolled over to the cage.

Troy didn't have to fake looking grateful. "Thanks, man."

But instead of opening the lock, the man kicked through the bars, smashing his boot into Troy's injured knee. And because Troy's hands were tied behind his back and he couldn't balance or catch himself, he went down, smashing into the hard cement.

*Dammit.*

His shoulder took most of the impact and throbbed with pain. His knee throbbed harder. *It better not be broken.* He still had plenty of fighting ahead of him, and then he'd have to run.

He struggled to his feet.

The guy was already back on his stool, back on his phone.

"Hey! Asshole!" Troy slammed his good shoulder into the bars so hard, they rattled. "You think you're a tough guy, why don't you step in here?"

He'd pick a fight if he had to, even if he'd get hurt.

Hurt was better than dead.

* * *

## Carly

Carly Montgomery's main goal for the moment was to fly under the radar and remain unnoticed. Actually, that was pretty much her overall life goal. Don't draw attention. Act normal. Don't let anyone see that you're crazy.

She stood at attention in Senator Wharst's office with half his security detail. The other half was on duty.

Every one of the six guys present was at least a head taller than she, and crazy built—bodybuilder muscles galore. As they faced the senator and his aide, uniform tough-guy looks sat on their chiseled faces, prime male specimens without a doubt. She could see why the housemaids were titillated, trying to chat up the guys at every chance.

Carly couldn't really relate to any of them. Standing next to the men on the antique Persian carpet, she felt like she was in some activity book for kids. *Which one of these is least like the others?*

They were a well-oiled team. She was the recent hire, the outsider. *The photo op.* On her first day on the job two weeks ago, the senator had just happened to walk around the grounds during her shift. He'd chatted her up, and the press had happened to be there to record everything.

SENATOR WHARST BELIEVES IN HIRING RETURNING VETS, the headlines read the next day, above a picture of the man smiling benevolently at her. That had been the first and last time he'd said boo to her.

Still, she was grateful for the job. Whatever his motivations were, she wasn't about to complain. Having work beat not having work any day of the week.

The senator now sat behind his gleaming antique desk—sixty-something, silver-gray hair, aristocratic features, the very picture of "distinguished." He handed a thin folder to his aide, who waited patiently behind him.

Then he looked up. "I want the security upgraded. How on earth did this guy get as far as the conference room? An intruder like this is absolutely unacceptable."

Senator Wharst being in his office close to midnight was nothing strange. From what Carly had seen so far, he often worked until the middle of the night.

"Yes, sir," the men said in unison.

While Carly blurted before she could catch herself, "I think we should call the police, sir."

She immediately wished she could suck the words back. Not that she hadn't spoken the truth. But now every eye was on her.

They should have called the cops the second they'd caught the intruder hours ago.

She'd been on break when the man had been apprehended, only finding out about him when everyone around her started running. Her earpiece must be acting up again, because she didn't even hear the alert.

The senator's aide, a twenty-something blond Adonis—it was almost as if all the staff had been picked with photo ops in mind—glared at her for speaking out of turn.

Nick, the head of security, stood at the far end of the lineup. He shot her a leave-this-to-me look. His hard gaze strongly suggested that she hadn't yet earned the right to have an opinion.

"The FBI is on the way," he said. "They're going to take him in. If we call the local police, the media will be alerted. They monitor the police channels. We want to keep this under wraps."

"I don't want this in the news," the senator cut in, wearing his best vote-winner smile, disarming and trust inspiring at the same time. "An attack on me will either paint me as a victim or a man hated enough for assassins to be stalking him. Not the image I'm trying for just when I'm about to announce my bid for the presidency."

Everything had a political angle here, probably even the color of the socks the man pulled on in the morning. Since Carly desperately needed the job, she just had to learn to live with that. "Yes, sir."

Wharst's gaze left her and moved from man to man. "I want you to find out how he got in and make sure this doesn't happen again."

"Yes, sir."

The senator nodded. "All right. Dismissed."

The security staff filed out, the men looking chastised and irritated in equal measure. They clearly resented being outsmarted by the intruder, then receiving the dressing-down from the senator.

Nick caught Carly outside the door. He wore an expensive black suit, while the rest of security had uniform navy suits the senator provided. The housemaids wore light blue, the kitchen staff white. Everybody had the appropriate uniform. Everybody knew their place.

As Nick opened his mouth to speak, Carly expected the boss to order her not to address the senator directly again but to go through him if she had anything to contribute.

Instead, he asked, "Can you take over guard duty in the basement for an hour or so? Jason needs to take a break. I have something to take care of, then I'll come down and you can leave for the day."

"Yes, sir." Another hour wasn't going to kill her. And she wanted to prove herself as a team player. She didn't want them to regret that they'd hired her.

So she headed downstairs, swung by the security office, grabbed a new headset, then strode down the long hallway, but her personal cell phone buzzed in her pocket. She stopped and looked at the number on the display, took the call. "Is everything okay, Mom?"

"I wish you would come home." Her mother spoke the words in the tone of a long-suffering martyr.

"Mom, it's midnight." Carly resumed walking. "We've talked about this."

"You know how bad stress is for my health." Her mother switched to accusation right on schedule.

"Then don't stress over it."

"You're sick too, you know. You should never have taken that job. You should be home recuperating. You shouldn't take any job, period." She paused before she added, "Hector's been asking about you."

"As soon as I'm ready to be a trophy wife, you'll be first to know."

Hector Merrick was one of her father's business associates, a man twenty years her senior.

"Don't use that mocking tone with me. I'm your mother."

"Sorry." She swiped a bottle of water from the pantry as she walked through what had been the servants' quarters when the sprawling Washington, DC mansion had been built over a hundred years ago. These days, only the housekeeper lived in.

"I want the best for you," Carly's mother said. "You should never have joined the army. Good Lord, with your height and those cheekbones—"

"Mom!" She couldn't deal with another lecture on her wasted life.

"Well, they broke you, then spit you out. You're very lucky that Hector is interested at all, with your sordid history. Not many men would want a burned-out soldier to be mother of his children, for heaven's sake, someone who *deliberately* involved herself in all that unpleasantness."

Carly bit her tongue. Hector was only interested in her because he wanted to take over Montgomery Funeral Services after her father retired. But pointing that out to her mother would be useless. Merrick & Montgomery was a dream Carly's mother wholeheartedly shared with Hector. They were the two largest players in the business in the Baltimore area. And Hector had dreams of total market domination.

"Are you still having hallucinations? You need a strong man by your side. In case you flip out and lose it."

Carly squeezed her eyes shut for a moment, infinitely grateful that her mother didn't know what happened with Patrick.

"I bet you still have those nasty nightmares," her mother went on without pause. "You need a man next to you in bed at night. You would sense his protection even in your sleep. I bet you would feel better."

A man in bed next to her at night was the last thing Carly needed. "I have to go, Mom. I'm at work."

"If you married Hector, you wouldn't have to work. I don't understand you, Carly."

That much was painfully obvious. "I'll call you later."

Carly hung up the phone and drew a deep breath. She wished she could explain herself to her mother, wished she had the kind of mother who'd understand. But if her mother knew the full truth, she would probably have Carly committed.

It wasn't just that Carly didn't want Hector. She didn't want to *mess up* Hector. She didn't want to *kill* him.

What happened with Patrick could never happen again.

Memories tightened every muscle in her body as she hurried down the stairs. She shoved back the images and deliberately relaxed her limbs.

She liked having a job. The job kept her sane. The job saved her from having to live under her parents' roof, where her mother would arrange daily "accidental" encounters with Hector.

Her new security guard position made Carly feel productive. Made her feel normal, even if she was anything but, even if she hadn't slept more than two hours at a stretch since she'd returned from Afghanistan.

She pushed the door open.

"About time." Jason slid off the barstool, then shoved his phone into his back pocket without looking at the man in the cage.

But Carly did, and blinked hard at the blood on the intruder's face.

"What happened to him?"

"Asked to use the bathroom. Tripped over his own shoelaces on the way back in." Jason shrugged, giving his shoulder muscles extra wiggle for her benefit. "Wiped the cement floor with his face."

"You could have cleaned him up."

As Jason strutted toward her, he tucked his shirt into his pants so it would mold to his oversized pecs. "He refused first aid."

She could believe that.

The man in the cage looked like one tough customer. His flint-gray eyes, cold and calculating, watched her without emotion. She could definitely see him as an assassin or domestic terrorist.

"Said anything yet?"

"We couldn't even get his fucking name out of him." Jason grunted. "How was the meeting? Did I miss anything interesting?"

"FBI is coming to pick him up."

"Good. I'm tired of babysitting." He stopped by her on his way out, the strong scent of his aftershave surrounding her. He lowered his voice as he said, "How about a drink this weekend?"

"I don't drink." She had enough other problems.

He looked at her as if he was considering whether she had some kind of a mental handicap. Maybe he'd never met a woman who didn't want to go out with him. Or never met anyone who said no to a drink.

His smile turned into a frown. "You're odd, you know that? Hard to figure out."

Perhaps compared to the maids who spent half their day trying to get the guys to notice them.

But Carly nodded cheerfully. "My mother says I'm one of those women who can't recognize a good thing when it's staring her in the face."

Jason's *that's it* expression said he was in full agreement.

As he climbed the stairs, she glanced after him. Great body—zero attraction. Unlike the maids, she wasn't mesmerized by muscle in a uniform. She hadn't felt attracted to a man in…She couldn't remember the last time.

Patrick had wanted her, and she'd been lonely, so she'd gone along with the relationship. A critical, and almost fatal, mistake.

She didn't love Patrick. She felt dead inside—maybe the legacy of war. Although she wasn't sure she'd ever believed in true love.

But she did believe in humane treatment of prisoners and a fair trial for all. She needed to believe in that because she needed something that separated her from the people she'd fought overseas.

She crossed over to the cage. "Would you like some water?"

The man pushed to his feet. "Thanks."

He had a deep voice, raspy, as if at one point he had suffered damage to his vocal cords. The deep-timbred tone tickled down her spine. A lot of women probably found that rasp sexy. To Carly, he was a criminal. Of course, some women were attracted to criminals. Not her.

He stood only a few inches taller than she but was nearly twice as wide across the shoulders. He had the body of a fighter. A wrestler? Or a boxer maybe? He looked like he'd be quick on his feet. She appreciated the steel bars between them.

Other than his piercing eyes, most of his face was damaged, his lips split and bloody. And he had plenty of old scars too under his new scrapes, a man familiar with violence.

With his hands tied behind his back, he couldn't grab the water, so she twisted off the cap, then fitted the small bottle through the bars and held it to his bleeding lips.

The beginnings of a stubble covered his square jaw. His Adam's apple bobbed up and down as he drank.

They stood close enough for her to feel his body heat. He smelled like sweat and blood, but didn't stink, just had the smell of fighting on him.

He drank down half the water, left the rest for later.

He watched her as she twisted the cap back on. "You're nicer than the others. New on the team?"

This close up, his voice sounded even deeper, raspier, sexier—a distracting combination with his fathomless gray gaze. He didn't look at her as a prisoner looks at a guard. He looked at her as a man looks at a woman.

She wasn't interested—in him or any other guy. She walked back to her seat.

He didn't take the hint. "How long have you been back from the war?" And then, at her questioning look, he added, "You move like a soldier."

She didn't like the idea that he'd been watching her that closely. She hadn't had a chance to assess how *he* moved. She'd only seen him tied up and locked in a cage.

"Maybe you could help me," he said.

She resisted rolling her eyes. "Unlikely."

"I don't belong here. It's a misunderstanding."

The mantra of prisoners in every jail around the world.

She raised an eyebrow. "You broke into the senator's home after dark, armed to the teeth. Are you going to tell me you came to clean the gutters?"

A hint of a smile appeared at the corner of his lips, softening the harsh lines of his face. "Would you believe me if I told you I came here on the side of justice, and the people who locked me up are the criminals?"

"Oh man. Shit. Why didn't you tell me sooner? Let me get the key." She did roll her eyes then. Shook her head. Looked him over. Did he really think she'd be that easy to play? She was a little offended.

"Here's the thing," she said. "You're right. I am a soldier. I just spent two tours of duty fighting foreign enemies. Frankly, I think people like you should appreciate our hard-won freedom and stop being jackasses. If you don't like a politician, go out and freaking vote. Hello, democracy."

He looked like he was fighting a grin at her impassioned speech, but the expression was gone the next second. Might have been a trick of the poor lighting.

"I didn't come here to hurt anybody," he said quietly. "My intentions were peaceful. I promise."

Right. His face was a testament that he did not lead a peaceful life. "You have a lot of scars. Are you going to tell me you got them shaving?"

"Got every last one of them working for the US government."

God, that raspy voice sent shivers down her spine.

He held her gaze as he spoke, not a blink, not a tic, no sign of lying.

A second passed. Two. Three.

He paced to the back of the cage, then came to the door again. Rolled his shoulders, watched her. He looked like he was thinking hard about what to say next. She didn't bother telling him to save his breath.

Although…Maybe he did move like a soldier. Hard to tell from just a few steps, with the way his hands were tied behind his back.

She squashed a sudden twitch of doubt even as she asked, "Working for the US government, doing what?"

"Hostage rescue," he said immediately, didn't stop to think about it, another indication that he might be telling the truth. "Would you believe it if I told you I used to be a Navy SEAL?"

She decided, mostly out of boredom, to play along for a few minutes. She might even gain useful information she could pass on to the FBI when they came for him. Maybe he *had* been on the right side at one point. He could be a SEAL who'd gone rogue. Stranger things had happened.

"SEAL, huh? That's hard-core. Were you good at it?" Plenty of people faked a background in spec ops for the glory. They loved bragging about the action they saw. Real spec ops didn't talk about their missions as a rule.

This guy's expression hardened at her question, his gaze shuttered.

She knew that look, had seen it on her friends' faces, had seen it on her own face in the mirror—the look that said they wouldn't relive their memories for any amount of money.

Maybe he *had* been in the military.

She tried to assess his old scars but couldn't see them well enough under the dried blood on his face. "How did you get hurt with the SEALs? You look like you got blown up."

His gaze hardened another notch. He turned away from her. Stretched his legs as he paced, then stopped. Rolled his shoulders again. Turned back.

She watched the tight set of his jaw, the determination on his face. "You want me to believe you, talk to me."

No harm in listening. Even if she wasn't inclined to believe anything he said.

His main goal was to trick her into letting him out. Then she'd lose her job. If she lost her job, she'd have to move back with her parents. She wasn't sure if she'd survive that.

# CHAPTER
# TWO

Carly waited the guy out. Seconds ticked by as tension filled the basement.

"Yeah," he said then. "I got blown up."

Those few rasped words made a key that slid effortlessly into the lock on the vault where Carly had shut away her memories. They came pouring out.

*Ratatatat. Gunfire. People shouting in a language she couldn't understand. The truck jerking around. She couldn't see anything. She was blindfolded. Pain, from her initial injury and the bite of hands holding her captive. Bam! The explosion. Flying. Hitting the ground with a pulverizing crash.*

The flashback lasted two seconds that felt like two years. She struggled to swallow the panic that choked her.

"How?" she asked, then realized she didn't want to hear the answer. Too late.

"Bad guys took a Canadian journalist. Sent her back to base decked out in a bomb vest."

She gaped. "Nina Norton?" She remembered that story. It'd been all over the news.

He stared at the bars, his eyes strained. "I disabled the timer, but it had a backup system, operated by remote."

He looked up into her eyes, his gaze a dark hole that led straight to hell, a journey she was familiar with.

He said, "Then suddenly, I saw the guy who had something in his hand that could have been the damned remote, but I hesitated a split second because he was one of our translators, and I couldn't comprehend that he'd crossed over to the other side."

Carly forced herself to draw a deep breath against the tightness that wrapped around her chest. Sweat beaded on her forehead. She could feel the explosion in her bones. Could smell the burning flesh around her.

"You okay?" the guy in the cage rasped. He was watching her closely, as close to her as the bars allowed.

She sank onto the barstool and forced herself to breathe slowly and evenly until her muscles relaxed.

"You had a rough time over there." His voice softened with sympathy.

She hated it. Who the hell was he to pity her? She wasn't going to respond, but for some reason, she ended up saying, "It's rough on everyone."

"Amen to that." His gaze never left her face. The depth of his eyes held dark shadows of things he'd seen. The dark path to hell was paved with them.

Her own eyes held the same shadows. Sometimes they spilled out and smothered her. Sometimes they filled her up until she couldn't breathe. Some nights, she fell into the dark hole and it swallowed her.

*Maybe he'd been there too.*

Maybe he'd lost friends, or parts of himself. It didn't matter. Wrong was wrong. He'd broken in with the intent of harming the senator. Why else?

"You blame politicians for what happened to you overseas," she said. "So you thought you'd kill the senator to make your point."

"I didn't come to kill the senator," he repeated his earlier claim. And then he said, in a quieter tone, "The anxiety gets better. If you were tough enough to survive two tours of duty, it's going to take more than a couple of flashbacks to take you down."

Those quietly spoken words of support surprised her. They were more than she'd ever gotten from her parents.

Not that this guy meant any of what he said. He was just messing with her head, trying to talk his way out of the cage.

"What's your name?" she asked.

He watched her silently. But then he said, "Troy Hill."

She went still. Had he decided to give up information at last? She had no idea why now, but she wasn't about to question it. She wanted to call in Nick, the leader of the security team, but was afraid Troy would stop talking, so she stayed in place and did her best to look encouraging.

"Working alone?" she asked.

His sharp gaze assessed her. Long seconds of tense silence passed before he decided to answer. "I'm working for the FBI. Investigating the senator."

Again, not the slightest nervous gesture betrayed that he might be lying, none of the usual tells she'd learned to look for. She'd guarded prisoners before, at the mountain base where she'd served. She wasn't an expert, but she wasn't a novice either. Rule number one: if a prisoner finally decided to talk, keep them talking.

"So you're undercover with the FBI, and right now you're breaking your cover, because…" She flashed an expectant look.

"I'm out of choices," he said reasonably. "Either you're involved in the senator's dark dealings, or you're an honest person in the middle of this mess. You're new to the team. Maybe you haven't been corrupted yet. Maybe you'll help me. It's my best bet."

His words held a certain logic. The man was convincing. Then again, criminals and crazy people often were.

"If you're FBI," she said, "then you're in luck. Your buddies are coming for you. The feds are on their way."

He swore instead of relaxing. "Listen, no way any law enforcement was called in. Whoever is coming for me, if they take me, I'm as good as dead. Wharst can't afford to let me live." His gaze pinned her. "My life is in your hands, Carly."

She didn't like that he used her name, made her feel like he was manipulating her. She wished Jason hadn't said her name in front of him. She rolled her eyes, keeping her tone dry as she said, "Nobody likes a drama queen."

His lips twitched, eyes flashing with amusement.

Then he half turned, wiggled his tied hands as he looked at her over his shoulder. "I'll cut back on the drama. But you need to get these cuffs off me."

Did she look stupid? "You need to stop talking."

But the sight of his hands restrained made her skin feel too tight. She rubbed her own wrists. Then dropped her hands as he turned back to her.

Resolution filled his gaze. "How about you call the FBI and confirm that they're coming for me?"

"Right. Because the FBI just gives out that kind of information over the phone to strangers." She shook her head. She'd had about as much bullshit as she had the patience for tonight.

She pulled out her cell phone and brought up the mystery novel she'd been reading, set to ignore the prisoner for the rest of her short shift. "Take a nap."

No way was she going to mess up this job. Plenty of vets went unemployed. She had friends higher ranking than her who worked parking lot security at the mall. And here she was, hanging out at a mansion. She knew a good gig when she saw it.

"I have to go to the bathroom," Troy said.

"Jason took you already."

"I promise you, he didn't. I didn't trip over my shoelaces on the way. You know that, right?"

She suspected it, which wasn't the same as knowing. Still, it bothered her. But she could do nothing about that now. "You'll have to wait for the next shift. I can't go into the bathroom with you."

And she wasn't going to let him out of her sight.

"I promise to behave."

She ignored Troy Hill, if that was his name, and read her book, even if she did find the man behind the bars distracting. His bullshit story kept echoing in her head. She had to work to keep her attention on the twisting plot on the screen.

"You have to let me out."

She kept reading. She read a lot these days, had a lot of sleepless hours to fill at night. She liked cozy mysteries, the puzzle aspect, the brain exercise they provided. Nothing bloody. She wasn't a fan of those high-body-count thrillers that were all about guns and revenge. She didn't find violence entertaining.

She sank into her current book—*Books of a Feather, a Bibliophile Mystery* by one of her favorite authors, Kate Carlisle—about a dead body found at a rare book library in San Francisco.

But before Carly could figure out if the bookbinder was the likely next target, Troy interrupted her again.

"Okay, you're new, but you've been here for a while now, right? A week or two, at least? You didn't get a sense that there's something off around here? Too many secrets?"

*Like the way the guys sometimes stop talking when I enter the room?*

She shook off the thought. Maybe they were telling fart jokes for all she knew, and stopped because she was a woman. She wasn't going to let Troy get to her.

Minutes ticked by; the multiple plot lines in the book grew more complicated. Turned out the homeless old friend wasn't the bookbinder's old friend, after all, but a total stranger who had lied to get into her house. Too bad the bookbinder didn't discover his deception until after he became victim number two. Carly read on, searching for clues on the pages.

Every couple of seconds, Troy would say something from the cage. And every time, she ignored him.

"Fine. You win. I give up," he said next. "Could I just have another drink? Please?"

And this time, she did look up. He was leaning against the bars, looking worn-out and beaten down. Maybe too much so. He suddenly radiated defeat. The look was all wrong for him.

Was he faking it? Was he trying to get her to let down her guard?

Her instincts prickled, but she was ready to stretch her legs anyway, so she set her phone down and picked up the water bottle, alert and watchful. She walked over to the bars. Hesitated.

He looked the picture of dejection, yet something about him spelled danger. She had that odd prickling feeling, like when you were out on patrol, moving down some narrow, dusty street, and suddenly the back of your neck starts itching a split second before a sniper on some rooftop starts sending bullets your way.

She held the water bottle but didn't put it through the bars. Instead, she gave the man a full and careful inspection.

All sparks had left his eyes, nothing but defeat and exhaustion in his gaze. His hands were still secured behind his back. He had no way to grab her.

His lips did look dry.

Okay. So maybe he really did just want water. But before she could twist off the bottle's cap, the basement's door banged open, and Nick appeared at the top of the stairs.

He seemed preoccupied, checking his phone, then checking it again.

"Everything okay?" she asked.

He came down the stairs without answering, still lost in his phone. Then he looked up at last. "Thanks for staying on."

"I don't mind."

"You weren't even supposed to be working tonight. Go get some sleep."

She nodded, then turned back to the prisoner with the water. She could make sure he got a drink before she left.

But Nick was next to her in a few more steps, and held his hand out for the bottle. "I'll do that. You go."

She had no reason to argue. Even if Nick was ticked that he'd been shown up by the intruder and refused him water, the FBI would be here for the guy soon. He wasn't going to dehydrate in the next hour.

Yet Carly felt an odd reluctance to leave him.

Nick raised an eyebrow.

*Right.* Better not look like an idiot in front of the boss. She handed him the bottle, then walked back to the barstool for her phone. "Regular schedule still in effect?"

"You have gate duty at oh-six-hundred."

*Better get some sleep.* Her gaze slid past the boss to Troy Hill. Frustration and anger flashed across his face, then hard determination. Then, in a split second, he turned into a dejected prisoner once again.

Carly blinked.

The man looked tired and beat-up enough to collapse.

Maybe the other expression had been a trick of the light. The bare lightbulb over the cage didn't exactly provide perfect lighting.

Still, unease ran up her spine. Something felt off but, again, she couldn't put her finger on what exactly.

She watched Troy for another second or two, then decided it didn't matter. Nick had things in hand. And the FBI should be here soon. Troy Hill was about to become somebody else's problem.

She hurried up the stairs, pretty much okay with the idea that she was never going to see him again.

* * *

**Troy**

Troy gritted his teeth as he watched the door close behind Carly. He'd been about to make his move when Nick the Dick interrupted.

*Idiot.*

Not Nick. Troy.

He'd dawdled around too much.

The woman's mix of strength and vulnerability had gotten to him. Somehow he'd convinced himself that she wasn't like the others. And he'd decided to see if he could get past her without resorting to violent measures.

He'd finally broken the plastic tie that restrained his hands, just before Nick came downstairs.

He'd been okay with luring Jason to the bars, reaching through, grabbing his collar, and slamming his head into the cage so hard the goon's neck would break. Then grabbing his gun, shooting off the padlock…But then Carly had come. Change of shift.

First thing Troy had noticed about her had been her bow-shaped mouth, the way she sucked in her bottom lip, then let it go, as if something had upset her just before she came down to report for duty. She was tall and lean, dark auburn hair in a tight bun at her nape, the clearest green eyes he'd ever seen.

She'd shaken off the initial upset by the time she reached the bottom of the stairs. And he noticed a more permanent shadow in her clear green eyes, more than a shadow…*a wall.* Or maybe even more than that, a whole defense system. Her muscles seemed to be always tense, her too-alert body language familiar.

Troy had a couple of SEAL friends with PTSD who walked like that, watched like that, always on the edge, on the balls of their feet as if they were ready at a moment's notice to lunge into a fight.

And Troy had hesitated. *Again.* Obviously, he hadn't learned anything from the past.

He'd counted on having a little more time with her.

She had a number of weaknesses he'd planned to exploit. She had the least amount of weight and muscle among the guards. She hadn't been there when they'd beaten him. Because the others didn't think she could handle it? She certainly seemed the kindest of the bunch, giving him water.

Among the guards Troy had seen so far, he figured she'd be the easiest one to rattle. But she definitely hadn't been a pushover. And she hadn't stayed long enough.

Nick the Dick would be a hell of a lot more difficult to tackle. He had forty pounds on Troy and two guns.

"I'm thirsty," Troy repeated. He needed to get the bastard within reach, close enough to the bars so he could grab him.

But the man just smirked, chucking the bottle into the corner and moving to the barstool. "Don't worry about it, buddy. You won't be thirsty that much longer."

# CHAPTER
# THREE

Carly stepped out into the night, scanned the grounds, and patted the two Rottweilers that ran up to her. Now here were two coworkers she could like without reservation. She took the time to give a good scratch behind the ears, grateful for the couple of hours of peace and quiet ahead of her.

"Off you go. Back to work." She waved them along after a few minutes, and they galloped off to do their duty.

She breathed in cool night air as she glanced at her watch. The intruder had messed up everyone's schedule. The afternoon shift had been asked to stay on. They'd spent half the night looking for an accomplice, looking for a bomb the man might have placed. They hadn't found anything.

Since she couldn't afford to rent a place anywhere near the senator's ritzy neighborhood, she had a one-bedroom apartment an hour's drive from here. *Not worth the drive tonight.* She had only five hours left before her shift.

She strode to the ancient Chevy she drove and picked up her duffle bag from the backseat. The security team had a room on top of the gatehouse for times like this. She headed that way.

She nodded at Jason, who was now manning the gate and would be there until she took her shift. "I'll be down in the morning. Try not to fall asleep."

He wiggled his eyebrow. "You could stay here with me and keep me awake." He flexed his biceps. "You know you're tempted."

She shook her head. "I'll wrestle down the urge."

"Think about it," Jason called after her as she plodded up the stairs.

But she was thinking about Troy Hill.

He'd been convincing. She could almost believe him. Of course, she knew better. The man would have said anything to break free. Without a doubt, he'd been scamming her in his gravelly voice, yet the image of his graphite eyes and his scarred and bloodied face stayed with her.

She reached the small, utilitarian room and locked the door behind her, dropped her bag, then stripped out of her clothes. She showered in the small stall in the bathroom, still trying to figure out the man in the basement.

*Had he really meant to kill the senator like Nick said?*

But then why had Troy gone to the empty conference room instead of the senator's personal quarters?

She dried herself off and lay down on the bed in nothing but a clean undershirt and her underwear. She closed her eyes.

As always, sleep played hard to get.

When she heard a car pull up to the gate twenty minutes later, she got up and looked out the front window. A dark, unmarked van stood outside—two burly men in the cab.

The driver didn't show ID at the gate—unusual and against the rules—but maybe the rules didn't apply to the FBI. Jason simply waved them through.

No markings or any kind of insignia identified the vehicle as belonging to the Bureau. The van didn't even have government license plates. A flat, plastic storage unit lay on top, the locks busted, the unit tied together with elastic luggage bands. Didn't look very professional.

The van pulled up next to the main building. The men got out, wearing camouflage pants and dark T-shirts. None of the Men in Black stuff Carly had expected. Before they even had a chance to knock, the mansion's side door opened for them.

Carly stayed at the window, her instincts prickling.

Ten minutes passed before the men reappeared, dragging Troy between them. Even from the distance, she could tell he'd gotten another beating since she'd last seen him. His nose was bleeding.

Maybe he'd resisted being taken from the cage.

His hands were in front of him now, metal cuffs glinting in the moonlight. The FBI had bound his ankles, a foot of slack in the rope so he could hobble forward, but not enough for him to step up into the back of the van. They had to lift him to toss him in. He resisted. Fell. One of the men kicked him in the head, the other in the ribs—viciously and repeatedly, even after he stopped struggling.

That didn't look like standard FBI procedure.

He was fully restrained, at the mercy of men who meant him harm.

Images from the past flashed through Carly's mind and stole the breath from her lungs. She could suddenly feel the metal cuff on her own wrist.

As the FBI locked the van's back door on Troy Hill, she shook her head and shut the past away.

But her pulse still raced. And she felt as if her insides were vacuum-packed.

She should go back to bed. But, really, what was the point? She stayed at the window. No way was she going to fall asleep tonight. She struggled with sleep on her best days.

She couldn't shake the image of Troy Hill—bloodied and beaten—out of her head.

She had looked like that once, not that long ago, had been carried off like that by the enemy. If some of the guys in her unit hadn't gone after her, she'd be dead. Dark memories swooped back into her head, vultures that didn't want to wait until she was dead, but came to tear her apart alive.

The van's motor started outside.

Nothing about this—not the van, not the men, not the beat down—looked like an FBI operation.

Something wasn't right.

Memories of her night in enemy hands played in Carly's head over and over. *If nobody had come to save me...*

What if Troy Hill had told her the truth?

Who was going to save *him*?

Instinct pushed her to do something. But what if it wasn't instinct? What if it was craziness, the same thing that made her an insomniac? The same thing that gave her flashbacks and made her tremble. The same insanity that almost killed Patrick.

She didn't want to be crazy. She wanted to be normal.

Was wanting to go after him normal behavior?

But even as she asked herself, she was dragging on her clothes. She checked her weapon, then hesitated again. Because, dammit, what exactly was she going to do? She wanted this job. She *needed* this job. If she didn't have this job, she didn't have anything.

But the FBI pickup didn't sit right with her. She could spend half an hour checking it out, just to set her own mind at ease. Nobody would have to know.

She pushed up the window quietly and climbed out onto the roof. She lunged and jumped to the top of the foot-wide stone wall that surrounded the property. The wall stood about two feet from the guardhouse, so the move didn't require much acrobatics.

A couple of hemlocks edged the gate on the inside. She stepped forward to the edge of the wall and crouched in the cover of one of the trees. The thick foliage blocked her from sight of the guardhouse and the grounds. *So far so good.*

When the van rolled through the gate, she glanced back at the guardhouse. Jason hadn't come out.

The van slowed for the speed bump that served as an extra security measure just outside the gate. Carly straightened and softly stepped over to the top of the vehicle. Since the speed bump jostled the van, the extra dip her weight added went unnoticed.

She squatted immediately and opened the storage unit, hanging on to it for support. Nothing inside but a couple of dusty tools. Once she folded her body into the space, she pulled the top down and hung on to the edge, leaving a small gap so she could see where they were going.

The van picked up speed as it rolled down the quiet street.

She would stay with them until they took the turn for Quantico, then she'd slip away at a red light unseen. She wanted to make sure they really were FBI.

But the van didn't head toward the FBI headquarters. They headed toward the Potomac River and stopped at the shipyard. The motor went silent. The two men up front got out, went around, and dragged Troy from the back, cursing at him.

The driver had cut the headlights, but the shipyard lights ahead provided enough illumination for Carly to see the two men march Troy toward a mid-sized fishing boat that bobbed on the water. They shoved him on board—not without a scuffle.

He fought at every chance, but with his hands and feet tied, he didn't get far. Knocking him off balance was too easy. And once he went down, the two men kicked the living daylights out of him again.

Only when he stopped moving did they finally leave him and hurry to cast off. They turned on the motor but not the lights, kept checking the harbor, kept scanning the water.

The longer Carly watched, the more the scene looked like something out of an old-fashioned mob movie, thugs taking their target out to sea to sleep with the fishes.

And she was almost relieved. Because this meant she wasn't a nutcase with paranoid delusions. She wasn't crazy. She was suddenly on a rescue op.

That actually calmed her. She'd had plenty of rescue experience from the military. She found her footing.

Since the men had parked the van in the shadows, she managed to slip to the ground unseen. She kept low as she snuck closer to the pier. Then she ducked behind a metal barrel when she reached the water's edge.

One man took the helm while the other shoved Troy below deck. He came back up alone, then joined his buddy behind the wheel. Since they hadn't turned on the lights, both men were probably needed to navigate.

She knew nothing about boats. Her family wasn't into vacations. You couldn't lock up a funeral home to spend a week or two on the beach. And she hadn't seen much water in the army either. She'd spent her deployments in the Afghan mountains.

The boat was a foot away from the dock. Then two. Then three.

She darted forward, ran along, and jumped. Then she hung on for dear life. If she slipped, the propellers would cut her. But her military training took over and pushed her to do what she had to do to achieve her objective.

Which was what?

Damned if she knew.

*Saving an innocent man. Maybe.* What did she really know about Troy Hill anyway?

She ducked behind a chum barrel just as one of the men lumbered her way to investigate what had rocked the boat.

"I don't see nuthin.'" He peered over the side. "Maybe you hit a floatin' log." He plodded down the stairs to the cabin below, came back up in two minutes. "We're fine. She ain't takin' on no water. Let's get the hell out."

He didn't sound like an FBI agent. Carly had still been half hoping they would simply cross the river and dock at some secret FBI facility. But instead, the boat continued downriver, moving through the city.

She reached into her pocket for her phone. Empty. The phone had fallen out, was probably in the storage container on the top of the van. *Great.*

She drew a deep breath, held it, blew it out slowly. Then did it again, pulling herself together.

At least she had her gun.

But would she shoot?

Maybe she was wrong. She didn't think so, but she didn't exactly trust her own judgment these days either. Sometimes she'd see something glint on a roof and become convinced it was a sniper. Or drive way around a pothole that looked like it might hide an IED. Sometimes her brain still confused the present with the past.

She wasn't in enemy country anymore. Everyone wasn't out to get her and the people around her. She was safe, back in the US. She had to be able to fit back into civilian society.

All she wanted was a normal life.

Except then, what was she doing on this boat?

*Oh hell.* Chances were, she was going to seriously regret climbing out that guardhouse window.

She drew another deep breath. *Fine.* She was here. At least nobody knew she was here. She would stay and observe. No action was necessary on her part at this stage. If anything changed, she could make a decision at that time whether to get involved and how.

Minutes ticked by as the boat cut through the water, passing through the lit-up capital, passing under the bridges.

"Goin' home after this?" one of the men asked the other up in the front.

"To Jenny's place. The wife thinks I'm doin' the night shift."

They shared a laugh, then the talk turned to the money they were going to make tonight and the women and the horses they were going to spend it on.

The river widened.

Carly shifted in the small spot she'd wedged herself into, unease creeping up her spine. She wasn't a strong swimmer. The lit-up houses on shore looked small and suddenly seemed as far away as the stars above.

Then the boat's motor cut out, and an eerie quiet enveloped the vessel. She held her breath as the two men walked toward the hatch. One went down; the other dragged a cement brick and heavy iron chains from the front of the boat.

She had a difficult time coming up with an innocent explanation for *that*.

Shoved from behind, Troy hobbled up the stairs. His face bled. So did his hands, the blood looking black in the dark. He held his shoulder at a crooked angle. He turned, and for a second, she could see him better in the moonlight.

Okay, the shoulder was definitely dislocated.

That had to hurt like hell.

He tried to lurch against the men, but being hog-tied worked against him. Still, he managed to knock one of them over the side of the boat.

The guy hit the water with a splash, the boat rocking a little.

"Don't fuckin' move!" The other man pointed a gun at Troy's head.

Carly could clearly see the silencer, heard the soft click as the safety was released.

The guy's buddy was climbing back into the boat, swearing his head off.

Carly's blood rushed in her ears. They meant to kill Troy, and they would do it right now, right here.

She grabbed her own gun, sprang up, pushed by instinct and training, aimed as she went, double-tapping the guy who held the gun. Clean shot to the heart, clean shot to the head. His dripping buddy pulled his own weapon, aiming it at Carly. She squeezed off two more shots and watched as the man folded to the deck.

Then she froze.

Her breath came in ragged gasps. Fear and confusion washed over her, realities blending, battle scenes dancing in front of her eyes, as she smelled the blood and the gunpowder.

She shook her head and blinked a couple of times. Then she forced air into her lungs before she moved up to the pile of limbs, keeping her gun ready. The two thugs lay dead, partially on top of their prisoner.

Troy blinked up at her, surprise on his scarred face.

She lowered her gun. "Are you okay?"

He sucked in air as he struggled to sit, rolling the bodies off him. "Been better."

She hesitated. Did she trust him now? How good could her judgment be when she hallucinated battle scenes at least once a day?

"Not that I mind being tied up and alone on a boat with a beautiful woman under the stars, but the cuffs are cutting off my circulation." His tone was mild, his attitude watchful.

She pulled her knife from her boot, freed his legs first. Then she had to search pockets to find the key to the handcuffs. Thank God, she found it on the first try.

She set Troy free, then held out a hand to pull him up, and he accepted the help, his long fingers folding around hers. A warm hand. Strong. Callused palm. A workingman's hand that should have felt rough on her skin, but instead felt…distracting.

As soon as he was on his feet, she pulled away. She kept her gun ready, in case he tried to tackle her, but he didn't.

*Okay.*

She gave him a minute to get blood flow back to all his extremities before she broke bad news number one. "We'll have to do something about that shoulder."

And the sooner, the better. Before the tissue got all swollen and made pushing the joint back even more difficult. She reached for his hand and gripped it tightly.

"Dare I hope all this handholding will eventually lead to romance?" he asked with a wry tilt of his lips.

A dark shiver ran down her spine, causing all kinds of inappropriate tingles. That raspy voice was going to be the death of her.

She yanked downward, hard, in one quick motion, and winced at the sound of his shoulder popping back into place.

His lips narrowed into a thin, straight line. His breath hissed out. A long second passed before he said, "Thanks."

She nodded. Time for bad news number two. "I can't drive a boat."

He smiled. "I can. Navy SEAL. Remember?"

She remembered, she just still wasn't sure how much of what he'd told her in that basement had been the truth. Although, the more time they spent together, the more she believed him.

He bent and searched the dead men, holding his left shoulder stiffly at his side, but still managing to be quick and efficient.

"No identifying documents," he said, frowning, as he straightened.

"Are you really with the FBI?"

"Yes, ma'am."

"Maybe you should call them."

"Wharst's goons took my secure phone when they caught me."

"I lost mine. Can't help you there."

"I don't want to use theirs." He indicated the bodies at his feet. Then he moved to the head of the boat. "Somebody had to have heard those shots. Let's get out of here." He started up the motor and began to turn the boat around.

She moved up behind him. The bodies kept drawing her gaze back, the black blood pooling on the deck.

He glanced over his shoulder. "You okay?"

She had to be. "I'm supposed to be adjusting to civilian life, not shooting people in the night."

Frustration swept through her, quickly followed by anger. She pushed some of that anger his way. "You can't be too good an undercover agent if they caught you. Didn't you pay attention in training?"

He'd turned the boat, and they were now going back up the Potomac. A few minutes ticked by before he responded.

"I was in the conference room, trying to place a bug. I figured, no security cameras, easy pickings. Right? The room has one entrance. The only way to reach it is to walk by the outside window. I thought if anyone was coming, I'd see them."

She knew which room he was talking about, and he was right. "So why didn't you?"

"The housekeeper's grandkids are short enough to fit under the window."

The kids, a gaggle of little girls, came by every day to visit their grandmother who lived on the premises.

"The second I heard noise at the door, I pulled my gun."

"They screamed like banshees," she finished the story for him.

"Then security rushed in and, at that point, the only way out would have been to open fire."

"So you let them take you instead of risking having the kids in the middle of a gunfight."

"I figured there'd be an opportunity to get away later."

"What happened to the bug?" Nick had said nothing about finding one.

Troy grimaced. "I swallowed it. Right now, somebody at Quantico is listening to my lunch being digested."

They moved up the river quietly for a while. She shot another glance back at the men she'd killed.

How was it possible that she was back to this again? Back to bloody violence and death. Maybe her mother was right. Trouble seemed to find her. Maybe she needed to stay home, play house for Hector, stay far away from any kind of action.

Not that staying at work would be a choice now. She would be out of a job. After only two weeks. She didn't look forward to a police investigation. In her experience, even a justified kill could heap a load of trouble on a person's head, even in war, let alone in the middle of DC.

She looked away from the bodies. She had really, really hoped that she would never have to pull the trigger again. "Do you know who they are?"

Troy kept his eyes on the river. "I'll have someone come and pick up the bodies. Maybe the lab can identify them by their fingerprints." He turned his attention to her. "Why did you come after me?"

"Saw them put you into the van. A couple of things seemed off."

"You saved my life. I couldn't get out of the metal cuffs. If you hadn't popped up, I'd probably be on the bottom of the river right now. Thank you."

The honest appreciation felt good, his raspy voice tickling something inside her. Since it made her feel strange, she brushed the sensation away. "No sense in getting all mushy."

He gave a flat grin.

She felt a responding tug on her lips that surprised her. She had very little to smile about. She'd just killed two men and lost her job. She was not looking forward to weeks of being interrogated by law enforcement, and then months or possibly years of "told you so" from her mother.

That last one, especially, was enough to make a girl consider tying that cement brick to her own feet and going over the side of the boat into the dark water.

# CHAPTER
# FOUR

Troy docked at the houseboat community where he lived. He should have been celebrating his escape, but instead, heavy tension sat on his shoulders as he watched Carly standing in the bow, holding on to the rail. He'd somehow managed to involve a civilian in his mission. *Shit.*

He didn't want a civilian on his hands. Not to mention two dead bodies. He'd gone to the senator's mansion for information. And because he hadn't gotten it, he would have to go back. But first, he had to deal with the clusterfuck on his hands.

He'd already dragged the bodies down below. A blue tarp covered the bloodstains on deck. As dark as the night was, he figured he'd taken sufficient precautions. The people in the other houseboats were tucked in for the night. Most of his neighbors were retirees.

He jumped to the dock and tied up the boat.

Carly jumped and landed next to him. Her auburn hair looked a few shades darker in the moonlight, the bun that had begun the night in military order now lopsided, a few stray locks curling around her chin.

She scanned the jumble of docks, the other boats, the small shops, and the road in the back. She assessed the terrain like a soldier.

She'd fought like a soldier too: decisive, her shots accurate even on the rocking boat. More than impressive. Unbelievable that she'd come after him to save him.

She looked strong and ready for anything, even now, but when she stepped under a light pole, the strain in her eyes and the quick jerk of her hand when a door slammed somewhere nearby, betrayed that she was fraying at the edges.

She kept three feet of distance between them—enough to go for her weapon, if needed. She still didn't fully trust him.

"Where are we going?" she asked.

"My place. I need to get my backup phone." And his backup weapon. "So how did you get from the mansion to the boat?"

As she told him, his respect for her grew by the second. She'd taken a huge chance. For a stranger. She involved herself in danger when it benefited her nothing. Her actions said a lot about the kind of person she was.

"Are they going to miss you at work?" He didn't want her to get into trouble or get hurt.

"My shift doesn't start until six. But I can't go back anyway." Her shoulders slumped. She glanced back toward the white boat and the blue tarp, then shot Troy a dark look. "I really needed that job."

He slowed. They were at his houseboat.

"This is it." He stopped in front of the weather-beaten aluminum plank that led to the deck. "1998 Harbor Master."

She looked at the houseboat as if she didn't know quite what to make of it. "I should go home."

Old Betsy wasn't that bad, was she? Sadly, Troy didn't spend enough time at home to do all the repairs she needed. Suddenly he was conscious of the torn awning and the mess he'd left this morning before he'd driven over to the senator's mansion.

He didn't mind the lack of refinement. Being here filled him with peace. He liked the solitude. He wanted a couple of days of nothing but fishing from the top deck. But first, he had a mission to finish.

"I'd like to talk to you some more," he said as a plan slowly formed in his head. "I'll drive you home afterwards."

He gestured at his home. "She was my grandfather's. A fifty-two footer. Twin inboard motor. Hop on board."

For reasons he couldn't define, he wanted her to like the boat.

He showed her his living room and the galley. Then he gestured toward the back. "The head is back there…bathroom," he switched to civilian speak. He pointed at the other door. "Bedroom. There's a smaller bedroom and bathroom below deck, but right now I'm using them for storage. They're stuffed to the ceiling with my boxes."

She shifted on her feet, an uncertain look in her eyes. Right. She didn't know him from Adam and wasn't comfortable being alone on a boat with him.

His appearance probably didn't help matters. He stepped over to the sink and washed the blood off his hands and face, although he wasn't sure if it'd be an improvement. Now all his scars would be on display.

The odd thought that she was the first woman on his boat popped into his head. *So what?* How was that relevant?

He turned his back to her and stripped out of his stained shirt, grabbed a clean one from the back of the nearest chair. He didn't have a lot of clothes. What little laundry he had, he hand-washed nightly, then lay the clothes out on the furniture to dry. Or on deck, if there was no wind.

Feeling a little more civilized without the blood, he opened the wall safe and grabbed his backup gun, tucked it in the back of his waistband. Then he pulled out his temporary FBI ID from the back of the safe and tossed it to her. "Good guy. See?"

She turned the ID over, nodded to him, and threw it back, her shoulders finally relaxing. "Why didn't you tell the senator's security who you were? Your cover would have been blown, but it would have saved you a beating. If Nick knew you were FBI, they would have treated you differently."

"Maybe." He wasn't sure. "I didn't want to ruin the whole investigation."

He grabbed his second phone, palmed the keys to his fully restored 1967 Chevy Camaro, black with white racing stripes—not exactly meant for undercover work, pretty much the opposite of low profile. But his black SUV sat a block from the mansion where he'd parked it before he'd been caught.

"What's your full name?" he asked conversationally as he stashed everything in his pockets. "I should know the name of the woman who saved my life."

"Carly Montgomery."

He liked the name. It fit her. *Carly* was feminine. *Montgomery* was the name of one of World War II's most important generals.

"Nice to meet you, Carly Montgomery." He gestured toward the head. "Feel free to use the bathroom if you need to clean up a little."

She hesitated.

"I'm not going to trap you in the bathroom for my nefarious purposes. I swear." He flashed her a smile. "I like rolling-around space when I'm seducing a woman."

Instead of blushing or shooting him a scathing look, she said, "Anything worth doing is worth doing right?"

"Navy SEALs sure as hell don't do anything badly."

She shook her head as she passed him, but she was smiling.

He liked her style. Almost as much as he liked the swing of her hips.

When the bathroom door hid her from view, he went into his bedroom, closed the door behind him, and dialed his FBI connection.

"Damn glad to hear from you," Agent Cassidy said.

With maybe more relief than Troy expected, so he asked, "Any news from Gabe and Jake?"

A weighty pause on the line. Then, "I just hung up with them. XO-ST caught up with Gabe in Kabul. Jake was still in the country, so between the two of them, they sorted those guys out. They'll be leaving Afghanistan today." Cassidy paused. "What happened to you?"

Troy filled the man in on everything, including Carly's participation, asked for a pickup for the bodies, the boat, and the van, and finished with "I want to bring her on board. After tonight, the senator's goons will step up security. Chances are I won't be able to get back in. She has a free pass to go in and out of the mansion as she pleases."

"The op is too delicate."

"She's a soldier, not a civilian. She's one smart woman. And she's already involved."

Silence on the other end.

"I vouch for her," Troy said. "If anything goes wrong, I take full responsibility."

Cassidy still hesitated, but only a second or two. "I'll run a background check."

After they ended the call, Troy grabbed his old prepaid phone that still had about fifty bucks on it, put himself in contacts, then dragged his battered body outside.

Carly was already out there, standing in the shadows at the railing, her arms wrapped around herself. She stared at the fishing boat with the blue tarp a few docks down. When she heard him coming she turned to him, a haunted expression clouding her face.

"I got a phone for you. You can use this until the FBI gets your old phone back to you." He lobbed the phone to her.

She caught it without effort. "Thanks."

"I'm number one on the speed dial."

She nodded.

"Family?" he asked, going for a sharp, but necessary change of subject. Whether or not she had three kids at home would make a difference in whether or not she might be willing to come on board with his plans.

"Parents in Baltimore."

"Husband? Children?"

"So far, I've been able to hold my mother back," she deadpanned.

He felt the corner of his lips tug up in a smile. "Lots of pressure, huh?"

"Volcanos have erupted from less."

He liked her style. Her honesty. Her bravery. That on a night like this, she was still hanging on to her sense of humor.

"So you live in DC alone?"

She nodded.

"No boyfriend?"

"None of your business." Then she muttered under her breath, barely audibly, "Not after the last one."

"What happened with the last one?" he asked.

She bit her lip as if she hadn't meant to say that out loud. Tension radiated off her and filled the air.

Then she finally said, "I got tangled in the sheets in the middle of the night." She was looking at her hands. "I had a flashback to something that happened in the army. I thrashed. Patrick woke up and leaned over me. I thought he was someone else." Her gaze suddenly clung to Troy's as if she was falling over a ledge into an abyss and he was the only link holding her, suspended over some dark vortex. "I tried to snap his neck. I actually broke his shoulder."

"That's pretty normal." He made sure his tone held no hint of judgment. "There are ways to work on flashbacks. They'll get milder. Have you done counseling?"

She nodded.

"Keep up with the meditation and the exercises they give you." Then he moved on from the subject to make it clear that it wasn't a problem for him.

"Roommates?" he asked.

"I can keep my mouth shut, if that's what you're getting at. And I don't have a roommate."

"Security clearance?"

She nodded. "Have to have that to be put on the senator's security team."

He asked a few more questions. Nothing in her answers made him wary or regret wanting to bring her on board. She'd gained his approval in record time. She'd demonstrated that she was open-minded, quick to act, capable of stealth, and, more importantly, knew right from wrong.

She seemed a little raw around the edges, but he didn't think that'd be unmanageable.

Her gaze moved across the scars on his face.

"Were you close to Nina Norton?" she asked, probably thinking it was her turn.

He frowned at her. "This isn't how this works. You're not evaluating whether or not I'm a security risk. I'm evaluating you."

"I'm evaluating whether or not to trust you."

Fair enough. "I was engaged to Nina Norton. And I couldn't save her from being blown up."

He didn't discuss this topic. With anyone. Ever.

But somehow, this was the second time he was talking about the explosion to Carly, in the span of a few hours. The first time, when he'd been in the cage, he'd told her about the explosion to play on her feminine sympathies. He'd been building a connection so he could talk her into setting him free.

He wished now that he'd kept his mouth shut, back then and now. Whatever she was going to say in response, he wasn't going to like it.

But she didn't get the chance to say anything. His phone buzzed with a text message.

*Carly Montgomery approved for mission assistance.*

"Let's go," he said, and was off the boat a minute later, hurrying to his car in the parking lot, Carly close behind.

He opened the car door for her, which earned him a funny look. He supposed in the army she'd gotten used to being treated like one of the guys. But when he went back around, turned the key in the ignition, and the engine purred to life, she actually smiled.

For the first time.

"Nice car."

"Thanks," he said, a little dazed.

To start with, she had a great body and a memorable face, but the smile put the whole package way over the top. She was ridiculously beautiful—all that auburn hair, the clear green eyes, that bow-shaped mouth—and need sliced through him, desire that he hadn't felt in a long time. And then he remembered his scars, the contrast between their appearances. He turned his face away, focusing on the road and the sparse traffic.

"So here's the thing…If you want me to, I'll drive you home. But I'm hoping you'll help me with the case I'm working."

"I'm still waiting for you to tell me what's going on," she said.

He glanced at the time. They had an hour before her shift would start at six a.m., and a ride to the senator's mansion that would take about that long. Enough time to fill her in on the basics.

"How would you like to moonlight for the FBI for a day or two? You return to the mansion as if nothing happened. Keep your eyes and ears open and report to me later at a pre-agreed location."

She considered him carefully. "I need to know what this is all about."

He began with the condensed version. "A while back, I worked for a private security firm on contract for the US government. We did international missions. On the last one, my team was sent to Venice, Italy, to pick up a Navy SEAL who'd gone rogue and killed several people."

She flinched. "PTSD?"

"Nothing like that. Turns out, he was the good guy. The men he killed had come after him first, to cover up a crime."

"How does that tie to the senator?"

"The same bad guy who tried to take out the good guy was also blackmailing Wharst. It all came out when we took the bad guy down."

Troy didn't want to name names, other than Wharst, whom she already knew.

"Blackmailed the senator with what?"

"Wharst's little brother was involved in something called combat tourism. The private commando company I worked for apparently also took rich civilians to war zones. These people were trained for a month, then put into real-life combat situations." Bile rose in his stomach along with fury. "Like a video game but in real life. Depending on how much they paid, they were even allowed kills."

She stared at him.

"One hundred percent confirmed." He turned left at the light. "The senator's little brother, Mitch, was involved. I'm looking to find evidence that the senator knew and turned a blind eye. I mean, we know he did, but we need proof that'll stand up in a court of law."

"That's why you tried to bug his conference room."

"And that's why he tried to take me out. He wants to run for president. He can't afford a scandal like this."

She looked like steam was ready to come out of her ears. "When we try to do everything right over there…Damned hard to prove to those people that we're not the enemy. Then idiots like that—" Her voice broke from fury. "For entertainment!" She swallowed hard, pinned her burning gaze on his face. "I'm in."

"One more thing." His fingers tightened on the steering wheel. "The senator knows that my team knows. His best bet is to take out everyone who has firsthand knowledge of his involvement. Without the three of us, nothing can be proved."

"So the three of you are in danger?"

"Us and some immediate family. A couple of women are currently at a safe house. That's why the senator's goons beat me at the mansion. They wanted everyone's location."

"Are the women in the US?" she asked, then shook her head the next second. "Never mind. It's better if I don't know. I'd like to think I'd be tough if caught, but everybody has their breaking point."

Troy drove through town, adding in some details and fleshing out the story to make sure she had the necessary information.

"So basically I'm looking for any hard evidence that proves the senator has knowledge of combat tourism," she said as he pulled the car over at the end of the street, about two hundred yards from the mansion.

"Look for anything with the name Brent Foley on it. That's the guy who was blackmailing Wharst. Or XO-ST. That's the name of the private security commando company that offered combat tourism—Xtreme Ops-Shadow Teams."

"How do I report back to you?"

"Don't call. I'll come to your place once your shift is over."

She gave him the address, and he memorized it.

She reached for the door handle. "Here we go."

He stopped her with a hand on her shoulder. "Are you a hundred percent sure? If they catch you, they won't be any kinder to you than they were to me."

"They won't catch me."

She slipped from the car and immediately moved into the shadows of the early dawn, then disappeared behind a tall hedge.

About a million second thoughts assailed Troy, as he thought *be careful*, but it was too late to say it.

Just a few hours ago, she'd followed a couple of armed kidnappers, hid on their boat, and attacked them in the middle of the night to save a complete stranger. Carly Montgomery was anything but careful. But at the moment, under the circumstances, she was the best person for the job. Ideal even, with her kind of access.

Troy watched the spot where she'd disappeared. *Stay safe.*

The last thing he wanted was another brave woman getting hurt because of him.

# CHAPTER
# FIVE

Carly snuck back into the small room above the gatehouse the same way she'd snuck out. Good thing she knew the location of every camera and motion detector on the grounds.

She checked her uniform. Almost dry. She'd rubbed a couple of bloodstains out with a wet towel back on Troy's houseboat. The stains hadn't been too bad. Troy had done the lions' share of the dirty work.

She washed her face again, mostly to wake herself up. Brushed her teeth. Combed her hair. The bags under her eyes were large enough to exceed airline carry-on limits. Not much she could do about that.

She reported for duty one minute early. Jason waited at the guardhouse door, yawning into the morning.

"Going home?" She stifled a responding yawn and tried to look bright-eyed and bushy-tailed.

"Yeah. Ready to hit the hay."

That made two of them. Hay, straw…honestly, she would gladly have slept on a patch of plain dirt.

*Okay. Stop fantasizing about sleep. Get to work.*

"Do you know who'll be on rotating duty with the intruder today?" she asked innocently, pretending she didn't notice that Jason had forgotten his gaze on her chest.

"FBI came to pick him up. You just missed them." He gathered himself and walked away with a halfhearted wave. He hadn't even hit on her this morning. He really was tired.

And he was a liar.

He had let the van through without checking IDs last night, and now he was lying about the FBI pickup. He had to be in on whatever was going on. Most likely, the senator's entire security team was in on it.

She couldn't trust anyone here.

She glanced out at the grounds. Everything looked quiet, no movement at the mansion save the guards. She wished she were on guard duty there. It'd make snooping around easier. But while she was stuck at the guardhouse, she would make the best of it and look for clues right here.

She wanted to help Troy Hill. She didn't want to let him down.

She pulled up the check-in log and read through it, going backward. The first oddity jumped out at her right away. The van that had come in the middle of the night hadn't been logged.

Which could mean that she was unlikely to come across anything valuable here. Evidently when a visit was on the shady side, security simply didn't log it. Nothing for her, or anyone else, to find.

She kept reading through the records anyway.

*License plate, time in, time out, name, reason for visit.* She scrolled down the screen, scanning row after row of visits from campaign aides and politicians, press, various deliveries and landscaping services, as well as employees.

Her arrivals and departures were there too. Staff used the same gate as visitors, but employees had to drive straight to the back lot after clearing the gate. They weren't allowed to pull up to the circular driveway in front of the mansion. They had to enter the house through the servants' entrance on the side.

She scanned the log carefully, but as fast as she could. Nick usually stopped by. The head of security didn't keep to a shift schedule but came and went. With yesterday's breach, he'd probably be here most of the day.

Would he call the men who'd taken Troy? He might. For confirmation that the job was completed. What would he do when he couldn't reach them?

Dry cleaning delivery pulled up to the gate in a yellow van. Carly let the young Korean guy through. He came twice a week. She logged the visit. He was in and out in half an hour, just a quick drop-off and pickup.

Right after the dry cleaner left, Jason meandered back to the guardhouse with a cup of steaming coffee. He leaned against the door frame. "Nick called a meeting for everyone who wasn't at last night's meeting."

"How long do you have to stay?"

He couldn't see the screen from where he was standing, so Carly kept scrolling and kept her attention on the names and dates. Nick might make changes to the schedule and pull her off this station. She wanted to scan at least six months' worth of backlog.

Jason said, "Meeting's in twenty minutes. How long was it last night?"

"Ten minutes? But it was with the senator."

Jason nodded, getting what she meant. The senator's time was precious. He didn't dawdle. Nick was more verbose. He liked being the boss and that people had to listen to him.

"If Nick was here all night, he'll want to go home too." She tried to be positive.

Jason rolled his eyes. "What's there to say, anyway? We fucked up. It's not like we did it on purpose. Bastard snuck in, but we caught him before he did any damage."

Carly kept an eye on the screen. She couldn't find anything suspicious in the logs, nothing to report to Troy later. Then again, the whole XO-ST team could have been here and she would never know it.

"What are you doing?" Jason stepped closer.

She looked up and flashed a mock frown. "I can't believe you went for coffee and didn't bring me any."

Was he involved in combat tourism? The concept was enough to make her want to strangle someone. It was an insult to the army she'd served and bled in.

He came around. She changed the screen. He stopped close enough so she could smell not only the coffee but also his morning breath.

"Were you up all night thinking about me? Should have called me up to the room." He pushed out his chest. "Admit it. You think about me naked."

"Honestly? I find you a little intimidating," she said to stroke his ego, and stepped to the side.

He flashed a pleased smile. "I think a lot of chicks do. Because of the way I look. But I'm just a big teddy bear."

He emphasized the word *big*.

He was definitely oversized. Bigger than Troy, yet in a fight, her money would be on the former SEAL. Hardness didn't come from just muscles. Troy Hill was hard to the bone, to his soul. He was the kind of guy who'd get blown up and keep going.

Jason was a mountain of muscle. Troy was a mountain of strength.

For the first time in forever, Carly found herself attracted to a man.

She was never going to think about Jason naked, but Troy Hill…. God, when he'd taken off his shirt on the houseboat, in his kitchen.

He hadn't turned on the light, but the windows let in enough moonlight, glinting off hills and valleys of muscles. And more scars, of course. She'd wanted to reach out and trace them.

Lust and need had hit her so hard, she thought her knees were going to buckle.

And that was just the superficial stuff.

He had a past as scarred as his body. A past that touched her heart. The woman he'd loved had been brutally killed, in front of his eyes.

But he hadn't let that tragedy destroy him. He kept on fighting. He was probably a hero a hundred times over. And fighting a senator right now? Talk about David and Goliath.

The stacked deck wouldn't matter to Troy. He put his life on the line to do the right thing.

Jason said, "So you live around here?"

If he was trying to wrangle an invitation to her apartment, he was going to be disappointed.

She let her gaze settle on Jason's wide chest. "You must have been in the military. Where were you deployed?"

He glanced down at his bicep, flexed it. "I thought about it, but I never enlisted. Somebody has to stay home and hold down the fort, right?"

*He hadn't been to Afghanistan.* "Absolutely."

"So you wanna—"

She cut him off. "You better get going, or you'll miss your meeting."

He glanced at his watch and backed away. "Shit." Then he strode off toward the mansion.

Carly looked after him. No connection to combat tourism, no Afghan or XO-ST link. Frustration pumped through her as she grabbed two protein bars from the drawer for breakfast.

She wanted, desperately, to have something to report to Troy later. She wanted to impress him, because he'd impressed her. She thought he was pretty damn great, and she wanted him to think the same about her.

She went back to the logs.

At nine, Brian, another guard, came up to give her a potty break. Guards at the gate got a short break every three hours and one long break for their main meal.

She ran up to the bathroom, freshened up, then—after a few longing glances at the bed—she went back down. "Thanks. Appreciated."

He was finishing some car magazine Jason must have left behind after his shift. She hadn't even noticed it, she'd been so focused on her computer spying.

"No problem," Brian said and stayed put.

Carly tilted her head and smiled at Mr. Tall and Blond. He wasn't as muscle-bound as Jason, but still well built. They all were. "You been on the job long?"

The two weeks she'd worked here had been enough to learn everyone's name, but little more beyond that.

"Couple of years."

"Must like it, if you stayed. Seems like a pretty good gig. I was considering doing either something like this or joining one of those private security commando teams the military hires to do contract work overseas. I'm glad I picked DC."

He nodded and walked away.

She swallowed a groan. So much for her subtly getting the man to admit that he'd been a mercenary before he'd come here and somehow connect the senator to all that nasty business.

Carly went back to double-checking the logs and made a note of the dates and times when the senator's little brother, Mitch, had stopped by for a visit. He was involved in all this, so keeping an eye on his comings and goings seemed logical.

As the hours passed, she was growing more and more dismayed at how little useful information she was able to gather.

By the time Brian came to give her a break for lunch, she was buzzing with impatience to get into the main building. She walked up to the mansion, in through the servants' entrance on the side, and poked around as much as she could on her way to the kitchen. Unfortunately, neither the bathrooms nor the laundry room nor the pantry were hotbeds of criminal activity.

Troy had been caught in the conference room. She meandered that way and noted the computer on the desk in the corner. She pushed a key to wake up the machine. A little window popped up to demand a password. She typed in 1234, which didn't work, then she was pretty much out of guesses.

To guess, she'd need to know who set the password. The senator? Nick? The IT guy? And what did she even know about any of them? Nothing.

She tried the desk drawers. All locked.

She glanced at the window. Nobody out there.

The housekeeper's grandkids weren't here today. Their parents had picked them up last night after their big scare. Carly wasn't going to get surprised by kids like Troy had been.

She picked a paper clip off the desk and bent it, tried to wiggle it inside the keyhole. She held her breath and focused all her attention on the lock and the stupid piece of metal that refused to do her will.

"What are you doing?"

The sharply spoken question startled her.

Nick stood in the doorway with a scowl on his face.

* * *

**Troy**

Troy rounded the senator's mansion in a rented black soccer-mom van that looked like all the other soccer-mom vans on the streets. He could drive by ten times and nobody would think anything of it. His Camaro was too memorable. Both his vehicles were off-limits.

His SUV was still parked where he'd left it last night, in case the senator's security detail had connected the car to their intruder.

A male guard stood in front of the guardhouse, watching the street. Troy didn't look at him straight on but through his rearview mirror that he'd tilted. The man rolled his shoulders.

Where was Carly?

Troy shifted in his seat as his cell phone rang. His FBI connection, Agent Cassidy. Troy drove on as he took the call.

He'd left Bureau headquarters an hour before, after he'd fully updated everyone on the new asset he'd brought in. "Anything new?"

"We got a match in the database on the two dead guys' fingerprints," the man on the other end said. "Minor convictions. Nothing to tie them to the senator or XO-ST."

"Of course not." Troy rubbed his thumb over his right eyebrow. "Would have been too easy."

"The van they left in the harbor failed just about every lab test. Gunpowder residue, drug residue, human blood from at least a dozen different people. Those guys were definitely not in the fishing business."

"Hired killers." He pulled into the parking lot of a golf store two streets up. Since the store stood on higher ground, he could see part of the senator's mansion from there.

"About that cell phone they got off you last night," Cassidy was saying. "We're seeing some activity."

That got Troy's attention. "It's a secured phone," he said, even as he thought, *every code can be broken.* "Can they access past calls?"

"Not supposed to. None of that info is saved to the phone or the chip…"

"But?" IT wasn't his strength. He'd been an explosives expert with the SEALs. That was the area where he'd had most of his training.

"The calls leave a binary fingerprint, so to speak," the FBI agent said.

"So the right person with the right skills can retrieve call records?"

"We only have one man like that at the Bureau. Chances of finding another person with that skill set…"

His heart sank. "But they did it."

"Calls went out from your unit to previous contacts. They were fishing. And nobody was stupid enough to give them anything. The good news is they think you're dead. Might take them days to figure out that last night didn't go as planned. They might not realize what happened until a week or two passes and their hired killers don't show up for the second half of their fee."

That would be a nice break, but Troy wasn't going to count on it. "This means they have the numbers for Jake and Gabe."

The three of them had regular briefings while the other two were overseas. He'd used the phone for every single one of those calls.

"Where are Gabe and Jake?" he asked.

"About to get on a military transport plane in Germany to head home. They've been instructed to destroy their units. In case some kind of a tracker code is sent to their phones from yours."

Troy relaxed for a millisecond. Then cold spread through his chest as a new thought occurred to him. "If the hacker has Jake's and Gabe's cell phone info through mine, could he peel back another layer and see who Jake and Gabe have been calling?"

"Theoretically, no." The man paused.

"Could your in-house hacker do it?"

A moment of silence stretched on the other end. "He could."

Jake and Gabe had probably called Jake's sisters at the safe house. Gabe must have called his sister and nieces. If their enemies somehow got lucky enough to pinpoint the location…"You have to move everyone from the safe house."

"I don't think—" the agent began to say.

But Troy cut him off, not giving a damn about the chain of command. "Send a team."

His fingers tightened on the phone as he looked at the mansion in the distance. They kept underestimating the senator, dammit. He was so much more dangerous than they'd thought.

Troy wanted Carly back. He felt as if he'd just thrown her into shark-infested waters. Why wasn't she at the guardhouse? They'd agreed that he wouldn't make contact while she was on duty. She would call him if she needed help.

Except, of course, if they caught her and took her phone from her.

"You need to move those women to another safe house immediately," he barked into the phone.

"All right," Cassidy agreed. "Okay."

Troy hung up, then dialed Carly. The call rang out. She didn't pick up.

He pulled out of the parking lot and drove back toward the senator's place, trying to figure out what the hell he could do to make sure she was safe, short of storming the mansion.

He never should have brought her into the op. What in hell had he been thinking? He'd been too focused on taking down Wharst.

He was acting just like Nina, who had always been so focused on her next newspaper article, she'd become careless about safety. And she'd paid with her life for that mistake.

And, God, after her death, Troy had been mad at her for so long. Mad at her, mad at himself, mad at the world.

That shit was *not* going to happen again.

He couldn't be so obsessed with Wharst that he lost sight of Carly's safety.

Whether Carly found anything useable today or not, she was out. Period. The end. Troy was going to find a way to bring down the senator without her.

# CHAPTER
# SIX

Carly slid the paper clip up her sleeve and straightened as Nick strode over. Had he crouched to sneak under the window?

When her phone buzzed in her pocket, she ignored it.

She plastered a smile on her face. "I was just wondering what the intruder was doing in here. Maybe looking for money? He probably tried the drawers. I wanted to see if he got in."

Nick watched her through narrowed eyes. "Did he?"

She bent to examine the desk. "The lock is scratched. He tried."

Nick yanked on the drawer. It stayed firmly in place.

She flashed a derisive grin, even as her heart beat in her throat. "So much for his burglar skills."

"You shouldn't be in here."

"Sorry. I just had this wild thought…" She hurried out of the room with an apologetic duck of her head.

Nick followed. He closed the door behind them with a hard click.

"I was just on my way to lunch." She headed toward the kitchen, but she turned back after a few feet. "Any news from the FBI? Do they know yet who the intruder is?"

Nick watched her for a second, his gaze cold and assessing. "Some petty criminal. He didn't even know whose house he was in. Saw a big mansion, figured it meant big money." He put on his boss face. "I want everyone to double their vigilance, understood? This can't happen again."

She clicked her heels together. "Yessir."

"The senator's privacy is paramount. He can't afford a media circus right now. You never heard of the intruder. You never saw anything. The guy was never here."

"Yessir," she said again, heading left while Nick went right and strode down the hallway toward the main part of the house.

*Crap.* She'd hoped to get farther than the conference room, but it wouldn't be good to get caught twice in one day.

She glanced at her watch. Then she glanced at her phone. She had a text message from Troy.

*U OK?*

She quickly texted back.

*@ lunch*

Then she put her phone away.

She had close to three hours left before her shift was over at three p.m. and she could talk to Troy. Hopefully his day was more productive than hers.

She was dragging from getting no sleep the night before, annoyed that she hadn't gotten anything remotely useful all morning. Then she turned into the kitchen, and…*ka-ching! Jackpot straight ahead.*

Mitch Wharst sat at the counter, flirting with the sixty-something cook. Marnie stood five feet four inches tall, as round as a grapefruit. She had the eyes of a hawk and the voice of a general.

"Nobody makes lamb chops like you do, Marnie. Are you sure you don't want to run away with me?"

The cook snorted. "I don't think that would make Arnold happy."

Mitch wiggled his eyebrows. Blond-streaked hair windswept as if he'd come from yachting, a white smile that probably cost more than her car, perfect aristocratic cheekbones—he was the kind of man Carly normally saw only in Ralph Lauren commercials.

He oozed his considerable charm all over the cook. "A vibrant young woman like you is wasted on a senior citizen. That's all I'm saying."

Marnie gave a bark of a laugh and shuffled back to the stove where a rich soup was bubbling, sending delicious puffs of steam into the air.

Carly relaxed her shoulders, strolled over, and took the barstool one over from Mitch.

His attention immediately refocused. "Hey, beautiful." He winked at her. "Where have you been all my life?"

He'd asked her the same thing when they'd first met last week, but now he showed no sign that he recognized her. He was an industrial-size flirt. She wasn't falling for anything he said. From what she'd seen of him last time—playing cricket on the front lawn with the housekeeper's grandkids—even he didn't take himself seriously. Unlike his older brother the senator.

Marnie came by and put a gourmet Angus burger with sweet potato fries on the counter in front of Carly, along with a large fruit salad and a bottle of water.

"Thank you, ma'am." She flashed the woman a look of pure gratitude. When somebody feeds you like that, you had better appreciate it. She'd eaten enough freeze-dried food in her MREs in the army to know a good thing when she saw it.

The presentation was so pretty, for a second she considered taking a picture of the food instead of eating it. It was a short second.

As she dug in, Mitch leaned closer. "A couple of friends and I are sneaking into the nature preserve for some extreme white-water rafting this afternoon. Come with us. We'll drive up as far as we can, then hike the rest of the way in. Rough terrain."

His eyes sparkled. "You can't tell anyone. My brother is obsessed with keeping me from causing a scandal. But if the chance is there, why not try everything? Life is too short to spend it in an office."

His white-toothed smile and enthusiasm were contagious. Like his brother the senator, he had a larger-than-life personality. He would have made a great movie star. He would practically jump off the silver screen.

She flashed him a friendly smile. "Already saw enough excitement to last me a lifetime. Thanks anyway. Just got back from my last tour of duty in Afghanistan a month ago. Ever been there?" she asked conversationally, pretending to pay attention to her food but watching him from the corner of her eye.

The smile slid right off his face. His lips squirmed as if he tasted something unpleasant. "A little while back. Quick business visit. Barely saw anything of the country." He slid off the chair and beat a retreat, calling a "See you around" from the doorway.

He seemed so harmless and was perhaps the most attractive man she'd ever met. Yet she would take Troy's somber eyes and raspy voice over Mitch's flirting any day of the week. Mitch seemed to live by the credo: "Do whatever you want as long as you're having fun."

She couldn't relate to Mitch.

She could relate to Troy. He was a military man; he committed. He had seen some seriously messed-up business. Unlike her, he didn't let it get to him. Maybe, if they hung around each other long enough, she could learn that skill from him.

Was the rest of Troy's body as scarred as his face and back? She choked on her fries. Not because the image that popped into her brain was scary. Just the opposite.

She washed down the food with some water, then made a mental note not to think of Troy naked again. She didn't need that kind of distraction.

She was absentmindedly staring after Mitch, which Marnie misinterpreted, because she said, "Handsome devil, our Mitch. Are you ready to take on all that heartbreak?"

"No, ma'am."

"Smart girl." Marnie turned to the sink.

Carly tackled the fruit salad, her thoughts circling back to Troy. Regardless of the scars he had on the outside—and she really wasn't going to think about those any further—he definitely had scars on the inside too. He'd lost the woman he loved.

Carly had no business being attracted to him. The last thing Troy needed in his life was a nutcase like her. She couldn't handle a relationship right now. She had no business being attracted to anyone. The solitude of her apartment fit her just fine.

Go to work. Go to the gym. Read in the evenings. She liked the predictability of her routine.

She finished her lunch, thanked Marnie again, then headed back to the gate.

Brian jumped up as soon as he saw her coming, his face and movements tense. "Good. I have to go." He practically ran by her.

"Are you okay?"

He didn't answer but strode to the mansion's side door and disappeared through it. As she watched, Billy came from around the building and followed with the same tense expression on his face.

Carly tapped her earpiece. She hadn't heard any call going out from Nick.

***

**Troy**

Troy headed down the hall to Carly's ground-floor apartment for their prearranged, after-shift debriefing. She got off work at three p.m. He'd waited until four to give her time to reach home. She was here. He'd seen her car in the parking lot as he pulled in.

The hallway didn't have enough lighting. The walls were marred by graffiti. It certainly didn't look like she was on her way to becoming a millionaire on her security guard salary. He wasn't crazy about her living in this neighborhood.

And that was before he noticed that her door stood ajar, the lock busted. His pulse leapt as he pushed through and found himself face-to-face with a well-executed karate kick she pulled back at the last second. He felt the wind of her sneaker.

She was pure action, eyes flashing, muscles bunched, fierce and ready.

Instead of being startled, Troy found himself aroused as he watched the flush of color in her cheeks. He needed to get a grip.

But not the kind of grip where he put his hands on her and ran his fingers through her soft hair, kissed her bow-shaped lips—

"Sorry." She stepped back. "I didn't expect you this early."

"What happened?" He took in the overturned furniture, pots and pans lying on the kitchen floor in a heap. A camouflage-pattern US Army coffee cup lay in pieces on the floor. His hands clenched. He stepped forward without thought, on instinct, ready to protect her. But, of course, he was too late.

He cursed.

"I don't exactly live in a high-security building." She played it down, but strain showed around her eyes, tension wrinkling the skin between her brows.

"I'm guessing they were looking for drugs or something they could pawn for drugs. They took the microwave."

*Only that?* The place was so sparse, it looked like somebody had backed a truck up to a window. She must not have had much to begin with.

"Want a soda?" She stepped over to the fridge. "Sorry, I don't keep any beer on hand. When I got back from overseas…I figured I better keep clear of alcohol. I wasn't in a good place."

He nodded, liking the forethought and the self-discipline, as well as the honesty, the unflinching way with which she admitted her problems. No games. "A cold soda would be great."

She opened the fridge door, and her lips flattened. "They took my leftovers." She grabbed two sodas, then slammed the door. "My favorite Chinese takeout, dammit."

He took the can she handed him. "Have you called the police?"

"This is the third time the place has been tossed since I moved in. The cops never do anything. It's the neighborhood I live in." A tentative look crossed her face, as if she was fighting with herself whether or not to say something more.

"What is it?"

"Probably nothing, but—The building had four break-ins in the last couple of months. Three times out of four, they hit my place. It's just coincidence, right?"

"Any other coincidences you noticed lately?"

She opened the tab on her soda can. "I keep getting faulty earpieces at work. I miss a lot of what's being said by the rest of the team."

The muscles in his jaw tightened. "They probably switch to a different channel to say things they don't want you to hear."

She nodded. Then gestured toward the mess with her drink. "I don't think they did this."

"Not every time. But I bet at least once. To make sure you really were who you said you were."

The thought that someone had violated her private space, that she'd had to come home alone to this, sent adrenaline pumping through Troy. He would have liked to spare her the stress, but he was too late to prevent it. The least he could do was help her get things back in order.

He set the furniture straight, ignoring his aching ribs that hadn't yet recovered from last night's beatings, then he picked up the broken slivers of her coffee cup and tossed them into the garbage. He moved to the living room, scooped some clothes from the floor and dropped them into the ancient reclining chair. Jeans, T-shirts, army fatigues, nothing fancy—her clean laundry, judging by the overturned hamper.

"You don't have to do this. I can do it later."

But he kept going. "Lets me work off some nervous energy."

She looked like she needed that too. She kept glancing at the door, at the mess, the muscles around her mouth tightening, then relaxing.

She stayed in the kitchen, and put the pots and pans away.

When she moved to the bedroom, he followed her, the two of them working silently side by side. He let her handle the spilled dresser drawers, turning the other way and busying himself with the ripped-off curtain while she reclaimed her underwear. Then he helped her make the bed. And tried not to picture her in pink cotton briefs.

He failed.

*Think of something else.*

Maybe this was where she'd beaten up her ex-boyfriend when she'd had a nightmare. Then the guy bailed instead of comforting her and making her feel safe. She deserved better than a weak-ass jerk.

But now she was alone at night with her memories. Troy didn't have the right to ask what caused her flashbacks, so he didn't. The idea of Carly lost in nightmares was a dull ache in his chest.

Since she didn't have much, restoring the place took all of twenty minutes.

"I really appreciate the help." She tossed the last pillow back in its place. Then she wiped a smudge of dust off her face. "Sorry. I was planning on taking a shower before you got here."

"Why don't you do that? I need to run out for a minute. We'll talk when I get back."

"If you don't mind the wait…"

"You have a gun?"

She shook her head.

He pulled his Glock 26 from the holster under his shirt and handed it to her. A good little gun for concealed carry. He preferred it over the MP9 because of the 10+1 capacity instead of 6+1. Four extra bullets could make a difference between life and death. "Take this into the bathroom with you."

Another woman might have hesitated, but she didn't. She took the Glock. "Thanks."

Hopping over to the hardware store on the corner took Troy thirty minutes. Installing a new lock and dead bolt on Carly's door ate up another ten. By the time she padded out of the bathroom in fresh T-shirt and jeans, hair wet, he was finished.

She checked the locks. "How much do I owe you for this?"

"How much do I owe you for helping me today?"

"That's—"

"Let's call it even."

"Thank you."

"You're welcome."

"It's not exactly an even trade." She dug her toes into the carpet, then looked up at him. "I got pretty much nothing today. I couldn't do more than look at the visitors' logs. I'll be in a better position tomorrow. I'll be in the main mansion."

"I'm having second thoughts about your involvement. I don't want you to get caught."

She drew back as if he'd slapped her. Her cheeks flushed. "I want to do this. I can handle it. The whole combat tourism bullshit is an insult to the army. I want to do something about it."

"The senator will be taken care of one way or the other. The FBI isn't going to let him get away with this. You don't need to be involved."

"It's easier for me to investigate at the mansion than it is for you. I'm supposed to be there. Nobody even notices me. I know the place better than you do."

All the reasons why he'd recruited her in the first place. She was capable. US Army trained.

"I'll be going in tomorrow night," he said. "The senator and his wife will be at another fund-raiser. The man knows no rest when it comes to chasing money." He paused. "I need you to draw me a blueprint of the upstairs, the private quarters."

"I'm going with you."

"You're not."

She held his gaze. "You can't really stop me."

He could. He could handcuff her to the radiator pipes right now.

Thinking about restraining her had been a mistake. Because now he was suddenly thinking about tying her down for purposes other than keeping her in the apartment. Not. Going. To. Happen.

In any case, being bound seemed to be some kind of a trigger for her. She'd said she'd had that bad flashback with the boyfriend because she'd gotten tangled in the sheets.

*Don't think about her tangled in sheets.*

"I make you a deal," he said.

She waited.

"I'll take you with me tomorrow, if you agree to move to the boat until this gig is over." As soon as he said it, he knew this was the answer. He could keep an eye on her at the mansion, and if she stayed on the boat, he could also keep her safe when she was off shift.

She stared at him as if he was nuts. "We met yesterday. Are you asking me to move in with you?"

"For safety reasons."

"You just put up new locks."

"I'd feel more comfortable if you were on the boat."

"You do know that I'm a soldier, right? I can take care of myself."

"I don't like it that there was trouble at the mansion, and right after, your place is burglarized. What if the senator's goons came here to make sure you're not an undercover investigator, to look through your stuff to confirm that you're really who you say you are?"

She looked around. "They couldn't possibly find anything condemning. So now they've confirmed that I'm who I say I am. They have no reason to mess with me."

"They could take you out just to be on the safe side."

The look in her eyes said she was working up more reasons to say no to him, so he added, "Don't think of it as me protecting you. Think of it as you protecting me. What if they track me to the boat? If that happens, it'd be nice to have backup."

She flashed him an are-you-messing-with-me-right-now look. But, after a few seconds, she turned and began packing a bag.

"You said you didn't find much at the mansion. Does that mean you found a little?" he asked once they were in his Camaro. He'd returned the soccer-mom van. If he needed another one tomorrow, he'd rent a different make and color.

"Security at the mansion doesn't log every vehicle that comes and goes," she said as they turned onto the boulevard. "They didn't log the van that came for you last night. Their official story is that the FBI got you this morning. We're all under a gag order. Nobody saw you. You were never there."

Troy kept his eyes on the traffic. The news didn't exactly surprise him.

By the time they reached the docks, Carly had filled him in on her day.

She searched the water as they got out of the car.

"The fishing boat is gone," he said. "The FBI took it by the time I came back from dropping you off at the mansion this morning."

She jumped on board old Betsy behind him and glanced around. "Looks different in the daylight."

"Not as bad as you first thought?" He loved his houseboat. Nothing fancy, but a real home.

"Worse," Carly said. "Way too much water."

He bit back a smile. "Not a fan of all things marine?"

"I don't see what there's to like about the water. Smells like fish." She wrinkled her nose.

He grinned as he walked to the counter in the galley. "Soda or coffee?"

Her eyes were puffy from lack of sleep. She looked like she could use another caffeine boost.

"Soda. It's my only addiction."

He tossed her a can from the fridge, and she closed her eyes briefly as she took the first long swallow. "My mother would kill me if she saw me drinking without a glass. Ladies never drink from the can."

He barely heard what she said. The sight of her with her eyes closed, head back, neck exposed, a soft sound of pleasure escaping her throat as she drank…

His body responded to her, to their proximity, to her body, to her voice. He forced himself to turn away.

He pulled a package of ground meat and an onion from the fridge, then a couple of peppers and tomatoes, a small zucchini and an even smaller summer squash. He felt like cooking. The clock on the microwave showed almost six. Time for dinner, anyway.

"So how did you end up in the army?" he asked her. "Big military family?"

"Funeral home empire. According to my mother. But not really. My parents are in the business." She watched him for a reaction.

He supposed not everyone accepted death as an occupation. He just kept chopping.

"I guess they're doing all right in the Baltimore area," she said, "but they're still small potatoes. Mom has dreams of world domination." She paused. "How about you? Descendant of Navy SEALs going back six generations?"

Not even close. "I grew up on a hog farm in Minnesota. My father was the foreman."

"Where are your parents now?"

"Both gone." And he missed them still. For a second, he wondered what his mother would have made of Carly. He was pretty sure she would have loved her.

He washed the tomatoes, then grabbed a pot to put on some water to boil. "What did your parents think when you joined the Armed Forces?"

"My father threatened to disown me. My mother wanted to have me committed." Her flat smile didn't reach her eyes. "My brother already turned his back on the business. He's an artist in LA. He's completely freaked out by dead bodies."

"And you're not."

"Death is part of life." But her voice was tight.

"I'm sorry you had to shoot the men on the boat because of me."

She held his gaze. Bleak secrets hid in the clear green pools of her eyes. "Ideally, I'd like to go the rest of my life without shooting anyone else."

"You saved my life," he said.

"Speaking of which—" She rubbed a hand over her knee. "Why haven't the police questioned me yet?"

"The FBI took care of the incident."

"Just like that?"

"They have bigger fish to fry." He dumped spaghetti noodles into the boiling water on the stove. Next he stirred the browning meat, then finished chopping the vegetables.

He strained the meat and dumped the vegetables in the skillet, added salt, pepper, and oregano, then stirred. Neither of them spoke again about last night, but they were both thinking about the blood and the bodies on the fishing boat.

When he finished cooking, they ate out on the deck, sitting in the shade, in the comfortable breeze that came off the water.

She thanked him for the meal before asking, "Where did you learn to cook?"

"From my mother. But not spaghetti. She didn't do Italian food. She was German. She made a dozen different kinds of sausages. She could make a hundred things out of pork."

She kept asking questions about Minnesota and the hog farm. Until she didn't.

At one point, when she blinked, her eyes didn't open back up. She fell asleep slouched down in her seat.

Her hair had come undone from its strict military bun and curled around her shoulders. With the water as backdrop, she resembled a resting mermaid.

She hadn't slept at all last night. He'd gotten her back to the mansion just in time to report for her shift. He'd caught a catnap this morning, but she'd had no rest.

Doing his best to block the pain of his injuries, he picked her up and carried her to his bed, laid her on top of the covers. The cabin was warm enough in the late afternoon, so she didn't need a blanket.

As he backed toward the door, her eyelids fluttered. He took another step away from her. She tossed, ready to wake up. He stopped. She settled down again.

He repeated the exercise with the same results.

Even in her sleep, she seemed to sense his presence, and it made her more comfortable in some way. He'd had his own bouts with stress and insomnia, anxiety brought on by memories of bloody violence. So he quietly dropped into his reading chair and stayed. He could let her nap for an hour or two. He could work on his cell phone until then, checking and answering messages.

He woke two hours later to the sound of his phone ringing.

"Gabe and Jake are back in the US. They're taking Allison and Jake's sisters to a new location as we speak," General Roberts said.

Carly blinked at Troy sleepily from his bed, her hair tousled. The sight flooded his body with heat.

"When they're done with that, they'll come to you so the three of you can wrap this thing up," the general continued on the other end.

"Yes, sir."

The line went dead, and Troy set his phone down.

Carly looked around. "How did I get here?"

"I carried you. You fell asleep."

"I never just fall asleep."

"Maybe it's the water."

Her eyes narrowed with suspicion. "And you what? Sat there and watched over me?"

"You hogged the only available bed."

She blinked the sleep from her eyes, brushed her soft hair from her face. She looked like a siren. Everything about her drew him to her. *Bad idea.* Didn't the sailors in the myth crash on the siren's rocky shores?

But maybe Troy didn't care.

"I nodded off too," he admitted. "We both had a busy night last night." He stood and stretched, winced when his ribs screamed. "Are you up now, or do you need a Sleeping Beauty kiss to come fully awake?"

He froze. He had no idea what had made him say that. He hadn't meant to, even if his gaze was straying even now to her lips. She was the first woman he'd been attracted to since Nina. Carly was the first woman in his bed here on the boat. Her presence here messed with his brain. And other body parts.

"Not if you value your front teeth," she said with a quick grin as she got up and pushed by him, leaving the bedroom and crossing the galley, moving outside.

He should have felt relief that she didn't take him seriously, but all he felt was disappointment as he followed her.

Better keep things light. "Could have been your lucky day."

She quirked an eyebrow and flashed him some sass. "Who says it isn't? Mitch Wharst asked me out earlier."

# CHAPTER
# SEVEN

"Mitch Wharst asked you out?" Troy's raspy voice dropped an octave, his eyebrows drawing together as he followed Carly outside. "And you didn't tell me this before?"

She glanced back at him. Waking up with him had been weird. Two solid hours of sleep. Very unlike her.

"Didn't seem related to your op," she said as she turned to the harbor again.

From the corner of her eye, she caught a dark blue van driving by the marina, eerily similar to the one that'd picked up Troy the night before, except this one didn't have a storage container on top.

What if whoever was in the van was involved with the senator? Could even be one of Nick's guys. They could recognize her. Or Troy, for that matter. They were out in the open.

Then Troy pulled her into his arms and turned her so she wouldn't be seen from the van, putting his back to the men and dipping his head to block her face.

"Tell the little bastard, over his dead body." His mouth hovered half an inch above hers.

She froze. *What? Oh, Mitch.*

Troy leaned another bit closer. The distance between them shrank to a quarter inch.

Heat speared through her, along with a sudden need that must have been lurking somewhere inside her for a while now, because it was making its presence known with a vengeance. Her mind fogged. His flint-gray gaze telegraphed a single intent, a single question.

In response, she pressed her lips to his.

His kiss was firm but gentle. He didn't crush her mouth as he kissed her, didn't demand. He coaxed her response out of her. Her body responded to him with an enthusiasm that was wholly unexpected.

And then he deepened the kiss.

The man made an Olympic sport out of kissing.

Granted, she didn't have a huge well of experience to draw from, but this was light years beyond anything she'd felt in a man's arms before.

In about a minute, she wanted more. Which was when she knew she was in trouble. She pulled away, then pressed her lips together.

"Look who's in a rush for dentures," she said in her best tough-chick voice and pretended like crazy that his kiss didn't swirl her needs and thoughts like a hurricane.

He looked very sure of himself as he said, "Stay away from Mitch."

Okay, now that was just plain insulting. "Do I look stupid?"

His gaze traveled the length of her body, and she felt as if someone was caressing her skin with soft feathers. "You look—" He bit off the sentence, then shook his head as if awakening from a dream. "I got the van's license plate. I'll call it in."

*Oh God.*

Her body cooled instantly. He'd only kissed her to keep her face covered. To make sure she wasn't recognized by whoever had been driving the suspicious van.

Except, her mind had melted and she'd responded to the kiss. *God, how embarrassing.* Dear Lord, let him think that she'd just been pretending too, if with a little too much enthusiasm.

Her lips tingled. She fisted her hands so she wouldn't reach up to touch them.

"Did you download the visitor's log by any chance?" Troy asked, obviously fully back on business.

She patted her pocket and came up with the pen drive. "I have the last six months, but I couldn't find anything suspicious."

He held out his hand. "Let me take a look."

As she gave him the pen drive, her fingertips brushed against his, and awareness shot through her. She yanked her hand back.

"How about this?" He tossed the pen drive in the air, then caught it. "While I look through the logs, you draw me a map of the mansion. What shift are you working tomorrow?"

"Morning. Same as today."

And between now and then stood an entire night, the two of them on the houseboat, alone, together. Nerves tingled across Carly's skin.

*Don't fall for this.*

*Don't fall for him.*

***

**Troy**

Carly slept in his bed.

Troy tossed and turned on the couch, feeling like a hapless human in a sci-fi movie, being drawn by tractor beams to an alien spaceship. He valiantly resisted, forcing his thoughts to the senator's mansion, the blueprint, where he needed to go, what he needed to do tomorrow night.

They'd spent hours going over the plan. They didn't quit until close to midnight. Tomorrow night, the senator's mansion would be theirs.

Troy wished he could go right now. Anything was better than lying on the couch and pining after the woman just one closed door away from him.

He wedged a foot between the pillow cushions to keep himself anchored.

And then the sound of her soft whimper reached him.

Not so soft, he realized. If he could hear her through the closed door and over the water that splashed around the boat…He sat up. The whimper came again.

She was having a nightmare.

He unwedged his foot and padded to her door. "Carly?"

She cried out, and the next second, he was through the door. And then he froze.

She must have been tossing for a while, because the blanket had slid off her. She slept in shorts and a T-shirt. The T-shirt was wrapped around her torso, up under her armpits, moonlight glazing the two perfect globes of her breasts.

Troy jumped back and closed the door behind him. And she whimpered again. And he swore under his breath.

Then he kicked the wall and smacked his good shoulder into it before he stomped off to the head to splash cold water into his face.

When he came out of the bathroom, Carly was waiting outside, her clothes—thank God—back in place.

With superhuman effort, he kept his gaze on her face. "Sorry if I woke you. Kicked something in the dark."

"I'm glad you woke me." Her voice sounded rough.

"Bad dreams?"

She nodded.

He leaned against the wall. "Want to talk about them?"

She shook her head, pushed past him and into the bathroom, and closed the door behind her.

He padded back to the galley and got a bottle of water from the fridge. He finished it to the last drop by the time she appeared. He pulled a bottle for her. "Water?"

She hesitated, but then moved toward him instead of heading straight to the bedroom. "Thanks."

"Maybe a drink will chase the nightmares away."

She twisted off the plastic cap. "At least I'm sleeping some. I'm usually a total insomniac."

"Seeing dead people?" He winced immediately, because that was a really stupid joke and an incredibly insensitive thing to ask, considering her military past and the two men she'd shot less than forty-eight hours ago. To save *his* stupid ass.

"I'm sorry." He turned his head and offered her his jaw. "Here. Just punch me in the face."

The lines of her face softened. "It's fine. I don't see dead people. I probably should. Maybe I don't have a conscience."

"You have a conscience."

Silence stretched between them. She fiddled with the cap instead of raising the bottle to her mouth.

"What do you see?" he asked.

"Shadows."

The pain in her voice cracked his heart.

He wanted to know more, but he didn't want to make her suffer by asking. He wanted to help. Would talking about it help?

"What are the shadows doing?"

She barely breathed the words. "They are bending over me."

The empty plastic bottle crunched in his hand as he crushed it.

"I was a POW." She avoided his gaze. "We went out on patrol. We took heavy fire. Some of our guns jammed from the sand. One man was killed, Dave Gardner. The rest of us were taken. Since I was a woman, the insurgents separated me from the others right at the beginning. I was put in the back of a different truck."

Every muscle in Troy's body tensed as he listened. The plastic bottle kept crackling as he gripped it tighter and tighter.

"I barely had time to panic when the truck blew up. In the dark night, the idiots ran over their own IED. I was thrown from the back of the truck." She took a drink.

"I don't know what happened after that. Next thing I knew, I was in a Taliban hospital with my left hand handcuffed to the bedrail." She rubbed her left wrist against her hip.

"How bad were you hurt?"

"Some burns and a broken ankle. I had the ankle in a splint." She took another drink. "I think they gave me drugs, because I drifted in and out. Towards morning, I woke to shadows bending over me."

He stood stock-still. The only other option was to put his fist through the nearest kitchen cabinet, and that would alarm her. So he reined in his anger.

"They were patients from the men's ward a floor below," she said. "They heard that an American woman was brought in."

*And her hand had been cuffed.*

Troy tossed the crushed bottle into the sink so hard it bounced back out. "You don't have to talk about this. I shouldn't have asked. But I just want to say this: I hope you killed the bastards."

"One held a pillow over my head," Carly told him. "I still don't know if murdering me was all they wanted or more. I fought them. I fought them the rest of the night. I fought them so hard, I almost broke my other ankle. I cracked a couple of ribs actually. Thank God they were sick too, hospital patients. If they had been guards or orderlies, I never would have made it."

He could see it like a movie in his head. The overwhelming force. Being hurt and having to fight injured. The dark room. The shadows that came to kill her.

He pulled her into his arms. "I'm glad you made it."

She held herself stiff for a few moments, then relaxed against him and slid her hands around his waist for support. "In the morning, my unit was there. They got me out. A couple of guys followed a hunch. I lived."

"You're tough. You're a warrior. If those bastards didn't break you, the nightmares won't. You're going to get over this."

She cleared her throat as she pulled away. "We need to get back to bed."

He held on to her hands. "I'd like to be in the bedroom with you. Like before. I'll sleep in the chair."

"I'm fine."

"For me," he said. "What you just told me is going to give me nightmares."

She shot him a look that said she knew he was full of shit. But she nodded. "I'll sleep in the chair."

"No."

"You are stubborn."

He nodded. "And at my age, I'm probably not going to change either."

That put a curve into her lips.

"We are adults, we could share the bed," he offered. No hidden agenda. He thought she could use the human contact.

"No. I told you what I did to Patrick."

"I'm not your ex. I can defend myself."

She finished her water and put the empty bottle on the counter. "Troy, you're welcome to the chair, if you think you can sleep on it. Not the bed. I'm sorry."

"That's okay. I'm not going to push. I want you to be comfortable."

She turned and walk toward the bedroom.

He went after her. Sleeping in the same room with her would be enough. Relief and something else flooded through him. He didn't examine the *something else*.

***

## Troy

Troy parked at the end of the street in a white road-survey van he'd borrowed from the Bureau for the day. He tried not to think of last night. Carly in his bed. The story she'd told him.

She was a pretty tough woman. Carly Montgomery was a survivor.

She was on house duty this morning, inside the mansion at last. While outside, Troy kept track of who was coming and going and tried to follow the ones he found suspicious, to see if they might lead him somewhere interesting. He watched an arriving white SUV, his thoughts returning to Carly as he jotted down the license plate number into the notebook next to him.

Tonight, they'd sneak into the mansion together and do a thorough search.

He shouldn't have kissed her last night, but he had a hard time regretting it. Desire had overridden his brain. *The excuse every idiot jerk out there uses. Dammit.*

But the idea of Mitch Wharst asking Carly out on a date had shorted out Troy's brain. *Not good.* She might be the first woman to awaken something in him since Nina had died, but Carly Montgomery wasn't his. He needed to remember that. She didn't want him. She didn't want or need anyone; she'd made that perfectly clear.

He was lucky she was still talking to him. She, of course, was a professional. She had promised to help, so she would see this mission to the end. But what if he'd killed the budding friendship that had somehow formed between them when they hadn't been looking?

*Hopefully not.* He enjoyed her company, both on and off the job. *Okay, so for future reference: hands and lips off.*

His phone buzzed in his shirt pocket. He figured the FBI, but saw a text message from Carly instead. *PCs and file boxes loaded into white SUV.*

He turned on the engine and waited. Could be Wharst was trying to have evidence destroyed. Could be he was donating old stuff to charity.

The white SUV pulled through the gate, two men in the front, one bald, the other more than making up for it in the facial-hair department. Troy waited a few seconds before he followed. He hung back, let another car pull in between them.

After a couple of turns, he was fairly sure they were heading toward the same shipyard where he'd been taken before, so he fell farther back to make sure they didn't spot him.

The men stopped in front of the shipyard twenty minutes later. The gate went up. They drove through.

Troy pulled up to the security guard in the weather-beaten shack. "Here to see about the job. They said I could go straight back to the office."

The man in a rumpled blue uniform looked over Troy's road-crew service van.

"Getting laid off next week." Troy peppered his tone with resentment.

The man nodded and raised the gate.

Since the white SUV had stopped, idling in front of a warehouse, Troy drove in a different direction and looped around the offices so he wouldn't look suspicious. He parked out of sight, then closed in on his target on foot.

The white SUV was gone.

The warehouse had three bays, all three roll-down doors shut.

Troy scanned the area, the dozen or so people out by the boats who minded their own business, and the guy who was stacking pallets nearby with a forklift. Nobody paid attention to Troy, so he rounded the building to find a window he could look through.

All the windows stood way too high above the ground, but he lucked out. Someone had stacked empty oil drums against the back wall.

Troy glanced around. Nobody back here to see him. He climbed the barrels to the window, carefully so they wouldn't bang against the corrugated steel siding and give him away. When he finally reached high enough, he peered through the dirty glass.

Abandoned machinery and boxes occupied most of the space inside, crates piled against the walls. More steel drums stood in the middle of the large warehouse. Three five-gallon red plastic gasoline jugs waited next to the barrels.

The men unloaded the contents of the SUV into the steel drums, file box after file box. All taped shut.

Troy called his FBI liaison and gave his location, asked for immediate backup, then settled back to wait. Except, the bald guy inside picked up a gasoline jug and began soaking the file boxes.

*No time to wait for the FBI.*

Troy picked up the barrel next to him, threw it through the window and, gun drawn, vaulted in.

The two men immediately opened fire, squatting in the cover of their SUV.

The easiest way to take them out would be to hit the SUV's fuel tank, but the explosion would destroy everything they'd brought to burn. Troy dashed behind the cover of a wide stack of crates and did his best to come up with another plan.

To his right, a row of used boat motors lined the ground, probably waiting for repair. They wouldn't provide any cover. To his left, an untidy stack of stained cardboard boxes stood about five feet high, containing screws according to the stamped labels—a much better alternative. That, at least, could stop a bullet.

He shot in the direction of the men as he dove behind the boxes. *Shitshitshit.* He managed to land on the shoulder he'd dislocated two days ago. *Man, that hurt.*

He filled his lungs, shook off the pain, and looked at the industrial lighting that hung on steel chains from the ceiling. From his new position, he could shoot that chain and bring the whole damn thing down on the men.

Except, before he could take the shot, the men split up, bald guy dashing left, guy with the Sasquatch hair to the right. They kept Troy's hiding place peppered with bullets as they went. By the time he could stick his head out again, he could no longer see either of them. They were probably circling back on him.

He needed a plan. *Okay.*

Step One: He had some time before they'd get to him, so he shot at the chains, and the light fixture fell with a loud crash onto the SUV, shattering windows and folding the roof down enough so nobody could get in on the driver's side. At least now they wouldn't be able to use the vehicle to ram him or to get away.

Step Two: He pulled a box from the bottom of the pile next to him as quietly as he could. He flattened himself into the space, then pulled the box back in place. The boxes hadn't been lined up neatly. The one that concealed him wouldn't be that noticeable in the haphazard mess.

Step Three: He waited, listening for an opportunity.

"Where is he?" A shout rang out to his right, but not close enough.

He hoped at least one of the men would walk by closer than that. He listened for the scraping sounds their shoes made on the cement floor.

They were searching through the warehouse, eliminating potential hiding places. Then one of them did stop right by him. Troy kicked the box aside and rolled out of the hole, just as Sasquatch was spinning around, his own weapon drawn. The two shots went off almost simultaneously.

Except the goon missed and Troy didn't.

He grabbed the dead guy's gun as the body hit the floor, then he ran to the back and ducked behind some metal shelving. He progressed along the wall, keeping in cover, inching closer to the evidence so he could secure it.

A shot rang out and hit the wall by his head. He ducked, scanning the place, but couldn't see the man. He moved forward, got shot at again. Okay. That gave him an idea for the guy's location: behind the green shelves. Troy moved forward and shot toward those. That kept the bastard down so Troy could reach the next bit of good cover, a large metal container.

"FBI," he called out. "Throw out your weapon, put your hands on your head, and slowly come forward."

"Eat shit," came the response, the man's voice betraying his exact location behind a double file cabinet.

Troy squeezed off a shot, hoping the bullet would go right through and hit something vital. No such luck. The man didn't cry out in pain. In fact, he laughed.

Troy positioned himself so he could dive forward. "Why don't you tell me what's in those file boxes?"

"Doughnuts. Why don't you call your cop buddies and have a party?"

As if the words had conjured them, sirens sounded in the distance.

Troy tried with "Listen, I take you out of here in handcuffs and all will be well. If the FBI storms the building, anything can happen. There'll be a lot of bullets flying."

"Go to hell."

"How about you go first and send me a postcard to let me know how the weather is?"

The man stepped from cover and came at him, guns blasting. *Where the hell did he get the second weapon?* Troy could only squeeze off a single shot before he had to crouch behind cover.

Judging by the yelp of pain, this time, he did hit the idiot. Not that a single bullet could stop him. The man swore and kept firing.

The sirens sounded right outside now, echoing off the walls, the earsplitting noise filling the place.

Troy darted to the left and ducked behind the SUV to use it for cover. He reached up and adjusted the side mirror so he could see without having to pop up and make himself a target.

The guy kept coming, squeezing off a hail of bullets. They were ricocheting off the cement floor, coming too close for comfort. Since Troy couldn't just stay down and hope for the best, he popped up and took the man out with a single shot to the chest.

Straight through the heart.

The fight was over.

But as the guy fell, his finger twitched, squeezing the trigger one last time. Whether he'd aimed for it or not, he hit the SUV's fuel tank.

As the explosion shook the building, Troy flew through the air. Flames licked his skin, heat seared his lungs, smoke clouded his vision. Time slowed, then sped up again, his body slamming into the cement floor that was covered with sharp chunks of metal and burning debris.

***

**Carly**

Troy wasn't answering his cell phone, so after her shift ended, Carly drove straight to his boat.

She found him lying in bed.

His thick dark hair was singed, his face scraped, his voice raspier than ever as he said, "Hey."

"Hope the other guy looks worse," she said lightly, even as anger bubbled up inside her. Anger and a sense of protectiveness, which was strange. It wasn't as if they'd been partners forever. But he was a decent man, on the side of good. She hated to see him in this shape.

She wanted to reach out to him, but she had a feeling he wouldn't like to be fussed over. She shoved her hands into her pockets.

"The other guys are dead," he rasped.

"Good." Satisfaction warmed her a little. "And the stuff they took from the mansion? Nick told me to guard the East Wing. I figured they had something going on, so I snuck over to the west side. Sure enough, they were carrying all that stuff out the back. Was it anything you can use?"

"I'd be willing to bet. But the evidence and I got blown up a little. There's a phone number for Chinese delivery on the fridge," he continued smoothly.

She swallowed the worry that had bubbled up her throat. "What, you're going to laze around in bed all night instead of cooking?" she joked, because if she didn't, she would have to cry at the sight of him. "I guess the honeymoon is over."

"I'll be up in a minute." He struggled to sit. "Damned nurse shot me up with drugs when she cleaned my burns."

The sheet slid off him, revealing a pile of bandages next to him on the bed.

She stepped closer. "What's that?"

He pulled the sheet back over them and flashed a completely fake smile that she supposed he meant to be reassuring.

"Troy?"

"I looked like a freaking mummy. I didn't want you to lose confidence."

"Are you crazy?"

"I didn't unwrap the burns on my leg."

Now that he was sitting, naked to the waist, she could see that his torso was all black and blue in between lacerations. "You broke those cracked ribs, didn't you?"

"Maybe a couple."

*Macho idiot.* She spotted a box of brand-new bandages on the table and brought them over. "I'm taping your ribs back up."

"Okay." Relief laced the single word. "I kind of regret undoing that."

She shook her head as she began, her arms around him, the scent of iodine in her nose, and beyond that, a more masculine scent, his.

Even the extensive bruises and scrapes did little to distract from his lean muscles. His body was a mixture of masculine beauty and destruction, a strange combination that reached her the way sheer perfection could never have. She ran her thumb over a particularly thick older scar.

"That must have been pretty bad." She didn't need to explain that she was talking about the explosion that had killed his fiancée.

He held her gaze. "I seem to be making a habit out of nearly getting blown to pieces."

"How bad was it the first time?"

"I died. The combat medics brought me back. I wasn't happy about that at the time."

"And now?"

He put his hand on top of hers and trapped it against his chest. "Is there a pity kiss somewhere in this for me?"

She bit back a laugh. Pity was definitely not on the list of things she was feeling for him: attraction, exasperation, confusion…

He leaned closer, his lips a hair's breadth from hers.

She could feel the heat that radiated off his body. She held her breath.

"There's something about you," he murmured.

"That's the painkillers talking."

"I think you're the kind of woman who could distract a man from a fair amount of pain."

"I'm the kind of woman who could *cause* a man a fair amount of pain."

He gave a strangled laugh, then dipped his head and took her mouth.

This so wasn't why she'd come here, she thought hazily as instant pleasure washed over her. She wasn't ready for getting tangled up with a man. Especially with this man. Although, at the moment, he didn't look to be up to serious tangling, which somehow quieted her nerves enough that she could fully enjoy the kiss.

She didn't remember kissing ever being this satisfying. Or maybe her guilt over beating up Patrick colored her memories of everything else she'd done with him. But, God, Troy could—

His stomach growled, interrupting the scary thought that he was somehow special to her and that he was beginning to mean something.

She pulled away. "Let me call for that food."

"Dinner can wait." His gaze darkened, betraying another kind of hunger.

Since every cell of her body responded to that look, she tried distraction. For both of them. "This messes up your plans for tonight."

"I'm going ahead with the plans."

"You were blown up today." She narrowed her eyes as something else occurred to her. "Do you have a concussion?"

"I'm not supposed to fall asleep. So, the middle of the night is the perfect time to visit the mansion. A little break-in will keep me awake."

"You're crazy, you know that?"

"Everybody's a little crazy."

"Not like this. I'm nutbuckets, but you're an entire swimming pool full of nuts."

He grinned. "We make a great pair."

She shook her head. "I think partnerships work better if at least one of the partners is sane. Since you have a concussion, I'm going to be the voice of reason today. I'll go into the mansion; you'll provide outside support. You can watch with night vision goggles and alert me if anyone is coming my way."

His grin melted. "I'm more of a take-charge kind of guy. I don't sit in the backseat."

*God, give me patience.*

"You. Were. Blown. Up." She enunciated carefully.

"It's not that bad the second time around. You kind of get used to it."

She swallowed a groan. "Could you please stop joking? Don't make me handcuff you to the bed."

"I'm not completely against *that*." Interest glinted in his flint-gray gaze. "Under the right set of circumstances."

She sighed. Refused to smile. Instead, she pinned him with her hardest look. "One day, you might wear down my defenses, but that day is not today."

"Fair enough," he rasped. "But just so you know, I'm really looking forward to that day."

# EIGHT

Carly snuck through the mansion. In her right ear, she had the earpiece Troy had given her. In her left ear, she had her security earpiece, so she would hear if any of the guards noticed anything amiss, if they were coming after her. In black shoes, black pants, and a long-sleeve black shirt, she should be able to pull into the shadows and go unnoticed.

Troy sat in a borrowed blue van in the golf shop's parking lot up the road, close enough to step in if she met with any trouble.

That had been a battle not easily won. He was just stubborn enough to attempt scaling the wall even with his broken ribs. She had to bargain hard to hold him back, and promised him all kinds of idiotic things like staying on his boat until the op was over and then finding a different apartment in a safer neighborhood after that.

She couldn't fathom why he would care. She wasn't foolish enough to think that a few kisses, extraordinary as they'd been, meant they had something between them.

"Entering the bedroom suite on the second floor," she whispered to him through the mouthpiece. She pushed in the door. "It's empty."

As it should be. They'd seen the senator leave in his limo with his wife an hour earlier. His solicitousness had surprised Carly: holding his wife's hand, shooting her adoring looks, opening the car door for her. He acted like a man in love. Maybe his career wasn't the most important thing to him, after all.

"Look for a wall safe," Troy suggested through their connection.

"Might take a while. Looks like the national gallery in here."

Enough moonlight filtered in that she didn't need a flashlight. The bedroom suite had to be close to a thousand square feet and included a sitting area with a fireplace, plus an extensive reading nook, in addition to the California king, four-poster bed that had steps leading up to it.

A state-of-the-art entertainment unit towered across from the bed. Oil paintings in elaborate antique frames covered the walls.

Carly looked behind every one of them. "No wall safe in the bedroom."

"How about a desk?"

"Everything but."

"Not even a dressing table?"

"Maybe in the dressing room." She moved toward a closed door in the corner that soon revealed a closet. She pushed into the dark space. The blinds on the windows were drawn here. She reached for her flashlight, closed the door behind her before she flicked it on. "Wow."

"Did you find something?"

"Just where the national budget has gone."

The closet was almost as large as her apartment. She panned the light over rows and rows of designer shoes. All men's. Then suits. Then tuxes. A display of Rolex watches. The senator's clothes and accessories filled as much room in the closet as his wife's on the other side.

"Check every panel. See if any of the drawers have double bottoms," Troy suggested, and she spent half an hour doing just that.

She brimmed with frustration by the time she finished, having gone over every possible hiding place and finding nothing. What if all evidence of the senator's involvement with XO-ST had burned up in the warehouse fire?

"I'm going to the offices," she told Troy. Senator Wharst and his wife had separate workspaces at the other end of this floor.

She turned off the flashlight before she opened the door to the bedroom. She didn't want anyone to catch sight of that light from outside.

But instead of the moonlit room she'd left just half an hour ago, she found herself in complete darkness. Someone had lowered the blinds in the bedroom while she'd been searching the closet.

She went for her gun, but too late. Hands grabbed her, wrested the weapon from her, at the same time others yanked the headsets from her ears, disconnecting her from Troy before she could warn him.

Her mouth was taped the next second, her hands and feet bound. Then she was picked up and carried out, down the stairs.

They took her to the same cage where they'd kept Troy before. Jason and Dan tossed her to the cement floor, the impact knocking the air out of her.

"I'm very disappointed," Nick said.

She looked from man to man, but the expression on their faces was cold and hard, even Jason's. She was nothing but the enemy to them now.

"What were you looking for?" Nick demanded as he bent and ripped the tape from her mouth.

"Jewelry. I need money to cover rent."

"Where's your buddy?"

"I work alone."

"Who were you talking to on your headset?"

"Go to hell."

He bent, grabbed the front of her shirt, and picked her up by the fabric, pulled her face close to his, his cheeks red with fury. "You don't want to play this the hard way."

Since she couldn't kick him with her feet tied, she spit into his face.

He slammed her to the ground, jarring her bones, and roared the words, "Who is he? Where is he?"

* * *

Troy

Their radio connection had gone dead, but not before Troy heard Carly gasp.

He put the van in gear and stepped on the gas, drove until he was just a few houses away, then parked. His phone buzzed as he ran through backyards, one after the other.

"Hey," Gabe Cannon said. "Jake and I are back in DC. Heard you got hurt. Want to get together for a cold beer?"

He sounded in a good mood. His confrontation with XO-ST must have gone well. Troy wanted details, but not right now.

"I'm busy rushing the mansion," he bit out the words without slowing. "Wharst's goons got Carly. My new partner," he added, not sure how much Cassidy at the FBI had passed on about that.

"I'll let the Bureau know." Gabe was all business in a split second.

The line went dead.

Troy pushed forward, compartmentalizing the pain. He'd acknowledge the pulsing agony later. He kept to the bushes until he reached the wall. He ran to the corner and scaled the stones where he could slip through between two security cameras pointed away from each other. Both the climb and thumping down to the grass on the other side made him see stars.

They could fix him when this was over.

He had one priority now: Carly.

He made it to the garage bay before the dogs discovered him—more curious than threatening. Maybe they smelled Carly on him and responded to the familiar scent. She'd been on his boat, in his car, had bandaged him. Or maybe he somehow still carried their scent, on his boots perhaps. He'd spent hours in their enclosure in the basement.

Earlier he had stashed a couple of Slim Jims in his pocket to hold him through the night. He held up the treats and signaled the dogs to sit, taking the alpha role, not letting fear show, not for a second. They followed his lead and obeyed. When he tossed their prize—as far as he could—they took off running.

He moved in the opposite direction, always keeping in cover.

Two guards stood in front of the main entry, so Troy decided to try his luck at the back. He was rounding the building when his phone vibrated in his pocket.

Gabe again. "You're going to hate this…There'll be an official FBI inquiry in the morning. Best they can do."

Troy bit back a curse. "It'll be too late by then."

"The op was for surveillance. Cassidy says you never had a search warrant. And no judge will issue a warrant based on Carly being missing for half an hour."

Troy let the next curse fly—not very impressive when he had to keep his voice to a whisper.

"Hey, don't shoot the messenger. Good news is, Jake and I thought we'd come and see how you're bungling all this. We're here."

"The guard dogs are having a snack at the east wall. Come in from the west. She's inside the mansion, probably in the basement. Expect about a dozen armed guards."

"Copy that," Gabe said, then ended the connection.

Troy slipped behind a boxwood bush.

Twenty feet of open driveway stood between the bush and the back door. Luckily, halfway in between, a Lexus sparkled darkly in the night. Troy made a short dart to the car. Nobody raised an alarm.

No guard at the door straight ahead.

Could be his first piece of luck.

Or a trap.

Only one way to find out which.

Troy drew his gun, ran for the door, then pushed inside, weapon trained at the back hallway that stretched in front of him. Empty.

He moved forward. He'd studied Carly's blueprints enough to know how to get where he was going.

The lights on the motion alarms he passed were green, which meant they were disabled. They were probably only turned on when the senator and his wife were on vacation and security was limited to the outside of the mansion.

Troy didn't have to worry about security cameras. The sprawling building had none. He'd figured that out on his first foray into the building. The senator probably conducted enough dirty dealings at the mansion that he didn't want video records which might be subpoenaed later.

Troy cut through the home gym. He heard noise up ahead, so he turned into a hallway on his left and took the narrow corridor to the kitchen. He ducked in there, waiting for the men to pass, but they didn't. They came right after him.

He glanced around and went for the nearest hiding place that could accommodate him: the industrial-size oven. He had to move a rack, silently, to fit in.

The men did a good job of searching the kitchen, but didn't look inside ovens or cabinets. When they left, Troy crawled out, his breath ragged from the pain of having to fold his large, broken body in the tight spot. He smelled like grease as he stole forward. That should help with the dogs on his way out. The worst thing that could happen—they might try to lick him to death.

He kept pushing forward, toward the basement stairs. The guard at the entrance to the hallway had his back to Troy. He was listening through his headset to the progress report from the sweep team. Keeping Carly's safety in mind, Troy stashed his gun. He stole up behind the man and zapped him with his own Taser, disarmed him, then shoved the limp body into a storage closet.

Nobody stirred. Nobody came to investigate the small noises.

Troy moved on silently to the basement door. No way to get through there without being noticed, so he gave up stealth. And he didn't do it halfway. He kicked the door in and started firing down the stairs, making sure none of the bullets would go toward the cage.

He wasn't particularly firing at anyone, just wanted to push the four men he could see—Nick, the head of security one of them—behind cover. He didn't want a body count. Not because he gave two shits about the guards, but because they were in the middle of DC at a senator's mansion. The FBI was going to string him up by his balls for this whole goatfuck as it was already.

"I just want to talk!" he roared over the gunfire, leaping down then ducking behind the cement block staircase. If he could get close enough to them to negotiate, he might be able to disarm them.

But the guards in the basement weren't interested in talking. They peppered his position with bullets.

Pinned by rapid gunfire, he had to shoot back.

He tried for non-life-threatening injuries and took down three of the men, while taking a bullet to his left thigh. Then the gunfire abruptly ended as Nick, the only man left without an injury, grabbed Carly from the cage and held her up in front of himself like a shield.

"How did you know she was in the house?" Troy played for time, hoping Gabe and Jake were somewhere near.

He didn't take his eyes off Nick to look at his injured leg, but the wound couldn't be too bad. His pants didn't feel soaked with blood. The injury burned like hell, but he could put weight on the leg without trouble. Most likely, the bullet just grazed him.

The guards were in a hell of a lot worse shape. He kept track of them from the corner of his eye. They'd pulled back into the corner, trying to stem the worst of the bleeding, letting the boss handle the rest.

Nick glanced toward the top of the stairs, probably hoping for his own backup. "After you broke in the first time, I thought we might have someone on the inside who couldn't be trusted. I put a bug in every security headset. They feed to the computer at the gatehouse. Every single thing anyone on my team said in the past two days has been recorded. I was hoping to catch a cell phone conversation."

Troy swore under his breath.

Carly had told him after she'd gotten in earlier that she was taking her security headset from the office, so she could be alerted if any of the guards spotted her. Except, the bug picked up her status reports to Troy.

"Let's negotiate," Troy offered. "Man to man. You lock the injured posse into the cage. Then maybe the rest of us will go up and get out of here."

A stupid plan. More security guards were probably waiting outside the basement door for Nick's signal even now.

Nick saw the advantage immediately. He gestured toward the cage with his head, and his men dragged each other in there, shooting Troy lethal glances. The last guy snapped on the lock.

*Good.*

"Toss out your weapons."

They looked at Nick. He nodded. Guns clattered to the cement floor, far enough from the cage to suit Troy.

Now he could keep his full focus on Nick. "Did you ever trust Carly? You searched her apartment. You messed with her earpieces."

Nick shrugged. "She was supposed to be the token army vet on the team. Good for photo ops, too burned out to notice anything or cause much trouble." He moved the barrel of his gun from her back, and pressed it against her temple, his eyes fixed on Troy. "Drop your weapon."

*Here we go again.* A standoff, and a woman he cared for was in the middle of the storm. But this time Troy didn't hesitate. He didn't wait for backup either.

He squeezed the trigger.

A red dot appeared between Nick's eyes a split second before the force of the bullet's impact spun him back. His body hit the ground, his gun clattering away from him. He didn't move again.

*Dead.*

Then Troy was at Carly's side, and she was in his arms. The men in the cage were shouting. He didn't care. He held her and thanked God for her.

She smelled like sweat and blood. Safe. He never wanted to let her go.

But the rest of the senator's security were out there, so Troy pulled back, looking her over. "Are you hurt?"

"Mostly surface damage. Nothing's broken." She sounded more frustrated than scared. "I couldn't get a single shred of proof before they caught me."

The faint, distant whining of sirens sounded, muffled by the basement walls.

Carly shot him a questioning look.

"No idea who that is. As far as I know, the FBI couldn't be bothered." He handed her his backup weapon from his boot, another Glock.

She grabbed the gun, then they headed up the stairs, covering for each other.

They ran into Jake Tekla at the top of the stairs. Carly whirled into a roundhouse kick as Troy called, "One of ours!" from behind her.

She pulled the kick—"Sorry"—but from the stunned look on Tekla's face, her sneaker might have brushed his nose.

"Jake," Tekla said, then, "Don't hurt me," with a sparkle in his eyes, and shot Troy a meaningful look over her head. The kind of look that said *Now I see why you're getting out-of-character attached here.* He ended with a cocky grin. "Tied up four men, stashed them in various rooms. What else do you need?"

Before Troy could answer, the window at the end of the hallway lit up. Cars with flashing lights were pulling into the yard.

He jerked his head that way. "Who's that?"

"Someone reported shooting at the senator's home to the FBI. I guess they had to come to check it out. Search warrant or no search warrant." Tekla grinned wider.

"Where's Gabe?"

"Out there, somewhere. He ran into dog trouble." Tekla was still watching Carly, evaluating her. "Gabe's our third musketeer. I try to keep him and Troy out of trouble, but you know how it is. Can't be everywhere at the same time." He gave a theatrical sigh that could have come straight from a long-suffering nanny to septuplets.

Too bad they didn't have time for a wrestling match.

"Let's move, Mary Poppins," Troy said. "Better go and give ourselves up before the SWAT team rushes the mansion and shoots us by accident."

They hurried down the hallway, then to the front door through the sprawling living room and foyer, stashed their weapons out of sight before they stepped out, arms raised into a flood of lights.

Keeping Carly behind them, Jake and Troy held up their FBI IDs.

"Drop your weapons!" A dozen shouts rang out from various directions regardless.

They complied.

Men rushed in, guns aimed until everyone's identity was confirmed.

"What in hell happened here?" Troy's FBI handler, Cassidy, yelled as he moved forward from the back, just as the senator's limo rolled through the gate with impeccable timing.

A handful of agents immediately ran to cover the vehicle, while others rushed inside to clear the building.

Troy put on his best butter-wouldn't-melt-in-his-mouth expression. "I was driving by on personal business when I saw several men attacking this woman on the front lawn. I had no idea who the residence belonged to. As a law enforcement agent, it was my duty to interfere."

"You realize you single-handedly messed up this op beyond repair?" Cassidy asked under his breath, face red with fury, jaw tightly set.

Troy didn't make excuses. He couldn't regret anything he'd done. He'd saved Carly's life, which was the only thing that truly mattered.

He looked back at her, caught her gaze, and his pulse sped up.

When did that happen?

"All clear." An agent came through the door behind them. "One casualty, half a dozen injured. I've called it in. Called for ambulances."

Cassidy nodded, then with a last I'll-nail-your-ass-for-this look, he walked to the limo, through the ring of his agents.

The back window went down, revealing the senator. "What is going on here?"

Cassidy introduced himself before responding. "There was an altercation on the premises, Senator. I'm going to have to ask you a couple of questions, sir."

"If it's unsafe, I don't want to be here."

"The mansion is secure, sir."

The man's personal guards got out of the limo first, opened the door for the senator on one side, his wife on the other, but the senator drew Meredith Wharst out after him and tucked her hand into his arm in a protective gesture.

Mitch, the senator's brother, left the limo last, with a *finally, some excitement* look on his face, scanning the front of the house, probably hoping to catch the tail end of the action.

The senator led the way inside in his thousand-dollar suit, his cold gaze promising that everyone involved would be out of a job by morning.

He strode straight to the conference room and, after letting go of his wife, threw himself in the oversized black leather chair at the head of the table. "I want an explanation."

"Yes, sir," Cassidy said, then, as he took a seat, he mouthed, *Don't say a word,* to Troy and Jake.

Two other agents came in. Everybody sat, except for the senator's two personal guards, who'd escorted him to tonight's function. Those two positioned themselves standing behind him.

"What is the meaning of this?" Wharst looked ready to have a stroke, lips thin, eyes narrowed, his right hand in a fist on the table. "Why is my house under siege?"

Cassidy hesitated, probably weighing political ramifications.

Troy glanced over at Carly who had a split lip, and a bruise darkening on her cheekbone from the guards' rough handling. And his tolerance for the senator's bullshit ran out all of a sudden.

They had no evidence, which burned him beyond belief. But he wanted the man to know that they knew what he really was behind the smarmy politician façade. He needed to wipe the smug look off Wharst's face. He shoved his chair back and stood before Cassidy could apologize.

"A couple of months ago, your yacht was impounded in Italy for transporting stolen goods. Isn't that true, Senator?"

The man pulled his spine straight. "Those crates were snuck on board. I had no knowledge of them."

"That's not what Brent Foley said before he died," Troy shot back before Cassidy could interrupt him. "Foley, in fact, indicated that you had full knowledge of the smuggling and you agreed to it because he was blackmailing you with something."

"I want my attorneys," the senator snapped at one of his guards who hurried out to make the call.

Troy turned to Mitch. "You were in Afghanistan last year."

Surprise had Mitch blinking. He hadn't expected to be included in all this. With the attention on him, he shrank back. "A quick business trip."

"So you had nothing to do with combat tourism while you were there?"

The blood ran out of Mitch's face, leaving him pale. He cast a panicked glance at his brother and pressed his lips shut.

"I want my damn lawyers!" the senator roared, slapping his hand on the table.

Gabe Cannon slipped into the room and gave Troy a nod. Carly cast him a curious look. Troy mouthed *Gabe* to her. Full introductions could wait until later.

Troy turned back to the senator's brother. "Tell me, Mitch, how much did it cost you to play the ultimate action game and shoot real people?"

"I never shot anyone." Mitch jumped to his feet, hands flailing as if he didn't know what to do with them. His gaze darted around, imploring them to believe him. He was a good-time boy, and the good times were ending, so he folded. "I swear. I just wanted a feel of what was going on over there. The experience. I couldn't kill a man."

"Shut up, you idiot." Wharst turned on his younger brother, his eyes bulging as he slapped the table. "Keep your stupid mouth shut."

"So you admit that you participated in combat tourism and that your brother, Senator Wharst, had full knowledge of it," Cassidy finally jumped into the fray.

But Mitch was more scared of his brother than the FBI. He dropped back into his chair and did shut up at last.

"We have nothing to say." Wharst had a better growl than his Rottweilers. "You will all regret this." He stood and shoved his chair back. "I want you to leave."

Gabe stepped forward with a laptop. "If you don't want to talk, how about you listen?" He ran his fingers over the keyboard. "I found this on the security computer at the gatehouse."

He must have opened an audio file, because the senator's voice came through the speaker.

"Fix this," he demanded of someone on the recording. "This whole mess has to go away, and go away now. I'll be announcing my run for presidency in less than six months. I don't want this hanging over my head another minute."

"Yes, sir," came the response. *Nick's voice?*

"Everybody who knows about this insane business has to be silenced." A sharp sound came through the recording, as if someone had slapped their palm on a desk. "I thought the trip would solve everything. He's out of control with his thrill seeking. He's bent on embarrassing me, and he will succeed sooner or later." He cursed. "My idiot kid brother was supposed to go to battle over there and get a bullet to the head. We would have said that he'd been visiting to conduct some humanitarian mission on my behalf."

Troy glanced at Mitch, who went another shade paler and stared at his brother, mouth agape. Mrs. Wharst began crying in the corner, burying her face in her hands. Senator Wharst stared daggers at everyone, a muscle jumping in his cheek. But he didn't move. He stood frozen, as if unable to believe that the gig was up, and he was caught.

And the recording kept going.

"I was supposed to get the sympathy vote. And when father's estate finally cleared, I would have inherited the full amount. It would have financed my run for office. That money could have made a difference in how this country is run. It shouldn't be squandered away on wild adventures."

"Yes, sir."

"But the stupid idiot can't even die." The senator growled on the recording. "That's what you get for working with coded messages. Some friend of his got shot instead—"

Senator Wharst reanimated at last, shouting, "It's a fake! That file is manipulated. That's not me!" He knocked over his chair as he rushed for the door. "I want my lawyers!"

The two FBI agents stopped him and escorted him back to his chair, as Gabe turned off the recording.

Mrs. Wharst sobbed openly. She headed for the door next, without looking at her husband.

"Meredith—" For the first time, the senator looked shaken, worry replacing fury in his eyes. He moved to go after her, but the FBI wouldn't let him.

And his wife walked out the door without ever turning back.

"Go after her," the senator snapped at his last remaining guard, and the man immediately left.

Wharst collapsed into his chair, stunned and lost, shaking his head as if not quite understanding what was happening.

Mitch stood, his face flushed now, the color back. His hands shook. He kept staring at his brother with disbelief, shock, and betrayal, like a kid who'd just found out Santa Claus wasn't real. Or a kid who'd just realized Santa hadn't come to the house to bring gifts but to smother him.

Then he finally squared his shoulders and turned to Cassidy. "I'll tell you whatever you need to know."

The two agents escorted him out. Cassidy went with them.

Carly's phone rang. She glanced at the screen. *My mother,* she mouthed to Troy, and stepped outside to take the call.

And suddenly, Troy, Gabe, and Jake were alone with the senator.

Troy took advantage of the gift. He let all his anger show in his eyes as he turned to the senator. "Let's make something clear so there's no misunderstanding. If you somehow manage to weasel out of the charges that are coming, we'll find you personally. We know you have connections; so do we. If you manage to come through this without the justice system actually delivering justice—*we* will. Personally. Swiftly. Painfully."

"Who the hell do you think you are?" Outrage strengthened the man's voice. "You three—"

Jake was closest to him. He reached out nonchalantly and pushed him back down, left his hand on the senator's shoulder as the man struggled. "If you send anyone after us or our loved ones, it'll be the last thing you do on this earth."

"To be clear," Gabe spoke up, and his voice had a cold hard tone that made even Troy uncomfortable, "we'd prefer you dead. It's a pretty strong preference. We wouldn't mind coming after you to make sure justice was done."

Troy and Jake nodded in agreement.

The senator stopped struggling to stand. But he still wouldn't shut up. "You can't talk like that to me." He seethed. "You don't know what I can do."

"You could go to sleep one night, all nice and cozy, then wake up in a chopper over the Middle East, dropped off behind enemy lines before you fully convinced yourself you weren't dreaming," Jake said, as if just talking out loud.

"Not that we couldn't do our own torture and dismemberment," Troy added, "but hey, give credit where credit is due. Those guys are pretty good at it over there."

"I'll definitely watch the video when they put it online." Gabe dropped the hard tone and sounded downright cheerful. "Probably even tape it."

The senator had no response for once.

"Our business is finished here, am I right?" Troy asked.

Wharst wouldn't meet his eyes. But he nodded.

Before anyone could say anything more, the two FBI agents who'd left with Cassidy and Mitch came back.

"Everything all right in here?"

Jake patted the senator on the back in a friendly gesture, then withdrew his hand. "Senator Wharst was just saying how he would like to make a full confession."

***

**Troy**

Troy, Gabe, and Jake sat around Troy's coffee table on the houseboat, Troy's phone between them on speaker.

Mandy, Jasmine, and Allison were driving up from the safe house in North Carolina. ETA: sometime in the morning. Judging by the way Gabe and Jake kept surreptitiously glancing at the clock, they were probably counting the minutes.

Carly had gone home. Her mother had driven down from Baltimore for a surprise visit. Troy doubted he'd see her until tomorrow. *Not* the way he'd planned things.

He wanted her on his boat, in his bed, in his life. He needed to tell her that.

But for now, he needed to focus on General Roberts.

"I have bad news and good news." The general's voice, coming through the phone, filled the cabin. "The bad news is, the FBI just fired all three of you. Mission accomplished or not, none of you were supposed to be inside the senator's mansion. You acted against orders."

The news left Troy unbothered. He'd already decided the FBI wasn't for him. Jake and Gabe didn't look destroyed either.

"By the way," the general asked, "how did you find that recording of the senator talking about setting up his own brother to be killed?"

Gabe leaned toward the phone. "The guard dogs didn't like me, sir. I ducked into the guardhouse by the gate for a minute to get away from them. I secured the guard there and took his earpiece so I could figure out what was going on in the mansion. I heard one of the security guys talking about how the mics were recording all day. I thought maybe they recorded something interesting. I got the computer password from the guard, found the file, and started listening."

"Well done."

"Thank you, sir."

Then Jake put in. "You said you had bad news and good news, sir?"

"The good news is…" The general paused as if for effect. "I have a job offer for you. All three of you."

They exchanged silent questioning looks.

General Roberts said, "While you were investigating, I managed to retire from the army. I was tagged by the Department of Defense to run a brand new unit. Are you familiar with Personnel Recovery?"

While the other two yes-sir-ed, Troy recited the textbook definition, "Personnel Recovery is the recovery of DOD civilian, DOD contractor personnel, or other personnel designated by the president or secretary of defense, who are isolated, missing, detained, or captured in an operational environment."

"Correct. The DOD is setting up a similar unit for civilians who disappear in a foreign country. Say a US businessman is kidnapped for ransom in Nigeria."

They all listened. Troy, for one, was definitely interested.

"We're calling the unit Foreign Recovery Team for now," the general said. "If you accept the offer, I'd like you three to be the first investigators."

They exchanged a look.

Honest work for an honest man, saving Americans—sounded good to Troy. He nodded.

Gabe nodded too. Troy knew he needed the money. He helped out his sick sister.

Jake looked between the two of them. He was guardian of his younger sister, Mandy, who'd be going to college next year.

"We're in," he said. "Thank you, sir."

"Excellent. I have in my hand a stack of files that need action ASAP. I'll see you at oh eight hundred at the DOD."

They ended the call.

"Another round of beer?" Troy offered, feeling more relaxed suddenly. He liked knowing what he was doing next.

Gabe nodded. "Thanks." He took out his phone and started hitting buttons. "I want to let Amy know that we're back in the country."

"How is she?" Troy handed him his beer. Amy was a single mom with three kids. And MS.

"Better every day. That new drug cocktail is a miracle."

"That's good to hear, man."

Jake stood. "I'm going to hit the head. I need a shower."

Troy headed out to the aft deck and sent a text of his own, to Carly: *U OK?*

He didn't expect a response. She was probably sleeping, or getting her mother settled. He just wanted to tell her that he'd swing by in the morning.

He wanted to talk. He wanted to tell her that he was falling for her. He wanted to kiss her. He wanted to make love to her. He wanted to convince her to move to the houseboat with him.

But before he could produce a strategy for convincing her, his phone rang. Carly. He clicked on the call.

"I'm going to Baltimore with my mother tomorrow."

She was whispering. Maybe her mother was sleeping already.

"For how long?"

"A while." Her voice dipped even lower as she said that.

Troy leaned against the railing and stared down at the water that swirled as darkly as his emotions. "Why?"

"I ran to DC to get away from things I didn't want to deal with. That's not how I want to live my life. I need to get myself together. I need to actually fix my problems."

"I could help."

"I know you could, and thank you for offering."

A pause stretched between them.

"But you need to figure this out on your own," he said, hating the concept, hating even more that he agreed with her, was proud of her for taking the bull by the horns. "I'm going to go out of the country for a while. I took a new job. Jake and Gabe too." He explained the basics.

"Stay safe," she said.

"You better believe it. I'm coming back so we can continue this conversation in person."

"The case is over."

Did she sound uncertain?

"We are not," he promised.

# CHAPTER NINE

*Three months later.*

Carly turned the burgers on the grill, standing steady on Betsy's gently swaying top deck. Stars sparkled in the sky. Excitement bubbled in the air.

For the past three months, Troy had been in Yemen to track down and rescue a kidnapped executive. Gabe had been in Ghana. And Jake had been in Peru. They were all due back today.

Jasmine Tekla, Jake's sister, closed her laptop on the table and looked toward the parking lot. "Okay. Where are they?"

She was such an exotic beauty, long dark hair, golden eyes, but nothing soft about her, from her combat boots and black stretch Lara Croft shorts to her sharp, intelligent gaze. She looked like a comic book action heroine. And she was a computer savant. She was the youngest of the three women on the boat.

"They should be here any minute," Allison Myers, Jake's girlfriend, said as she set the table.

She wore a Mondini Construction T-shirt with her jeans, blonde hair in a long ponytail. She'd been at some corporate function. She headed her own construction company. And she'd just started a major charity for the equality of women in third world countries. Yeah. Impressive.

Carly felt decidedly unremarkable next to them, still unemployed, although at least she'd finally decided what she wanted to do next. For the first time in a long time, the thought of her future filled her with hope and even excitement. Jasmine's and Allison's high-energy and positive vibes were contagious.

"I just want to say, I appreciate you guys," she told them over the grill. "And our friendship."

"Forget it." Jasmine tucked her laptop into her bag to make room on the table for another place setting. "We're sworn sisters."

Carly grinned. *That* had happened about a month ago, after a couple of bottles of good red wine when Jasmine had double-dared them at two in the morning to skinny-dip off the side of the boat. Giggling around in the dark water, both Carly and Allison came to the conclusion that they'd missed out on a lot by not having sisters. So Jasmine adopted them on the spot, citing her status as the sister with the most experience.

Of course, she and Allison were going to be sisters-in-law soon anyway. Carly felt honored to be included in the circle. For the first time since she'd moved to DC, she felt at home.

Jasmine got up to dump some more ice in the beer cooler, then turned to Allison. She cleared her throat. "Do you think you could keep my brother busy tonight? I mean when we go back to the hotel?"

Carly tried not to grin as she pulled the corn off the grill.

Allison didn't bother holding back a knowing smile. "I'll try for your sake. Sneaking out to party?"

Carly had a different guess. "Sneaking over to see Gabe."

Jasmine put on her I-mean-business face. "I'm tired of strained phone calls when he changes the subject every time I tell him that I'm not wearing anything. It's time for him to get over the fact that I'm Jake's little sister."

Allison exchanged a Gabe-is-toast look with Carly.

"You are so not entitled to criticize my plans." Jasmine shook her head at Carly. "I've been here when Troy called for your nightly video chat. Talking about phone sex…"

"We do not do that!" Although, Troy did call every night. Ostensibly, to check on his boat. But, invariably, they'd end up in soul-deep conversations.

"Oh, please." Jasmine gave a champion eye roll. "You two take veiled flirting to new heights. Just the look in his eyes would qualify for an R rating."

Before Carly could come up with a snappy retort, a familiar black SUV pulled into the parking lot, followed by two other cars.

When the car doors opened almost simultaneously and Gabe, Jake, and Troy appeared, the three women on the houseboat gave a collective sigh of relief.

Hearing on the phone that their missions had gone well was one thing. Seeing them all uninjured—or mostly uninjured, Jake did limp—was what they'd been holding their breaths for.

Jasmine ran down from the top deck and into Gabe's arms as he reached the houseboat. Allison dove into Jake's at the top of the stairs as he came up. Carly waited by the grill, suddenly feeling awkward.

When she'd gone to Baltimore to spend some time with her family, she'd given up her seedy DC apartment. She wanted to make a new life for herself, and part of that process was getting her parents to see eye to eye with her. While her mother began to accept that Carly's life was her own, Carly learned that Baltimore was no longer her home. Her heart brought her back to DC.

Troy had offered her the use of his houseboat while she figured out her future.

"What's all this?" he rasped as he strode over and dropped his duffel bag on the deck next to her.

He was still larger than life, the carved image of a quintessential rugged hero, a warrior angel, watchful, scarred, overpoweringly male—the object of all her fantasies.

Her heart leapt. "We made a welcome-home dinner."

The sexy smile he flashed her thrilled her. She lost control of her thoughts. And her nipples.

They poked at her shirt in an embarrassingly obvious way. She hoped he'd think from the breeze that came off the water.

She nudged the burgers around for something to do other than melt into a puddle at his feet. "So I take it the mission went well?"

"One kidnapped CEO retrieved, with barely an ear missing. And that's about as much as I can tell you. Sorry. No details." His gaze traveled over her. Hesitated on the nipples. "How have you been?" His eyes glinted with mischief. "Lonely for me?"

"We had wild girls-only parties."

When Allison and Jasmine had first shown up to visit her, they claimed it was just to "hang out," but Carly had a feeling Troy had asked them to check on her. And then they'd become friends. And then they'd become sisters.

"Thank you for letting me live on the boat." Betsy's gentle swaying on the river calmed her. She slept through most nights these days. In Troy's bed.

When she dreamed, she dreamed of him, which she so wasn't going to admit. Ever.

"My boat is your boat."

His raspy voice and the deep longing look in his eyes reached inside her and filled her up.

Jake put down Allison and picked up Jasmine next, twirled his sister around too. "And where's our youngest sis?"

"Out on a date," Jasmine said when her feet finally touched the deck again.

Jake's posture stiffened. "I don't remember authorizing that."

Jasmine punched him in the shoulder. "Next time, I go off on some exciting mission, and you stay home and try to hold her back."

Troy kept smiling at Carly, even as he called to the others. "Burgers are ready. A lot of good food was prepared for us here. Let's appreciate it."

That drew everyone to the table.

Carly brought the meat. But she didn't sit down with the others. "Before we start…" She cleared her throat and tamped down her nerves. She looked at the men. She wanted to say something before all the beer was drunk. "I figured out what I want to do for work. I'd like to join the Foreign Recovery Team. If you guys could help me get in."

Troy choked on his Budweiser.

"I have the background," she hurried to say. "I've been looking for a job since you've been gone. I can't find anything to save my life. It's not like the senator is going to give me a good reference." Especially since he was in jail, awaiting trial, bail denied, along with over a dozen XO-ST commando soldiers who'd been charged with being involved in combat tourism.

Troy put a hand on hers. "Carly, you have to—"

Jasmine stood up and cleared her throat. "Actually, I've been thinking the same."

"No," Jake and Gabe said firmly at the same time.

She put her hands on her hips. "Sexist much? Are you saying we couldn't handle it?"

The men looked at each other and smartly stayed quiet. None of them were going to touch that live wire.

Allison sat up a little straighter. "Actually, I have an announcement too."

"You're a businesswoman. Please, be reasonable," Jake begged.

She gave him a quiet smile. "We're going to have a baby."

A cheer went up, and then suddenly everybody was patting everybody else on the back. Jake gave Allison a kiss that earned catcalls and wolf whistles, and a few get-a-room suggestions.

Allison winced at Jasmine and Carly. "Sorry I didn't tell you guys. I wanted Jake to be here when I first said those words."

They had her in a sister group hug the next second, a babbling, incoherent mess of joy and support. And then she asked them to be godmothers.

Carly had tears in her eyes. "Of course." She felt as if her new family was forming right in front of her eyes.

"Yes!" Jasmine shouted, with a side look at Gabe that said she was going to do everything in her power to make sure they were next.

Much later, after the mountain of food had been eaten to the last bite and all the congratulations had been warmly accepted, after the party ended, Carly sat with Troy under the stars, alone with him on the houseboat.

"I have one more piece of news," she told him to fill the silence that suddenly crackled with all sorts of tension. Okay, not 'all sorts.' Mostly just sexual.

"I don't think I can take more. Have mercy." But he was grinning.

"I rented a new apartment." She hadn't wanted to assume. They weren't a couple. He'd said she would be welcome to stay as long as she wanted, but coming back from a mission, maybe he would prefer his privacy.

She stood. "Actually, I should be leaving too."

Disappointment flashed in his eyes. "You should stay. Just tonight. At least."

She hesitated.

"I have some injuries. I might need some help with the fresh bandages."

She still didn't say anything.

"We kind of downplayed how rough we had it out there. I'll probably have nightmares. It would be nice not to have to be alone in the night."

She smelled a rat. Troy loathed admitting any kind of weakness.

"Listen to all that whining," she teased.

He stalked her. Caught her. Held her.

"I've been thinking about coming back home. A lot."

Her heart rate sped. "And were they happy little fantasies?"

"Very. Actually, in those fantasies, when I got home, you stayed."

"Were you delusional from blood loss at the time?"

"I missed you," he said in a raspy whisper, leaning in.

And, *oh, what the hell*, she let him kiss her.

"Just because you're fresh from the fight and all that," she told him when they pulled apart a few heated minutes later. "You're practically a hero, blah, blah, whatever. It doesn't mean I'm going to faint at your feet."

"Good. I would never make love to an unconscious woman. What kind of creep does that?"

He flashed her a blinding grin. She didn't believe in swooning, but she might have swayed a little.

She didn't protest when he picked her up and carried her to his bed. The bed where she'd slept for months, where she'd sometimes held long conversations with him over the Internet and gotten to know him, made friends with him, fallen in love with him.

He laid her down and then joined her on top of the covers.

She would have been lying if she said she hadn't entertained a few fantasies about a similar scenario. Except reality was turning out much better. She gave up pretending that she didn't want this as much as he did and tugged his shirt out of his pants.

The sight of his scarred, magnificent torso made her swallow. She ran her fingers over his old scars. There weren't any new ones, just a few scrapes. *Thank God.*

"Sorry," he said. "I know it's not fun to look at." He tugged the shirt back down. "I should probably keep this on."

She wouldn't let him. "Don't be stupid."

"It's ugly."

The toneless way he said those words made her think he was quoting somebody. "Not to me."

Warmth softened his flint-gray gaze as he watched her and accepted her declaration with a slow nod.

Then he kissed her.

He pressed a chaste kiss to one corner of her mouth, then the other. Then he rubbed his closed lips over hers, nudged her, waited.

She didn't want to make him wait any longer. She kissed him back.

"My turn," he whispered when they pulled apart a long minute later. He went for the hem of her T-shirt. "I get to check for new injuries too."

"I didn't go on an op. Where would I get injured?"

"You could have slipped on deck. Technically, I could be held liable since I'm the boat's owner. I have to confirm that you sustained no injuries while you resided on my property. Common sense. And legal stuff," he added.

She arched an eyebrow. "Legal stuff?"

"Criminal liability."

"Are you making this up?"

"Maybe?"

He smiled so sweetly, so unlike his usual somber self, that she let him pull the T-shirt over her head.

"Talking about liability… That's a heart-attack trigger right there." He ran the pad of his thumb over the edge of her pink lace bra.

She suddenly felt shy under his admiring gaze. "Jasmine and Allison took me shopping. They said my military-issue underwear was appalling."

"And they know what kind of underwear you have, how? You had an underwear party? The three of you?" His gaze darkened. "I don't suppose anybody made a home video?"

She swatted him. "They helped me unpack after I moved here." Then she bit her lip. "There also might have been a single incidence of skinny-dipping."

His eyes widened comically. He opened his mouth to say something as his finger stilled on the front clasp, but then the clasp popped open from the pressure and he didn't say anything.

He kissed her again, long and deep, trailed kisses down her neck, over her collarbone, working a winding path to her nipples.

Heat and need shot through her as he nibbled.

His left arm supported his weight, while his right hand went to the buttons of her jeans. He undid them with agonizing slowness, slipping his long, capable fingers inside her panties. He glanced down.

"They match." He sounded breathless.

There had to be some snappy comeback or snide remark to that but she couldn't think of any.

"It's been a pretty long time for me," she told him instead.

He held her gaze. "Same here. We should be able to figure it out. If we can't, I'll download some pictures from the Internet. There might be an instructional video somewhere that we could watch together."

She gave a weak laugh. "I think we can manage."

He came up to his knees on the bed and pulled down her pants and underwear in the same smooth move, baring her completely. His eyes hesitated on the old battle scars on her hip. He softly drew the pad of his thumb over them. "Are you sure you want to join the team? How are you doing with the flashbacks?"

"Gone."

"Nightmares?"

"Not for a while." She wasn't sure why. Maybe it was the gentle rocking of the boat. Or maybe Gabe's smell on the pillow made her feel safe while she slept.

"Why undo all the progress?"

"I wouldn't be going into battle with bombs and tanks. We'd be investigating. Tracking and surveillance."

"And the odd armed confrontation. Do you want to risk getting hurt again?"

"I'm a warrior at heart, same as you. Even if I ran away from it…the fight would find me. It did at the mansion. This is who we are. This is what we do."

"Sometimes," he agreed. "But at other times, *this* is what we do." And then he moved up alongside her body and kissed her again.

As soon as she opened her mouth, he swept in, and her eyes fluttered closed. Heat swept through her, made her back arch on the bed. Her heels dug into the covers.

He explored every corner of her mouth as carefully as if he was on a search and rescue mission.

She bent her knees. He let his weight settle between them, against her pelvic bone. His hard places pressed against her soft spots. Arousal pebbled her nipples.

He must have had some nipple radar, because he pulled back, kissed her lips again, then moved down. He gave a masculine sigh of pure contentment. "It's good to be home."

"It's good to have you home."

"I think this homecoming is about to get even better." He dipped his head.

His hot lips encased her nipple, and he sucked it into a turgid peak while she squirmed under him. When she was so aroused she was tugging at his boxer shorts, he simply moved to the other nipple.

He took his sweet time, driving her senseless.

"Torture is against US military law and the Geneva Convention." She could barely gasp out the words.

He moved his lips down her abdomen. "How about, if you let me torture you, I'll let you torture me back."

He kept going. She was in no condition to negotiate, so she simply surrendered.

He parted her with his tongue.

She whimpered.

He licked her up and down, then around, then up and down again. And again, his large hands under her, lifting her so he could feast.

The orgasm rode through her like a military freight train.

When she quieted, he moved up over her body and switched their positions so she was sprawled on top of him. He spread his arms to the side. "I'm all yours. Do your worst."

"Protection?"

"Nightstand."

She covered him. Then she straddled him and guided him into her, stretched to accept him, as he gradually entered her. She was nearly ready to come again by the time he was fully buried inside her.

She arched her back, head thrown back as she ground herself onto him, her breasts protruding toward him, soft moans escaping her mouth. She rode him. And felt power. Felt in control. Felt sexier than she ever had.

She leaned forward a little, and his left hand came up to cup her breast, his thumb brushing against her nipple. His other thumb went lower and pressed into her, rubbed against her swollen clit.

"This is it," he rasped. "You know that, right?"

She rode harder, on the edge, thinking he was talking about his orgasm. She wanted to get there together.

But he said, "Look at me."

So she did.

And then he said. "I love you, Carly. This is it for us. This is the beginning of forever."

Her body contracted, pulsed, squeezed him. He groaned as he came, and she keened, and then collapsed on top of him.

His arms folded around her.

"I love you too," she whispered into his neck, her heart clamoring, beating against his.

His fingers meandered down her back. Reached her buttocks. Squeezed. Began an erotic massage that sent a new bolt of pleasure through her.

She groaned. "I can't come a third time tonight. You're going to have to give me a break. It can't be done."

Carly felt more than heard Troy's deep chuckle.

He flipped their positions again, his gaze burning into hers. "Maybe they didn't teach this in the army, but never issue a challenge to a SEAL."

She seriously had to stand up for the army here. And she would. In another minute.

Troy distracted her by rubbing his lips over hers. "Tell me more about that skinny-dipping."

*The End*

***

But it doesn't have to be...
Read on for your bonus FREE short story.

# SEAL
## SURRENDER

A short story by Dana Marton

Jasmine pushed her coins into the vending machine at the end of the hallway and waited for the can of soda to drop. She had a room at the Marriott. Her brother was at the same hotel, sharing a room with Allison one floor above. The cookout on Troy's boat had been great, but they'd taken off after a couple of hours. The way Troy and Carly were looking at each other, those two definitely needed time alone together.

Jasmine tried not to be jealous.

"Hey! Yo, babe!"

She glanced over her shoulder at the trio of frat boys headed toward her.

"Why aren't you at the party, girl?"

The party was at the end of the hallway, music thumping through the closed door so she could hear it all the way here. Since the floors were concrete under the carpet, the beat vibrated under her feet. Hard to believe nobody had complained at the front desk yet.

One of the guys, a surfer-dude type, streaked blond hair, waxed chest, and Hawaiian surfer shorts, strutted up to the icebox next to Jasmine's vending machine and began filling the small plastic garbage can he'd brought. The other two, dark haired, both with gym muscles and spray-on tans, focused on Jasmine.

"How about a mojito? They're a killer," the one with the Justin Bieber haircut promised.

"I just got a soda, thanks." Except the can wasn't dropping.

The third guy—who for some inexplicable reason was dressed as an elf from Middle Earth, complete with fake ears and a bow and arrows—went down to his knees and put his hands into the drop tray, tried to reach up.

His movements were slow and uncoordinated, as if maybe he'd been smoking more than cigarettes.

Surfer dude finished with the ice machine and set his garbage can down, then came to help.

Before Carly could protest, all three were working on getting her soda to drop from its perch. The effort was comical, not enough room for three of them, especially with their spectacular lack of coordination.

Then they tried one of Elf Boy's fake arrows, and they bent the shaft.

"Are you kidding me right now?" Elf Boy pulled out the bent arrow and just sat on the ground, staring at it sadly, as if someone had slapped his puppy.

They laughed at him.

"Boys?"

They didn't hear her.

"Boys!"

Now she had their attention.

"Please step back."

She looked at the machine, at the spot where the can was hanging. Then she executed a roundhouse kick, not at the glass, but at the exact point where the shelf met the side of the machine, providing a large enough tremor to free her drink.

Surfer Boy stared. "That's hot."

Bieber Hair smiled with full enthusiasm. "Room 696." The smile turned into a leer. "Perfect room for a party, right? Get it?"

She flashed him a look that hopefully communicated how utterly unimpressed she was. She grabbed her soda can and headed in the opposite direction from the party. Her room was far enough down the hall so she should be able to sleep.

"You're breaking our hearts!" Elf Boy shouted after her, waving his bent arrow in a way that struck Jasmine as possibly symbolic.

She kept walking.

She'd gone to parties like that, not even that long ago. She'd gone out with guys like that. She'd thought they were fun.

Then Gabe Cannon had come back into her life and ruined her for all other men. Definitely ruined her for boys.

She strode into her room, put her drink on the nightstand, and threw herself on the bed, staring at the popcorn ceiling as if the haphazard pattern held the answer to all of life's questions.

Gabe was here somewhere in the building.

She lifted her butt, pulled her cell phone from her pocket, and dialed him. "Would you like to come over?" she asked as soon as he picked up.

Silence. Then, "I don't think that's a good idea. Your brother is in the same hotel."

Just his voice had the ability to make her melt in bed.

But if Gabe didn't stop thinking about her as Jake's little sister, she was going to snap one of these days and strangle both men. "I have full faith in Allison to keep Jake busy. All night long."

Gabe said, his voice a little rougher, "I'll see you at breakfast."

Frustration burned through her. "I might not get up that early. There's some kind of a frat party down the hall. I just got invited. I'm going to check it out."

"Jasm—"

She hung up on him.

Then she punched the mattress. Then she flailed like a two-year-old throwing a fit in a grocery aisle. She might even have screamed through clenched teeth.

When she finished, she got up, drank half her soda, slammed the can down, and strode to the closet, a woman on a mission. She yanked her shortest skirt off the hanger, the lowest-cut tank top from the shelf, and bent to pick up five-inch red pumps, the only pair of real heels she owned, bought on impulse at the mall that afternoon with Gabe in mind.

The shoes looked great, dammit. They made her legs look ridiculously long and slim. And somebody was going to see her in them. Those shoes were not meant for the back of a hotel closet.

By the time she was done with those frat boys, they'd be a puddle of drool, slowly soaking into the carpet.

Gabe had rejected her one time too many. It hurt. Every single time.

They'd had one lopsided sexual encounter months ago when he hadn't even taken off his clothes—although that hadn't stopped him from bringing her to a roaring orgasm. Multiple times.

Since then: nothing.

He even refused phone sex.

He had some insane idea that he was being gallant and protecting her reputation or purity or whatever. That he could not corrupt his friend's little sister. She was sooooo over it.

Today was the first time she'd seen him in three months. She'd flown into his arms. He'd kissed her breathless.

A kiss that promised: Tonight is the night. Or so she'd thought.

He was kissing her all the way up in the elevator once they'd gotten to the hotel. Allison had to go back to the car for something and Jake had gone with her, so Gabe and Jasmine had gone upstairs alone together. Gabe had seemed fully with the program. Then the elevator dinged when it reached Jasmine's floor, and the door opened. She'd stepped out.

"Good night, Jasmine," he'd said, and didn't get off behind her.

She couldn't believe it.

She wasn't going to stay in her room and pine for him all night, dammit. She brushed her hair, leaving it loose, then she grabbed all the little bottles of alcohol from her minifridge to contribute to the party.

She pushed her room card into her bra.

Ready.

She marched down the hallway like a runway model. Okay, wobbled like a slightly tipsy sailor. She wasn't used to the heels. But she made it, and the party door opened before she could knock.

"Hey, babe!" Surfer Dude reached for her, grabbed her elbow, and pulled her in. He grinned at her armload of mini bottles. "Thanks for the reinforcements." He held up the empty plastic bucket. "I'm going for more ice. Be right back. Enjoy the party."

He pushed her deeper into the room crowded with at least two dozen college kids, then hurried off.

Bieber Hair saw her first. "Yo! Babe!"

He stretched babe into two syllables, his gaze drinking up every inch of her. He spread his arms. "Come to Daddy."

She was at least five years older. The whole situation was ridiculous. What the hell was she doing here?

A twiggy girl dressed like a manga character took the bottles from her. Somebody else shoved a mojito into her hand. Bieber Hair handed her a brownie from the tray next to him.

She was half done with the mojito, pretending to listen to manga girl's long story about a hair extension disaster, when the chanting began. "Tits! Tits! Tits! Tits!"

And the tops came off, the girls wiggling their breasts like one of those Spring Break videos. Every phone was out. Even the girls were taking selfies of themselves, the music pumping, everybody laughing and hooting, jockeying for the best angles.

Jasmine turned. She was out of there. She wasn't about to hang around long enough for the dick pics.

Bieber Hair grabbed the bottom of her tank top and yanked it up. "Come on, babe. Don't be shy."

Another boy tugged her strap down her shoulder. Before she could blink, her left breast was exposed.

Cameras flashed.

She had a drink in one hand and the brownie in the other. She was about to drop both and start knocking heads together when she was suddenly caught from behind, lifted, shifted, then she was tossed over an improbably wide shoulder, her head dangling down, her eyes inches from Gabe Cannon's jean-encased ass.

She recognized his ass.

That's how bad she had it for him.

The party parted before him like the Red Sea before Moses.

Then they were out in the hallway. Her breasts were pressed into his back, one of them still naked. She wiggled.

A large palm came firmly across her butt—smack!—and stayed there.

Shock held her speechless. Arousal made her wet. Outrage had her biting his ass. Just sinking her teeth in right through the denim.

"Ow. What the hell, Jasmine?" He set her down in front of her door, his scowl as dark as a black hole at midnight. His hard gaze slipped to her bare breast. His Adam's apple bobbed. "Key?"

She stuck her chin out. She still had the mojito glass in one hand—contents spilled—and the brownie mushed in the other. "In my bra."

With a look of titanium-clad determination, he reached for the unexposed breast, his long fingers sweeping under the lace, and came up with her key card while she struggled for breath.

He opened the door. Looked back at her.

"Don't you dare," she snapped.

A quick nod. Then, instead of carrying her in, he gestured for her to go first.

She marched in like the queen of Sheba. Tossed the brownie in the trash, the glass on the dresser, then finally covered up and turned to face him.

She pointed her index finger at his face. "Do not put hands on me."

"You've been begging me for months to put hands on you."

He had a point there. Still, he'd handled her like a macho caveman. And it wasn't so much that she didn't like it. Maybe it was that she liked it, and she was embarrassed to admit it. She was a Generation Y-er, for heaven's sake.

But, oh God, her knees were going weak at his caveman imitation, in violation of every feminine doctrine ever invented.

The party room had been crowded with two dozen people, but her room had less air in it. Gabe's presence took up all the available oxygen. He was big, and man, and testosterone, and sharply real, an irresistible force.

She wanted him to take off her tank top. And her skirt. And she wouldn't have minded at all if he put his hand back on her ass.

"I think we should wait," he said, as if he'd read her thoughts.

She groaned. "Wait for what? Jake is okay with us together. I swear."

"Until we get married. I'm going to ask Jake for permission."

Part of her was dancing the conga; the sane part said, "What century is this?"

"I love you," he said.

Which slightly dampened her urge to choke him.

"I love you too." She took a step closer.

He went down on both knees. "Will you marry me?"

As she tried to catch her breath, he reached out and pulled her to him, gently pressed his face into the softness of her abdomen.

She slipped her fingers into his thick hair. "Yes."

Then she slid down too, until they were face-to-face.

He kissed her. One soft brush at a time. One soft nibble at a time. One soft taste at a time. Just a little pressure here and there until somehow his mouth owned her, and hot need pulsed between her legs.

Gabe's kisses very nearly made up for his foolish ideas about a chaste courtship. His kisses were more passionate, more intimate than some sex she'd had in the past. He was a master-of-his-realm type of man, and she was clearly his realm now, because he mastered her, no other word for it.

She gladly let him, sinking into the pleasure of his lips.

"I want you," she whispered when they came up for air.

"What if I don't live up to expectations?"

"I'm willing to give you the opportunity to improve," she deadpanned.

A bark of laugh escaped him. "God, I love you, Jasmine."

"Then make love to me."

"Are we engaged? One hundred percent? Officially?"

"Yes!"

He grinned, picked her up, and lay her gently on the bed. "I've thought about this a million times. I have a million fantasies."

"Was throwing me over your shoulder and spanking me one of them?"

His gaze bore into hers. "Yes."

Need throbbed through her so sharply, it should have shredded her clothes. She whispered, "What else?"

"I had this fantasy that I came home, you tempted me into your room, and stripped for me."

She scrambled up, pushed him down at the foot of the bed, and then she stood between the pillows on the other end. Then she stopped. God, was she really doing this?

"Music?" she stalled.

He pulled out his phone and put on a soft, sultry tango, looking at her like she looked at the pastry shop window she passed in the mornings. Like she fully intended to taste everything and come away with powdered-sugar-dusted chin.

He licked his lips.

And the room's temperature suddenly shot to the triple digits.

Her hips swayed.

Passion darkened his eyes.

She fidgeted with the bottom of her tank top. Then she committed and inched the material up, little by little, revealing a finger's width of skin at a time to his hungry gaze. He'd already seen all her scars. None of that mattered.

She tossed the tank top.

Her bra was little more than a scrap of purple lace.

Left strap first. Then right strap. Then she reached back and popped the clasp, caught the bra from falling, and playfully tried to shoot it at Gabe like a rubber band.

She shot herself in the face, nearly taking an eye out. "Ow."

Gabe reached out, pulled her down, and rolled her under him. "As a safety measure. I think I need to intervene before you hurt yourself."

"You have no patience," she complained, rubbing her nose.

He pulled away her hand and kissed it. Then he kissed her lips.

Her naked breasts pressed against his chest.

"Take off your shirt," she whispered.

He quirked an eyebrow. "Want a striptease?"

She thought about it. More heat flooded her. "Some other time. I have no patience either."

The man could move fast. He was down to his boxers by the time she fully caught up with the fact that they were finally getting naked together.

He was ripped, tanned, scarred—straight off the cover of a romance novel.

And he wasn't given to hesitation either. His lip closed around her nipple, and his fingers pinched the other one almost simultaneously.

She arched her back under him, liquid need pooling at the V of her legs.

His hard length rode her pubic bone, pressing against her clitoris through her skirt and underwear. A few more minutes of this and they'd probably burn off her.

Her eyes rolled back into her head, and her fingers dug into his hair, everything going way too fast. And she wanted it faster.

She bucked against him.

One of his hands snuck down and hooked up her skirt, his fingers stealing inside the wet lace of her underwear. His fingertips caressed her, slipped inside, massaged, tugged, rubbed, tapped.

She screamed her release loud enough for the party kids down the hall to hear her.

Before her body stopped pulsing, she was naked, and he was naked, and he was protected, and his hard length was slipping inside her.

She couldn't catch her breath.

"I can't," she gasped. "It's too soon." She needed time to come down from the heights.

"I'm a SEAL," he murmured against her lip. "I'm not familiar with the concept of can't. As a SEAL's wife, you're just going to have to try harder."

He was right. She so wasn't a quitter. She wrapped her legs around him, tilted her pelvis and helped him slide in all the way.

Then she flexed her vaginal muscles around him and squeezed.

He groaned. "That's the spirit."

"Am I good enough to be a SEAL's wife?"

"Definitely military grade." He kissed her.

He moved in a way to maximize her pleasure, rubbing her everywhere at once, until she was half out of her mind with the need to come again.

But then he slowed. "I want you to pick a date."

*Who? What? The wedding?* "Now?"

He stopped completely.

She squirmed, then stared at him with disbelief. "Are you blackmailing me with an orgasm?"

"I need a date."

"Next summer."

"Too late."

She squirmed again, desperate. "Next month?"

"The first of the month."

"Okay. Deal."

And he finally moved again. And then she shattered around him as his own release pulsed inside her. She felt blown apart and put back together. She was flying through space. Or maybe the stars were flying through her.

Gabe had put her into a whole other state of being. She couldn't catch her breath.

He rolled them to their sides and held on to her.

She gasped for air. She could barely speak enough to say, "You fight dirty."

He groaned. "Don't say *dirty* when we're naked in bed. Now I'm thinking about all the dirty things I want to do to you."

She caught her breath at last. And curiosity immediately took over. "Like what?"

"Give me half an hour, and I'll show you a couple of them."

"What are we going to do until then?"

"Plan the wedding," he said, and tilted up her chin so he could kiss her again.

***

If you'd like to read more about General Robert's new department
and the men and women who find and rescue Americans
who disappear abroad, check out these full-size novels.


FORCED DISAPPEARANCE –a nerd romance—(available
now at www.danamarton.com/book/pop/19)
FLASH FIRE –a Navy SEAL romance—(available
now at www.danamarton.com/book/pop/20)
**GIRL IN THE WATER** –a jungle romance—(coming soon)


<u>Titles in the Bestselling Broslin Creek Series:</u>
DEATHWATCH, book 1 (www.danamarton.com/book/pop/13)
DEATHSCAPE, book 2 (www.danamarton.com/book/pop/14)
DEATHTRAP, book 3 (www.danamarton.com/book/pop/15)
DEATHBLOW, book 4 (www.danamarton.com/book/pop/16)
BROSLIN BRIDE, book 5 (www.danamarton.com/book/pop/17)
DEATHWISH, book 6 (www.danamarton.com/book/pop/18)
DEATHMARCH (coming soon)
DEATHTOLL (coming soon)

Thank you for reading my books! To be notified when my next title comes out, please sign up for my New Book Alerts on my web site at danamarton.com. I send out a one-page note, once a month tops (and sometimes not even that frequently), so I promise not to overwhelm your email! I also always notify my readers of upcoming sales and giveaways. I, together with a couple of author friends, raffle off a $100 gift card nearly every month.

Would you have a moment for a quick review? Authors live and die by their online reviews. Would you please consider leaving a review? Just your honest opinion. Even a single sentence would make a real difference to me. The more reviews, the more visibility some retailers give the book. Thank you!!!!

Wishing you all the best,
Dana Marton
Author

www.ingramcontent.com/pod-product-compliance
Lightning Source LLC
Chambersburg PA
CBHW070826190726
48292CB00006B/2122